Lover, Killers and Diamonds

ANGEL JONSON

Lover, Killers and Diamonds

Published by Angel Jonson.

Requests for reproduction should be addressed via email to: angel.jonson07@outlook.com

Cover design by pro_ebookcovers.

Autor photo by Brent Hughes Photography.

Book design by Angel Jonson.

ISBN-13: 978-0-9983341-2-7

Printed by CreateSpace, An Amazon.com Company

Dedicated to my grandmothers,
who thought me
how to be a good man.

CONTENTS

CHAPTER 1

I woke up at 6:00 a.m. in the morning. I went to bed at 10:00 p.m. last night and I had a good dream. After thirty minute of exercise, I took a shower and I prepared a bowl of mixed fruits for breakfast: cantaloupe, watermelon, apple, blueberry and grapes. The phone started ringing at 8:30 a.m.

"Are you sleeping?" Jimmy asked me.

"No, I am ready to leave my apartment."

"Don't forget 7000 Preston Road. You will see a long wall with big a gate."

"Thanks Jimmy. I will be there at 9:15 a.m.

I was at 7000 Preston Road at 9:00 a.m. I pushed the bell.

"Who is this?"

"My name is Carl Hope and I am here to pick up three boxes."

"Come in, I will open the gate."

She was outside the door waiting for me. "Hi, I am Carl Hope. Nice to meet you."

"I am Michelle", she said and smiled.

"Come in the house, my father is waiting for you."

I entered the living room and I stopped for twenty or thirty seconds. It was a huge space, around 80 feet long, 50 feet wide and 15 feet high. In the center of the room was a big sofa and a table. Many large paintings were hanging on the walls.

"Are you surprised?"

"Yes."

"Who built this house Michelle?"

"My grandfather, but I am not sure exactly which year. You need to ask my father. My grandfather moved from New York and he opened a Construction Company in Dallas." I looked at Michelle and I smiled.

"Why are you smiling?" she asked me.

"I will tell you later."

"Why, you don't tell me now?"

"Because, this is a long story."

"Is it a secret?"

"I don't have any secrets in my life. I am very honest and direct man, Michelle."

"My father has talked about you, but this is the first time I am speaking with you. I am sorry, if I hurt your feelings asking about secrets."

"You didn't hurt my feelings, but I have a question, where is your father?"

"Hi is in his office. Do you want me to take you to his office?"

"No. I will wait here. You have many family paintings, I would like to look at them while your father comes here if that is Ok with you."

I was looking at the paintings, when somebody asked me "Are you Carl Hope?"

"How do you like me to call you?"

"Carl or Hope. I will be happy, if you call me Carl, since my grandmother named me Carl. If you call me Hope, I will be proud, because this is my family name.

"What is your name sir?"

"Jimmy didn't tell you my name?"

"No sir."

"Young man, this is not important for business. I am the owner and the boss of the company you work for. My name is Ethan Dreyfus. My great-grand father came from France. He was a banker in New York. My grandfather worked on Wall Street. My father Louis Dreyfus moved from New York to Dallas in 1938. He started this business in Dallas and he built this house. My grandfather was a banker, my father was builder and I am an architect. Each of us made a different choice. Remember, the choice is yours, not the family."

"Mr. Dreyfus, you have a lot of experience. I like to spend more time talking to you, but I must take the three boxes I came for and go back to the office. I have a lot of work."

"Carl Hope, work will never finish. When you finish my project call me."

"Sir, I will finish it on Friday or Saturday."

"How do you know that you will finish on Friday or Saturday? This is a short time Carl!"

"I know that I will need to work very hard, but I am determined to finish."

"Are you sure?"

"Absolutely sir."

"If you finish on Friday or Saturday, we will have a party on Sunday to celebrate."

"Is it OK with you Carl?"

"Yes sir. It will be a pleasure to visit with you again."

"Do you like to talk to me now Carl?"

"I can't sir. I have to go."

"Do you think that you are polite? You are in my house, I am your boss and you don't like to speak with me."

"First, I came here to take three boxes. Second, now, I know that you are the owner and the boss of the office where I work. If you think that you are my boss, I need to tell you that I never have had a boss. I work for somebody and I get paid.

"What would you do if I fire you now, Carl?"

"This is your choice sir. Call the office and tell them that I am fired. I will pack up my things and I will leave."

"Oh boy, are you joking?"

"I am not sir."

"I will fire you in Saturday, if you don't finish the project. Michelle, could you show Carl the boxes?" and he left living room.

"Follow me, Carl."

Michelle tried to help me with the boxes, but she had hard time lifting them.

"You are a girl Michelle they are heavy. You shouldn't do that. Let me do it" and I picked and dropped three boxes in a car.

"Are you coming on Sunday, Carl?"

"If I finish the project, I will. If I don't your father will fire me and I will leave the office."

"I will pray to God that you do. You must finish the project on Friday or Saturday Carl."

"I will Michelle. I love my job. Bye Michelle."

"Bye Carl."

I was in the office at 10:30 a.m. I closed the door and I looked at the boxes. I started my plan with the hours I have to work on the project. Today I have eight hours. Tomorrow is Tuesday and I need to work ten hours. Wednesday ten hours, Thursday ten hours and Friday ten or twelve hours. I have three boxes and fifty hours. I must wake up at 6:00am, exercise for 30 minutes, take a shower for 30 minutes and have breakfast for 20 minutes. I must be in the office at 7:45 a.m. I will have lunch between 12:00-1:00 p.m. I must leave the office at 7:00 p.m. I will have two hours for shopping and dinner. I must be in bed by 9:00 p.m. I have five busy days on front of me but I am feeling excited about it. I have nine years of experience. I know I can do this.

I was 17 years old, when I moved from Knoxville, Tennessee to Manhattan, New York. I love my grandfather, because he helped me when I decided to move to Manhattan. I was a little boy when my grandfather told me "I will be proud someday with you grandson." There are four people that I love very, very much: grandmother, grandfather, Uncle Mark and my mom Julia. I was thinking about them, when somebody knocked and opened the door of my office. It was Jimmy. He asked me "How many weeks do you have to make the deadline for this project?"

"I have five days Jimmy."

"Oh my God! Five days! You must have a plan for every hour if you going to make it."

"I have a good plan, Jimmy, but I need some help."

"Tell me what I need to do Carl."

"First, I will close my office between 8:00-12:00 p.m. and 1:00-7:00 p.m. I need you tell the people in the office not to knock on my door and ask me anything for five days. Second, could you buy lunch for me every day this week? I will have lunch between 12:00-1:00 p.m. and I will speak with you. That is it, Jimmy."

"Do you need somebody else to help you Carl?"

"No. I need to complete the project by myself, so I will know every detail."

"OK Carl. Today for lunch you will have chicken with rice and mushroom soup. Sue was preparing that for me, I will ask her to pack for you too. Tomorrow, I will bring lunch for both of us. You know that Sue cooks very well. If you want any special food, I will tell Sue and she will cook it for you?"

"No Jimmy, I will be happy to eat the food Sue prepares."

"You must start to work now, you don't have time ", Jimmy told me and he left the room.

I opened the first box. The first think I saw was a folded list. I started to read. It was a numbered list with all the pieces for the project. I counted 123 pieces. Next, I found the blueprint of the project and the 123 pieces. Not too bed. Every piece was numbered. I started looking through the pieces. I started slow with the first twenty pieces, after that became easier. I looked at my watch, it was 6:30 p.m. I have placed 79 pieces. It was a good start. I picked up the phone and I called Jimmy.

"Could you give me Michelle's phone number?"

I wrote down the phone number and I called Michelle.

"Mr. Dreyfus house, may I help you? I am Robert."

"Hi Robert, this is Carl Hope, ,may I speak with Michelle?"

"She isn't here. Do you like to speak with Mr. Dreyfus?"

"No Robert, I will call later and I hang up the phone."

I left the office at 7:00 p.m. I got something for dinner and I was in my apartment by 8:00 p.m. While I was eating the phone rang twice, but I didn't' pick up. On Tuesday morning, I was in my office at 7:00 a.m. Jimmy was in my office, waiting for me

"Carl, you don't have time, but I need to tell you two things. First, Michelle called me twice last night and asked for you. She didn't tell me for why she called. The second time she sounded unhappy."

"This is Michelle's problem Jimmy. Don't worry about that."

"What is the second thing, Jimmy?"

"What time do you like to have your lunch?"

"At twelve o'clock. I don't want to waste more of your time. You need to work Carl."

"Thanks Jimmy" and I started to work.

At 12:00 p.m. I was in the break room. Jimmy has already unpacked the lunch. The food was on one of the tables and he was waiting for me. We started to eat. Jimmy asked me "Do you think that Michelle likes you?"

"I don't think so Jimmy. I met Michelle yesterday and I spoke with her for one hour. She must be crazy, if she thinks that I like her."

"Michelle is very rich Carl."

"This is good for her, because somebody will marry Michelle or her money."

"That someone can be you. You will have a chance to take her money, if you marry her."

"I think that you are crazy Jimmy. I will never marry for money. I will make money. I don't need to marry for money."

"What If Michelle is in love with you Carl?"

"Hey, I told you, that I met Michelle one time. I have never met her before."

"May I tell you something Carl?"

"Sue fell in love with me, the first time we met but she told me that several years after we got married. She never told me why she married me. You know that I am not an attractive man."

"You are very loving husband and father Jimmy. You never spend money or have sexual relationships with other women."

"You are right Carl. But now I have something to say about you Carl. You are an attractive young man. You don't have any problem to find beautiful women."

"I have a lot of them Jimmy. I have sex with them. I never had a long term relationship with a woman. I never have told of woman that I love her. I tell them, that I have good time with them, but I don't think that I will marry them."

"You don't have experience, you don't understand people Carl."

"I think that I have Jimmy. I was 12 years old when I started to observe people and understand their behavior. I learned about life from my family, relatives and friends. They had different lives."

"What happened when you were 13 years old?"

"It's a long story Jimmy. It is 12:50 p.m. I need go back to work. I will tell you about it another time." Jimmy's mouth was open. He wanted to ask me, but I left the breakroom and walked very fast to my office. I didn't want to speak with anyone, so I closed the door. I knew that Jimmy will ask me again. He was a curious person. I know that Jimmy has a simple live and he was asking many coworkers about their private life. But honestly, he never asked me. If Jimmy asks me again, what happened when I was 13, I need to have an answer. He has been a good friend and coworker, so I can't be rude to him. But now I need to work.

I finished the first house of the project at 6:30 p.m. I was tired and I left the office. While I was driving, I started to think what happened when I was 13. I saw something that was eroding my respect for my father, but it didn't become a big deal until few years later. I got in a big trouble with my father and the school, when I was 17 years old.

I was in a chemistry class, when the teacher asked me "Carl, do you want to be in class and do you like chemistry?"

"I don't want to be in class and I don't like chemistry."

"Why, Carl?"

"Because, you are a teacher but you are a liar" I took me bag and I left the class. I was at home at 10:00 a.m. At 10:15am my father came home too.

"Have you lost your mind?" he asked me.

"Your teacher, Larisa, is a very powerful in the school. She is a very influential political person in Knoxville. You have created a big problem for me Carl because offended your teacher like that today."

"I don't think so father. You have a good relationship with your lovely teacher." My father tried to hit me, but my grandfather entered the room and stopped him.

"What are you doing son?" grandfather asked him.

"Do you know, what Carl said to his teacher?" my father asked my grandfather.

"I know and I want to know why Carl said that. Come with me grandson."

"Father, this is my son and Carl needs to respect me when I am talking to him."

"May I tell you something son? I noticed that you lost Carl's respect, four years ago. I need to know what happened between you and Carl."

We were in grandfather's car. He was driving when he looked me and asked "What happened four years ago, Carl?"

"Do you want to know everything or in general?"

Grandfather smiled and said "You are a smart boy. I love you for that grandson, but start talking now. I need to know everything."

"You are the first person, to whom I am telling this story grandfather" and I started to speak.

"You know that I like to swim, so I go to the pool any day during the week when I can. I was in the swimming pool. I finished and I was ready to leave. Nobody else was in the pool when I was leaving that is why I was surprised when I heard heavy breading. I saw my father having sex. When they finished, the woman asked my father if he had prepared divorce documents."

"Larisa, I have a stupid son and a wife. You have two smart children. You are smart too Larisa. If I divorce, what are we going to do?"

"I will divorce my husband too Wyle. I will marry you and we will live together. This is my dream Wyle."

"Do you have the same dream?"

"Larisa, I don't have enough money to support a family of five. My father has a lot of land. If he dies, I will sale the land and I be rich. When I am rich and I have money, I will marry you."

"How long did you spy on them?"

"Three years."

"Why did you stop?"

"Every day was the same, grandfather. She asked if my father was divorcing my mother, he told her, that he will marry her, when my father dies and sales the land."

"Do you have proof?"

"I have, many pictures of them having sex."

"Where are the pictures?"

"In your house."

"How long have the pictures been in my house?"

"Two years. They were in my room, but my father noticed that I am loosing respect for him, so he started snooping in my room. I saw him few times leaving my room when I got from school early."

When we arrived in my grandfather's house, he asked me "Where are the pictures, could you give them to me?"

I went to get the pictures. When I came back to the living room, grandfather was speaking with Uncle Mark on the phone.

"Why you didn't tell me that your brother has been having a sexual relationship with this woman for six years, Mark? Oh my God, this is so bad Mark. Did Wyle ask you for my land? Five years ago he did! This isn't good news for me Mark" and grandfather hang up the phone.

Then he turned to me and said "You are right Carl. Mark told me the same story and he advised me to leave Knoxville because your father has asked the chief of police to arrest me and you because I took you with me. The chief of police told Mark, that you and I have 24 hours to leave Knoxville. If we don't leave, they will arrest us. Give me the pictures Carl."

He looked the pictures. He laughed "You are a pretty good photographer, Carl. Where do you want to continue high school?"

"I want to go to Manhattan, New York."

"How much money do you have in your saving account?"

"I have thirty two thousand in my saving account grandfather."

"Carl, I will make a call and have the phone on a speaker, so you can listen. Don't say anything." Grandfather picked the phone and he called.

"May I speak with John Cristal?"

"Who is calling?"

"My name is John Hope. Just a moment, Mr. Hope, I will tell Mr. Cristal that you would like to speak with him."

"Hey Hope, what are you doing?"

"Hey your grandson has created a big problem in the school. Larisa, the teacher called me. She told me, what your grandson told her. I don't know what to do Hope. Do you have any idea what we can do?"

"I will tell you what to do, Cristal. You must prepare documents to move my grandson to a high school in Manhattan, New York."

"Are you joking with me?"

"No Cristal. I am not."

"Could you tell me your fax number? I want to send you a picture?"…

"Oh my God. Hope, this is very dangerous."

"I told you, that I am not joking. If I don't have documents tomorrow by 9:00AM, I will give one of the pictures to the local newspaper."

"Hope, Manhattan is an expensive area. Do you have enough money to support your grandson to leave there?"

"My grandson has thirty two thousand dollars in his savings account. I have seventy an additional five thousand dollars in a savings account for my grandson's college and I will give him four thousand every month for living expenses. We are old political enemies Cristal, but in this moment we have to be friends. You need to keep your chair Cristal. I must move my grandson. Do you understand me?"

"I understand Hope. I will call you between 4:00 p.m. and 5:00 p.m."

"Hey, Carl it is lunch time. What do you like for lunch?"

"I like soup, grilled chicken and a salad grandfather."

"Good choice for lunch Carl."

After lunch my grandfather told me that he will take one hour nap and if the phone rings, I should not pick up. Grandfather woke up at 3:30 p.m. Cristal called at 4:30 p.m. Grandfather had the phone on the speaker. Crystal said "Tomorrow at 8:30am, I will wait for you and your grandson in my office. I will give you an envelope with documents. I spoke with Jerry Shapiro. He is a supervisor in the Manhattan School District. Your grandson will live in Shapiro's apartment. Your grandson is an "A" student. Shapiro told me that the Manhattan high school will be the best for your grandson. See you tomorrow morning."

Grandfather picked a phone and called someone named Jonathan.

"John Hope is calling."

"Hey Jonnie boy."

"I am OK Jonathan, but I need to use your private jet tomorrow morning between 9:30-10:00am to go to New York. Two people. After I arrive in New York the jet is free, because I don't know which day I will return back. See you tomorrow morning Jonathan."

"We need to get ready for tomorrow Carl. Do you need to take something from your father's house?"

"No. I will buy everything new."

My grandfather and I woke up at 6:00am in the morning. We went to Cristal's office at 8:15 a.m. He was there.

"Come in boys" Cristal told us.

"Hope, I have good news for Carl. Everything is OK. Take this envelope. Don't open it. Mr. Shapiro must open the envelope. When you arrive in New York, you need to call this phone number. It is the phone number of Jerry Shapiro. He will tell you, what you need to do. I know that you are in a hurry, but I like to tell you what happened. I called at 3:00 p.m. and I asked Shapiro for Carl. He asked for Carl Hope's high school grades. I sent him Carl's grades. After thirty minutes Shapiro called and told me that Carl Hope is approved."

"This is an amazing boy. I want to see him. When can he come to in New York?"

"Tomorrow."

"When he arrives in New York, he must call me."

"Boy, I wish you a big success in New York and Cristal shook my hand. Good luck Carl."

Grandfather and I were at the airport at 9:15 a.m. At 9:45am, we flew to New York.

I got home feeling very tired. I need to get some rest. I looked at my watch it was 8:45pm. I was confused when the phone rang Where are you now Carl, I asked myself? Who is calling me at 8:45pm? I didn't feel like talking, I didn't pick up the phone. I wanted to sleep, so I went to bed.

Wednesday and Thursday were the same. I woke up at 6:00 a.m. I had lunch at 12:00 p.m. I left the office at 7:00 p.m. and was in a bed by 9:00 p.m. Friday, I was in an office at 7:00am and Jimmy was waiting for me.

"I need to tell you, that last night Michelle called and she asked about you. Ethan called later and he asked me to give him the phone number of your relatives. I gave him the phone number of your grandfather in Knoxville. I am so sorry Carl. I told Ethan, that, he needs to call you and speak with you not to bother your family."

"Don't worry Jimmy. I need to work."

Later, when I and Jimmy were in the breakroom for lunch he told me that Michelle called him at 10:00am this morning and she asked about me.

"Could you call her Carl?"

"I don't have time Jimmy", I need to work and I left the breakroom, before I finished my lunch. I finished the project at 5:15pm. I looked at the project. I was so happy, that I told Ethan that I will finish on Friday and I did. Somebody knocked and opened the door. It was Jimmy. He looked at the project and said "Amazing job Carl! There are three beautiful houses. The first is 3,500 square feet, the second is 5,200 square feet and the third is 6,700 square feet. How much will the company sale this project for, Carl?"

"Between twenty and twenty two millions Jimmy."

"This is a lot money Carl. Did you see that Ethan used a lot of ideas from the projects you have done before?"

"I saw that, Jimmy. But, I am glad that Ethan used my ideas."

"Are you sure?"

"I am sure Jimmy. I will call Ethan to tell him, that you have finished."

"No Jimmy. I don't like to speak with Ethan, Michelle or anybody else. My body needs alcohol and a woman. When I leave the office, you do what you want to do."

I picked the phone and I called a taxi.

Jimmy looked at the project and he asked me "How do you know that the project cost twenty or twenty two millions dollars"?

"I spent five days to do this project. There are three beautiful houses. I know every detail. Ethan will be stupid, if he sales the project under twenty millions."

The phone rang and I picked up "The taxi is waiting for you Mr. Hope."

"What can I do for you Carl?"

"Take my car to my apartment" and I left the office. After thirty minutes I was in a topless bar.

"You look very tired boy, what can I do for you, the bartender asked me?"

"Could you give me a double whisky, Chivas Regal, please?"

"OK boy. My name is David. "

"Call me Carl."

David gave me double Chivas Regal. I drank it and I ask for one more.

"Carl it is only six o'clock. The night is young. Take it easy. You are starting to drink early. If you continue with this tempo, after one hour, you will be drunk. Do you want that?"

"No David."

"Do you like company Carl?"

"Of course, but it depends on the price and the service."

"How much do you want to pay for all night and a good service?"

"One thousand for all night, and five hundred for a good service."

"OK Carl. I will call her. She is special and she works with rich people." David made a phone call.

"Kate, this is David. I know that you are off tonight, but Carl is a good customer. He will pay you one thousand for all night and five hundred for a good service. Carl, Kate asked what time?"

"She should be here by eight o'clock."

"She will be here at eight o'clock Carl."

"Thanks David."

"I need to reserve a table for you. Which table do you want Carl?"

"Any one that is on a corner. I don't like traffic."

"Go to the table Carl. It isn't healthy to stay for two hours on a bar."

I moved to the table and I told David that I don't like another waiter.

"Is it OK David?"

"Don't worry. It is OK Carl. This is my job and I want to be your waiter."

Kate arrived at eight o'clock. She was beautiful. She was about five feet and eight inches tall, and she weighted around one hundred twenty five pounds. Kate had a middle size bosom.

"Could you turn a little Kate?"

"Of course."

Kate had a fantastic ass.

"Are you sizing me?"

I stood up. I took and kissed her hand.

"My name is Carl .You are so beautiful Kate."

"You are a gentlemen Carl."

"Could you tell me, what is my price?"

"One hundred twenty five pound diamond. If you want to know, what your price is, you need to ask a bank."

"You are joking Carl" and we laughed.

"Hey Kate, I will tell you joke. Two friends were drinking coffee and talking. One of them complained that he has short sex and he asked what he has to do so he can have sex longer time and the other man gave him an advice."

"When you start having sex, don't think about sex, but think about something else. Strat thinking that you have taken a taxi and you are going to a restaurant. You enter the restaurant and a waiter asks you, what you like to drink. You order whisky and wait. When waiter brings you the whisky, you finish sex, but you had fifty minutes or one hour of sex by then, because you took a taxi, entered restaurant ordered and waited for whisky."

"They meet again after one week and the man who gave the advice asked what happened."

"Nothing buddy. I started with the sex and the waiter gave me the whisky."

Kate laughed and she asked me "Are you the man who gave the

advice or man who asked for the advice?"

"You will need to find out that yourself, Kate. After we have sex, you need to tell me, which man I am." We laughed.

"This is very funny."

"What do you like to drink?" David asked Kate.

"I like French Champagne" Kate replied.

"What about you Carl?"

"I prefer French Chardonnay."

"Do you like a glass or bottle Carl?"

"Bottle for both and I like fish for dinner."

"Do you have salmon from the Cooper River in Alaska?"

"I don't know Carl. I need to ask the chef."

"What would you like lady?"

"The same that Carl ordered, but I have question David, what is better for fish, Champagne or Chardonnay?"

"Chardonnay is better, but it is your decision Kate."

"I will drink Chardonnay too. Thanks David."

"My pleasure Kate. I will be your servant tonight. Ask me any time, this is my job."

"Oh my God. I feel like a princess". I and David laughed and we said together "You are Kate." David left to work on the order. I looked at Kate.

"What Carl?"

"I am very happy Kate. You are a beautiful, smart, honest and an attractive woman."

"How do you know that? I have been with you for thirty minutes Carl."

"I was 12 years old, when I started to learn about people. I have 14 years of experience now."

"Are you twenty six?"

"I am, but I am feeling and thinking like I am thirty six. Do you believe that Kate?"

"Of course, I believe. Cheers Carl!"

"Cheers Kate!"

Around 11:30 p.m., we left the bar. We were in my apartment at 12:00 p.m. The moment we walked in the living room Kate said "I don't want to talk, I like to have sex with you Carl." We went straight to bed. Kate was very professional in the bed. She taught me something new too.

I woke up and I looked at my watch. It was 9:15 a.m. Kate was in the kitchen. "Good morning sir."

"Good morning lady."

"I need to tell you Carl, that last night I had good sex and now I know that you were the person who gave the advice in your joke. Your breakfast is ready. I have prepared eggs, bacon, mash potatoes, salad and orange juice."

"You know to cook. Who taught you Kate?"

"I am from Midland Texas and I spent a lot of time with grandma. She was my teacher. I like to talk about that Carl. I had a wonderful life in Midland. My family isn't wealthy but they have enough money for a good life. I finished two years of college and I found a job in Dallas. I make thirty four thousand dollars a year. My boss is a good man. A gentlemen. We had a party at work. A man around fifty asked me to dance. I love to dance. When the music finished, he asked me if I wanted to have sex with him."

"How much are you paying, if I have sex with you?"

"One thousand and five hundred now and one thousand after we had sex."

"I told him that I was joking and I left. I continued to drink and dance. I was almost drunk, when he came to me and told me "OK lady, two thousand now and one thousand later."

"Why not sir, I am ready. We met to have sex for one month. We used his condo in downtown. He paid me after sex. We had a schedule. He called me at eleven or four o'clock and I was there at twelve or six o'clock."

"After one month, we had another party. A gentlemen around sixty five offered me five thousand for sex. I accepted. After six months I had five gentlemen that called me regularly."

"Did you have problem with your boss?"

"No Carl. My boss never asked me anything about my private live. He loves me like his daughter."

"How do you know that Kate?"

"Every year for Thanksgiving, Christmas and Fourth of July, I celebrate with my family in Midland. Well, for Thanksgiving I was ready to leave Dallas, when my father called me and said that he doesn't like me to visit anymore and he hang up the phone. I spoke with my mom and she told me, that my cousin George was in Dallas and that morning. When he returned to Midland he spoke with my father. After that my father was mad. I was alone for Thanksgiving. This was very bad for me. A disaster Carl. She started to cry."

"You told me, that your boss is a good man."

"Yes Carl. He gave me for Christmas three weeks to spend in Midland, but I told him that there will be no more Midland for me. He never asked me what happened Carl. The Next day his wife called and she invited me for Christmas. I had a wonderful Christmas. I have been with them many times. I tried to change my live, but my gentlemen scared me with IRS. They told me, if I stopped the IRS will ask me, how I bought a condo for $150,000 with the $34,000 I make a year. I don't like to have problem with the IRS, so I continued."

"Is it true Carl?"

"I don't know Kate. IRS is the IRS. You never know. IRS is very powerful. Your gentlemen have a lot of money. When you are between them it is dangerous, but do you like to stop Kate?"

"I like to stop Carl. I don't know how to stop this?"

"Carl, you speak a lot about your present and future. You will have a wife, children and prosperity. I will never have husband and children, if I am woman, that has sex for money. I need to have a normal live. Could you help me?"

"Are you sure about that Kate?"

"I am sure Carl."

"Well, first you must change your voicemail and stop to pick up the phone. If the gentlemen call you in the office, you tell them that you are busy and you must work until 9:00 p.m. You must ask your boss, if you need to leave before 9:00 p.m. Second, you need to continue your education."

"What kind of business does your company have?"

"Business advice."

"I assume that almost all are lawyers Kate."

"Almost Carl."

"Do you like to become a lawyer too Kate? You can study at SMU."

"Why not? I have the money."

"If you become a lawyer, the gentlemen will think before they ask you to have sex with them."

"Do you have problem to take one day off?"

"No Carl. I told you, that my boss never asks me, when I want to take off. I work very hard."

"Could you take off and go to SMU on Monday? Ask them,

what application you need, so you can continue your education to become a lawyer."

"I will Carl."

"May I ask you Kate, how did you keep this secret for three years?"

"The gentlemen used me Monday to Friday between 12:00-1:00 p.m. and 6:00-8:00 p.m. I never have sex with them on Saturday and on Sunday. They were with their families."

"Why did you say, they used you Kate?"

"I am a sex machine for them. They used me to have sex. They are an ATM for me. I take money from them. It is simple Carl, Sex-money, sex-money, for three years."

"Did you think, that I used you last night Kate?"

"Nooo…! Last night was different."

"Why Kate. What was different?"

"Because, I had sex with you. For the first time in the last three years, I had an orgasm. I wanted to have more and more sex. I wished that time stops, so that will be together in a bed forever."

"I don't understand you Kate."

"I have sex with gentlemen but I never have orgasm or feelings. I am an iron machine for them. Are you ready to have sex now Carl?"

"Yes, I am ready Kate."

"I am sorry, but I have to leave now. I will call you Monday Carl."

"You forgot something Kate. There are $1,500 On the table for you. It is for last night and a good service."

"Thank you for your advice. I know how I can get rid of my gentlemen."

"You take your money Carl. I forgot to tell you that Michelle called and asked for you. I told her that you are asleep. She asked me what I am doing in your apartment. I told her that I am Kate and last night I had good sex with you. Michelle hung up the phone. Is this a problem Carl?"

"This is Michelle's problem, not mine."

"Carl, my name is Katrina Cooper." She kissed me and left the apartment.

I don't think that Kate realizes that she has a big problem. I need to help her. The phone was ringing. It was Michelle.

"Hi Carl, tomorrow at 6:00 p.m. in my house."

"You called me for that?"

"Yes. Do you like to speak with me Carl?"

"No Michelle, I am busy now" and I hung up the phone. After ten minutes the phone rang again. It was my mom.

"How is your live Julia?"

"The same Carl. I called you, because I spoke with Ethan Dreyfus. He called me and he asked for you."

"Do you have problem with Ethan and how long have you known him?"

"I don't have problem with him, Mom. I met Ethan last Monday. I have worked for the company for two years, but I never knew that Ethan is the owner. Ethan is strange, Mom. Why, he didn't meet or speak with me until now? I think that I am a good architect. Do you think that he behaves that way because there is something in his past?"

"Ethan had to deal with many problems in his past Carl. I don't want to tell you, because you live in Dallas. If you were in New York, I would have told you. Why did you left New York, you have everything here?"

"Do you think that I am a bad boy, Mom?"

"I never said that Carl. You are good boy. Many people, including myself, have things in their past they don't want to talk about unless there is a compelling reason."

"Mom, you know that I never ask people personal questions and I don't like to speak about the past. I know that you know about my past because you are my mom and you had to know what kind of boy I am. I am so happy that you are my mom Julia."

"You are a an adult now and working in the Dreyfus family business, so you need to know that I had a sexual relationship with Louis Dreyfus. Ethan Dreyfus is his son. I and Louis were planning on getting married but he left for Dallas. Tomorrow, when you go to the party in the house of Ethan Dreyfus look at face and the eyes of Louis Dreyfus and his wife."

"I will Mom but I need to tell you that I stopped to observe people closely after I moved to Dallas. This was in my past and I don't like to do that anymore, but I will make an exception and I will do t for you."

"Thanks Carl. I know that you love me and you will do everything for me."

"You are right Mom. Are you scared for me?"

"Before I spoke with Ethan, I wasn't but now I am. You must come back to New York Carl", and she hung up the phone.

"I don't know what I need to do but something is wrong. Mom never hangs up the phone before she tells me that she is sending me a kiss."

I picked the phone and I called Ethan.

"This is Dreyfus."

"I will come tomorrow for the party at 5:30 p.m. sir."

"See you at 5:30 p.m. Carl" and he hung up the phone.

I thought about to my past, and how I met Julia. I lived in Jerry Shapiro's apartment. When I came in Jerry's apartment, he told me that I had two choices. I can have my room or I and Max can share Max's room. Max told Jerry that he wants me to stay in his room. I and Max lived together for three months. When I arrived in Jerry's apartment, Max had B and C grades in school. I taught Max, what he needed to do in school. I had one rule. I listened very carefully the teachers and I remembered what they said. Max listened to me and he improved his grades to B and A. Jerry was happy and he told me "When I saw your grades, I knew that you are smart. I was hoping you can help Max and I decided to move you to New York. You did a good job Carl. You and I had a good result. Max changed his grades in school, you live in New York."

"Thank you so much Jerry, I will never forget that." We had dinner in Jerry's apartment when I met Julia for the first time. We ate and spoke. Julia asked me "Are you German boy?"

"No Mss. Shapiro."

"Your family came in USA from Germany. My mom, grandfather, father and I were born in USA. This is three generations."

"Shut up Jerry. Do you know how many Jewish people Hitler killed?"

"Six millions Mss. Shapiro."

"Do you why Hitler killed them?"

"He killed them to steal their real estate property, diamonds, gold, silver and everything of value."

"How do you know that?"

"I read their history. Jewish people are hardworking and peaceful, but the Egyptians', the Roman Empire, Hitler and Stalin tried to destroy the lives of the Jewish people."

"Why did you read about the Jewish people?"

"Because, they know how to make money."

"How old are you?"

"Seventeen Mss. Shapiro."

"Call me Julia."

When I finished school, Jerry told me "My mom likes to see you Carl." We went to her apartment. Julia told me, to follow her. We went to a nice room. She asked me if I like it. I said that I did.

She replied "Since you like it, this is your rom. You will live in my apartment."

"The view is beautiful. I can see Central Park, Mss. Shapiro."

"Call me Julia."

"Thank you so much Julia" and I started to leave with Julia and became her son.

CHAPTER 2

It is Sunday morning. I am drinking coffee and I relaxing on the sofa. I had a very busy week. I finished a good job. The project is ready for a presentation. If Ethan Dreyfus gives me to present the project, I will have a chance to show my expertize. If Ethan chooses Jimmy or he decides to present the project himself, they will have a problem, because they don't know the details. I know that. Oh my God. I am so stupid. I have been working for two years for this company and I had completed many projects, but I never given a presentation. They have used me. I am in the same boat as Kate. I give ideas, complete projects, and get paid for it.

Why did Jimmy tell me now that Ethan Dreyfus have used my ideas? He never told me that before. Jimmy was polite last week. Mom called me and she told that she had sexual relationship with Louis Dreyfus. Now I am wondering.

Who is Louis Dreyfus?

Who is Ethan Dreyfus?

Who is Michelle Dreyfus?

Oh boy, so many Dreyfuses. If I call and ask Mom, she will tell me, who the Dreyfus family is. But why Jimmy never told me about them? I have been many times in Jimmy's and Sue's house. Sue didn't tell me too. Maybe the Dreyfus family has a secret. Mom told me that Ethan had a problem in his past. The phone rang and I picked it up. It was my grandfather.

"What are you doing? I called yesterday but you didn't pick up the phone?"

"I was extremely busy at work last week Grandfather. Today I am free."

"I called you, because I spoke with Ethan Dreyfus on Friday morning. Ethan asked for you. He told me, that he is your boss. Is Ethan your new boss? I knew that Jimmy is your boss. What is going on?"

"I don't know either. I met Ethan Dreyfus for the first time last Monday and he told me that he is the boss and owner of the company I work for. Ethan is a very strange Grandfather, but Ethan's daughter is even stranger."

"Hey Carl, do you have a problem in Dallas? If you have problem, I and Mark will come to help you."

"I don't have a problem Grandfather."

"Carl, I told Dreyfus that you lived in Knoxville until you were seventeen years old. After that you moved to New York and you lived with your mom Julia Shapiro. Ethan Dreyfus was surprised. I wanted to give him Julia's phone number, but Ethan told me, that he knows it. I was surprised that he knows Julia. I am very proud of you. Ethan told me that you are an amusing architect. I need to tell you, that Mark called on Thursday and he asked for you. He gave me one hundred thousand dollars for you. Could you tell me what I to do with this money?"

"Keep the money for me. When we meet, you will give them to me. How is Mark doing?"

"He is good. He has many customers from New York. I think your friend Dino send him many customers after he bought a car from Mark, but you know Mark, he doesn't like to speak about business. The big news about Mark is that he stopped to chase women. Now, he is a loving husband. Your grandmother is scared for Mark." We laughed.

"What is Grandmother doing?"

"She is OK. I keep her busy, because she keeps me busy. You know your grandmother and I laugh a lot. Carl, I think that Julia is lonely. I talk to her regularly. I try to joke, but she told me that after you left New York her live isn't good. You must think about that Carl."

"You are right Grandfather. I spoke with Julia yesterday, she wasn't happy. You know how much I love her. I need to do something. She deserves better live."

"I don't like to give you advice, because you are big boy Carl.

Do you need to tell me something Carl?"

"No Grandfather."

"Bye Carl."

"Bye Grandfather" and I hang up the phone. Now I know that Julia spoke with Grandfather. She is scared for my live, because Grandfather told me that, if I have problem, he will come to Dallas. I don't have a problem. I live in Dallas now for one year and ten months. I have a simple and quiet life. Why did Dreyfus called my grandfather and Julia?

Jimmy was right when he told Dreyfus, if he needs information for my past, he should speak with me. I gave Jimmy my Grandfather's phone number for emergency and I can't believe that he gave it to Dreyfus. I am wondering how does Ethan Dreyfus know Julia's phone number?

I never told Jimmy about Julia. Too Many questions and I don't have any answers. The phone was ringing and I picked it up. It was Michelle.

"Hi Carl. Do you have time to speak with me?"

"Of course, I do."

"Why did you hang up the phone on me yesterday?"

"Today is new day, different from yesterday Michelle."

"What is different Carl?"

"Yesterday, I had good and calm life. I didn't have questions for my past, present and future. Today, I have many questions and I don't have any answers."

"Can I help you Carl?"

"Maybe. But, first I need to know what your problem is."

"Carl, I love you. For the first time in my live I am in love with a man."

"Why, Michelle?"

"You don't know me and I don't know you. You saw me only one time."

"I don't know why Carl. I have one question, but I don't have an answer. Hey, see you at six o'clock."

"I will come at five thirty Michelle."

"See you at five thirty" and Michelle hang up the phone.

Strange girl. I don't know what she wants. Maybe she will tell me when I see her at the party tonight. I took my keys and I left my apartment. After thirty minutes I was in the Galleria shopping mall. I was looking for jewelry. I entered a store with diamonds.

"May I help you sir?" the salesman asked me.

"I want to buy earrings, a bracelet, a ring and a necklace."

"Do you want a set sir?"

"Yes please, but I have only five thousand in cash with me."

"What is your name boy?" an older gentlemen asked me.

"My name is Carl Hope sir."

"You are speaking with New York accent. Are you from New York Carl?"

"I was born in Knoxville Tennessee, but I graduated from a high school in Manhattan and University in New York City sir."

"Where did you live in Manhattan Carl?"

"I lived for three months in Jerry Shapiro's apartment and seven years in Julia Shapiro's apartment. Julia is my mom sir."

"Call me Cristal."

"What are you doing in Dallas Carl?"

"I am an architect. I work in the company owned by Ethan Dreyfus."

"Is he your boss?"

"No sir. I work in the company he owns. I don't have a boss sir."

"Do you know somebody by the name Cristal in Knoxville Carl?"

"I know John Cristal sir. He helped me to move to New York."

"John Cristal is my second cousin, Carl."

"Could you please get three coffees Bill?", Cristal told the salesman.

"This set is eight thousand, but I will give it to you for four thousand and five hundred Carl."

"How is Michelle?", Cristal asked me.

"I spoke with her this morning and I will meet her at 5:30 p.m. We have a party in the house of Ethan Dreyfus tonight. I bought the jewelry for Sue, Jimmy's wife. Do you know Jimmy, Cristal?"

"Yes, I know Jimmy. We had a party and Ethan introduced me to Jimmy and Sue. Jimmy is a fox, Ethan is wolf, but they have been working together for fifteen years. I like to tell you about Michelle, Carl. She is a smart girl. She has a degree in business administration from SMU. Now, she is continuing her Master's there. Every Jew wants to marry his son to Ethan Dreyfus' daughter, but boys are stupid Carl. They call her crazy and they will marry her only for the family money not for her. This is so bad.

After a car accident, Michelle's mom was in a hospital and I believe that somebody killed her there."

"How do you know that Cristal?"

"She died three days after the accident in the hospital. The Doctor that took care for her told me that somebody killed Michelle's mom, a professional. The doctor is my first cousin. But, this is in the past. We need to look forward in the future. I think that Michelle loves you. Somebody needs to help her. I think that you are the somebody that can do that Carl."

"How do you know that Cristal?"

"You are a very different boy. If you marry Michelle, you will marry her, not her money. Carl, you have a big and a good heart. You lived with Julia and she made you a very smart boy."

"Thank you for the kind words Cristal, I will tell Julia."

"Sorry Carl, I have to attend to another customer now." Cristal gave me his business card and said "Call me Carl". He started to speak with another customer. I left the store.

It was lunch time and I looked for a restaurant. I saw pizzeria and I decided to eat there. I entered and I could not believe it. Dino, my brother was inside.

"What are you doing in Dallas, Dino?"

"Hey Carl, mama-mia. Finally, I saw you. I called you many times. I spoke with Jimmy three times. He told me that you are very busy and I should call you on Friday after 6:00 p.m. I called, but Jimmy told me that you left at 5:30 p.m. Is it true Carl?"

"Yes, it is true Dino. I was very busy. I had a project and I finished it at 5:00 p.m. on Friday and I left the office at 5:30 p.m."

"Carl, I know that last Friday night you were in a topless bar. I was there last night. Everybody spoke about Kate and Carl. I asked the bartender who is that guy Carl?"

"Carl Hope man. We had fun last night with Kate and Carl."

"I introduced myself, and I told him that you are my brother and that we are from New York. He was confused that I am an Italian and very different from you."

"Hey bartender, I will tell you a story, how Carl saved my live and after that, my family told me, that Carl is my brother. I told the bartender, how an Irish cleaner tried to kill me but you saved my live. The bartender laughed a lot. I think that he didn't believe me. But that is the past how is your live Carl?"

"Dino, my live is simple. Job, women, sport…etc."

"Are you lonely Carl?"

"I try to keep busy. I love Julia and New York and I know that she is lonely."

"Carl, Julia hates Dallas. When I told her that I have trip to Dallas, she told me that she hates Dallas.

"I lost one lover in Dallas. If you see Carl tell him that he must return to New York, I am so lonely."

"She misses me Dino."

"She love you so much Carl. Could you return to New York?" Dino started to cry.

"Oh, no Dino. My brother can't cry. I will return to New York."

I ordered lunch. We eat and talk.

"Can you tell me about you and your family?"

"I bought a new apartment in Manhattan. Julia told me that since I work in Manhattan and I must move to Manhattan. Julia found an apartment. She made a deal and helped me with twenty thousand dollars."

"How many times I said Julia Carl?"

"I forgot Carl."

"My wife works in the Manhattan School District. Jerry Shapiro helped her to get the job. Do you understand Carl?"

"I understand Dino. I must return to New York."

"May I tell Julia that Carl?"

"Tell her Dino."

"I am so happy Carl. You and I will be together in New York, just like the old times. Hey, you didn't tell me, how much the project cost?"

"Twenty or twenty-two million Dino."

"You know what you work for Carl. I make fifty six thousand and my wife forty two thousand, but we live well. My wife and I are waiting for a second child. Julia is very happy for us. Are going to marry someday Carl?"

"Of course, I will marry, but I don't know when. My flight is at 5:20 p.m. I need to live Carl."

"Do you want me to drop you off at the airport?"

"No Carl. Just drop me off at the hotel. I have a shuttle that will take me to the airport." When we arrived in the hotel, Dino took my head in his hands and he kissed my forehead. He told me "God bless you!".

"What are you doing Dino?"

"Ask Julia. She told me to kiss your forehead and say God bless you Carl!"

He left my car and entered the hotel. I don't know how long I was standing out of my car, when somebody ask me "Are you OK sir?"

"Yes. I am OK." I entered my car and drove to my apartment. I didn't know what to think. I was like a robot. I asked myself "What is wrong Carl? Why Julia is scared for your live?"

Last Sunday was perfect. I had good time with Becky. I met her in a swimming pool two weeks ago. She looked very good and I told her, your body is fantastic. If I spend time with your body in bed, I think that you will be happy and I will be happy.

"My name is Carl."

"I like you too boy. You look very good too. It is a good idea if I spend time with you in bed. My name is Becky." We were together for a week. She told me that Miami Beach is the best place to relax and enjoy.

"You told me that you swim many days of the year. Miami will be perfect for you. If you come to Miami, this is my phone number. Call me. I will be happy to see you. Cheers Carl."

"Cheers Becky."

"Do you like more wine Becky?"

"No. I want sex" and we were in bed for three hours. Later she said "I am leaving tomorrow Carl" and she left Dallas on Monday.

I had busy five days but I had fantastic night on Friday with Kate. I must think positive. I took a shower and I left my apartment at 5:00 p.m.

I arrived at Ethan Dreyfus's house. Ethan was outside.

"Hi Carl."

"Hi Ethan. Where is Michelle? I have flowers for her?"

"She is inside. Sir, I would like to look at your parents' paintings, but don't tell Michelle about it."

"I will not Carl."

"Come in Carl. I will show you four paintings. Two are in the living room and two in my office."

"Hi Carl."

"Hi Michelle and I kissed her hand.

"You are a gentlemen."

"Yes, I am" and I gave her the flowers.

"Thank you so much Carl."

"It is my pleasure."

"Can you give us some privacy Michelle? We will be in the living room and my office."

"I will stay away from the living room and your office father" and she left the living room.

I saw that Michelle listened to her father.

"When you are finished with the living room, you come to my office Carl. My office is on the second floor, third door to the left, I will be there. I don't understand Carl. My parents have been dead for twenty five years, but it is up to you" and Ethan left the living room. I looked at Louis Dreyfus' painting. He had blue eyes that looked far in the future. Louis had a long and calm face.

"Do you think that I am a killer boy?"

I quickly turn around. Nobody was in the living room.

I replied, "I don't think that you are killer sir." I was surprised. I spoke with a person, who was dead for twenty five years. I moved slowly my eyes and I started to look at Ethan's mother. She was different. Her eyes were dark brown and calm. She had an oval face and she was smiling. She looked like a person, who liked to spend most of her time with Louis and Ethan. She trusted Louis. Now I know, looks like somebody killed Ethan's parents. This is a mystery. Who killed them twenty five years ago? Ethan told that they have been dead for twenty five years, he didn't say that they were killed. I left the living room and I looked for Ethan's office. I was on the second floor. I saw that an open door. I knocked.

"Come in Carl."

"Did you ever talk to your father after his death?"

"How do you know that Carl?"

"Because, your father asked me If think that he is a killer."

"Well. I was drunk one night. I looked at my father's painting and I asked him. Why did you kill my mom?"

"I didn't kill your mom. You must stop to drink Ethan."

"I told him that he is a mother faker."

"What are you doing Ethan?"

"I turned around and I saw Sue. I spoke with my father Sue."

"What did he tell you?"

"He didn't kill Mom and I must stop to drink."

"This is a painting. How can a painting talk to you?"

"I don't know Sue but he told me."

"You are a drunk Ethan. I will take Michelle with me if you don't stop."

"What do you think Carl, am I crazy?"

"That means that I am too Ethan. Because your father spoke to me too."

"Do you think, we must ask a psychiatrist?"

"Maybe someday we will go to ask a psychiatrist, but now I want to know something. Do you have a picture of your parents' dead bodies lying on the ground from the police?"

"I have. Just a moment I will give them to you."

I looked at the picture.

"Do you have a ruler?"

I toke the ruler and measured. There were forty nine feet between the bodies.

"Do you have an injury description of the bodies?"

"Yes." He started to read, but I told him.

"I will tell you what I see on the picture, you can compare to the injury descriptions. Your mother had broken legs and pelvis but she didn't have broken head. Your father had broken head, neck but he didn't have broken legs. Is it correct?"

"Yes Carl."

"What floor they were staying on?"

"The room had a terrace and was on the ninth floor."

"Somebody killed your parents. First, they dropped your mom, because her body on picture is near the hotel. Second they threw your father because the body is forty nine feet from your mom. If your father killed your mom, he will have problem to pick up and drop your mom, but two people were able to do that easy. If your father jumped from terrace his body would have been fifteen to twenty feet from your mom. Two people threw your father. Your parents were killed."

The doorbell started ringing.

"This is Jimmy, Carl. I don't want, Jimmy to ask me, why you arrived early. I like us to continue this conversation tomorrow morning at nine thirty, but I don't want Jimmy to know that."

"I will tell Jimmy, that you are off tomorrow morning." We left the office and entered the living room.

"Hey, it looks like you arrived early Carl."

"What were you doing with Ethan?"

"I called Carl, Jimmy. I wanted to give him $100,000, but Carl told me that if we sale the project for twenty million, he will take a check."

"What about me?" Jimmy asked Ethan.

"I forgot your check in my office Jimmy. I will go to get it."

"I will get the check father, you stay here."

"No Michelle, you waited for one week to see Carl. Now Carl is here. You spend time with him, get to know him."

I asked Michelle "Why did you wait one week for me?"

"I wanted to see you, because I love you Carl."

"What should I do with the other girls, Michelle?"

"I don't know Carl. This is your problem. I don't have boys to worry about."

"This is your check Jimmy."

"Thank you Ethan." Jimmy took his check for $100,000 and he started to laugh saying "Twenty million!"

"Are you joking with me Carl?"

"OK Carl, if we sale for twenty millions, I will give you five hundred thousand bonus."

"Do we have a deal? "

"It is a deal, Ethan."

"How much I will get?" Jimmy asked Ethan.

"Zero Jimmy. You took your check."

"Why did you change your mind?"

"You have never given a check before a presentation. If we don't sale the project for twenty million, I don't have to pay a hundred thousand to Carl. I will save money."

"Do you think that I am stupid Jimmy?"

"I don't think that you are stupid Ethan, but Carl told me, that if you sale for less than twenty millions, then you must be stupid."

"Is it true Carl?"

"It is true. If you sale for less than twenty million, you are stupid Ethan."

"Thanks for telling me that."

"My pleasure, Ethan."

"Could you please give me a double shot of whisky Robert?"

"You never drink and drive Carl", Jimmy told me.

"I will leave my car here."

" Did you get a permission from Ethan?"

"Do I have your permission Ethan?"

"Please, Please."

"This is not funny Carl. This is serious" Jimmy told me.

"I am so sorry Ethan, but I have to go."

"See you later."

"See you Carl." I stood up and try to live but Michelle jumped and caught my hand.

"Carl give me your key. I will park your car in the garage." She took the key and told me to sit and relax. I sat and Robert gave me a double shot whisky. Michelle parked my car and she came back to the living room.

"You are very stupid Jimmy. Carl worked five days to fix that project, you took one hundred thousand check for nothing, after that you tried to kick out Carl from my house. Who do you think you are Jimmy?"

Jimmy tried to say something but Sue told him "Shut up Jimmy". I looked at Michelle and told her "You are good girl Michelle."

"Do you think that Carl?"

"May I ask for your help, Michelle?"

"I am listening Carl."

"I was told that you have been studying at SMU for five years."

"Who told you that?"

"A little bird told me, that you are continuing your studies at SMU."

"You are kidding with me Carl. I don't but this isn't important. What can I do for you Carl?"

"Tomorrow morning, my friend Kate will be at SMU. She likes to continue her education there too. Could you help her?"

"I don't want to help her because Kate is a prostitute."

"She isn't a prostitute Michelle."

"Did you sleep with Kate last Friday Carl?"

"I have been with Kate but this isn't important. I am man and I need woman in my bed."

"How did you know, that I have been with Kate?"

"I spoke with Kate on Saturday morning and she told me, that she had sex with you."

"I told you that I am man and I need sex. What do I need to do for you, so you will help Kate?"

"You have to sleep with me."

"I promise Michelle. I will sleep with you."

"No, you must have sex with me."

"But you said sleep and that what I agreed too."

"You decide Carl. If you have sex with me, I will help Kate."

"Do I need a permission from your father?"

"You have it Carl" Ethan told me.

"What do we do now Carl?"

"I like to have sex with you and you have permission from my father."

"Hey, Kate needs to move somewhere for one month, because she is selling her condo. Could you take her Jimmy?"

"Kate is a prostitute. I don't want her in my house."

"Our house dear", Sue told Jimmy.

"I will take her Carl."

"Me too." Ethan told me.

"What do you think about Kate?", Jimmy asked Michelle.

"I don't know now. I need to speak with her, before I can be sure."

"Could you call Kate? I want to speak with her Carl."

"Give me the phone book and a phone Michelle."

I called David, but Michelle put the phone on the speaker.

"This is David, may I help you?"

"Hey David, this is Carl."

"Hey Carl last night was very funny. Dino from New York was here. We spoke for you and Kate, when Dino asked me who is Carl. Carl Hope, I told him. Dino told me, that you are Dino's brother. He told me the story, about the Irish cleaner who tried to kill Dino, but you told him if you like to kill Dino, he must kill you first. The Irish cleaner told you that he will kill you both. You told him that it will be bad for him because you are from the Smoky Mountains and your family will clean three generations of the Irishmen's family. Then we spoke about Kate, but Dino told us that you have a girl in New York. Her name is Vicky. He said that her legs are four feet and one inch long. If you have sex with Vicky, before you start with her, you will finish in your pants. Is it true Carl?"

"It is true David."

"Oh my God. Dino didn't lie?"

"He didn't lie David."

"Are you rich Carl? Dino told us that you are. I know that you have money, because you spent a lot of money on Friday, but Dino told us that you have millions. It is hard to believe it because you are young Carl."

"I don't know how rich I am, but I have around sixteen million David."

"Did you pay Kate one thousand five hundred?"

"I paid her in cash, but she returned my money, because I gave her advice."

"I am a little confused Carl, but tell me, what I can I do for you?"

"You must find Kate and tell her, that Michelle will help her at SMU."

"Give me her full name and birthplace Carl?", I asked.

"Katrina Cooper and she was born in Midland, Texas."

"Can you give me your phone number Carl?"

"I am not at home right now. I am at a party. She will have to call here."

"Hey David, my name is Michelle and the party is at my father's house" and she told him her phone number.

"Oh boy, looks like you have a new girl tonight. Carl don't go to bed with her. You must be near a phone, because Kate will be calling you in twenty-thirty minutes."

"I will David."

"Who is this Irish cleaner Carl?, Michelle asked me.

"He wanted to kill me, but now he is my best friend. His name is Roger."

"How much did you pay to have sex with Vicky?"

"Hey, this is my privacy Michelle. What is your problem and why are you asking me about my private live?"

"I am sorry, if I have upset you Carl."

"You didn't upset me and I will tell you. The first time I was with her I paid three thousand, after that she never took my money."

"How does he know that she has four feet and one inch legs?", Michelle asked me.

"I measured her legs with a ruler and her legs are four feet and one inch long. It takes me fifteen minutes to get to kiss her pussy, when I start to kiss a finger on her leg."

"Oh my God. After this perfect description, I need to be with a woman."

"May I invite a woman my daughter?"

"Of course. This is your house father."

"Could you please give me a double shot whisky Robert?"

"You have not had a drink for ten years", Sue told Ethan.

"I remember, Michelle was 12 years old, now she is 22 years", Ethan replied.

"I feel very happy tonight, so I want to have a drink. Cheers Carl."

"I want too" and Michelle took a glass of wine and she said, cheers to everybody."

"Cheers Michelle", we all said. The phone was ringing. Michelle picked up.

"This is Michelle, may I help you?"

"Hi Kate. Carl is here. Carl for you" and Michelle gave me the phone.

"Kate, you need to speak with Michelle. She has been at SMU for five years, I will give her the phone now" I tried to give the phone to Michelle, but she told me that she will take the call in her bedroom. They started to speak and I hang up the phone.

"How did David find Kate?", Jimmy asked me.

"I think that David used the police, because he asked me for Kate's full name and birthplace."

I asked Ethan where the is box I brought with me.

"The box is on the table", he replied. I toke the box and I gave it to Sue.

"This gift is for you Sue. Thank you for the excellent lunches last week."

"What is this Carl?"

"A jewelry for you, Sue."

"I see, but this is very expensive."

"For you, this is nothing. You deserve much, much more."

"Can I see it Sue?" Ethan took and looked at the jewelry.

"This set of jewelry costs eight thousand dollars, Sue."

"I paid four thousand five hundred Ethan. If you don't believe me, the invoice is in the box. If Sue doesn't like the jewelry, she can exchange it."

"Where did you buy the jewelry from?"

"From the Galleria. The seller was Cristal. He gave me a good deal."

"Cristal divides every penny. I think that something has gone wrong with him."

"Cristal said that he knows you Ethan."

"Of course, he knows me, but why did Cristal gave you this big discount? What happened between Cristal and you Carl?"

"Well, Cristal asked me where I lived in New York and I told him, that I lived in Jerry Shapiro's apartment for three months and then I lived with Julia Shapiro for seven years. Julia is my mom and I will go back to New York. You are right Ethan, the price was eight thousand."

Sue put the jewelry on and she jumped and kissed me.

"Do you think that I am a Princess Ethan?"

"Now, you are a diamond Princess, Sue. If somebody wants to ask you for something, he must pay hundred thousand."

"Hey Ethan, this is my wife."

"Of course, Sue is your wife now, but nobody knows tomorrow Jimmy." Sue raised her wine glass and told us cheers.

"Carl gave me back my life. Thank you so much Carl."

"It is my pleasure. You are the diamond Princess and I am your jester."

Jimmy asked me, "Can you tell me Carl, how did you make sixteen millions dollars?"

Ethan and Sue laughed and Ethan said, "Are you jealous Jimmy?"

"I am not Ethan."

"OK Jimmy. I am like Clyde from Bonnie and Clyde, but with a twist. I and my girls did fifteen bank robberies."

"I am serious Carl. I want to know the truth."

"Do you want to know everything or in general?"

"I want to know everything Carl."

"Hey Jimmy, we are in a party, I don't like it to be about Carl's past."

"Shut up Ethan."

Well, here is the short version. I was nineteen years old. We had a party. Somebody asked me if I have five thousand to invest on the Market.

I replied "I don't understand your question! My name is Carl."

"My name is Joshua. I work on the New York Stock Exchange. I am a broker. If you invest five thousand now, after two three years you will have thirty or thirty five thousand."

"OK Joshua, I will give you five thousand in cash."

"Not now. You need to come to my office. I need to prepare contract and you must sign it. Which day is good for you Carl?"

"Monday after three o'clock I have time", and I gave Joshua my name, address and phone number. I asked my mom, what the New York Stock Exchange is. She told me that smart people make a lot of money on the Market.

"What is a broker, Mom?"

"Person, why works with your money."

"Do you want to invest on a Marked Carl?"

"I will invest Mom."

On Monday, I was in Joshua's office. Joshua gave me the contract. I read it and asked, if he can change the contract.

"No problem Carl, I will change it. What do I need to change?"

"I want to invest one hundred thousand dollars."

"I need fifteen minutes to change the contract. While you waiting for me, do you like some coffee, tea or water Carl?"

"No. I am OK."

I was looking out the window from the Joshua's office when somebody asked me, "Who are you, Joshua needs to work, and he does not have time to waste with friends?"

"I am client sir", and I told him "Could you close the door please on your way out?"

I signed the contract and I was getting ready to live, when the same person entered the office and he asked Joshua, "Who is this boy?"

"My client sir?"

"How much did he invest?"

"One hundred thousand sir."

"How old are you boy?"

"Nineteen sir."

"Give me the check Joshua?"

He called and he spoke with my bank. "Sorry boy. Everything is OK Joshua." While he was leaving Joshua's office he told me, "I will never forget what you told me."

He smiled and closed the door. I invested one hundred thousand, now I have eight million now Jimmy.

"Can you tell me about the Dealership?"

"How did you know that Jimmy? I never told you about it."

"Are you spying on me Jimmy?"

"I am sorry Carl, I told him." said Ethan .

"Don't worry Ethan."

"I am waiting Carl."

"Oh no Jimmy, give me a break", said Ethan.

"I will tell him Ethan. Cheers everyone." Sue and Ethan raised their glasses, Jimmy didn't.

"Are you ready Jimmy?"

"I am ready Carl."

I was in my third year in the University. My Uncle Mark called me and he asked for an advice. He told me that somebody was trying to close his dealership. "They offered me two millions dollars Carl. They were pushing me to sale. What will I do if I sale it?"

"Mark, don't be scared. Give me two days. I will call you."

I called my broker Joshua and I told him, what happened with my uncle.

"I need Mark's full name and phone number. I will speak with my boss. He loves you Carl. He refers to you as "Could you close the door?"

Joshua called next day and told me, "Carl, Mark must sale. They will give Mark two million and three hundred thousand. Your grandfather has a lot land around Knoxville. He needs to take surveys of the land. Next Thursday, you, John and Mark need to be in my office at nine o'clock in the morning."

Mark sold for two million three hundred thousand. We were in Joshua's office on Thursday. Joshua's boss told me that I need to create a project for a new dealership. Grandfather prepared survey for the building of the dealership and Mark invested the money. After six months, we had a new dealership. We invested four millions, now the dealership is worth sixteen million.

"Did you understand Jimmy? It is simple, invest and invest again. Any questions Jimmy?"

"I don't have any more questions, Carl."

"What kind of man are you Carl?", Sue asked me.

"I don't know, but after ten years, I must have one hundred million dollars Sue."

"I believe you Carl", and she stood up and kissed me again.

"What are you doing Sue, this is my boy!", Michelle said to Sue.

"Carl is yours Michelle, I have a husband."

"Daughter, if you continue to be so pushy with Carl, he will leave Dallas and he will never return to our house."

"Is it true?", Michelle asked me.

"Of course, I will disappear Michelle."

"I love you and I like to kiss you Carl."

"What about my privacy Michelle?"

"This is a free country. I want to tell you about Kate, Carl."

"You didn't answer my question."

"May I sit on your lap Carl?"

"Of course. She sat and she told me. Kate isn't a prostitute. She wants to study to be a lawyer."

"Oh my God. What is Sue?"

"You are a Princess."

"I am Michelle."

"May I touch the jewelry?"

Michelle stood up and touched the jewelry. She returned back and sat again on my lap. She continued to speak and she moved her ass on my lap.

"Oh Carl, I feel something."

"Of course, you feel. For ten minutes you have been moving your ass on my lap. It woke up."

She jumped off my lab and said "Kate told me that Carl is a good horse. If you are a good rider and keep a good rhythm, he will run between forty to fifty minutes. Carl is good at sex Michelle."

"I am a jester."

"No Carl. You are good horse."

I laughed and I said "Cheers!".

"This isn't good for you, if somebody calls you a horse", Jimmy told me.

"I don't care what people think about me. I know who I am. The fox is a smart animal Jimmy. The fox hunts rabbits underground and duck around the lake. The fox has enemies. Hunters and wild animals. The fox has to think, hunt and avoid it's enemies. You don't think Jimmy. The first hunter will kill you. You aren't a smart fox."

Jimmy jumped and he told me "I am not a fox."

"That is what I think Jimmy, but it is up to you. You need to say cheers now."

Robert stood up and he told Ethan, that it is 7:30 p.m. and he needs to get the dinner table ready.

"Robert sit down, I will get the table ready", Michelle told Robert.

"I have a very heavy casserole in the stove Michelle."

"I will help her Robert."

"Thanks Carl."

Michelle and I entered the kitchen.

"Hey Carl, if you need a condom, I have some in my car", Jimmy told me.

"Thanks Jimmy, I will make French love with Carl", everybody laughed and Ethan said, "hey daughter, you are very honest about such a private matter on front of so many people".

"I am father."

I helped her to move casserole from the stove and I try to live, but Michelle took my head with her hands and she kissed my mouth for a long time. I was surprised.

"You need to go back to the living room, they are waiting for you Carl."

"Hey Carl, you finished very fast."

"She didn't like me Jimmy."

"If you marry Michelle, you will be very rich."

"I don't like to marry for money Jimmy, I like to marry the woman I love."

"What is the difference?"

"I don't like someday my children to tell me that I married their mom, because she is rich."

"Do you love Michelle, Carl?"

"Why do I need to love Michelle, Jimmy?"

"You work in the company that Ethan owns and he is your boss. Ethan is Michelle's father."

"I never have a boss Jimmy. I work in a company, but I don't think that you or Ethan is my boss. I have worked in the company for one year and ten months. Why you didn't tell me, that Ethan is the owner and your boss Jimmy?"

"Ethan is your boss too, Carl."

"I don't think so Jimmy, but I told you that you are a stupid fox."

"What is the problem with who the boss is?", Ethan asked me and Jimmy.

"I will tell you father, what the problem is."

"You and Jimmy think that you are smart, because you use Carl. You think that Carl will stay in the company and he will create projects and you and Jimmy will make good money from his projects. Carl works for the company to gain experience and Carl will leave."

"How did you know that?" Ethan asked Michelle.

"The first time I met Carl, I told him that your father built this house and he had a Construction Company in Dallas. Carl smiled. Now I know why Carl smiled. He will open his own Construction and Investment Company. Carl wants to make millions, he doesn't need your cheap salary father."

"Is it true Carl?"

"It is true Ethan."

"You never told Michelle that?"

"No, I didn't. Michelle concluded that analyzing my face and my words. She is smart. You must be proud with her Ethan."

"What will we do if Carl leaves Ethan?", Jimmy asked.

"Don't say ,we, Jimmy. I work at home and I use Carl's ideas and I make projects. You must work Jimmy."

"You have two children and a beautiful wife", I told Jimmy.

"This isn't your problem Carl?"

"Of course, this isn't my problem, but if Ethan kick your ass out of the office what would you do Jimmy? You have a family, you must support your family. Your children and beautiful wife, they deserve that."

"Why did you say that Sue is beautiful?"

"Do you like to have sex with Sue, Carl?"

"Never Jimmy. I respect Sue a lot. I love your children. I have many women. Why do I need to have sex with Sue or you think that I am a sex manic?"

"I don't think that you are a sex manic, because you love my children and Sue. You are my best friend. I don't know what to do Carl."

"You must start to use your brain. If you work, you will be busy. People, who work, they are busy and they don't have time to look, what other people do. They want to work more and more. They want to make more and more money. They want to have better and better live. This people think positive. You have a lot free time. You look at what people do in the office. You spent a lot of time asking them, what they did in the office and out of the office. They tell you, because you are their boss, and they are scared. You never ask me, because you are scared. You know that if you ask me, I will tell you. Mather fucker who are you to ask me?"

"Is it true?", Ethan asked Jimmy.

"Carl is right. Carl has such a personality and I am afraid to ask him. Carl works very hard and he makes good projects, but I don't understand, why he wants to make millions."

"Not for me Jimmy, I will make money for my wife and my children. They must have money. I would like one day when I am eighty years old, my children and grandchildren to tell me "We are proud with you. You are the best husband, father and grandfather. You built this world for us." That is it Jimmy. I am twenty six, but I think for the time when I am going to be eighty. Maybe, I am crazy, but I am Carl Hope."

Michelle clapped and she said, "Carl, you live in another world, they will never understand you. I understand, because I think the same as you. I think for love, children and husband. I like to live forever with them. I want my children to be prosperous. I love you Carl, because you and I think the same."

"Oh my God! I don't believe that two different people can think the same."

"Do you believe that?", Jimmy asked Ethan.

"I don't know what I need to say, but young people live in a different world Jimmy."

"Do you love me Carl?"

"At this moment, I don't love you Michelle. I need time to get to know, but I applauded you for your speech, nobody else did."

"I will wait. Doesn't matter how long it takes you Carl." I stood up and I kiss her lips long. Michelle pulled my body closer to her. I felt her.

"I don't know what to do Michelle."

"Nothing Carl. I am not ready for sex. I like to have sex, but I am little scared, because I am a virgin. I am so sorry Carl."

This is OK Michelle.

"Carl, do you think, that we have a problem, because I am virgin?"

"I don't think so Michelle. Maybe you have a problem, if you have sex when you are fifteen, sixteen or seventeen. You are twenty two. You keep your virginity to have sex with the man you love."

"I love you Carl and I like to have sex with you, but I need time, because I don't have experience."

"I understand Michelle."

"You don't need experience to have sex daughter, you take Carl in bed. He knows what to do." Everybody laughed.

"Hey Michelle, Carl, we have a party. Cheers for love", Sue said. Everybody raised their glasses and said cheers.

"Are you going to sleep in Ethan's house tonight Carl?"

"No Jimmy. I don't want to be running fast early in the morning while Ethan is chasing me and calling me "Mother fucker, my daughter was a virgin last night, this morning she isn't. I will kill you."

"You are wrong Carl. I will not be surprised, if my daughter tells me early in the morning "My father wake up, last night I raped Carl and now I am not a virgin."

"I like that my father, I will think about that."

Robert told us that dinner is ready and we moved to the dining room. Robert cooked very well. The food was delicious. I looked at my watch. It was 10:30 p.m. I called and ordered a taxi. Michelle wanted me to stay and sleep in her house, but I told her that I need to go back to my apartment. The taxi arrived and I said good night to everybody. I kissed Michelle and I entered the taxi.

"I will drop you in your apartment Carl."

"Yes. You gave me your phone number on Friday night, but I don't remember your name."

"Call me Frankie. I work with my son. When I work at night he is off, he usually works during the day. I will give you his phone number."

"Tomorrow morning at 9:00 a.m., I need to come back to this house. I need to take my car. Could you tell your son to pick up me at 9:00am?"

"I will pick up you, because I know your apartment and the house where I need to drop you."

"Thanks Frankie."

"Do you have an enemy Carl?"

"I don't know Frankie."

"A Black Cadillac is following us. I saw the same car around your friend's house. I will change direction to see if it follows us.'

Few minutes later Frankie said "Carl, the Cadillac is continuing to drive behind us. What do you want me to do Carl?"

"I don't have an idea Frankie."

"I have Carl. I will stop at the shopping center and I will call my son. He will drive the taxi. If the Cadillac follows my son, I will follow the Cadillac with the car of my son."

"Do you have a problem to walk from the shopping center to your apartment?"

"I don't have a problem to walk Frankie. This is will be a good exercise after dinner."

"See you tomorrow morning at 9:00 a.m. Carl."

"Good night Frankie."

CHAPTER 3

It is Monday morning. I woke up at 6:30 a.m. I have about two hours before 9:00 a.m. I started my regular morning exercise and I was going through what happened last week. Now, I have learned that Ethan is the owner and the boss of the company I work for. Mom is right. Ethan had a big problem in his past. Maybe today I will find out, what that problem was, if Ethan decides to trust me and tells me. Last night Ethan drank for the first time in ten years. Maybe, he stopped, because he had a big problem with Michelle, but she was twelve years old when Ethan stopped to drink. I will never ask Ethan because I have a rule to never ask people for their private life. Jimmy is a total opposite of me. Cristal was right when he told me that Jimmy is a fox, but I know that Jimmy is a stupid fox. Last night Jimmy lost control, Sue saw that and she tried to protect Jimmy's image. Jimmy understood and he changed his position towards me and Michelle very fast. Looks like Sue and Jimmy have a big secret too. I think that Sue depends on Jimmy but this isn't my problem. Sue is my best friend. She knows that.

The question is, who is Michelle and why does she loves me?

It seems to me that she doesn't have a mental problem but I can sense that she has some problem in her life especially dealing with boys. Cristal told me that boys liked Michelle's family money, but not her. I don't understand that, she is a pretty girl.

Honestly, Michelle looks so sexy but I am not ready to have sex with her. Maybe someday I will. The phone rang interrupting my thoughts. I picked up. I couldn't believe it. I was thinking of Michelle and she was calling me. Like she was reading my mind.

"May I see you this afternoon?"

"I am sorry, but don't have time, I am busy."

"You are a bad, a very bad boy."

"I am Michelle. Could you kiss Kate and tell her that I am sending her a kiss?"

"I will kiss Kate, because I am not jealous Carl."

"This is good for you. If you were jealous, you would never have said that you love me."

"Is it true Michelle?"

"Yes Carl. I love you and I am not jealous, but I am busy too" and she hang up the phone. This was good for me, because I didn't have time. I looked at my watch. It was 8:45 a.m. I put on some clothes and I left my apartment. Frankie was waiting for me.

"Good morning Frankie."

"Good morning Carl. How are you feeling this morning?"

"I am good Frankie. I exercised, took a shower, had breakfast and I spoke with Michelle. I had a good time on Friday and Saturday too. During the week I worked and at night I stayed in my apartment. Last week, I was very busy. I finished a project, but if the company sales the project for twenty million, I will make $500,000, so my hard work was worth it"

"You are making good money Carl. My son and I have to work for seven years to make this money."

"How many days of the week do you work Frankie?"

"Sometimes, I work seven days a week. I need to make and save money. I live in Plano. I bought a house with three bedrooms and two baths, but my son will marry and I need to buy a house with four or five bedrooms. You didn't ask me, what happened with the Cadillac last night Carl."

"I forgot Frankie, so please tell me."

"I followed the Cadillac. There were two people inside. They went to a big house. The house was big, similar to your friend's house. This is the address."

"How much do you need to save to buy the new house Frankie?"

"I need nine thousand."

"If you don't have this money, I will give them to you."

"Thank you so much Carl, my family will be happy I will never forget that."

We arrived at Ethan's property. Ethan was outside. Frankie jumped and opened the door.

"Thanks Frankie."

"My pleasure, my King."

Ethan laughed and said jokingly "Are you a King Carl?"

I gave Frankie five hundred dollars, but he told me, that I don't need to pay. I left the money on the seat and closed the door. And asked him "What is the difference between five hundred and five hundred thousand?"

"Three zeros Carl."

I introduced Ethan to Frankie.

"My friend Frankie will be looking around your house for some time Ethan. Don't be alarmed about that."

"Do you want the money now?" I asked Frankie.

"Not now, when I am ready, I will call you."

"Ethan, Frankie needs nine thousand to buy a new house. I promised to give him the money, but since I am going out town, you give Frankie the money."

"No problem, Carl I will do that for you."

"Ethan, you know many bankers. Could you help Frankie to get a good rate for his mortgage?"

"I will. Frankie, this is Ethan's phone number. I will give yours to Ethan." Frankie left Ethan's property and Ethan told me to come in.

"Could you bring two coffees to my office Robert?"

"One coffee Robert. I don't like coffee right now, may be later."

I sat on a chair. Ethan asked me "Why did you tell Frankie's to look around my house?"

"Last night a black Cadillac followed us" and I told Ethan what Frankie told me about the car and where it went.

"How did they know that you were in my house Carl?"

"The only people that knew that were me, you, Jimmy, Sue, Robert and Michelle."

"I don't know, but this is the address where they went with the car."

"Carl, this is the address of Scott Colman. Frankie is wrong."

"Frankie is right Ethan."

"Can you tell me who Scott Colman is?"

"My father and Scott were partners, but when my father died, Grandfather sold to Scott my father's share for very cheap."

"Why did he sell it cheap?"

"I asked three times my Grandfather, but he never told me."

"Do you know how much the share was worth at the time and how much did Scott pay?"

"I don't know. Grandfather told me "You must forget the company". I became an architect and I opened this company, the one you work for now Carl."

"How is your relationship with your Grandfather?"

"Before my father's death, I had a good relationship. After that, I hated him, but he had been dead now for three years."

"Why did you hate him?"

"After my father's death, Grandfather invited four people in the house. Two were from New York, the other two were from Dallas. They were looking for something everywhere in the house. I didn't know what for, but they were in the office when one of them asked Grandfather, what to do with the books."

"Throw them on the floor boys, who cares for books."

"I love to read books and I didn't like that at all. I took a gun, entered the office and told them "If you don't live now, I will kill you". Before they left the house, I told Grandfather "If you come back in the house, I will kill you. Never ever come back here stupid Grandfather." He looked at me and told me "You are stupid grandson and your father was very greedy". After that, I never spoke to him. I didn't invite him, to my wedding and when Michelle was born. I am close with my uncle Simon. He is a good man. I love him and he loves Michelle and me. Simon cried so much for my father. He cried every times he saw me. Simon was in my house when my wife gave birth to Michelle. I told him "Simon no more cries. My father is not coming back. We must look to the future". After that, Simon never cried. I lost three people, who I loved."

"Somebody killed them for a reason Ethan."

"Now I know that my parents were killed, but my wife died after a car accident."

"Most probably the same people killed her in the hospital Ethan."

"How do you know that Carl?"

"Cristal told me. The doctor who took care of your wife in the hospital was his cousin. He told Cristal, that your wife was killed by professionals. I think that the deaths of your parents and wife were connected. You must give me every document you have. I will need some time to analyze them."

"Did you know that Julia and Louis had a sexual relationship?"

"I was fifteen or sixteen when my father told me about Julia. He said "Ethan, I love your mom, but when I lived in New York, I had the first love in my life. When I came to Dallas she never followed me. I told you, because I don't want somebody else to tell you about her. Her name is Julia Shapiro."

"Did your mom know that Louis and Julia had a sexual relationship?"

"I think she knew. When Louis told me about Julia, I was surprised, but we never spoke again about that."

"I was twenty or twenty one when I met Julia's daughter Debby. I had a sexual relationship with her, but she asked me all the time about my father, so I left her."

"Do you think that your mom hates your father, because he loved Julia?"

"Before yesterday, I thought that my father killed my mom and I hated him for that, but now I know that he loved Mom. My mom was very powerful and I listened more to her than anybody else when I was a child. I didn't listen to my father, but he loved me so much. I think that Michelle looks more like my father's family. On Friday, I called Julia and left a message."

"Did she call you back?"

"She called me on Saturday and she told me about your parents." Robert entered and he asked, "Do you like coffee Carl?"

"I like coffee now Robert, thank you."

"If somebody asks for me, I am not at home Robert."

"I know that Ethan, I will say that you are out."

Ethan asked me, "Do you think that Michelle has a mental problem?"

"I don't think so. Michelle is a normal person, but she has growing up without her mom. I am sure you are a great father, but you are man. She is very sensitive like a little animal afraid for his life."

"She was able to read your thoughts."

"Because she is sensitive and smart too", Ethan.

"I will speak with Michelle. I like to know what happened to her."

"All I can tell you that she was in New York and when she came back, Michelle told me "You aren't a good father and husband." I said to her, your mom is dead and I don't have a wife. Why did you tell me that I am not a good husband?"

"Because you didn't save my mom. She is dead and I will die too. I didn't let Michelle to go back to New York."

"How old was Michelle at that time?"

"Fifteen."

"Michelle doesn't believe you, because somebody told her something different about her mom's death than you have told her."

"I will speak with Michelle."

"Don't do that Ethan. She will close even more. She needs to open her heart and brain. She must do that. Now she is twenty two and she will change."

"How do you know that?"

"I was the same. I was twelve years old when I started to observe people. Julia was the first person who asked me "Can you read my thoughts Carl? Could you tell me what I think?"

"I told her what she thought."

"You are right Carl", she confirmed.

When I was twenty four I stopped.

"Do you think, Michelle loves me Carl?"

"She loves you, but she doesn't believe that you will save her live, because you didn't save her mom."

"Your coffee Carl."

"Thanks Robert."

"Do you think that Michelle will be safer with Carl than with me", Ethan asked Robert.

"Yes sir. Michelle thinks that she is safe with Carl. She told me that you didn't save her mom."

"Why you didn't tell me that Robert?"

"If I told you, would you believe me Ethan?"

"I wouldn't have."

"I am so sorry, but I have more to tell you."

"Do you remember when Frank Colman's wife Emmy came late one night?"

"Yes, I remember that Frank called and told me that Emmy

must stay in my house, because Frank was in California. I didn't find that unusual, because my wife and Emmy were friends."

"Well, this wasn't normal Ethan. Emmy told your wife crying, that Scott Colman tried to rape Emmy and Scott's wife saw that."

"How do you know that?"

"Your wife asked me to keep this between us, because you will fire me. At your wife's funeral, Scott Colman told me "Robert, Ethan is next."

"You might be right Robert. Now I understand why Frank bought a new house when he returned from California and moved there very quickly"

A phone was ringing.

"Mr. Dreyfus house, may I help you?"

"Robert, this is Jimmy."

"Is Carl there?"

"No Jimmy. Carl isn't here."

"May I speak with Ethan?'

"He isn't here too. You are a lair Robert. Ethan and Carl are inside."

"Can you wait for a moment Jimmy? I will get my gun and kill one stupid fox. I will be a hero for every hunter" and Robert hung up.

"You are my hero", Ethan told Robert.

"I am" and Robert left the office.

"You must help Sue, Ethan. Jimmy is out of control."

"I made many mistakes in my past. I spent twenty five years and millions of dollars for nothing. You made the right decision for thirty minutes."

"Should I ask Michelle why she is scared Carl?"

"Yes Ethan, but you need to be honest with her."

"I think that Michelle suspects that I might have something to do with that."

"You tell her that we spoke about your past and that I helped me get clear understanding about some events in your past. I think that you and Michelle will have a good conversation Ethan."

"Thank you Carl."

"This is your ticket to New York. Wednesday morning at 10:00 o'clock is your flight. You know Julia. She called and said, "I need to kiss my son. You need to buy tickets for Carl and Michelle to come to visit me in New York. We have the presentation for the project in Frank Colman's office on Tuesday at 3:00 p.m. in the afternoon. You will present the project. You need to be in Frank's office at 2:30 p.m. in the afternoon. This is the address. I will give Michelle her ticket on Tuesday night."

Robert told us that the lunch is ready. We sat down and started to eat. He cooked a wild duck. I tasted it and I said "It looks like it was marinated in spices for at least twelve hours. Is that correct?" I asked Robert.

"Yes Carl. A wild duck needs to be marinated."

"How did you know that Carl?"

"My Grandfather is a hunter and sometimes he killed wild ducks. My Grandmother use to prepare them the same way as you did Robert."

"Do you like to hunt Carl?"

"No Ethan. I love animals. I believe that animals are better than humans."

"One time when I was with Grandfather he killed a fawn. I asked him, "Why did you kill this beautiful fawn Grandfather?"

"Because, I am a hunter."

"After that I never went with him to hunt. He taught me, how to use a pistol. Last time I scored ninety nine from one hundred. The instructor told me, "You use a pistol very well."

"I replied, "Ninety nine isn't good instructor. One hundred is good.""

"Are you scared Carl?", Ethan asked me.

"No, I grew up in the Smoky Mountains, Ethan. My grandfather told me, "If you meet a wild animal, you must stay quiet, don't move. If you are scared the wild animal will feel that and it will attack you. If you are not scared the it will leave you alone."

"Carl, last night you said that Kate was born in Midland. Scott Colman was born in Midland too, but Frank Colman was born in Dallas. What do you think about them Ethan?"

"I have business with Frank and I have a good relationship with him. We are best friends. My father loved Frank very much. Every time he saw Frank, he gave him money. My father told me that Frank will be a good businessman. I don't know Scott. I see him sometimes in Frank's office."

"If I have a chance, I will kill Scott" Robert told me and Ethan.

"May I hire you to be my cleaner Robert, you will kill all my enemies?"

"I will pay you five thousand every month Robert."

"Why not? This is a good idea Carl."

"Oh my God. I have a killer in my house" and we laughed.

"Hey, when I go back to the office, if Jimmy asks for you Robert, I will tell him to be careful with you, because you were a killer before and that Ethan doesn't know that."

We finished lunch.

"I need to leave, Jimmy is waiting for me. Hey Robert, when you see Michelle could you kiss her from me? If Michelle asks you why, tell her that I am sending her a kiss."

"Oh boy, you like to joke a lot", Ethan told me.

I took my car and I left Ethan's property. I was in the office. Jimmy was waiting for me.

"I like to speak with you Carl."

"Come to my office Jimmy." We entered the office and I closed the door.

"I want to tell you what happened this morning. First, Robert wants to kill me. Second, a Black Cadillac followed me and then parked in our company parking. Two people spoke with Kelly. When they left, I asked Kelly, why these people were following me and if they were asking questions about me. She said that she didn't know who I was talking about."

"Kelly, I saw you speaking with them."

"She said that the two people were asking about you Carl not me. I didn't believe her. They asked for me, they didn't ask for you Carl. Do you believe that Robert will kill me Carl?"

"Robert use to be a killer."

"How did you know that Robert was a killer?"

"Last night I saw that Robert carried a gun and I asked Ethan why was Robert carrying a gun?"

"Ethan told me that Robert was a killer."

"You need to ask Ethan, who Robert is Jimmy."

"I am scared for my live Carl."

"Don't be scared, you need to work Jimmy. You need to use your brain."

"What do I need to do Carl?"

"You need to work on your projects."

"I will, but if I have a problem, you need to help me."

"You need to ask everybody in the office Jimmy."

"You are right Carl."

"I must use my brain and he left my office."

Now I know. They don't know my car and they don't know where I live. My office phone was ringing. It was Sue.

"I like to speak with you. May I see you at 3:00 o'clock in the coffee shop Carl?"

"See you there Sue."

I saw Kelly and I told her "I will leave the office and I will be back on Wednesday morning."

"If somebody asks for you Carl I will tell them that you will be back on Wednesday morning."

I am going to New York that day, but I didn't want anybody in the office to know that.

At three o'clock I was in the coffee shop. Sue was there. I kissed and asked her "What happened with Jimmy?"

"He is scared. That is why I called you Carl. Last night when I and Jimmy went home, for the first time in my life, I saw Jimmy very scared and he spoke incoherently. I was scared for the children. The babysitter looked at me and said "Don't worry dear, he is drunk." I asked her to leave early and I paid her. When I came back in the house, Jimmy was crying. I kissed Jimmy and I took him to bed. We had sex. After that Jimmy slept. I couldn't sleep the whole night, but I don't have any idea what to do."

"I was sleeping when I heard the children saying "Mom, wake up". I opened my eyes and the children told me that Jimmy was very angry. Where is he now? I asked the children. "He left the house Mom." I called and asked Kelly, where Jimmy is, but she told me that Jimmy isn't in the office. Do you think that Ethan will fire Jimmy?"

"I don't think so Sue. I spoke with Jimmy and you are correct. He is very scared. He asked me what to do. I told him to use his brain and focus on his work."

"I need to tell you something Carl. Before I married Jimmy, I had a big love. When he graduated the University, I had one more year to go. We were planning to get married, but he disappeared. I spoke with his mother and she told me that he left the house two days ago. I thought that he was with you Sue. He called me after ten days and he told me "Sue find another man" and he hung up the phon. I cried for one week when my mom told me "Sue you need to continue your education. There are many men in the world". I met Jimmy in a bar. I was drunk. After the bar we went to Jimmy's apartment. In the morning, Jimmy asked me to marry him. I thought that he was kidding and I told him that maybe someday I will marry him, but first want to graduate from the University. He asked me to have dinner with him the next day and I accepted. The following night in the restaurant Jimmy asked me if I want to marry and he gave me an engagement ring. I accepted. Now I understood. He told me, I want to marry. He didn't ask me to marry him." Sue paused, took a deep breath and continued.

"After we married I became nothing. Jimmy didn't let me to continue my education. I had two children very fast. Jimmy decided everything. I was a nobody. I don't know what to do. If you have an idea, tell me Carl?"

"My advice will be for you to speak him. You must finish University and start to work. You speak with Michelle too. She loves you and she will help you."

"Sue, what happened when Michelle was twelve years old?"

"Ethan was drunk and Michelle called me for help. After twenty minutes I was in Ethan's house. Ethan was in the living room and he was speaking with a painting. I took Michelle and Robert to my car. I went back in the house and I said "Ethan, you must stop to drink, otherwise Michelle will live with me or she will go to New York." Michelle lived for one week in my house. Ethan stopped to drink and he started to work from the house. Ethan took Michelle back. Jimmy became the boss. For the last ten years Ethan has been working from home and Jimmy has been the boss. I need to speak with Jimmy to see how he is doing."

Sue left. When she returned, she was angry.

"You are right Carl. Jimmy is scared. He told me that two people were in the office and asked for him. A black Cadillac is waiting outside the office."

"They will kill me Sue."

"I told Jimmy, that I will come to the office to pick him up."

"Sue, you need to speak with the people inside the black Cadillac. If they don't leave, you call the police".

"I will ask them to leave", Carl. She stood up and kissed me.

Sue left and I followed her. She spoke with the people in the black Cadillac. They left and I followed them. The black Cadillac entered Scott Colman's property. I know now. Scott Colman likes to know, where I live and what car I drive. Tomorrow I will tell you Scott, I told myself. I was in my apartment at 6:00 p.m. I decided to go for a swim in the morning. I was in a bed by 9:00 p.m. I woke up at 5:30 in the morning. At 7:00 a.m. I was in the swimming pool. I swam for two hours. I was outside the swimming pool when Michelle asked me "What are you doing here Carl?"

"I swam and I am getting ready to live."

"How many times have you been here?"

"I have been here many times, in the last two years. I never saw you before."

"Of course, you didn't. You were looking for some macho man. I am a simple man."

"No Carl" and Michelle put her hand in my swimsuit and she touched me. I was surprised and aroused.

"I like the what I felt in there Carl!"

"Michelle, if you like it, take it and carry it with you."

"No Carl. You carry it. I like to use it. See you later" and she jumped in the pool. I looked in the swimming pool, nobody was there except her. It was a joy to watch her swim. She was a good swimmer. After few minutes I left. I drove and found a place for breakfast. I had some yogurt and fruits. When I finished breakfast I asked the manager to use the phone. I called Kate's office and I asked to speak with her.

"I need to see you Kate."

"Come to my office, my boss wants to meet you."

I was in the office shortly and I asked for Kate at the lobby. "Kate's office is on the third right door sir." I entered and closed the door.

"Oh boy. Do you need something?"

"No Kate", and I told her what happened in the swimming pool. "Carl, this isn't good. This is a public place."

"I know, that is why I need your advice as a woman."

"Carl, I spoke with Michelle yesterday and I told her that she needs to be more aggressive if she want to get your attention, but Michelle is dangerously aggressive. I will speak with her about it."

"If you speak with Michelle before I do, you need to tell her that this is not the way to go. You need to use strong language, Carl."

"Michelle loves you and she will listen to you. She will think that If she doesn't stop, she will drive you away from her. Michelle is so sensitive and honest. Everybody knows and loves her at SMU.

They prepared my documents for one hour and half. I will start school in August. I am so happy Carl. Hey last night I called you, but you didn't pick up the phone."

"I am sorry, but I was tired and I was in bed by 9:00 p.m. I am so happy that you will start school Kate. Hey, you told me that you were born and lived in Midland. Do you know Scott Colman?"

"I think that my father knows him, but you know that I don't speak with my father. My boss said that Scott was born in Midland, but I don't know Scott and I never met him."

"I need to speak with your boss Kate."

"Come with me Carl."

We entered the office of her boss.

"Boss, this is my friend Carl, you wanted to meet with him."

"My name is Dan Hoffman. Kate told me that you gave her a good advice. The advice will help her. You are a smart man. Do you like coffee Carl?"

"Yes sir. Call me Dan. "

"Could you please get two coffees for us Kate?"

"Can you give me the name and phone number of your father and close the door Kate?"

"His name is Ned" and Kate told me the phone number and she closed the door. I called and put the speaker on.

"This is Ned Cooper, may I help you?"

"Hi Mr. Cooper. My name is Carl Hope."

"Why did you call me?"

"I want to ask you about Scott Colman, because he was born in Midland and you live there."

"Do you work for the FBI Hope?"

"No sir. I am an architect."

"How did you find my phone number?"

"Kate, your daughter gave it to me."

"I don't have a daughter Hope."

"What do you want to know about Scoot?"

"Today at 3:00 p.m. I will meet Scott and Frank Colman, so I would like who I am meeting with."

"Frank is a good man, but Scott is a Devil." Ned laughed and he asked "How old you are Carl?"

"I am twenty six sir."

"Call me Ned. You must be careful with Scott."

"Do you want to speak with Mr. Dan Hoffman, Mr. Cooper?

He wants to speak with you."

"OK give me Hoffman."

"How are you Mr. Cooper?"

"I am well Dan."

"Mr. Cooper, I am the owner of the company Kate works for. "

"Do you want to come to my house Dan?"

"Which day do you want me to come to your house Ned?"

"Can you come this weekend?"

"OK. I will come with my wife on Friday afternoon, but I don't know your address Ned."

"Take Kate with you Dan, she will bring you over. Carl, you are invited too."

"Thanks Ned, but I have business with Scott and Frank Colman so I really need to know who I am dealing with."

"Carl, every time Scott comes to Midland, he has two or three boys with him. They are killed or disappear, but I will tell you a story. I was eighteen or nineteen. Scott was middle age. When I met Scott he asked me if I needed money."

"What do I need to do Mr. Colman?"

"You must kill somebody boy."

"I will kill you first Colman." Colman pissed in his pants. They were wet. After that, he never spoke to me.

"See you Friday Dan" and Net hang up. I stood up and opened the door. Kate was waiting outside with the two cups of coffee.

"Come in Kate. Is your father a hunter?"

"He spends a lot of time hunting."

"Could you tell me how much is one good rifle for a hunter Dan?"

"Good rifle costs three or four thousand Carl."

"Take this four thousand and buy a rifle for Ned."

"Four thousand is a lot of money Carl. How much do you make a year?"

"One hundred seventy thousand, but I will get a check for five hundred thousand this afternoon."

"Kate told me that you are rich, now I believe it. Carl, you were asking about Scott. He is a bad man. His son Frank is good. Sometime I have business with Frank. I never had any business with Scott, but my friend told me that Scott is dangerous. You must be careful with Scott."

"I am so sorry, but I need to leave Dan."

"When you have time call me, I would like to speak with you Carl."

"I will call." I kissed Kate and I left the office.

I was in the lobby of Frank Colman's an office at 2:15pm.

"Good afternoon lady, my name is Carl Hope. Where is the conference room for the Dreyfus' project presentation?"

"Go to the fourth door on the left. Are you the presenter? Are you scared Mr. Hope?"

"Carl is never scared Monica." I turned and I saw Michelle.

"This morning I touched Carl's erection."

"Michelle is joking Monica."

"I am not joking."

"Thanks Monica. I need to find the conference room and get ready for the presentation."

Michelle walked with me and we entered the conference room together. Ethan was inside and he asked me.

"Are you ready Carl?"

"I am ready, but I need five minutes to speak with Michelle." He walked fifteen feet from us. I think that Ethan knew what happened this morning. I asked Michelle "How many hands do you have Michelle?"

"Two Carl" and she laughed.

"Can you put one hand in your rear, and the other in your mouth? I am a gentleman, I am not a street clown. You must stay ten feet away from me. You should be ashamed at yourself for what you did this morning and said now to the receptionist." I need you to stay ten feet away from me. I turned and walked toward Ethan. He asked me "Are you ready now?"

"Now I am ready Ethan."

We were talking about the project when Michelle came to us. "I asked you to stay ten feet away from me Michelle, you must do it." She tried to say something to Ethan, but he told her "I am busy Michelle, not now". She counted ten feet from me and stood there looking at me.

Jimmy came and he asked me "Why is Michelle staying there Carl?"

"I asked her to stay in a ten feet distance from me Jimmy."

"Who are you to tell Michelle, what to do?"

"Jimmy it is good for you to keep out of this."

"Hey Ethan there is Emmy and Kris Colman, I will say hello to them and he left us."

"You may scare many people today Carl."

"If Scott Colman comes, I will start with him Ethan. He laughed and told me, "Good luck Carl". I walked and I looked at the project, when somebody told me, " I heard that you are Carl Hope boy."

"Yes, that is me sir."

"My name is Frank Colman."

"Nice to meet you Frank."

"How much do I need to pay for this project?"

"If you want to make a good profit, you need to pay twenty two million Frank."

"I want a good profit. "

"How do you know that I need to pay twenty two million?"

"Every house in the project costs between $400,000 and $700,000. The houses will be bought by people who make from $300,000 to $600,000 or more a year. If you build one thousand houses and you have a profit of $150, 000 on each house, you will make $150,000,000. You will pay twenty two million and you will have profit of $150,000,000. You will need to buy a cheap land in California, Oregon, Washington State or Colorado, but you must buy a lot of land for a new development in different states Frank.

"Can you help me Carl?"

"I will come with you Frank."

"You need to ask your boss Ethan, if you can come with me."

"I don't have a boss, I just work in Ethan's company."

"Nobody knows you in Dallas Carl, but this morning I spoke with "close the door" from New York and I asked him for you. I borrow money from him. He is my banker, and he works on Wall Street. He told me that you are a smart and honest young men. He advised me to work with you if I want to make good money and trust the price you give me. OK boy, I will buy the project. Do we have a deal?"

"Yes, we do Frank" and we shook hands.

"I would like to introduce you to my wife and my daughter Carl. Emmy and Kris, this is Carl, my future partner."

I kissed Emmy's hand. "You are a real gentlemen Carl."

"I am lady." I shook Kris' hand.

"I am so sorry, but I have a presentation now, so I have to go", Frank told us and he toke the microphone.

"Ladies and gentlemen, I bought the project. Ethan, please come to my office to discuss the details." Ethan looked at me and I raised my shoulders.

"What happen with Michelle? She has been standing for twenty minutes in the same place and not moving", Emmy asked me.

I look at Michelle and I told Emmy and Kris "Excuse me ladies" and I walked to Michelle. I walked to her I kissed her cheek.

"I am sorry Carl, I better not talk. I am embarrassed."

"Michelle, you need to think before you do or say something."

"I like to speak with Emmy and Kris Carl." Michelle and I walked to them.

"How are you Emmy?", Michelle asked.

"I am good, thank you."

"How is your life Michelle?"

"The same Emmy, except that I met Carl and I love him."

"You need to make some changes in your life Michelle."

"I am trying Emmy, but it is very hard for me. You know, after my mom died, I grew with my father. I didn't have a mom to teach me about boys and now I have a problem. This morning I did something wrong, and I told other people about that, and they laughed at me. If I had mom, she would have told me that what did is not good for me and the boy."

"Don't worry about that Michelle. I am sure that Carl will forgive you."

"I love Carl, Emmy, but he doesn't love me."

"I think that someday maybe not too long from now, Carl will tell you that he loves you and he will ask you to marry him."

"Mom, what about me? Kris asked.

"You don't have a chance with Carl dear. Carl needs a wife, who will spend time with him and his children. He needs a wife who will listen to him. Dear, you like to spend time shopping and husband who listens to you. You will never listen to your husband. I think that Michelle is the right woman for Carl and she will marry him."

"Thank you Emmy."

"What happen here, why don't we have a presentation?"

Everybody looked towards the man that was speaking.

"This is Scott Colman", Emmy told me. He was with two people.

"Ask your son, he is in the office." Emmy replied.

"Shut up Emmy, I don't know why my son married you. You are a cheap prostitute." Scott turned and he walked to Frank's office.

"Emmy, I need to speak with you." Emmy and I moved towards the end of the conference room, so we can speak without being heard.

"You must help me."

"Of course, I will. What do I need to do for you Carl?"

"You must know a person in Scott's house who can give you information for Scott. Where he travels, what car and airplane he uses. I know, this is not easy, but if you pay good money somebody will tell you. I will give you the money to pay that person."

"I have money Carl, but I have a question. Do you plan to kill Scott?"

"I never killed anyone, but if I have a problem with Scott, I will kill him."

"How do I will give you the information you asked for?"

"It will be easier if you tell Ethan, since you speak to him regularly. I will get it from him."

"I hate Scott Carl. If I have a chance, I will kill him."

"This is my job Emmy." She went back and she started to speak with Michelle and Kris. I was alone, when Scott walked to me and he asked me.

"Are you Carl Hope?"

"I am sir."

"Do you knowing, who I am?"

"I don't sir."

"I am Scott Colman and I am the owner of this company."

"Nice to meet you Scott" and I tried to shake Scott's hand, but he told me "I don't want to shake the hand of a clown".

"This is your decision Scott."

"My son Frank paid twenty two million for this trash."

"Don't talk like that for this project Scott. It is a good project and modern with a great potential."

"How do you know that joker?"

"Scott, you are an old man. I saw a stain on your shorts. You must keep your pants dry."

Scott couldn't tell, if it was true. Scott left the office with the two men. Emmy came and she kissed me on the cheek. She whispered "I will do anything for you Carl. For the first time, I saw a man who scared Scott."

"I need to leave the office, but I don't want somebody to see that. Could you come with me and talk until we reach the door Emmy?"

I got in my car and stared driving to my apartment. While driving I looked at the mirror. Of course, the black Cadillac was following my car. Before my car entered the gate of my building, the black Cadillac passed me and entered first then turned to the left of my apartment. Now I know, that they know my car and my apartment, but they don't know what I am thinking. I turned to the right and I stopped at the public phone. I jumped out of my car and started pressing on the hood until the alarm stared to whistle. I called the police. I told them that two people with black Cadillac are trying to steal my car and I gave them the address. I cleaned the phone handle with tissue and jumped back in my car. I was parking my car when I heard firearm shots. I walked towards the direction where I heard the shots and saw that the policemen and people from the black Cadillac were firing at each other. I entered my apartment. The shots continued. After ten minutes they stopped. I knocked on the door of my neighbor and asked "What is happening Gloria?"

"I don't know. Somebody was shooting."

"Could you stay with me, I am scared Carl?"

"I will stay and I entered Gloria's apartment."

"Do you like coffee Carl?"

"It is too late for coffee, but if you have wine I will have some wine. I had a busy day and the wine is good for relaxation." She brought two wine glasses with wine.

"Cheers Carl! We are neighbors for year and a half, but we never have been together. We spoke four times when you traveled to New York and you gave me a key to look after apartment, but you never invited me to spend time with you.'

"Gloria, I am so busy, but I have a principle. I never have intimate relationships with my friends, at my work or with my neighbors. Many people use their job and neighbors to have sexual relationships."

Somebody knocked on the door. Gloria opened. A policeman told her that a man called the police and he wants to speak with him.

"I didn't call and I don't know who did, but I want to know

what happened?"

"We killed two criminals, but they killed one policeman. I am sorry lady, but I need to check the other apartments."

We drank and spoke. I looked at my watch.

"It is 10:00 p.m. Gloria. I need to leave."

"Could you stay with me, I am scared Carl?"

After one hour we were in her bed.

I woke up and I looked at the watch. It was 6:15 a.m. Gloria was sleeping. I left and went to my apartment. I took a shower and I put some clothes in a bag. I went back to Gloria's apartment. She was in the kitchen. She asked me "Are you leaving?"

"I need to leave, because I have a business trip."

"Are you going to give me your key?"

"Yes Gloria. I will be away for one or two weeks. If something is wrong and you need help, you call this phone number. Kate is my friend."

"I will, but I need to ask you, are we going be together in the future?"

"I don't think so Gloria. We had good time last night together, but we don't have a future. I am so sorry, if I hurt you."

"You didn't hurt me. I had a good time with you last night and I hope that we will be good friends."

"Thanks Gloria. "I kissed her and left her apartment. When I arrived at Ethan's house, Michelle and Ethan were ready to leave.

"May I park my car in your garage Ethan?"

"Of course Carl. Michelle, please park Carl's car."

I took my bag and Michelle parked the car.

"You have one bag only Carl?"

"Michelle, did you forget that I am from New York?"

Robert was outside and we told him good bye.

"I will miss you Carl", Robert told me. Ethan drove and nobody spoke.

"What are you thinking about Carl?"

"Could you tell me, what I should be thinking about Michelle?"

"Last night Carl, I came to your apartment. Nobody was there, but your car was there. You were missing."

"How do you know where I live?"

"My father and I asked Jimmy to come with us. He told us where you live."

"Why did you do that Ethan?"

"Michelle said that you have a problem, but she didn't tell me what the problem is."

"You shouldn't do that in the future Michelle."

"I love you Carl and I was scared for you."

"This is my privacy Michelle but I will tell you. If you marry me and you chase like that after me, you will catch me with another woman and you will want to get a divorce. I don't see a point for us to marry at all."

"Could you tell me, where you were last night?"

"Well, when I parked my car, I heard shots outside my apartment. I was scared and I cried. I didn't know what to do, when a woman told me "Don't be scared and don't cry boy. You can spend the night with me. I will save your life."

"You are a bad, bad boy Carl. I told my father and Jimmy, that we shouldn't be so concerned about you and that I am sure you are having sex somewhere, while we are worrying about you."

"You didn't believe me last night, do you believe me now father?"

"I believe you and I know that you are right, but you must think before you decide what you want to do. Carl said that he had sex last night with somebody. Do you want to marry him?"

"Of course, I want to, but Carl must want to marry me. We are so different. Carl has girls and he has sex with them. I don't have boys and I am a virgin. But now I know that if I marry Carl, I will never ask about Carl's past and I will never chase him." We laughed. We arrived at the airport and Ethan told Michelle "Could you give me a minute with Carl?"

"I will father", and she left the car.

"They tried to kill you last night Carl." Ethan told me.

"I know that Scott Colman's people tried to kill me."

"Do you think that they will try to kill me and Michelle?"

"I don't think that Scott people will kill you, but maybe they will kill Michelle to hurt you."

"We have a problem Ethan. Scott knows me, you, Julia and Michelle. I know only Scott. I am suspecting that there are more people involved in this game. I need some time and more information."

"Carl, I have arranged for you to meet my uncle on Friday at 3:00 p.m. in New York. You need to ask him. His name is Simon Dreyfus. He has more documents and information for you. Simon loved my father very much. He was different from Louis. Simon loves Michelle too. He will give you a credit card. I told him that you need to have this credit card. When you use it we will know where you are and if you have a problem we will help you. I saw how you analyzed the documents, we have looked at them and didn't see anything. I am sure that you will see something we could not, may be because is our family and we can't. Emmy told me that she is certain that you will catch and cut a big head."

"I will Ethan, because I don't have a choice. Them or me. There is not a middle way for me at this point."

"This morning I spoke with Julia and asked her to have Michelle in her apartment. Do have a problem if Michelle stays in Julia's apartment?"

"No Ethan, but I think that Michelle will be safer, if she stays with me. I understand Michelle, and I will try to help her. Last night God saved my live, because I felt that I have a problem. I didn't know what the problem was, but I felt that, and I now I am very conscious about my surroundings. This is the reality for me now. I have accepted the game and I must finish it. I am still analyzing and I don't have experience in this game, but I am sure that I am one step ahead, because I believe in God, they don't."

"How do you know that Carl?"

"I have never killed a person, but they killed three innocent people, your parents and your wife. They killed your parents for information, your wife to punish you. I am starting to believe that this game is for a lot of money, at least hundred million dollars. That is what I feel Ethan. I need to leave, Michelle is waiting." We left the car and Michelle asked Ethan "Do you give Carl the check, father?"

"I forgot Michelle." Ethan gave me a check and I put it in my pocket. Michelle asked me why I didn't look at the check. "This isn't important for me, how much the check is Michelle."

"Give me the check Carl." And I did.

She looked at the check and grimed at her father.

"Father, you got twenty two million, but you gave Carl one million. Carl deserve two or three million. Next time I will make the deal Carl." I was surprised at her reaction.

"I think that you will be a good wife", I told Michelle.

"I will be Carl." We laughed. Ethan kissed Michelle. I and Michelle entered the airport. At 10:00 a.m. we flew to New York.

CHAPTER 4

We were in the plane flying to New York. I closed my eyes and I was thinking of Julia, Jerry, Dino, Vicky and New York. Michelle asked me if I was thinking about Julia and my friends. "Yes I am Michelle, you have read my mind again. These people have been in my life for many years. I love them and they love me. I love New York. I was seventeen when I came to New York. I grew up in New York as a teenager, but I love the Smoky Mountains too, because I was born there. I assume that you love Dallas, because you were born and grew up in Dallas. I am sorry that I am not very talkative. I am tired and I need some rest. If you like to talk I will listen."

"I want to tell you what happened last night Carl. I didn't need to see you. My father wanted that. He was scared for you. I didn't know why. He was very happy when he saw you alive this morning, but I want to tell you about last night. Ethan toke me and Jimmy, because Jimmy knows where you live. We saw your car and Jimmy checked your apartment. Jimmy told us that nobody was in your apartment. Jimmy said that we must call the police and ask for you. I told them that you are most probably with a woman somewhere. I asked Jimmy if he would like to be the light in the room there."

"You are a good girl Michelle, I know that and thank you for telling me."

"Do you want to hear the rest?"

"Yes please, I am listening."

"Ethan was angry and he told us that we need to get in the car.

Ethan didn't want Jimmy to call the police. When we entered the car Jimmy said that he will speak with you tomorrow. He said that he wanted to know what kind of man you are. I told him "you had two years to ask Jimmy. Carl is never coming back to the office. He closed the page in Dallas. Today was the last day of Carl in Dallas."

"Carl has to work in Dallas for two more months, he has a contract Ethan."

"You must forget the contract Jimmy."

"May I ask you Jimmy why did you wait to ask Carl in the last two months of his contract, if he wants to extend it with us?"

"I don't think that this was important, Ethan."

"You are lying Jimmy. You waited, because if Carl asks, you will tell him that the company isn't making enough money, so if he wants to extend the contract he will have to take a pay cut. We thought that we used Carl, but it looks like he used us. He has enough experience to work anywhere. On Monday I will be back in the office. You need to clean your office, because I will take your office. You need to move in Carl's office. On Friday I will buy new office furniture. You have to work now Jimmy and Sue must go back to the University to finish her education. I will find a job for Sue to work part time."

"Ethan dropped Jimmy at his house. Ethan drove, but we didn't speak. When we went home, Ethan told me that when he was in Frank's office, he was surprised when Frank asked him "Where did you hide this golden boy until now Ethan? Frank and Carl will make hundred million dollars" and Frank gave me checks for twenty two million. Now I know, why Louis loved Frank. Every time Louis met Frank, he gave him one hundred dollars. Louis knew that Frank was smarter than me. I listened more to my mom. If you marry Carl you need to listen to him. He will be a good father for your children. After that he gave me the ticket to come with you to New York."

"Have a good time with Carl and you must decide for your live. You are a big girl."

"In the morning Ethan called and asked Julia if I can stay in with her and she said "Yes". After that I heard what my father saying to Julia "If you were my mom, I would have been a better man. I would have understood my father Louis "and Ethan hang up the phone. I didn't understand that comment from my father Carl. Do you have any idea why he said that?"

"I know Michelle, but I will tell you that in New York, because this is a long story."

"Could you start now Carl, we have two hours before we arrive?"

"How did you meet Julia?"

"I was seventeen when I arrived in New York."

"Why did you leave the Smoky Mountains?"

"They kicked me out of school, because I told that teacher that she was a liar."

"Why did you tell her that?"

"When you were talking I didn't interrupt you! I don't want to interrupt me now."

"I am so sorry Carl."

"Could you continue Carl? I will listen."

"No. I need to sleep" and I closed eyes.

When I opened my eyes, Michelle asked me "You slept for one hour how do you feel now?"

"I am better Michelle. I have never slept before in the plane. I had a good sleep."

"Do you like to continue?"

"Continue what Michelle?"

"Telling me about your life in New York."

"Oh my God. You don't stop pushing me. You are so aggressive Michelle."

"Why do you need to know about my life in New York, I never ask you for your life in Dallas?"

"If you ask me, I will tell you Carl. "

"Many people think that you have a mental problem, but I know that you don't. You have problem with your life. You don't know what to do with your life. You look at the life of other people and you ask them questions. If you have your own life and you are busy, you will never ask other people about their life."

"You are right Carl. I have a simple life. I want to know, because if you have a problem and I want to help you. I want to save your life Carl."

"Michelle, you need to open your heart and change your life. You must stop to read what people think. If you tell me about your life in New York, when we get to Julia's apartment, then I will stop trying to read what people think Carl. Do we have a deal?"

"Deal Michelle."

We arrived at the New York airport and took a taxi. After one hour, we were in the building of Julia's apartment. I pushed the bell.

"Don't you have a key Carl?"

"I have, but what if Julia has a boyfriend in the apartment with her?" A man's voice came from the inside, "The door is open".

"What are you doing here Grandfather?"

"Who are you boy, I am here to see Michelle?"

"I am here Grandfather" and Michelle kissed him. "Come in daughter" and mom kissed Michelle. I laughed and entered my room.

"May I come in?", Julia was knocking on the door of my room.

"Come in Mom." She embraced and kissed me.

"Finally, I saw you and you are alive. I was scared for your life Carl."

"I hope that you are staying in New York, because I don't want you to go back to Dallas?"

"I am planning on staying in New York. I will never leave you for a long time again Mom."

"Carl, I will kiss your cheek here, I didn't want Michelle to see that. You are a big boy."

"I know that Mom. I need to speak with you in your office."

"You wait in the office Carl, I need to talk to John and Michelle for a minute."

I was waiting in the office looking through the window when Julia entered and closed a door. She asked me "Were they trying to kill you Carl? I saw the news this morning."

"Yes Mom."

"Why Carl? You have a quiet life in Dallas and you don't have any enemies?"

"I don't know Mom, but you need to tell me everything for the last sixty years."

"I told John and Michelle that I will not be with them for one hour. We will have to continue tomorrow Carl, if are not finished."

"Well, Louis Dreyfus was the biggest love I my life. We were preparing to get married. It was Friday. Louis came to my father's apartment and told me "I must speak with you, I will wait at our place in Central park". After thirty minutes I was there. I tried to kiss him, but he told me "Not now Julia. Tomorrow, I am leaving New York. I am moving to live in Dallas Texas. Are you ready to come tomorrow with me or you need time to get ready, so and when I am back in New York next time we will go together to Dallas?"

"Louis, you can forget that, I will never leave New York."

"He didn't say anything. He left Carl. I didn't believe it. I thought that he will call letter and apologize, but he didn't. The next day I called and asked for Louis, but his brother Simon told me that Louis left New York and he is in Dallas."

"I thought that you knew that Julia".

"After one month, Louis came to New York. I and Louis were in a hotel. We had sex. I tried to convince Louis to come back to New York, but he told me "Julia, you have two choices. I and you live in Dallas or you live in New York and I live in Dallas." I told him again that I will never leave New York. When I woke up in the morning, Louis wasn't in room. He left.

Ten days later I met Simon and I asked for Louis, he told me "Louis is getting married next month Julia." I didn't believe it. Louis closed the door for me. I never saw Louis after he married. Louis gave me a chance, but I didn't take it.

Few months later, I was in a restaurant when a man who I didn't know very well asked me to sit to have a drink with him. We drank and spoke. After the restaurant we continued in a hotel room and we had sex. We woke up at 9:30 in the morning. He kissed and asked me "Do you like to marry me Julia?"

Why not? and we were married four weeks later. I was pregnant. After eight months Jerry was born."

I clapped and said "Bravo".

"What is that Carl?", Julia asked

"Sue married Jimmy the same way as you did but there is a difference. Jimmy told Sue, "I want to marry you". Your husband told you "Do you like to marry me Julia?"

"Oh my God. You analyze what people tell you Carl?"

"You are correct Julia. This will save my life."

"One hour Carl, I need to go back in the kitchen."

We finished dinner and Julia started to clean the table, but Michelle said that if Mom has talk to me, she will clean the table. "Thanks Michelle" Mom and I went back to her office.

"She is a smart young lady, Carl. What do you think?"

"Mom, you had sex with Louis Dreyfus, Ethan Dreyfus had sex with Debby. Are you ask me to have sex with Michelle?"

"The answer is that I don't need to have sex with Michelle."

"You are very arrogant, Carl."

"I am Mom. I don't want Dreyfus, but you must continue with your story."

"Who told you about Debby and Ethan?"

"Ethan told me Mom."

"Well, we married and bought this apartment and Jerry was born. My husband, I don't want to say his name. For us he is the joker. The joker returned to the house and he told me "German Nazi is looking for people to spy for them. They are around the Dreyfus' apartment. I think they are spying on Dreyfus." After three days one Nazi was killed inside the building of the Dreyfus apartment, and life continued Carl.

Debby was born and everyday was the same. I didn't love the joker, but I have two children and they grew with us. Before I got married I was an aggressive woman, but after that I was a different person. At home I was quiet. I was more aggressive at my job. One day when I was home, the joker came and he told me "Your lover killed his wife and then committed a suicide. This was big news in Miami Beach Julia. They killed them for information. Before were Nazi, now KGB, Stasi Mafia and now a businessman from Dallas. They all are trying to steal the diamonds from Louis Dreyfus" and he left the living room.

I went to Miami and I stayed there for three days. I spoke with a detective, I cried and offered him money. He told me" I am sorry, but if I tell you anything, the shark will kill me and he will kill my family too."

"Did you remember the name of the detective?"

"I know his name Carl, but when I finish, I will give you everything."

"When I came back to New York the Joker asked me, "Do you have news from Miami?"

"Are you spying on me?", I asked him.

"After one week the joker had a car accident and he died. When we finished with the funeral, we returned to the apartment. I cried."

"Why are you crying Mom, he was a Devil", my daughter told me.

"What did you say Debby?"

"Mom, he pushed me to have sex with Ethan for information."

"Then when I married, he blackmailed me. He said, "Debby, if you tell that your Mom that I pushed you to have sex to spy on Ethan, I will tell your husband about it. Can you believe that Carl?"

The joker used his daughter for information. After that, I have never been to the joker's grave. The joker's brother was in the apartment and he asked me, "Why are you doing this, he was your husband Julia?"

"You must ask Debby" and I left the apartment. Now I speak with his middle brother, nobody else from the joker's family talks to me."

"I can't believe that after twenty five years somebody started this again. I taught that is was over. One think I don't understand is why they didn't kill me Carl?"

"Why do they needed to kill you?"

"It looks to me that they are after the Dreyfus's family. You are in the Shapiro family."

"Then why are they trying to kill you Carl?"

"Because, I was in Ethan Dreyfus house and I spoke with Ethan. I think that there is a connection between Ethan, you and Simon."

"Why do you think that?"

"I never had problem in Dallas until you spoke with Ethan. I was in Ethan's house and Ethan spoke with Simon. After that, they tried to kill me. I am a new person for them, but they think that I know something. I don't know anything. I need to find that something before they kill me. I must know who is behind that something. I have to find out what the something is."

"I don't understand Carl, why are saying the word something so many times."

"Oh my God, Mom. I think that the that something is information. They killed Louis and his wife for information."

"What is the information that Louis and Louis wife had?"

"We will speak more tomorrow. It is getting too late now Mom. We need to get some sleep."

"I will give you some documents now." She gave me an envelope and told me, "Carl promises me, you will be very careful and stay alive."

"I promise Mom" and went to the living room. I said good night and went to my room.

I was in bed when Michelle knocked and asked me "May I sleep with you Carl?"

"Come in Michelle." She was laying in the my bed next to me. I took her head from the pillow and put it on my chest. We didn't speak. For the first time in my life I was with a woman in bed and I didn't know what to do. Michelle was sleeping peacefully.

I woke up and looked at my watch. It was 5:30 in the morning. Michelle was sleeping and her head was on my chest. I put head gently on the pillow. She didn't move. She was asleep.

I made coffee and went to the office. I was looking at the books on the shelf, when Julia knocked and asked me "May I enter Carl?"

"Come in Julia." I continued to look at the books.

"Why are you looking at the books Carl?"

"I think that there is something in those books. I think that the joker was keeping information there. The joker is dead, but the information is still here."

"Did you or somebody looked at the books after the joker died?"

"No Carl. Before the joker died Jerry and Debby lived on their own. I was the only person dusting them, but I never remove them."

"What do you like for breakfast Carl?"

"Bacon, eggs and Greek salad Mom." She left the office.

I started checking the books on the top shelf, first. I removed the books one by one and checked the wall behind them. One book looked different. It had hard cover. I saw pages, but the book was a box with drawn pages. You couldn't open to read it. I set on a table and turn on the lamp. I started to investigate the book. I saw a very small hole. I toke a pin and I placed the pin in the hole. The book opened. Inside the book was an envelope. Michelle knocked and asked "Could you open the door?"

"What do you want Michelle?"

"I need to see you. Please wait for me in the living room or the kitchen, I will come there." I closed the book and placed it on the same place, but not all the way to the end of the shelf.

I left the office and went in the kitchen. Michelle asked me "Why did you lock the door Carl?"

"Why are you asking stupid questions like that? The office is a place for documentation and sometimes you don't want everyone to see it."

"Hey, this is a lady. Don't speak to her in that tone",

Grandfather told me.

"I am sorry Michelle, please don't ask so many questions. I have something very important in my mind."

The atmosphere in the room became tense. Mom tried to break that and she asked me "Where do you want to have your breakfast Carl, here or in the living room?"

I looked at Mom and replied, "I want to eat here Mom."

I was still angry with Michelle, so I told her, "You never ever ask me, what I am doing. Do you understand Michelle?"

"I understand Carl. I am sorry."

"I don't accept your sorry Michelle. I told you. You must think before you start to speak or you must keep your mouth zipped."

After breakfast, I asked Julia "What are you planning to do today Mom?"

"I will take John and Michelle shopping" and they started to get ready to leave. "When we are ready and decide to come back, I will call you."

"Thanks Mom." They left and I locked the door. I went back to the office and I started to check the books again. I found a second book that looked the same. The top shelf had four books that were the same. I took the first a book and I opened it. I found an envelope and took out everything from it on the table. I took piece of newspaper and I read it "A Nazi was killed In Manhattan. His name was Otto Weber." Julia already told me that. Next, I took a letter and I read "Otto Weber has a son who lives in Switzerland with his mom. His name is Hans Webern and his mom is Anna Weber." Oh my God looks like the joker had a mental problem. He wrote Otto Weber and Anna Weber.

"Why did the joker wrote that Otto Weber and Anna Weber have a son Hans Webern?"

His name must be Hans Weber. Maybe, they adopted Hans, because Julia is my mom, but her name is Shapiro, my name is Hope. I took and read next the letter. It said "Julia had a problem with Louis. She didn't want to leave New York. Louis left to Dallas. I must marry Julia. I need to find out what happen with the Dreyfus family diamonds."

Next letter. "Lucas Dreyfus from Paris told the Nazi about the diamonds. Lucas was in Oswiecim in 1943, but he disappeared and he came back to Paris in 1948. Louis Dreyfus was in Zurich Switzerland in the spring of 1950 and in the summer of 1951.

Pavlov worked for KGB. He has more information for Lucas and Louis, but he doesn't want to meet with me." I opened the next book and I read the first letter. "The shark is smarter and more aggressive than Pavlov. The shark wanted to know, what did Louis do when he was in New York. The shark asked for Simon and his father, what they did, where they traveled and what is their business, but I didn't have any of this information. Louis and Julia met in New York. Julia never met Louis again after he left her. I must invent some story, because the shark is very dangerous. I need to know, why the shark works for the KGB and who told him for the diamonds and Louis. The shark has information that Louis has a business partner in Dallas. Why does Louis's need a partner? He has enough money for business?"

Next book. "Pavlov disappeared. The shark said that he killed Pavlov. I don't believe it, but the shark said that if I lie to him, he will kill me. Ethan Dreyfus was in New York. Debby must have sex with Ethan and she needs to ask him for Louis. I told the shark that and he was happy. The shark told me, that I am smart, but if Julia finds out she will kill me. I need to be careful with Julia. I met a new KGB, Konev. He is different from Pavlov and the shark. I met Konev and Hans Weber from Stasi. Hans asked me for Otto Weber, his father. He wanted to know what happened with Otto in New York. Now I know that Hans Weber who is from West Berlin and Hans Webern who is from Switzerland is one and the same person. Otto Weber was smart. Hans has dual citizenships. Hans is West German citizen and Swiss citizen. If Hans has problem in West Germany, he will move to Switzerland. I told Hans that Dreyfus' family killed Otto because they think that Otto Weber knew where the diamonds are. I have a letter from German people who live in New York and they told me that the Dreyfus' killed Otto. I have this letter for my security, in case they try to kill me." I stayed and looked at the letter. It looks like the joker had a serious mental problem. He wrote what he was thinking on paper. Why did he needed to keep this information? The only reason I can think of is that the joker wanted to find and get the diamonds for himself. He didn't need to keep letters for that. It seems to me that this was dangerous for him. I need to ask Mom for the joker.

Next letter. "The shark and Konev are becoming more aggressive. They want to get the information they are looking fast. They don't have time. They don't want to wait. The shark told me that Louis and his wife will be on vacation in Florida. We must finish this job. I asked him, where is Hans, but he told me. "I killed Hans, because Otto Weber knew where the diamonds are and he told his wife. He was in New York to take the diamonds, but Dreyfus' family killed him. Now, Hans wants to take the diamonds". The shark is crazy. He will kill Louis, but he didn't kill Hans. Hans works for Stasi."

Next book. I opened it and I took a letter and I read "They killed Louis and his wife. They killed two other men, one in New York and the other in Dallas, but a third man from New York disappeared. I must save my life. The shark will kill me. I have a lot of information and I know many people who are after Louis in order to get the diamonds. I am scared."

I checked each book on the shelf. I didn't find another book with letters. Of course, I didn't, because they killed the joker. I placed every book back on its ordinal place. I looked at the shelf and the books. Everything was looking the way it looked before. I took the envelopes and left the office. I entered my room, I took a backpack I put the envelopes inside. I also put two construction projects I created when I was in the University. I covered the letters with the projects.

I was in the living room when the phone started ringing. I picked up "We are on our the way back Carl."

"Thanks Julia." I removed the security bolt on the door and was waiting for them . They came after twenty minutes. As they walked in Julia asked me, what I want for lunch.

"I am leaving Mom" and I asked Michelle for my check.

"The check is my room Carl."

"Could you give me the check Michelle?"

"I will go and get it for you Carl" and she walked to my room and tried to open it, but the door was locked. She took the check from her room and when she gave me the check, Michelle asked me "Why did you lock your door?"

"I had sex with my girlfriend and she is taking a shower."

Grandfather told me that he has a check for me and he handed it to me. I opened the door of my room. Michelle was behind me.

"Why are you behind me Michelle?"

"I need to check the bathroom. I took my backpack and left the room. She came running behind me and said "There is no girl in the bathroom".

I replied, "She is a dove, so she flew out the window Michelle". I left the apartment. I found a public phone. I called Joshua and I asked to meet with him.

"I will be waiting for you Carl." I went to Joshua's office. He jumped and grabbed my hand.

"So long Carl. I don't remember when was the last time I saw you. It was maybe seven or eight months ago. Are you coming back to New York?"

"Yes Joshua, I am not going back to Dallas. I will stay forever with Julia in New York."

"Every time I met her she asked me the same question."

"Why did Carl leave New York? Maybe, I am not a good Mom, Joshua."

"How is she now?'

"She is busy with grandfather and Michelle Dreyfus."

"Hey Carl, Dreyfus family is very rich. Do you love her?"

"I don't know what to say, but if you want to meet her, I will introduce you. She might tell you that she loves you." We laughed. I gave him the two checks for total a of one million.

"How long did you work to get this money?"

"Nine days."

"My father is right. He told me. "Joshua, you need learn to make money like Carl does".

"I told him that If he wants you to be his son, he needs to ask Julia."

"Don't say that Joshua. If I ask Julia, she will kill me." We laughed and I told him that his father is right. I asked Joshua that I have two projects from Dallas and I need to put in a safe box at the bank.

"Could you help me with that Joshua?"

"I will Carl" and he picked up a phone and called. "Greg, I have a friend. He need a safe box. Could you help him? His name is Carl Hope. Are you ready to go to the box now Carl?"

"I am ready Joshua."

"Greg is waiting for you. He works in Bank of America. The bank is not far from here" and Joshua gave me the address.

"Tanks Joshua" and I left for the bank. I was there in few minutes and I asked for Greg. He gave me an application. I filled and signed. I got the key and put the letters in the box. I thanked Greg's for his help and I left the bank.

I went back to Julia's apartment. I said "Anybody Home?", but nobody answered me. I entered my room and closed the door. The phone was ringing, but I didn't pick up. Julia knocked and on my door and said, "it is for you Carl". I picked up. It was Roger.

"I must see you after twenty minutes in our place."

"I will be there Roger." I told grandfather that he needs to come with me. Michelle asked me if she can come with me, but I didn't answer her. Julia understood that Michelle has problem with me and Julia told her "Michelle, they are men and they have man job to do some times. The same as we women have women job to do."

Grandfather said that he is ready. "Mom don't wait for dinner, John and I will eat out. I don't know what time we will finish" and we left. We were walking and speaking. Grandfather told me "Carl, your grandmother told me that any woman that wants to control you will have a big problem, because you are a wild man, a Hill Billy. I told her that you are a soft man, because you aren't a hunter. Now I know that she is right. I will apologize to her. Julia told me that Michelle is very rich Carl."

"I don't need her money Grandfather, I know how to make money. I don't like somebody to die, so that I will be rich."

"Why did you say that Carl?"

"Because, if Julia says that to Grandmother she would tell her that I am a man I don't need to take money from Michelle, because I know how to make money. "

"You are wild man Carl. You hurt me when you said, that somebody has to die. It always reminds me of what your father said."

"If you die he will be rich."

"You never forgot that Carl?"

"I will never forget that Grandfather."

"Do you hate your father Carl?"

"No Grandfather. I don't hate people. Remember he is still your father Carl."

"You are wrong Grandfather. He is your son."

"Why don't you like to spend time with Michelle?"

"She reads my thoughts. Michelle loves people when they say good thinks about her. If you think badly for her, she will hate you. Grandfather, you love Michelle and you think that I will marry her and that is why she loves you. If you think that she isn't a good girl, she will hate you."

"Does she have a mental problem Carl?"

"No. Michelle has problem with her life. She grew without a mom. Her mom died when Michelle was twelve years old. She grew with her father. I am happy, because I grew up with you, Grandmother and Julia. Now I am a macho man" and I laughed.

"You are Carl."

"Could you tell me more about Michelle?"

"Not now Grandfather. This is a long story." We entered the restaurant and I saw Roger. He was sitting on a table in a corner of the restaurant. He looked uncomfortable at my grandfather.

"Don't worry Roger, this is my Grandfather." He stood up and shook my hand and Grandfather's hand.

"It has been a long time Roger."

"This is true Carl."

"How is Dallas?"

"No more Dallas for me Roger. I am back in New York for good."

"I am glad to hear that Carl. New York is New York. I love this city, but you need to know that they know that you here and you will meet Ethan's Uncle Simon tomorrow at 3:00 p.m. I called to see you and decide what we are going to do."

"This isn't good news Roger."

"I know that Carl. They tried to kill you in Dallas."

"How many people know that you are in New York?"

"Many people know that I am in here, but only three people knew, that I will meet Simon tomorrow at 3:00 p.m. Myself, Ethan and Simon."

"Do you think that Ethan told somebody?"

"No. I trust him."

"Who is Uncle Simon?"

"Tomorrow, I will meet him for the first time."

I ordered three beers and then we ordered dinner. The waiter left with the order and we continued to talk.

"I have an idea Carl. Tomorrow morning at 7:00 you need to call Simon and tell him, that you need to meet him at a coffee shop at 9:00 a.m. Do you know where the Argo Tea Café is?'

"I know Roger."

"I will be there before 9:00 a.m. and I will scout the place, to see if anyone is waiting for you and Simon. If you have problem, I will send you a paper note with one word "Yes". You and Simon must go back to Simon's apartment and check to see if there is anything out of place on his phone. If you find something, don't touch it. Tell Simon that I will come and check the phone myself. Depending on what I find, I will tell you what we need to do next."

"Roger, I don't have experience dealing with such situations now, but I will finish this job."

"Carl, you said that you will finish this job. You must say, "I will kill them".

"You are right Roger. I will kill them."

The dinner arrived and we eat and talked. It was around 10:15pm when we finished dinner and left the restaurant. As we were walking out Roger told me," you must kill them, otherwise they will kill you Carl" and he said good night.

"Good night Roger."

My grandfather and I walked back to the apartment, but we didn't speak. When we got in I told him, "good night". I locked the door of my room. I was in bed when Michelle came to the door of my room and asked me if she can to come in the room. I didn't answer her.

I woke up at 6:00 a.m. Julia was in the kitchen.

I said "Good morning Mom" and I kissed her.

"Mom, do you thing that something was wrong with your joker?"

"Are you asking me if I think that I was married to a crazy man?"

"Did you find something Carl?"

"Yes Mom."

"Do you have documents, that make you believe that something was wrong with the joker? May I see these documents?"

"No Mom, I remove the documents and I don't want you to see and read them."

"Why, don't you show me the documents?"

"I will never show you the documents, because I love you Mom, but tell me what was wrong with the joker?"

"Well, I recall that one time when the joker was in the office, I entered to ask him, what he likes for lunch, but he didn't answer me. He was writing something on a paper. I asked him, "What are you writing?" "Nothing Julia" and he burned the paper. After that, I never saw him writing when I have been in the house. That is it

Carl."

"I found four books, but the books were not real books, they were actually boxes. I found letters inside them."

"Oh my God. The Joke spied on me?"

"Why did the joker spied on me. I had a simple life. I didn't have other man?"

"The joker spied on you because of Louis."

"But I don't understand, Louis left for Dallas, and I never saw him again. What do we need to do? I am afraid that this is the reason you are danger Carl?"

"Right now I don't know Mom, I am hoping that I will be able to tell you in the afternoon. If they continue to chase after me, Michelle must go back to Dallas for her safety. If you go with Michelle, I will be very happy Mom."

"Ethan and I got you involved in this dangerous game and now I must listen to you Carl."

"I will speak with Michelle for going back to Dallas. I need to make a call from a public phone, and I will be back for breakfast."

I called Simon and told him, that I will wait for him in Argo Tea Café at 9:00 a.m.

"I know this place. See you at 9:00 Carl." Simon is smart, he didn't ask me, why I changed the place and the time. I went back to the apartment.

We were sitting and having breakfast when Michelle asked me "Why did you have to use a public phone Carl?"

I didn't answer. Mom told Michelle that she must think before she asks me, but Michelle continued.

"Why Julia and I must go back to Dallas? You didn't to ask me, if I want to go back to Dallas Carl."

"If you continue with this line of questioning, I don't want to speak and see you again. Do you understand me Michelle?"

Michelle looked at me. She was scared.

"I understand Carl. I will stop, but you need to speak with me."

"You are a good girl Michelle."

"I promise that I will come to see you and speak with you."

"I will be good Carl. My father told me that I must listen to you. I promised him that I will."

"I know that Michelle."

Kate was right that Michelle loves me and she will listen to me. I was ready to leave. Michelle didn't ask me, where I am going.

Mom smiled. Grandfather laughed. I was in Argo Tea Café at 9:00 a.m. A man waived his hand and he said "I am here Carl." He stood up and shook my hand.

"How did you recognize me Simon?"

"I knew who you were, because I have seen you many times in the Jewish community in Manhattan. This is a credit card for you. It doesn't have a limit. If you decide to spend hundred thousand dollars, you can."

"Why you and Ethan are giving me this credit card?"

"We spent millions for the last twenty five years and we have zero result. You told Ethan what happened with my brother and his wife in thirty minutes. For that reason we decided to give you this credit card. We are stupid, and you are smart. Life is more important than money. My family has a lot of money, but Louis is in the grave. My brother was more important than the money. You lose money and make money. If you lose your live you can't get it back. Death forever Carl."

"You are right Simon. I am so sorry for Louis."

"You changed my live Carl. When Ethan called and told me that Louis didn't kill his wife and committed suicide, I was so happy, because finally I know that Louis didn't do that. They were killed. I don't know how to tell you, but it was very difficult to live thinking that my brother was a killer."

"Simon, I have a question, do you know who the shark on Wall Street is?"

"Are you kidding?"

"Carl, if you ask anyone who works on Wall Street who the shark is, they will tell you that I am the shark." We laughed.

"Simon, I have information that Otto Weber was in Manhattan to spy on your family. Every Jew thinks that your family killed Otto, but I know that German people who lived in New York at the time killed Otto."

"Oh boy, how do you know that? Most people believe that my family killed Otto."

"I have a letter, Simon. Before Thursday I knew that only one person was my enemy, Scott Colman. Now, I know that more people are involved in this game. Some of them may have stopped, but others, I think, are continuing. I think that, because they tried to kill me. If somebody says that I am crazy, I don't know what to say, but I feel that, this game is for at least hundred million dollars."

"I don't understand you Carl."

"I suspect that this deadly game has something to do with diamonds Simon. Somebody wants to get the diamonds from the Dreyfus' family. For that reason they killed your brother and his wife. They were looking for information to find where the diamonds are. They are scared and that is why they tried to kill me, because I told Ethan, how they killed his parents. They know that I will find the information and I will take the diamonds."

"Carl why do they want to kill you now?"

"It makes more sense to me that they use you to find the diamonds, then they will kill you and take them."

"Looks like you think the same as them Simon. I will never take the diamonds, because the diamonds belong to the Dreyfus' family. I am an honest man. When I find them I will give the diamonds to you and Ethan. Everybody will know that you and Ethan own the diamonds. Now, nobody knows where the diamonds are. If they find them, they can take them, and they will be the owners. They will keep that a secret. You and Ethan will lose the diamonds. That is why they are perceiving me as a big problem. When you have a problem, what do you do Simon? You clean it. They will kill me the problem is gone."

"Did you know about the diamonds Simon?"

"Many people in my family talk about them, but I have never seen them so I didn't believe that they exist. I believe they do Simon and I will tell you that I know five people who were around Louis: Scott Colman, Pavlov, Shark, Konev and Hans. Scott was Louis' partner. Do you know how much your father sold Louis' share for?"

"I don't know Carl. I had a very hard time with my father when Louis died and he sold the shares, I asked him why he sold so cheap the shares of Louis, he told me that this business is nothing. Then he asked me where are the diamonds are and that they are worth hundred million dollars."

"I didn't understand him. I thought that he was crazy because Louis died."

"The diamonds exist Simon. They are somewhere. Louis knew that, but they killed hm. Now nobody knows where they are."

"How did you find out about the diamonds Carl?"

"Lucas Dreyfus from Paris told people about the diamonds.

Lucas was in Oswiecim and he told the Nazi's. Lucas told them to save his life. I think that he lived in Russia after Oswiecim. KGB kept Lucas for the information, but he didn't know where the diamonds were. Carl, Lucas died in a car accident in Paris."

"Which year did Lucas have the car accident and he died Simon?"

"I think that Lucas died twenty five years ago."

"Three weeks after Louis died. They killed Louis. After one week they killed Julia's husband, three weeks later they killed Lucas."

"Why did they kill Lucas and Julia's husband Carl?"

"Because, Lucas and Julia's husband had information for the killers. I think that the shark is the boss Simon, because he ordered the killings of Louis and his wife."

"Carl, I think that Adam knows who the shark is."

"Who is Adam, Simon?"

"You don't know Adam, Carl?"

"I don't Simon."

"Adam is Joshua's father. Joshua is your broker."

"Joshua never told me that his boss is his father."

"I know that the boss is "close the door"."

"I know that Carl. Adam told me how he met you."

"Hey Simon, now I that I know Adam, who is Eve?" We laughed.

"Carl you are so funny. Ethan told me that you are funny and I can see that this is true. "

We laughed when somebody put a paper on our table. I took and looked at the paper. The writing said, "Yes".

"We will have to go to your apartment Simon." On the way Simon asked me, "What do you think about Michelle, Carl?"

"Michelle needs to improve her life. She has good qualities. She is pretty and honest. She is educated, but she has problem with boys."

"You are right Carl, but I don't know why. Do you have any idea?"

"She reads people's thoughts. This is bad for her. Michelle must stop that. If she doesn't stop, she will have problem with her brain. Now she is only twenty two. Michelle is young has time to change her life."

"Are you going to help Michelle, Carl?"

"Not now Simon. We have more important job to do first. We must save our lives and kill our enemy."

"You are right Carl." We entered Simon's apartment and I asked where his office is. I checked the phone. Of course, inside the phone I found a small piece that looked out of place. I showed it Simon and told him "My friend Roger will come here and he will tell you what to do. You must listen to him. I don't know what to do with the piece I found inside the phone. I need to go and tell Roger". I left.

Roger was outside the building waiting for me. I told Roger what I saw and that Simon is waiting for him.

"When I finish with Simon I will come to Julia's apartment. I need to speak with you Carl. Are you going back to Julia's apartment now?"

"I am not Roger. I must speak with Adam first, but you go there and wait for me."

Roger went up the stairs to Simon's apartment. I was walking and looking for a phone. I saw one and I called Joshua.

"I must meet with your father today."

"Give me fifteen minutes Carl."

I called after fifteen minutes. "My father is waiting for you. Come to my office." I was in the office in 30 minutes. When he saw me Joshua called and said, "Carl is here". Adam came pretty quickly to Joshua's office. I asked him "Where is Eve, Adam?"

"She is watching the apple Carl." Adam and I laughed, Joshua didn't understand.

"Joshua, could you please bring three coffees"

"What is new Carl?" Adam asked me.

"I don't have good news and I need some information."

"What I can I do for you Carl?"

"Who is the shark on Wall Street?"

"Everybody there believes that he or she is a shark, but one person in particular has the reputation of being the biggest shark."

"Who is that?"

"Well, he has a lot of money and political power. He is very dangerous. I know that Adam. He killed Louis Dreyfus. He killed many people. He gives money to politicians to have this power. If he doesn't have protection from politicians, he will be nobody."

You have money too Adam. Simon has money. Julia Shapiro has money too."

"Many people have big money, but they use their money for legitimate business. The shark uses his money for criminal business. Do you think that KGB agents give money to politicians for elections?"

"I don't think so Adam."

"Carl, it is very dangerous to go against the shark. My advice is for you is to stay away from the shark."

"I don't have a choice Adam. I must kill him."

"Are you crazy, Carl?"

"The shark will kill you and me. I don't want to listen anymore" and he tried to leave.

"I need to tell you Adam. I have behind me two rich families with hundreds of millions of dollars. Julia and Simon are behind me. Maybe the shark kill me, maybe I will kill him. I know that one of us will die. I think that I have a good chance. I am certain that I will kill him. Adam, you will lose the respect of two rich families, if you don't help me."

"What do I need to do Carl?"

"You know the politicians who take money from the shark. You must tell them that the Shapiro and the Dreyfus family will give them more money and they must distance themselves from the shark. If the shark loses the political power, it will be easier for me to kill him."

"I know that you are crazy Carl, but now I know that you are serious about this. It is dangerous and crazy, but I will help you. I believe that you will kill him. This is between me and you Carl. I don't want Joshua to know anything about it."

"I will not tell him, and thanks Adam."

"Come in Joshua", Adam asked Joshua.

"What kind of business does Simon have?"

"Simon has a lot of properties in New York. He owns many buildings in Manhattan. He gives them for rent and he has a lot of money on Wall Street, father."

"Are you going back to Dallas Carl?", Adam asked me.

"I am staying in New York and I will work anywhere in America and the world."

"What is Frank doing?"

"Frank bought a project from the company I worked for in Dallas and we will be working together."

"If you and Frank need money call me. I need to go back to

work Carl", and Adam left. I spoke with Joshua for fifteen minutes and I left the office.

I stopped and bought two plane tickets for Julia and Michelle. They will depart on Sunday morning at 10:00 from New York to Dallas. When I returned to Julia's apartment Roger was there waiting for me. Roger and I went to the office and I closed the door.

"Carl, the people who were spying on you and Simon were not very professional, but they heard and now know what you, Simon and Ethan are doing. They are one step ahead. I told Simon what he needs to do."

"Roger do you have people who can make a passport? I need one Irish passport with and Irish name born in 1964. One West German with the name of Hans Weber that was born in 1938. I need the passports by this Sunday. This is my picture for the Irish passport. For the German passport the person on the picture needs to look around fifty five. You must get ready to leave with my Grandfather. You must stay for three to four weeks in my Grandfather's house. The house is in the Smoky Mountains. You need to be hear on Sunday morning at 10:00o'clock."

"Do you have idea what we need to do Carl?"

"I have an idea. I have information for the person that is the shark."

"I don't understand Carl, you said "the Shark".

"Roger, A shark is a fish. "The Shark" is person who has business and makes a lot of money on Wall Street. But now I don't want to speak about that. I need to be sure one hundred per cent, who is the shark. I don't want to kill an innocent person, because there are many sharks on Wall Street" and we laughed.

"See you Sunday at 10:00 Carl", and Roger left Julia's apartment.

I took glass with whisky and sat on the sofa. "What is this Carl?" Julia asked me.

"Whisky Julia, I need to have a drink, because on Sunday I will be free."

"Oh my God!"

"I will be free Julia."

"Grandfather, could you call Jonathan and tell him that there will be one more passenger on the plane on Sunday?"

"I have two tickets for Julia and Michelle."

"Where are we going Carl?"

"You and Julia are going to Dallas."

"Do you have any more questions Michelle?"

"I have Carl, because made a decision for me and Julia. You didn't ask me, if I want to go to Dallas. Where are you going Carl?"

"I am going to the Smoky Mountains, with my grandfather."

"Why are you going to the Smoky Mountains? You should to come with Julia and me to Dallas?"

"I have a love in the Smoky Mountains, Michelle. I miss her."

"Who is your love in the Smoky Mountains Carl?"

"My love is doe Michelle. I love her and she loves me."

"A Doe is an animal, Carl. For you, doe is an animal, for me doe is my love."

"Are you crazy Carl? I don't understand you."

"You will never understand this world until you change your life Michelle. You must stop to read people's minds. After that you will understand, why I love the doe."

"I need to speak with my father Carl."

"Of course you do."

I called Ethan. "Michelle likes to speak with you Ethan."

"I don't want to speak with my father Carl."

"No Michelle you must. Go in your room and pick up the phone." They started to speak and I hang up the phone.

"My God. You have grown so fast Carl!", Grandfather told me. "I can't believe it. Can you believe it Julia?"

"He grew up with two cultures John. First, Carl is a Hill Billy from the Smoky Mountains. Second, Carl is a Jew from New York. Carl never have been scared and he knows how to make money. I am proud of him."

"Me too Julia." Mom and John started to cry.

"Why are you crying? I am alive" I asked them.

They smiled. "You are right Carl. We need to be happy", Mom told me and she took a wine glass.

"Do you like whisky John?"

"Give me a glass with whisky Julia. We need to celebrate." Michelle came back to the living room and I asked her.

"Do you like wine Michelle?"

"I would like some wine and my dad said that you are right. I need to change my life. I am so sorry Carl."

"This is OK Michelle. I forgot all about it, but you must think for your future. Don't waste any more time. Start changing your life. You need to start now Michelle."

"I will Carl."

After dinner we sat and drunk. "Do you like more wine Carl?", Julia ask me.

"No thank you! I am ready to go to sleep Julia." I stood up and said good night to everyone. Grandfather was little drunk and he said, "Hey Carl, maybe Michelle likes something from you".

"Maybe someday Grandfather, not now."

"I am a virgin John and I am not ready for sex. Carl is right. Maybe we will have sex someday." We laughed and I went to my room. I didn't lock the door. I knew that Michelle told the truth. She wasn't ready for sex.

I woke up at 7:00 o'clock in the morning. Julia was in the kitchen.

"Do you like coffee?"

"No Mom. When Michelle wakes up, I like to take her out. We will have breakfast, coffee and will go for some shopping."

"Are you taking John with you?"

"If he wants to. It is up to him if he wants to join us."

When John came to the kitchen, Julia told him that Michelle and I are going out. She asked him" Are going to join them?"

He said "I would like to. I need to buy something for my wife." About an half an hour later Michelle was ready and we left the apartment. We went to a coffee shop close to a shopping area. We had a nice breakfast. After we finished, we went to the shopping center.

Out of nowhere I heard someone calling my name, "Hey Carl what are you doing here?"

"I was looking for you Vicky. This morning I told Julia that I want to see you and God sent you. I embraced her. I have not seen you in a while" and I kissed her.

"Oh boy you know the effect your kisses have on me. I am ready. We will need a hotel room."

"Not now Vicky, I am with John and Michelle."

I introduced Vicky to John and Michelle. Grandfather kissed Vicky's hand.

"You a gentlemen like Carl, Mr. Hope."

"When he was a little boy, Carl grew up with me and my wife. We taught him well. You are so beautiful Vicky."

"Thank you Mr. Hope."

"How did you know his name?", Michelle asked Vicky.

"Carl's last Name is Hope. John is Carl's Grandfather. I guessed." "Michelle, you have a beautiful name", Vicky told Michelle. "Thanks Vicky. I am sorry for my stupid question. I need to keep quite."

"It is OK Michelle. Are you planning to buy clothes today?"

"I want to, but I don't know what I need to buy Vicky."

"I will help you, if you want me to."

"Sorry Carl. I think that Michelle and I will have go for some girl shopping ourselves. It will be boring for you. We will be back here after one hour."

"Take you time Vicky. We will be waiting for you two here. "

"Thanks Carl", and Michelle kissed me. They left.

Grandfather asked me "Did you sleep with Vicky, she is so beautiful Carl?"

"Hey, this is private Grandfather" and I laughed. We decided to take a walk and I saw a diamond store. I looked through the window and I saw something that caught my eye. We entered the store.

"May I help you sir?"

"Of course, I would like to buy this diamond collection."

"How much?"

"The collection is ten thousand and four hundred sir."

"Could you wrap it for a gift, please?"

"Oh boy, you love Michelle so much?"

"Common Grandfather."

"Could you tell me, for young or old lady sir?"

"They are for my grandmother, lady."

"Give me ten minutes sir."

"This is very expensive Carl!"

"Grandmother is more expensive to me. I love her. Don't you?"

"Don't say that Carl. You know that I love your grandmother."

"I know. I am kidding Grandfather." The salesgirl gave me the box with the diamonds. I paid and we left the store.

"My I ask you Carl, when will she wear these diamonds?"

"On my wedding."

"I understand Carl. So should we get ready for a great – grandchildren?"

"You should, Grandfather."

"Hey Carl, I am so happy. I will be a great-grandfather, but you must have sex with a woman."

"I will try, but she needs to want to have sex with me", I laughed.

"I think that Michelle is ready Carl."

"She isn't Grandfather. If you don't believe me, ask her."

Vicky and Michelle came and Michelle told me "Vicky chose and bought everything for me Carl. She is so generous."

"Don't worry about that Michelle, this is nothing", Vicky told her.

"Can you give us a little more time Carl?", Vicky asked me.

"Of course."

"Michelle has a beautiful hair, but I think that she needs to change her hairstyle. What do you think Michelle?"

"I would love that Vicky."

I asked grandfather, if he wants to wait or he will be going back to the apartment.

"I am tired Carl. I will take taxi and go back." I stopped a taxi and opened door. I started talking to the driver without looking at him. He replied "Hey Carl, do you remember me, I am Rado?"

"Of course, I remember you. You are Rado Zlatanovich or Rado Golden." We laughed and I asked him "What happened with your son?"

"He finished high school and is going to study to become an architect. My son told me that since you helped him with math and physics and you are an architect, then he wants to be an architect too."

"I am so glad to hear that Rado", and I asked him to drop Grandfather and I gave him the address. Rado gave me a business card and told me, "If you need a taxi call me."

"Give me Michelle's shopping bags Carl, I will take them to the apartment." I took Michelle's shopping bags and I put them in the taxi. Rado and Grandfather left.

We went to the hair salon. The moment we entered in somebody said, "May I help you Vicky?" and he kissed her hand.

"You are so sweet darling." and Vicky kissed him back.

"You look pretty and I love you darling, but now this girl needs to change her hair. This is Michelle. She is a new model. We have a show this evening and you must get her ready for it."

"I will Vicky" and he took Michelle's hand and they walked to a chair. "They are so sweet Carl, I love them."

"I know that you are smart Vicky. I have been many times with you."

"Do you like to continue Carl? I would like to spend some time in bed with you Carl."

"I am very happy when I am with you Vicky."

"I know that Carl. Honestly, I love you. You are the man that I will never forget. Did you miss me these two years?"

"Now I am back and will stay and work in New York, Vicky."

"What do you think about Michelle, Carl?"

"Are you jealous Vicky?"

"I have never been jealous Carl. You never ask me for my boys and I never ask you for your girls. This is why we have this special relationship. We like to look in the future. We don't like to think about the past."

"You have been the best woman in my life. You know that very well Vicky. I had a big problem with Julia when I wanted to marry Edit. Julia told me, "Carl, Vicky is so smart and beautiful, if you marry her, I will be happy."

"Are you going to marry me Carl?"

"Now, I can't think about that, because I have a problem. When I resolve it I will have time to think about marriage."

"I will be very happy, if someday you marry me and we have children. Mom told me that you are the best man for me and if I marry you, she will be very happy too. My mom and dad told me many times that I need to speak with you, but you were in Dallas. Now, you are in New York. I don't know, why people keep asking me, "Vicky, when will you marry Carl?". I told them. "Carl will never marry a KGB." We laughed.

"I really need to speak with you Carl. Do you have time tomorrow or next week? I see that you are with Michelle now."

"Tomorrow after three o'clock I will have time. Julia and Michelle are leaving to Dallas. Come to Julia's apartment after three o'clock."

"May I stay all night Carl?"

"I think that this is a great idea Vicky. I should buy some chocolate, to gain some strength." We laughed when Michelle came. She looked so different. I couldn't believe it!

"You look so beautiful Michelle!"

"Thank you Vicky."

"What do you think Carl?", Michelle asked me.

"You are beautiful" and I kissed her and reassuringly said "I think that this is a an important step in the right direction to change your life."

"I promise to continue Carl". We talked for few more minutes exchanging goodbyes and Vicky took a taxi.

"Do you like to walk or you want us to take a taxi Michelle?"

"I want to walk" and she told me, "I think that Vicky will be my friend forever Carl. She encouraged me to take the first step to change my life. I will never forget that."

We were walking in silence for a while, when suddenly from nowhere Michelle asked me, "Do you think that I look like Edit?"

"I don't understand you Michelle!", I replied very surprised grinning at her.

"The man, who changed my hair style, told me that you had a serious relationship with Edit and that I look like her. So far I have figured out that you had sex with Kate, Vicky and Edit. I wonder, how many other women are there Carl? But then who I am to judge your life? I must focus on my life. Kate said that I need to go get you to go to bed with me. She said that you know what to do in bed, but I don't have any experience. I have no idea what to do. I must teach myself. When I am ready I will take you to bed. For the time being you shouldn't be scared that I will jump in bed with you."

"Hey, I will be patient, I wait for you to take me to bed." I was looking at Michelle trying to figure out how to react to this. She smiled. I smiled. Then we both laughed. I felt that Michelle tried to open her hart to me. She looked relived. I thought that this was very good for her.

"I love you so much Carl. I will be very happy, if someday I marry you and we have children."

Oh my God what is going on with these women today? I don't understand why all of a sudden they all want to marry me. I have not had any thoughts of marrying Vicky or Michele. I have so much in my mind about the shark. May be they are feeling that I am in danger. First Vicky told me, now Michelle. I have not told me that the shark or somebody else is after me to kill me. I need to get back to the problem at hand first "The Shark".

I told Roger that I have an idea, but the truth is that I knew that

I have to kill him. I didn't know how, when or where. Michelle was saying something, but I was deep in my thoughts. I was thinking for the shark, Scot, Pavlov, Hans and Konev. If I tell anyone that the shark is KGB and he uses politicians to have power and make money, everybody on Wall Street will laugh and tell me, that I am young and stupid boy. I had to find more information to connect the dots behind this whole mystery. I was going through my head where to start. I was going through the names assessing who might be willing to talk to me. If I try to speak with Scott, I have zero chance. Pavlov and Konev live in Russia. Hans lives in Germany or Switzerland. Then it dawned on me that I have one person, that may talk to me, the detective that lives in Florida. The detective told Julia, that he was scared and if he said anything, the shark will kill him. Maybe, the detective knows the shark. At that moment I realized that we were back on front of the apartment. I told Michelle that I am tired and I need to relax. I went to my room and closed the door. I was in bed and closed my eyes.

CHAPTER 5

I was in bed looking through the documents that I took from Ethan, Simon and Julia. Every document had the name of the detective who investigated Louis' and his wife death. The detective's name was Lorenzo Falsone. In the documents I got from Ethan and Simon, I read the name of Scott Colman and that he was Louis's business partner, but I didn't find the names of Otto, Pavlov, the shark, Hans and Konev. I didn't find any information about the fact that the same day when Louis and his wife died, two people were killed in Miami Beach. I think that Lorenzo Falsone covered something. First, he said that Louis killed his wife and committed suicide. This wasn't true. Second, he never said anything about the two people that were killed near by the hotel the same day where Louis and his wife stayed. Lorenzo didn't say anything else to Julia, because fears that the shark will kill him and his family. The joker wrote that the shark will kill him too. It is clear to me that "The shark" is the boss. If I kill the shark, I will save my life and I will find the diamonds. Only two people spoke about the shark, the joker and Lorenzo. The joker is dead. I must speak with Lorenzo, if he is alive. Mom knocked on the door and she asked me, what I wanted for dinner, but I know that she was in my room out of concern, because I was in my room for a long time.

"Come in Mom."

"How old was Lorenzo when you met him?"

"I think around thirty. He told me that I am beautiful and he likes to have dinner with me. I told him that I am a married woman and I am too old for him. He is an Italian, Carl."

"You didn't want be unfaithful to the joker?" I laughed.

She told me 'Of course, I didn't, because I loved the joker" and she laughed.

"I spoke with Simon. He told me that you joked the whole time, when you met the other night."

"Why do you need to kill the shark?"

"If I don't, the shark will kill me Mom. The shark killed many innocent people."

"I came in your room to speak to you about that. Simon called me and he told me that the Dreyfus family and money are behind you. I asked Simon why does Carl needs the Dreyfus family and money behind him?"

"Because, the shark wants to kill Carl, but I believe that Carl will kill the shark. Julia, we need to give money to politicians and Adam will tell us who they are."

"After that, Adam called me. He was scared."

"Julia, Carl wants to kill the shark."

"Carl will kill the shark Adam", I told him.

"The Shapiro family and money are behind him."

"Now that I spoke with you I feel more comfortable Julia. I will help Carl" and he hang up the phone.

"I don't understand why Adam needs to help you Carl?".

"Why do I need to give money to people Adam tells me to? What if I don't like them Carl?"

"The shark has a political power, because he gives money to politicians and they support him. If we give more money to same politicians they will distance themselves from the shark. If the shark loses the political support he has, he will lose his power on Wall Street too. That will make it easier to kill him. I am hoping that Lorenzo will give me more information for the shark or what happened to Louis and his wife."

"Why did Simon tell me that you changed his life?"

"Because Simon thought that Louis was a killer, now Simon knows that he is not. I told Simon that the shark ordered that."

"How do you know that?"

"The joker wrote a letter. For me, the joker letters are golden chickens Julia. Joker's letters confirm that the shark is the boss. The joker was a close friend with the shark. After they killed Louis and his wife, the shark killed the joker, because the joker had a lot of information and the joker knew the shark."

"Why didn't he kill Lorenzo, Carl?"

"Lorenzo is a detective Julia. He isn't stupid. I suspect that he has incriminating documents for Scott and the shark. If they kill him, these documents will end up in the newspapers. The shark doesn't want that. I think that the shark has given money to Lorenzo to keep his mouth shut. Remember Julia, you offered Lorenzo money, but he didn't take them, because he took money from the shark."

"Are you flying to Miami tomorrow, Carl?"

"Yes Mom. I need to speak with Lorenzo."

"Why do you think that Lorenzo will give you information?"

"I have a lot names and I will tell Lorenzo, that if he doesn't tell the truth, I will tell the shark that Lorenzo gave me this information and the shark will kill Lorenzo and his family."

"Carl, you should be working for FBI or CIA."

"No Mom. I am working for the Dreyfus family" and we laughed. Michelle knocked and asked if she can to come in.

"Looks like that the Dreyfus family has arrived. They must check what I am doing." Mom and I laughed then I said "Come in Michelle".

"Why are you laughing?", she asked.

"I told Mom that you are now Edit, but she doesn't believe it."

"What do you think Mom, is this young or old Edit?"

"Edit was five years older than you. Michelle is four years younger than you. I am sorry Carl, but I prefer Michelle."

"Hey Michelle, if someday you and I marry, you will not marry me for me, but you will marry me for my mom."

"Do you want have sex with me Carl?", Michelle asked me.

"If my mom is holding a lantern in the room with us, I do. She can see that you are a virgin."

"This isn't funny Carl, you are hurting Michelle."

"Don't worry Julia, I know that Carl is joking. I love you Carl."

"I know that Michelle."

"I will be happy, if someday you and Michelle get married".

"I know why you want me to marry Michelle, Mom. Now I am half Hill Billy, half Jew. If I marry Michelle I will be one hundred percent Jew, because if marry a Jewess, I will become one hundred percent Jew."

"Who told you that Carl?"

"Jerry told me that. When I wanted to marry Edit." Jerry said, "If you marry Edit, you will be fifty per cent Hill Billy, fifty per cent Jew. If you marry Jewess, you are will be one hundred percent Jew." We laughed.

"You must take marriage seriously Carl. It is not a matter to joke about."

"I will Mom." I told Mom that I need to make a call and she left the room. I called Rado and told him that I need a taxi tomorrow morning at 7:00 o'clock. "The same address where you dropped Grandfather Rado."

After dinner I said good night to everybody and I entered my room. Rado picked up Julia, Michelle and me at 7:00 in the morning. We arrived at the airport at 8:15 a.m. I kissed Julia and Michelle and told them, "Ladies, have a good trip and call me when you arrive In Dallas."

"We will Carl." Mom was traying to be strong, because Michelle was with her. Me and Rado went back to Manhattan. When we got to the Julia's apartment building I said to Rado, "You need to wait fifteen minutes for me here".

Roger was in the apartment speaking with Grandfather. He gave my one passport and he told me that if I need the West German passport I will need to wait three weeks.

"Tell them that I don't need the passport."

"That will not be necessary. If I don't ask again they know that I canceled the order Carl. Why didn't you check the passport Carl?"

"I don't need to check. I will use this passport for emergency only Roger."

"What do you want me to do in the Smoky Mountains Carl?"

"You must be ready to enhance the taste of a wine when the time comes."

"Are you talking about a poison Carl?"

"You are correct Roger."

"After we finish this job, what do I need to do for you Carl?"

" I will open my own company. I would like us to work together Roger."

"I am onboard, as long as we are not going to have to deal with criminal people Carl."

"You can count on it."

"I do not want anything to do with criminal people, never have been."

"I would like to have a quiet life, a wife and children." We embraced like brothers.

We were at the airport and I told Rado that he needs to wait. Me, my grandfather and Roger entered the airport. I told them, "Have a good trip" and they entered the gate.

I bought a ticket to Miami. After that I found a public phone and called Becky. Somebody picked up the phone and I asked "May I speak with Becky Hodler, please?"

"Who are you?"

"My name is Carl Hope and I would like to speak with Becky."

"How do you know her?"

"We were friends in college."

"Who is calling Marko?"

"Your friend from college Carl Hope is on the phone."

"I am picking up the phone, Marko."

"Hey boy, this is Becky. I can't believe it. I have not heard from you in ages. What is going on?"

"Can you to talk to me in private Becky?"

"Sure, his is my mom's home. Marko may have a problem, but I can kick his him out of the house."

"I will arrive in Miami tomorrow afternoon, between 4:00-4:30 p.m."

"Could you give me airline and the flight number?"

"American Airlines 1732, from New York to Miami."

"Can you reserve hotel on the beach for me Becky?"

"My parents have a big house Carl. If you like you can stay in my parents' house. The house is close to the beach."

"Will your parent be Ok with me staying in their house? I am little uncomfortable imposing like that."

"Don't worry Carl. I told you what I will do with Marko, if he doesn't listen. I insist that you to stay in my parents' house."

"We will talk about that tomorrow Becky."

"I will be waiting for you boy" and she hang up the phone. When I entered the taxi Rado was angry. I asked what happened.

"Many people wanted me to drive them, Carl. I told them that I have a client and I am waiting for him. They told me that the my taxi sign doesn't work. Looks like I need to change the lamp. After I drop you, I will do that."

Rado dropped me and I told him. "Tomorrow morning at 10:00 I will be waiting for you here Rado."

"I will be here Carl, you can count on me. You are one of my favorite customers and you pay well."

I entered the apartment and started getting ready for Vicky. At three o'clock the bell was ringing. I opened the door. Vicky gave me flowers and she told me, "For you honey."

"Vicky, I am a man."

"No Carl. Tonight you will be my girl. You must listen and you do what I want. I will fuck you and spend more time on top of you than you have imagined. I will never forget my first night with you Carl. You were very generous with your body. When we finished, I felt that my body was done. You paid me three thousand dollars. I gave the money to the first homeless I saw on the street. He told me, "God bless you daughter". I told him, "Thank Carl, not me." After that I never have sex for money. You changed my life Carl. Now I am so happy and I have sex, but not for money."

I kissed and told Vicky that I am glad to hear that.

"You are beautiful and smart. You must open your own business Vicky."

"I have been thinking about it and that is why I am here Carl. I need to talk to you about my future."

"Would you like some champagne?"

"No Carl. I think it is too early in day for drinks. Maybe, I will drink coffee, but I need to take you to bed first." She took my hand and we entered my room. Vicky took off my shirt in a snap. My shorts followed. Before I can blink, I was naked. I took off her bra and kissed her abdomen. Vicky took off her bikini. She pushed me gently to the bed and started kissing my body. %My erection was growing. Vicky was on top of me. I let her to do what she wants to do. She decided to ride me. I felt my erection sucked in her. "Don't move Carl" she ordered me. Her body started to move forth and back. After that up and down. Slowly she started to make a circular motion. I don't know how long that was. Finally, her body started to quiver. I heard Vicky's and my voice. The voices were high. We climaxed together. I felt like I was shot. My heart was beating very fast. She kissed me and put her head on my chest. I kissed Vicky's head.

"Carl, I want you inside me forever." I embraced and kissed her head. I don't know how long we stayed like that. I didn't move. At some point Vicky said, "I need to take a shower Carl." When Vicky came back, I have not moved.

"What happened boy, did I kill you?"

"Almost Vicky. Your body killed my body. I must do more exercise and eat chocolate."

"I will make coffee. You take a shower Carl." When I entered the living room she kissed me and gave me coffee.

"How do you feel Carl? Are you alive?"

"I am, but I feel different. I like to stay with you forever Vicky."

"You may like that Carl, but KGB doesn't. We will have to spy for KGB. KGB will be after us and between us."

"I will kill anybody that wants to be between us."

"That won't help us. KGB will send somebody else Carl. They will never stop. My father told me that he is certain that you will be a very rich one day and that will give you a big political power and I will be rich too being your wife. I told my father that I don't like you to spend your life worrying for my safety. There are many sick people that work in KGB and they have killed many people for nothing."

"Do you think that I am sick too? I never killed anyone Vicky", my father said.

"You must ask Mom, don't ask me father."

"Nowadays Russia is changing slowly Vicky."

"How long it will take Russia to change?"

"Maybe ten, twenty, thirty years or never. Nobody knows that daughter. Maybe, you are right Vicky, but you must promise me, that you will never go back to Russia. You grew up in New York. You will never understand the Russian people and they will never understand you. They will use you as a prostitute or kill you. These are two different cultures. Russia and USA are so different. You are lucky that you grew up in the USA Vicky."

"I now that I am very fortunate to have grown up and live in the USA father. My mom and father told me to speak with you. I promised them and I am here. Carl, you must tell me what to do!"

"My advice for you is to open a business Vicky."

"What kind business should I open?"

"I will tell you. For example. Your first full name is Victoria. Women are crazy to buy from Victoria's Secret. Victoria's Secret has many beautiful models. You are too Vicky. You are model, but not very famous in this business. Nevertheless, you know this business and you know many designers that make clothes. You must open a boutique for clothes. I think that many designers will work with you to sale their clothes. You must find and rent a place in Manhattan. My friend Simon Dreyfus has many properties in Manhattan. You need to ask him for help. I will help you, if you need money."

"Mom and Dad were right . This is a great idea. You have a solution for me."

"May I continue Vicky?"

"I am sorry Carl, I should listen. When I was in the University, I had a friend, who tried to stay in America. He told me, that if he invests in business, the government will give him a permit to stay in America. I didn't ask him any more questions, so I don't know how and where you need to invest. You need speak with an immigration lawyer. You also need to ask him, how long you will need to wait for a green card, if you marry an American citizen."

"Maybe, I marry you Carl."

"Who knows Vicky?"

"Do you believe that I am a KGB Carl?"

"I don't believe that Vicky. If you are a KGB, then I am a CIA. If we marry and have children, the children will be smart and dangerous. They will cut iron when they piss." We laughed and Vicky asked me "Why are joking for everything all the time Carl?"

"Because life is more fun that way Vicky. You must enjoy, that you are alive."

"Why did you say that Carl?"

"Because, at this moment I have a problem, but when I resolve it, I will enjoy my life again."

"What is your problem Carl?"

"Many people are after me but I don't know why."

"Who are these people Carl? I may be able to can help you?"

"Do you know Pavlov, the shark or Konev?"

"I don't know who Pavlov is, but I heard about the shark. I met Konev in Kremlin in Moscow. I was there with my parents. I was very surprised when Konev asked me "What is Carl doing Vicky?"

"Carl is good in sex Konev."

"I know that Vicky, Carl is a good boy."

"My father knows Konev very well. He told me that Konev is a good person. I don't know if that is true, because he is KGB. Carl, my father told my mom that shark wanted to know what will happen if he goes back to Russia? He told him that they will kill him, because he is a traitor who works for KGB and CIA."

"You were born in Russia and now you are an American citizen. You keep Russian citizenship for emergency, but nobody in America knows that. You have double citizenship and you are a double agent. Nobody likes that, because you killed many Russian agents and innocent people shark."

"That is what I know Carl."

"Tanks Vicky" and I kissed her.

"Do you have more questions Carl?"

"No Vicky, this is enough. I will make something for dinner, you get the wine Carl. Hey, you deserved the flowers you were a good girl Carl."

"Thanks. Next time I will be a better girl Vicky." We were eating and talking.

"Why don't you ever speak about your past Carl?"

"Past is past Vicky. Past never comes back. You need to remember the past, but you must look and think for the future. I have a plan for myself for the next twenty five years. I will make hundred million dollars. I will marry and have children."

"How many children do you want Carl?"

"I think that two or three children, but God will decide. Our life is in God's hands."

"Where are you planning to live?"

"New York, of course. I love Julia and like to live with her and my wife in New York."

"What will happen, if your wife likes to live outside of New York, are you going to follow her?"

"If there is a compelling reason, I will follow her. Family needs to be flexible and should be for the benefit of the family. This is very important for the children. For example, I am who I am, because my grandparents and Julia were my mom and father. If I lived with different parents, I would have been different."

"What are you going to do Carl if Julia tells you that you need to marry me?"

"I will, but when I start to kill many KGB, I will ask her how many more KGB, do I need to kill Mom?"

We laughed and Vicky said "You never asked me for KGB Carl?"

"Vicky, this is your live. You decide what to do, not me. What kind of KGB, am I Carl? Many people think, that I work for the KGB, because, my father is a diplomat."

"They know that every diplomat works for the intelligence services."

"My father is in a high position in the KGB, but he never has killed people. He only spies on people. Two years ago he told me "If they return me to Moscow, you must never go back to Russia. They will kill me, but my daughter and my grandchildren will live in the USA. You and your children will have a future. In Russia you don't have a future Vicky." I believe him Carl, because my father knows how the KGB system works in Russia."

"Cheers Vicky. No more KGB and other people. We need to speak for us. For your life and the future of Vicky. For my life and my future. We are young people and we need to use the system. We should not allow the system to use us."

"You are right Carl. I need to get a permit and stay forever in the USA. You need to make money. Do you think that I will have a problem to get a permit?"

"No Vicky. You have brain and education. You have a college degree from a good University and you have two choices. You either open a business or you marry. Don't be afraid. I promise, that I will help you Vicky."

"Thanks Carl. I believe you. Tomorrow, I will meet with Simon and ask him for help. I will tell Simon, that I need a place to open a boutique. Hey, Simon Dreyfus' family is from France. Boutique is a French word. The name of the boutique will be, "Vicky's Boutique for Women." We laughed.

"Life is so much fun with you Carl." She took my hand and told me, "Come with me to bed my girl, I have more surprises for you."

I had many surprises in bed that night. Vicky used my body very well. I know that she loved me so much and she wanted to make my happy. She did that. I was happy. When I woke up at 6:30 in the morning, her hand was on my chest. I moved Vicky's hand and kissed her cheek. Vicky was looking so sweet in her sleep. I made her breakfast. I made fruit salad, cup of milk and espresso. Vicky entered the kitchen.

"Good morning Carl" and she kissed me.

"You remembered what I like to eat for breakfast!"

"Of course I remember, I will never forget, what you like for breakfast, lunch and dinner."

"Can I call Simon, Carl?"

"You shouldn't call him, but somebody is listening to Simon's conversations on his phone. You must see Simon in his apartment. This is his address" and I wrote it down for her.

"When you see Simon, you need to tell him that Carl said that I must see you in your apartment, because somebody is listening to your phone. Vicky, until now only three people knew that. You are the fourth. Simon will know that you are my close friend and he will help you."

"Carl, yesterday you said that you have a problem. Somebody tried to kill you."

"Yes Vicky."

"Carl, if you need more information for KGB, you must ask me. I don't have information, but my father has."

"I think that if you stay far away from this game will be better for you and me Vicky, because I have names, but I don't have faces. I promise, that if I need your help, I will ask you."

"In the past KGB used to kill people in car accidents or bullet in the head. Now KGB kills people with poison or bullet. You need to know that Carl."

"May I call my father?"

"Of course, Vicky."

She called. "Dad everything is OK. He will help me. I will call you letter" and Vicky hung up the phone.

"My father said "Hi". You were asking me for the shark and Konev Carl. If you kill the shark, many people in Russia will be happy."

"I am going out of town for two or three weeks. I don't want you to worry about me Vicky."

"I know that you are smart. You will finish this job easy." We finished breakfast and Vicky was ready to leave.

"Can you promise me something Carl? I would like to have one more night with you like this one!"

"I promise Vicky! I will be so happy to have one more night like this." She kissed me and left the apartment.

I gathered my luggage for my trip to Miami. I left the apartment. Rado was waiting for me. I got in the taxi and asked him to take me to Bank of America and I gave him the address. I entered the bank and saw Greg.

"Hi Carl. How can I help you?"

"I need to access my box Greg." Greg got me quickly to my box. He sensed that I was in a hurry, but he didn't ask. I took the box to the private room and put the Irish passport in it. As I was leaving, Greg told me "Joshua told me, what kind of man you are. When you come to the bank ask for me Carl."

"Thanks Greg, I will" and I left the bank.

"You must drop me at the JFK airport Rado." I didn't feel like talking. I was gathering my thoughts for my trip to Miami. We arrived at the airport and I gave Rado two thousand.

"Carl, you gave me yesterday one thousand. Why did you give me three thousand, for few trips? This is a lot of money."

"This money are for your son Rado. He starts school and he needs money for books and clothes. Could you tell him hi from me?"

"I will Carl. Any time you need a taxi, call me."

"I will."

I walked in the airport and checked in for my flight. I entered the plane and sat on my sit. I took a magazine and started reading, when somebody asked me "Do you remember me Carl?"

I looked up to see who was talking to me.

"It's me, Sisi."

"I didn't think that I will ever see you again Sisi."

"I am sorry Carl, but I am little busy now. I will be back later."

I went back to my reading when Sisi came and told me, "Carl take your bag and follow me." She gave me a sit in first class. I looked at her, ready to ask why, but she told me "Don't worry. I spoke with my boss. I will ask my boss if I can serve in first class. I like to spend time with you. I know that I will have fun time with you." I looked around. There were several empty seats. I just realized that I have never have sat in first class before. I know that I can afforded. Sisi distracted me from my thoughts. She came back all smiles and told me "I just got permission to serve in first class Carl. What do you like to drink, whisky, vodka, wine or beer?"

"Thank you Sisi, but I never drink, when I fly. Can I get some orange or apple juice?"

"It looks tom like you had a busy night", and she smirked at me.

"Why do you say that Sisi?"

"I know your type Carl. A strong man like you needs to have sex on a regular basis."

"You are correct Sisi, but last night was different, I was a girl."

"Oh my God. I would like my boss to hear this story Carl. I told him that we will have fun. She came back with her boss. I am listening boy" and he sat next to me on the empty seat looking at me. I started my story.

"Yesterday afternoon, I opened the door of my apartment and I saw flowers on front of my face and the voice behind the flowers said "For you Carl".

"Why?, I asked her. I am a man!"

She said "Because, tonight you will be my girl." I told them what happened in bed.

"She fucked me two times."

"You didn't move?", the boss asked me.

"I didn't have to boss. My body stayed in the same position. She was on top of me. I was inside her when my erection touched something inside her and, she told me "Oh my God. I will die." When we finished, our voices sounded like we were dying."

"How did you manage not to move?"

"She did all the moving moved with her pussy. My body didn't move."

"This is amazing boy."

"I told you boss, you will hear some amazing stories."

"You are right Sisi. I will tell my wife about this. She needs to learn to have the same sex with me."

"I don't believe that she can do that boss."

"You stay with Carl, Sisi, I will take your shift. Have a good time with Carl."

"I spent with you only one night in Dallas, but I remember that night often. We didn't speak the whole night, because we were busy having sex. I didn't give you my phone number, because I thought that there is not a chance that I will ever see you again. I was very surprised when I saw you tonight in the plane. At first I didn't believe that it was you. I didn't know what to do. I was not sure if you remembered me. I live in Los Angeles. I am so happy that you remember me, so I would like you to have my phone number so you can call me if you are in Los Angeles. Why are you flying from New York today, you said that you lived in Dallas that night?"

"Sisi, I am from New York, I worked in Dallas for the two years. This is my phone number in New York."

"Why are you going to Miami?"

"On vacation. I worked very hard in the last two years and I decided to take a break for two, three weeks."

"Where is your girlfriend?"

"She is busy with another man. This is a free country. Everybody has control of their life. I don't have control over my girlfriend. She is quite aggressive and she needs more than one men."

Sisi laughed and asked me "Do you think that someday, you will change your life Carl?"

"I don't know Sisi. Maybe, you will marry me and you will change my life."

"Who knows Carl? If I have a chance, I will marry you. I know two good things about you. First, you are good at sex. Second, you are very funny and I think that you have money. Every woman likes good sex and rich husband, but I don't believe that you will marry me." She paused then she asked me "How old you are Carl?"

"In about four months, I will be twenty seven."

"Do you think that my life is bad Sisi?"

"You need to ask my boss, Carl. I am a young girl. I am twenty three and I don't have that much experience."

As she was saying that her boss was coming our way, so I asked him "Hey boss, do you think that my life is bad?"

"I don't think so Carl. You are in the company of many beautiful women. You are young, strong and have money. I am guessing that you are making at least two hundred thousand a year. This is good money. Don't tell Sisi that you are rich. She will try to take you to bed and ask you to marry her."

We laughed and the boss asked Sisi "Are you having a good time with Carl?"

"I don't boss, because Carl and I haven't used the restroom together."

"The restroom is too narrow. I think that Carl likes a bed better."

"Have you had sex in a restroom in a plane Carl?", Sisi asked me.

"No Sisi, your boss is right. The restroom is too narrow. I am a big man, but maybe next time we need to think about it."

"Next time we will use the restroom", Sisi told me. Everybody laughed in first class.

"How many women do you have Carl?", Sisi asked me.

"I don't know Sisi. I have never counted, but I have many beautiful girls, including you Sisi." Everybody applauded and repeated "Sisi, Sisi".

"Hey guys, we are scaring the pilot with all that noise", Sisi's boss told us. He came to me and told me that is time to prepare for landing.

Thirty munities later we arrived in Miami. Sisi kissed and whispered "Call me Carl."

Her boss shook my hand and told me " Thank you for the good time, I enjoyed it. Have a good vacation Carl."

"Thanks boss." I left the plane and entered the gate. Becky was waiting for me. She embraced and kissed me.

"I can't believe that you are here on front of me Carl. I thought, after that beautiful week with you in Dallas, I will never see you again."

"Are you in Miami to see me or you have another reason?"

"Both Becky. I need to see you and I need to meet somebody."

"Why were the passengers laughing when they were exiting the plane?"

I told her what happened in the airplane. Becky laughed too at the story on the way to her car.

"What do I need to do for you Carl?"

"I need to meet Lorenzo Falsone. He was a detective twenty five years ago. If Lorenzo is still alive, I must speak with him. If he asks for money, I will give Lorenzo, as much as he asks."

"Are you working for somebody?"

"No Becky. It is for my mom."

"Carl, you came from New York?"

"I am from New York. When we met I was working in Dallas, but now I went back to New Your and I going back to live there." We stopped on a marina and walked towards the boats. The water was calm. We sopped on front of a boat and Becky said "This is my dad's boat. If I find Lorenzo, I will bring him here. I will call you after one hour, you must come here to meet with him. I don't like anybody to know that. This is between you and me Carl."

"Thank you. May I kiss you Becky?"

"Of course, but we don't have time for anything else. They are waiting for us. We need to get to my parents' house." We left the marina and drove for five minutes to get there.

We entered her parent's house. A young guy was walking toward us. He said "Hey cowboy, how are you feeling in Miami?"

"I don't know, because I arrived one hour ago, I assume you are Marko."

"Yes, I am Marko cowboy."

"Why are you calling me a cowboy?"

"Because you are from Dallas, Texas."

"You are wrong Marko. I am from Manhattan, New York."

"Are you kidding with me cowboy?"

"No, I am not, but if it makes you happy, I will be from Dallas."

"If you make French love to me, that will make me happier."

Somebody said "bravo" and applauded.

A beautiful middle aged woman was walking towards us.

"My name is Peggy boy." As she approached she was holding her hand for a handshake, I took her hand and kissed it.

"Nice to meet you Peggy. It is my pleasure to be in your house."

"Are you from France Carl, because I heard that you said French?" and she laughed.

"Marco was interested in something related to French, but he will have to wait for later. I am from New York. I am not from France Peggy."

"Hey cowboy do you know that Becky is my wife?"

"Of course, she is Marko. Two stupid people living together."

"Mom, I am not stupid and I am not married, I am engaged to Marko."

"You don't tell me that. You need to explain to Marko that."

"Come with me Carl, I would like to show you your room."

Peggy took me through the hallway and we entered a bedroom. She told me "Marko is very stupid. I hate him. You need to help Becky Carl. When you are settled, come back to the living room, I will be there."

I took a shower and went back to the living room. I saw there a middle aged man. He said "My name is Jack Hodler. Marko told me that you are from Dallas."

"Do you know Frank Colman from Dallas cowboy?"

"I know Frank Colman. We will be partners. He bought a project that I designed. I am good friends with Emmy, Frank's wife. She is a beautiful and smart. She helps Frank a lot. For some reason Peggy reminds me of her, smart and beautiful."

"You are right cowboy. Peggy is beautiful and smart."

Becky was standing on the corner. I walked to her and kissed her.

"Don't worry Becky, everything is OK."

"Hey cowboy, why did you kiss my wife?"

"Today, Becky is your wife, but tomorrow nobody knows Marko."

"Do you know who I am cowboy?"

"I don't Marko, but you are a very short man to fight with me."

"This is my house and I will kick your ass out of my house cowboy", Marko told me."

"Is it true that Marko owns this house Jack?", Peggy asked.

Jack was angry. "Marko stop talking. This is Peggy's house. Maybe, she will kick both of our asses out of the house."

"Do you like to go to a restaurant in Miami Beach tonight Carl?", Jack asked me.

"This is a great idea Jack."

"How about an Italian restaurant Carl?"

"That is fine, Jack."

We took to Jack's car and thirty minutes later Jack was parking his car. When we entered Jack asked me if like to sit inside or outside on the patio.

"It is a great evening Jack, I prefer outside."

I took a chair and offered Peggy to sit.

"Do you remember Paris, Jack?"

"I feel as if I am in Paris, and Carl is my lover"

"May I kiss you Carl?"

"Of course Peggy and she kissed me." Jack and Becky laughed, Marko didn't. Becky and Jack understood that I and Peggy like to make Marko nervous. Marko looked at us with a stupid look. It was obvious to me that Marko was lacking higher education. I asked Marko, "What did you major in College?"

"I have an associate degree cowboy. This is enough for me, because I am smart. I decided that it will be a waste of my time to get a bachelor's degree. I am a vice president of a company already without a college degree and I don't have a boss."

"Jack is your boss Marko", Peggy told him.

"Maybe after one year I will be the boss of the company,

Peggy." He tried to continue, but the waiter arrived and asked what we would like to drink.

"For me, Jack and the cowboy a round of tequilas, for the women beer."

"I don't like tequila Marko. I will order something else" and I asked the waiter to give me the white wine list.

"Of course sir."

"Call me Carl."

"Hey cowboy, you speak like a civilized man."

"I have a bachelor's degree in architecture a and I am from New York Marko."

"Do you know Dino Capaci Carl?", the waiter asked me.

"Of course, Dino is my brother."

"Do you know Dino's wife?"

"Yes."

"You said that your name was Carl."

"Are you Carl Hope?", the waiter asked me.

"Yes, I am Carl Hope, but how did you know my last name."

"Dino and Marisa were here and Dino told me that he has a very rich brother, Carl Hope, in New York."

"What is your name waiter?"

"Call me Filipe. My great-grandparents came from Italy, but I have never been there."

"Cold you ask the chef, Filipe, what will he recommend from the menu, the salmon or the white fish?"

Filipe gave me the wine list and I told him that I like chardonnay from France.

"Hey waiter, I order three tequilas, but you didn't bring them. Instead, you are spending your time speaking with the cowboy. Do you know, who I am? I will speak with manager and I tell him to fire you. You must know and remember me, I am Marko."

"Do you have problem?", Becky asked Marko.

"I don't have a problem, but you will have problem, if you had sex with Carl." Everyone on the table was quite. Peggy broke the silence. She asked Jack, "Is Becky your daughter or not Jack?".

"Marko is just kidding Peggy."

"Hey, I know that Marko went to China. Marko brought the spaghetti to Italy."

"Have you been to China Marko?"

"I never been there."

"Of course, I forgot that this man was Marko Polo from Italy, you are stupid Marko from Miami. I am so sorry Marko."

Peggy and Becky laughed when the manager came and asked what the problem is. Marco said, "I ordered three tequilas, but waiter didn't bring them."

"We have many tables Marko. You are a rich man and I am sure that you won't have problem to pay for a special waiter, just to serve you."

"How much I need to pay?"

"You need to pay two hundred dollars."

"I don't need a special waiter", Marco replied

"I will pay sir" and I gave two hundred to the manager and told him that I like Filipe to be my special waiter. Filipe arrived with the order and he placed the tequila on front of me.

"I don't like tequila Filipe, give it to Marko."

"You will have to wait for the wine Carl."

"No problem Filipe."

"What do you like for appetizers?", Filipe asked us.

Marko ordered grilled marinated chicken and French fries for himself, Jack, Becky and Peggy. I ordered calamari and Greek salad. When Becky and Peggy heard what I ordered they told Filipe ,"We like the same that Carl ordered and we will drink chardonnay, we don't like beer", Peggy told Filipe.

Marko laughed and said "Jack, looks like we have one more girl on our table tonight. Either me or you will have to take this girl to bed."

"Carl is for you Marko, but you need to be careful in bed. Nobody knows who will be the woman," Jack said.

"Who are you and why are you manipulating my wife and daughter to agree with you Carl?"

"Why do you think that I am manipulating Peggy and Becky Jack?"

"Because, Marko ordered tequila, beer and food for everybody, but when you ordered, Peggy and Becky changed the order."

"Jack, I never drink tequila and why did Marko ordered food for me?"

"Because, Marko is paying for this dinner."

"I am sorry Jack, but I don't like anybody to order and pay for my dinner."

Filipe arrived and told me that the white fish is better.

"I assume that you are from Miami, Jack. You must know that fish is better for dinner than anything else because is a light food. Light dinner is good for the stomach and the heart. They can process it easy. When you sleep your body needs to relax. Wine is good for the absorption of the food in your stomach. I am from New York and many people in New York order New York stake for dinner, I don't, because the stake is too heavy for dinner. After dinner, you go to bed and this is a problem for the heart. If you eat stake for lunch, then you are active for the rest of the day, which allows your stomach to process the food easily and you have less problems with your heart."

"Are you a doctor Carl?", Jack asked me.

"No. I am an architect, but I read about everything."

"I believe you Carl." Jack turn to Filipe and said, "fish and wine for everybody". Peggy laughed and said "I am sending a kiss darling".

Filipe brought the wine and poured in each glass. Jack said " Cheers everybody, live is good with Carl". Jack tried to talk to me about business, but I told him that we are having a nice dinner, not a meeting to be speaking for business.

"Tomorrow, we can talk for business."

We eat and talked. The fish was delicious. When Felipe came to ask, if somebody need something, I gave him one hundred dollars and asked him to give it to the chief for the good meal. Becky left the table two times and went outside the restaurant and spoke with few people on the street. Marko asked Becky, why was she speaking with these people. She told him, "This isn't your business Marko. I do what I need to do."

After dinner, Marko invited us to continue the evening in a night club, but Jack said that we have business tomorrow morning and he returned us all to the house. I said good night to everybody and went to my room. I woke up at 6:15 in the morning. At 6:45 I was on the beach. I look to the left and then to the right. I chose a point on the left side of the beach that will be my mark to turn around and swim back. I jumped and started to swim. I felt good and I found my tempo. I love to swim. I was feeling like a shark. Oh my God. I will be the next shark. I was kidding with myself.

I finished my swim and I went back to Jack's house. Peggy, Jack and Marko were on a table having coffee. "Good morning" I told them. "Good morning Carl", they replied.

"What do you like for breakfast?", Peggy asked me.

"Cold you make me an omelet and a green salad Peggy?"

"Why are you so meticulous about everything Carl?", Jack asked me.

"Not everything, Jack. I know that my face and skin will change with time, but I need to keep my body as healthy as possible. I don't need to have belly and I want to keep my muscles strong."

"Are you keeping your body in such a good shape for women Carl?"

"I don't Marko. For women I keep something else in shape."

Peggy laughed, but Jack and Marko didn't.

"Please excuse me, but I need to take a shower", I told them and I went to my room. When I returned to the kitchen, Peggy told me, "Jack and Marko are waiting for you, but you need to finish your breakfast first." I finished and I took cup of coffee and went to the living room.

"Do you have a friend on Wall Street, who invests money and gives credit?", Jack asked me.

"I have Jack."

"I need to borrow fifty or sixty million dollars. I found land for development and I need the money. Can you call your friend, I like to speak with him?"

"I don't like to make the call Jack, if Marko will be present."

"Marko go to the office, you need to work. I will come to the office in two hours and check, what you did."

"Jack, I don't like to hear these words again."

"You must move your ass Marko, because I will kick your ass out of the office and my house."

After Marko left, I picked the phone and called Joshua and asked for Adam.

"He is in my office Carl."

"Joshua can you please leave us alone, I need to speak with Carl."

"Hi Carl."

"Hi Adam."

"I have good news for you. The shark is scared, because the system started to work. You were right. I think after one month, the shark will be nothing. He is a fat fish, you are shark. I am happy, because you are my friend Carl. I don't like to waste my time speaking unless it is about making money. I need to go back work Carl."

"Hey Adam, actually I called you for business."

"If you are asking for Frank, he was approved for one hundred fifty millions for the first state and one hundred million for other states. Are you in Dallas Carl?"

"No. I am in Miami, Adam. I am in the house of Jack Hodler. He needs to speak with you. I am going to put the phone on a speaker." Peggy came to the office.

"How do you know Jack Hodler, Carl?", Adam asked me.

Jack replied before I can say anything, "Hey Adam, this is Jack. My daughter invited Carl to my house."

"What is the name of your daughter Jack?"

"Her name is Becky. Hey Jack, how long, did Carl swim this morning?"

"Carl swam for about two hours. He is a very strong man, Adam."

"Hey Carl, are you going to marry Becky?"

"This sounds good Adam. I like that. My name is Peggy. I am Jack's wife. Hey Peggy, you need to look out for your daughter. She will jump with Carl in bed. I will be happy if that happens, Adam."

"Hey, we need to be talking about making money, not about my private life."

"You are right Carl."

"How much, do you need Jack?"

"Between sixty and seventy million."

"If Carl can see the land and tell me, that it is good for development and we can make money, you will have the money with a good rate Jack."

"I am afraid that I have to go for a meeting now to make more money. Talk to you all later. " and Adam hung up the phone.

"Do you have time to look at the land today Carl?"

"I don't have time today, but tomorrow morning after 9:00, we can go to see the land."

"Thanks Carl."

"You opened my eyes", Jack kissed and told Peggy.

"I am so sorry honey, I will never do that again."

"Don't worry, everything is OK dear", and Peggy kissed Jack.

"I am going outside to the swimming pool."

"May I take the phone outside to the swimming pool Peggy?"

"Of course Carl. When I finish my conversation with Jack, I

will come to join you outside at the pool too. It will be nice to relax and look at the sky."

Peggy came after a while and lied on the lounge chair next to me. She said, "I like to tell you my story. Do you want to hear that, Carl?"

"I will listen, but I don't feel like talking much Peggy."

"I just need you to listen Carl. I had a very hard time in the last four months. I was ready for a divorce. You know that Becky is a lawyer."

"I didn't Peggy, but I know that now."

"How come you didn't know. Becky told me that you have spent an amazing week together in Dallas!"

"That week we never spoke about our private or business life. Becky and I were busy during the day. At night, we had fun and sex. We were happy and wanted to spend our time together in bed."

"How did you meet Becky?"

"I met her at a swimming pool. She was looking at my body, I was looking at hers. I broke the silence and I told Becky that like her Body."

"Me too boy", she replied.

"I am Carl."

"My name is Becky."

"In was late in the afternoon, so I asked Becky if she wants to go to dinner with me. She said "I would love to", while staring at my eyes. I knew at that moment that she likes me and I was hoping that we will spend more time together than just a dinner. We spent one week together and we had a good time. Becky has a fantastic body. She is perfect in bed too."

"Hey, I am her mom."

"That is why I am telling you that. You must be proud with your daughter. She is a lawyer, beautiful and good in bed too."

"Becky told me the same story and she said that you are perfect in bed too. Then she said "but I will never see him again Mom."

"And yes, I am proud of Becky, but she has a problem with Marko."

"Do you think before you say something about somebody Carl?"

"Of course Peggy, but sometimes I hurt people, even though I tell the truth."

"Now I know that Becky has many problems and she is confused. She doesn't know what to do. Yesterday, you told me, that I need to help Becky. I will try Peggy, but that depends on what Becky wants to do. I need to be honest with you, I don't have plans to marry Becky. She is a good girl, but I think that we have different vision for life. Becky is a lawyer and beautiful, but she lives with a simple man. She won't have good reputation if she listens to Marko, but Marko thinks that he is a macho man and Marko never listens to Becky. You saw what happened last night in the restaurant."

"You are right, Carl. I am sorry and now I know that you think before you speak, but I am her mom."

"I know that Peggy. My mom is the same as you. I had big problem when I decided to merry. I was twenty two years old when I told mom that I am going to marry. She told me the truth the way she saw it and I understood that she was right."

"Did you listen to your mom?"

"I listened to her Peggy. I love my mom."

"This is the difference between you and Becky. Becky loves me too, but she doesn't listen to me. She listens to her father."

"I would like to tell you more Carl. Do you want to hear the rest of my story?"

"Absolutely."

"I was in the living room and listened when you called and spoke to Becky. She was very happy, but she had a difficult conversation with Marko and Jack. They didn't want you to come in the house. That made me angry. I told them "You must stop. I would like to see this boy in my house, after that I will decide. Maybe, I kick Jack's ass out the house."

"I don't understand Mom. I am considering divorcing your father Becky, but I would like to meet Carl. Based on what you have told me he seems like an interesting young man."

"When Jack saw that I was angry, he told Becky to invite you in the house, to please me. Jack knew that I will kick his ass out, because he had sex with Marko's relative four months ago and Jack paid her five hundred dollars. If he can perform well in bed for me, I will tell him that I had good sex with him and I he made me happy and I am tired. If he wants more, he needs to look for another woman."

"This is so funny Peggy." We laughed.

"How did you know that she Marko's relative?"

"I was born and grew in Miami. I have lived in Miami for fifty years. My friend called and told me what happened, because Marko doesn't have a zipper on his mouth, but I think that Marko wanted to hurt me. Marko hates me Carl, because I stay between him and Becky. I am between Marko and Jack too. After my friend called and told me what happened, I picked up the phone and made a call to somebody I had a good relationship with a while back, so I called him. Hey boy, do you remember me?"

"I will never forgot you Peggy. You will stay forever in my hard." "How many more do you have in your hard boy?"

"Do you want to have a good time with me tonight boy?"

"I will be very happy to."

"We met in a hotel and I did everything he wanted. I had the same sex, as I had twenty five years ago with Jack. This boy was my lover, but I chose and married Jack. I returned home at 9:00 in the morning. Jack and Marko were in the living room. I told them good morning. I entered the bedroom and locked the door. Jack knocked and said that he wanted to speak with me. I told him to go and speak with Marko's relative and never ever enter this room."

"For four months I didn't speak with Jack and Marko. Becky tried to ask me, but I told her that I don't want to discuss this with her. It is my problem. I know what to do, you must take care of your macho man Marko."

"Do you think I should divorce Jack, Carl?"

"I don't think so Peggy. A divorce will be very hard for you and Jack. I think that Jack loves you."

"Oh boy. You are such a positive man. All of my friends tell me that I need to get a divorce, but you are right. Jack told me that he will never do that again. I need to ask Jack, how many times he had sex with Marko's relative." We laughed.

"You are so funny Peggy." The phone next to me was ringing. I picked up.

"I need to see you at 12:00 p.m."

"I will be there."

"I need to leave Peggy. When I return we will continue. I like to hear the whole story."

"I will be waiting for you Carl."

I went to the boat that Becky showed me earlier. I waited outside for few minutes. Then I decided to go inside to wait for

Becky and Lorenzo. A man entered the boat. When he saw me he said, "I am Lorenzo. Beaky told me, that your name is Carl Hope and you want to speak with me." As he said that the boat engine started. I looked questioningly at Lorenzo.

"I told Becky to take the boat somewhere", Lorenzo told me. "What do you need to know boy?"

"I need to know who the shark is."

"I don't know who the shark is."

"I know that the shark paid you a lot of money twenty five years ago to keep your mouth shut. He killed Louis Dreyfus and his wife and you were the detective that declared that Louis killed his wife and then killed himself."

"Are you a detective or are you working for the FBI?"

"I am neither. Julia is my mom. She told me that she spoke with you, twenty five years ago. Louis was her lover before he got married but she never stopped loving him. She offered you money at the time, but you told her, "If I say anything Julia, the shark will kill me and my family".

"Why are you asking about this after twenty five years?"

"Because the shark tried to kill me Lorenzo. If I want to be alive, and I must kill him."

"Do you know other people that are involved in this Carl?"

"I know Scott Colman, Pavlov, Hans and Konev. Three people killed Louis and his wife. The shark and Scott killed two of them, one was from Dallas, the other from New York, but the third disappeared. I need to know who the third person was. After twenty five years they started again Lorenzo. I don't know who these people are."

"I am hearing these names for the first time in my life Carl."

"I don't think that you are telling me the truth. I think that you know very well these people Lorenzo. You need to know that If the shark kills me, you and your family will be next, because the shark will think that you have told something to somebody. If I kill the shark, nobody will touch you."

"Why I should believe you that you will kill the shark?"

"I don't have a choice. If I don't kill the shark he will kill me. You are a detective and you know that one of us must die."

"The third man disappeared in Sicily. He is from New York."

"How long have you been working on this case?"

"Ten days. Becky told me that you are smart. Could you sit

down? I will tell you everything I know." I did as he requested.

"The shark and Scott Colman paid for the killing of Louis and his wife. I know that, because I heard when Konev asked Scott talking about it.

"Who ordered to kill Louis and Louis's wife? What are we going to do now? We didn't get the location of the diamonds Scott."

"The shark ordered it. He said that Ethan knows where the diamonds are."

"You are so stupid Scott. You want to get Louis' business at a very low price. This business is four, five million dollars. The diamonds are hundred million. Do you understand how much money we are losing Scott?"

"You must ask the shark, why he ordered to kill Louis and his wife, Konev?

"Where is the third man, because they killed two?"

"He disappeared, but we know that he is from New York and we will kill him in New York."

"Do you know his name and where he lives in New York Scott?"

"His name is Bruno Corso, but we must kill him fast, because he is from Sicily."

"If he disappears in Sicily, what are we going to do? Do you have an idea Scott?"

"I don't have an idea, but this is the shark's problem. He should have thought about it before he ordered to kill Louis and his wife. This is problem for us Scott, because now we don't know where the diamonds are" and Konev left. Scott gave me money and he said "The shark is giving you this money to change the evidence and the official reports. You must say that Louis killed his wife and then he killed himself. If you don't do that, the shark will kill you and your family Lorenzo."

"I changed the evidence and my report, because I didn't have a choice Carl. I was sorry for them, but there was nothing I can do for them . They were death."

"Did you ever see the shark or received any letters from him?"

"No Carl. I know Scott and Konev."

"You never saw Hans?"

"I never heard of him."

"Did you try to find Bruno Corso, Lorenzo?"

"I sent my best friend in Sicily to find Bruno Corso, but he disappeared and I never saw or heard from him. After that I stopped to think for the diamonds. I understood that this is a dangerous game. The diamonds exist, but I don't know where they are."

"You are smart Lorenzo. When I finish this job, you need to work for me."

"Do I have to kill people Carl?"

"No Lorenzo. You are a detective, not a killer. I want to invest in the Caribbean Islands. You know that the mafia is everywhere and crime people too. You will travel with me and investigate the risk of my investment."

"You are a miracle man Carl. I would love to do this for you."

"I need to tell you about Marko. You are staying in the house of Jack and Peggy. Becky is engaged to Marko. Marko is very dangerous. This is a big problem for Becky. She is beautiful and smart, but Becky didn't think before she raised her legs up. It is too late to stop Marko. If she doesn't marry him, he will kill her.

"Why will Marko kill Becky? People cancel engagements all the time Lorenzo!"

"Because he wants to take over the business of Jack and Peggy. He wants to divorce them. I am guessing that he is planning to pay somebody to kill Peggy. Everybody will point the finger to Jack, because he divorced Peggy. The people will think that Jack killed Peggy to take one hundred percent of the business, because now Peggy has fifty percent and Jack has fifty percent. Marko will pay to send Jack in jail, so Marko will be the owner of the company one hundred percent."

"You are forgetting Becky, Lorenzo."

"Marko manipulates Becky very easy Carl."

"Are you sure that Marko wants to marry Becky, because he wants to use her to take the business of Jack and Peggy?"

"Yes Carl."

"Oh my God. We all think that Marko is stupid, but he is smart Lorenzo."

"He is Carl."

"You need to tell Becky that we have finished and she needs to take the boat back. I will stay inside Lorenzo. I don't want somebody to see that I am with you and Becky. I will leave later, after you and Becky have left the boat." Becky returned the boat back. Becky and Lorenzo left. After fifteen minutes I left the boat too. I went back to the house. Peggy was waiting for me.

"Do you have good news Carl?"

"I am so sorry Peggy. The news isn't good for you and I told her about my conversation with Lorenzo in regards to her and her family."

"I have been feeling that, but I didn't want to believe it Carl. Don't tell Jack and Becky what I told you."

"I can't tell them Carl, because they will tell Marko."

"You are right Peggy. Now, I don't want to have problem with Marko. When you finish your job in Miami, you can stay in my house if you want. Are you planning to go back to New York?"

"When we finish looking at the land you want to show me tomorrow, I would like to go to Bahamas for four or five days. I need a vacation, but I will be looking for business opportunities too."

"Hey Carl, Jack and I have a house there. The house isn't far from Nassau. Do you like to stay in my house in the Bahamas?"

"I would like that very much Peggy, but only if you don't tell Jack and Becky. I know that you will never tell Marko."

"Are you flying there tomorrow afternoon and which day are you planning to leave?"

"I am flying tomorrow afternoon and leaving on Monday afternoon."

"Hey Carl, may I come with you, I need a vacation too?"

"Of course Peggy, but you need to ask two people for permeation, Jack and your lover, because after you have a vacation with me, you will want to leave both of them." We laughed.

"Carl you are so funny, I love you so much. Now I have a daughter and a son."

"If my mom hears that, she will kill you Peggy. You must tell my mom, that I am Becky's lover." We laughed and I told her that I need to make a phone call, but I need some privacy.

"Do you like to call from Becky's office? I am going there to for a meeting with Becky's boss."

"Why not Peggy, I will see my love Becky."

We got in Peggy's car. I noticed how confident she was.

"You drive very well, Peggy."

"Hey boy, I know every street in Miami. I started to drive when I was seventeen years old." I decided to stop staring at Peggy and looked out from my window at the colorful buildings. Peggy was in her own thoughts. We didn't speak.

We got to our destination about twenty minutes later. As we entered Becky's office Peggy told me "I need to introduce you to Becky's boss Carl."

We went towards an office. Peggy knew her way around. We were on front of an office and the door was open. A man in gray suit was sitting behind a desk. We walked in and Peggy said "Hi boss, I would like to introduce you to this young man. This is Carl Hope, from New York. He is my new boyfriend. What do you think, do I have a good taste?"

"Peggy, he looks very strong and capable of spending a quality time in bed with you, but you are an attractive girl, and I bet you can kill Carl in bed." We all laughed a lot and we had tears in our eyes when Becky came in.

"What are you doing here Mom?" Becky asked Peggy.

"This is my new boyfriend dear."

"He looks very good Mom. I am willing to give you my boyfriend Becky, because your boss said that I will kill this good boy in bed. I like him too much, so I don't want to kill him. You try him in bed, maybe my he will be alive after sex with you dear." We laughed.

"I am engaged to Marko, Mom", Becky said.

"I will give you my boyfriend for thirty minutes Becky. You go and check him in your office dear. I will be glad to take him to my office for thirty minutes. Boy, follow me." We got to Becky's office.

"Do you want me to stay with you or I you would like me to leave Carl?"

"You can stay, but please keep the door closed." I called my grandfather and told him "You need to call Jonathan and tell him that I need the jet for next Tuesday afternoon from Newark Liberty airport to Palermo Sicily" and I gave him Becky's phone number. "If I am not here tell Becky at what time." Then, I called Ethan's office and told Ethan, that I will fly overseas next Tuesday, but I don't like Julia and Michelle to know that.

"Good luck Carl and he hung up the phone." Becky looked and asked.

"Who are you Carl? What have you got yourself involved in?"

"I can't tell you much right now for your own good. When I

finish this job, I will call you and you need to tell Lorenzo, "Carl is ready to work with you now."

The phone was ringing. I picked up. It was my grandfather. "Tuesday one o'clock" and he asked me. "Do you need to speak with your brother?"

"Not now Grandfather, I am busy. Carl, your grandmother said you "Hi" and she is waiting for a great-grandchild. She is looking every day at diamonds you gave her."

"If I have time I will marry and have a child. Grandmother will have to wait for one year."

"I will tell her" and he hung up the phone.

I called Joshua and told him that I need to speak with Simon. "He is here Carl, in Adam's office. I will fetch him for you."

In few minutes Simon was on the phone. "Hey boy, how is your vacation?"

"Simon just listen to me carefully, I am flying to Palermo Sicily next Tuesday. I need to go there with Tony Capaci. He is Dino's grandfather. You need to arrange this form me."

"Can you give me the Dino's phone number and what I have to tell Tony?"

"I have to meet Bruno Corso in Sicily. Tony Capaci is from Sicily. If Tony comes with me he will help me, when we are in Sicily. We will fly at 1:00 p.m. on Tuesday. I will be in New York on Monday afternoon."

"Do you want to say something to your friend Vicky, because we are working together and we found a place for her boutique?"

"Vicky told me about it last Sunday night."

"You need to kiss Vicky and tell her that she is beautiful and smart girl."

"I will Carl", and Simon hung up.

"Do you think that you and I have a future Carl?"

"You are honest and beautiful. You have education. You are a lawyer Becky. I don't understand why you choose Marko for your husband?"

Becky was thinking about her answer when we heard a voice in the hallway.

Becky looked at me and said "This is Marko, Carl. You need to stay here. I will deal with him. You need to wait in my office. After two minutes go to my boss's office." She left and I did as she asked. I entered the boss's office and Peggy asked me, "Did you finish, because Marko came and was looking for Becky?"

"Everything is OK Peggy." We were speaking when Becky and Marko entered. Becky's boss said that Becky needs to go to Dallas. She has to leave on Thursday morning and return on Monday. He looked at Marko and said, "Do you want to go with Becky Marko? I will buy two tickets?"

"I need to work, buy only one ticket. I need to stay in Miami."

"I don't want to go to Dallas", Becky told her boss.

"If you don't go to Dallas, I will fire you Becky."

"Becky, you need to go to Dallas", Marko told her.

"I will go to Dallas, but I am not happy about it." She and Marko left. Peggy smiled and said, "Tanks boss" and we left his office.

"Do you know a diamond store near by Peggy? I need to look for something?"

"Sure thing, Carl. I will take you there."

She stopped and we entered the store. I asked Peggy to help me.

"How old is she Carl?"

"The same as your age Peggy". She looked around for few minutes and she chose a set that had a necklace and earrings.

"Could you put it on you, I need to see how the diamonds will look on?"

"How do I look Carl?"

"I don't have words to tell you."

"You are beautiful Mrs. Hodler."

"How did you know my name lady?", the salesgirl replied.

"Many people in Miami know you. Marko, your son in-law, is a frequent customer here, but he buys cheap staff. I told him that, and he said the they are for Becky and Peggy and they OK for them. "

"How much do I need to pay lady?"

"Four thousand seven hundred, sir." Peggy tried to take off the diamonds.

"I bought the diamonds for you Peggy."

"This is a very expensive gift Carl."

"You deserve more."

"Thanks Carl."

We left the store and Peggy told me, "Now, we need to go to my office." When we entered Peggy's office, everybody looked at her in surprise. Two ladies said in unison, "You look like a Princess Peggy."

"Who bought these diamonds for you? We know that Jack and Marko are cheap, so it must be someone else."

"You are so right ladies. Meet my new boyfriend, Carl. He bought the diamonds for me. I am planning to divorce Jack and marry him." We laughed.

"There is champagne in the refrigerator. Let's have a drink for me and my boyfriend. I will be back in the office next week. I need to work guys. Cheers."

"Cheers Peggy."

Jack came asking what is happening.

"Today we are celebrating Jack. I will be back in the office next week."

"Do you want that Jack?"

"Of course and he kissed Peggy."

"Hey Peggy, what happened to Carl?"

"He is young. Carl needs to find a young girl." Everybody applauded.

"Can I have you attention please. Today we have to celebrate, no more work, more champagne. Come to my office Carl."

Me, Peggy and Jack entered the office and Jack closed the door.

"Do you think, that I have problem with Marko Carl?", Jack asked me.

"Marko is dangerous for you Jack. If he has a lot of information for your company, this is not good for you and Peggy, but don't fire Marko now. When Peggy takes control of the company, you won't have a problem to fire him, but Becky marrying Marko may become an issue. I don't know what to tell you. This is a family problem Jack."

"Why did you have sex with Marko's relative?"

"It was a stupid mistake. I was drunk Peggy. You know that I love you" and Jack kissed Peggy.

"I love you too Jack, but you created a big problem. If Carl was not visiting us, I would have divorced you. He helped me cool my head and realize how much our divorce will hurt our family. We need to focus and save our family and business."

Marko entered the office without knocking and asking Jack, why people were celebrating.

"First you need to knock on the door Marko. Second, I am

back in the office", Peggy replied coldly to him.

"Is it true? What happened?", Marko asked Jack.

"Peggy is my wife and she was the boss of the company before. Peggy built this company. She owns fifty percent and I own the other fifty percent. Peggy is your boss now Marko."

Marco turn to Peggy smiling "You have beautiful jewels, I never saw them before Peggy."

"Marko, you bought them for me, don't you remember?"

"Really!", Marco replied in disbelieve.

"No Marco, the one you bought were cheap jewels for Becky and me."

"I am going to join the celebration for the new boss too" and Marko left the office of Jack.

"You never told me that Marko bought jewels for you and Becky."

"Marko bought for his mamacitas Jack, but you paid five hundred to have sex with one. There isn't a big difference, between you and Marko."

"Here is what I want you to do Jack, if Carl says that land is good, you need to go to New York on Thursday and be back on Monday. You must take Marko with you."

"If Becky tells me that Marko needs to stay in Miami, what should I tell her Peggy?"

"I would kick Becky's and Marko's asses out on my house Jack. You have always approved everything Becky wanted, no matter if it was right or wrong. Becky loves me, but she doesn't respects me. Now, she must know that I am her mom and she needs to respect me. Now, I know what to do with our business, you, Becky and Marko. Peggy Hodler, from twenty five years ago is back. Do you understand me Jack?"

"I understand Peggy. When I married for you, I knew that I would have a good life, if I listen to you. After twenty five years, you are the same Peggy. I love you so much. I know that I have brought two wrong things in our life, Marko and his relative. I trust you Peggy and I need to support you. I know that Carl is a better choice in bed than me. He is young."

"Do you think that we could have the same sex, as we had twenty five years ago, Peggy?"

"Hey, hey, Jack. Peggy is my future business partner. If I have sexual relationship with her, we will be twenty four hours in bed.

You need to work twenty four hours Jack." We laughed.

"You are so funny Carl", Peggy said and kissed me. Peggy and I went back to the house. We were in the swimming pool when Becky and Marko came in the house. They came to the swimming pool and Becky asked "Mom, where are your jewels?"

"I have many dear."

"Which one are you talking about? As you know, I have many."

"The ones that Carl bought for you today. The diamond jewels."

"How did you know that Carl bought jewels for me? I never told you that dear."

"Marko told me, Mom. He told me that Carl is your lover and you have a sexual relationship with him."

"This isn't your problem Becky. This is a problem for your father, but I need to tell you that your father had sex with Marko's relative and Marko himself has many mamacitas. He bought jewels for them, but he told everyone that the jewels were for you and me. You need to ask Marko, where the jewels are. Don't ask me dear. This is very important for you Becky."

"Carl, I need to talk with you."

"Talk here dear. I would hear what you have to say Becky."

"I will Mom. Why did you buy jewels for Mom?"

"I love her Becky and it is normal to buy something for the woman I love."

"But, Mom is old for you Carl."

"Of course I am old for Carl, you are young and good for Carl, Becky. When you decide to have sex with him, could you ask Marko to watch?" Peggy laughed.

"Mom, this is not funny."

"Of course dear. The sex is a feeling. I tried with Carl and I am feeling very good now dear."

"I need to tell Jack, what is going on in his house. "

"Marko, you need to take your relative with you when you speak with Jack. I think that Jack would feel good about it. Did she make French love to Jack? If she didn't, the why did Jack paid five hounded dollars? I did that to Carl and he bought me jewels."

"What I do you want me to do Peggy?", Marko asked.

"You have two choices Marko. First, you marry Becky and you must work in the company to make money for her and your children. Second you, Becky and Jack go away and leave me alone."

"What do you want to do Marco?", Peggy asked.

"I want to work in the company for Becky and my children Peggy."

"This sounds good. You are a good boy Marko."

When Jack came back at home Marko asked him "Do you know that Carl is Peggy's new lover, Jack?"

"Of course Marko. Carl is young and strong. Every woman would like to have sex with him."

"But, Peggy is your wife."

"If she divorces me, she will be free, but you must take care of Becky, and don't worry about Peggy."

"You are right Jack, I need to take care of Becky."

"You need to have sex Marko", Peggy told Marko and she laughed.

"May I sleep tonight with you Mom?", Becky asked Peggy.

"Tonight and tomorrow night, you can sleep in my bedroom, but on Monday, you and Marko need to leave my house. I give you three days to leave or I will kick your ass out of my house Becky. I need to spend more time with jack."

"Of course Peggy. After Becky returns from Dallas on Monday, I and Becky will move somewhere."

"This is a good decision Marko."

I felt that the family needed to sort things out, so I said good night and went to my room. I felt asleep immediately. I woke up at 6:00 in the morning. I swam for two hours. I took a shower and finished fast my breakfast. Marko and Becky weren't in the house. As planned I went with Peggy and Jack to see the land that Jack wanted to do the development on.

"This is the land Carl." I looked around for a while trying to access if this will be a good investment.

"How long do you need to drive to get to a beach from here?", I asked Jack

"I don't know Carl."

"Can you drive me to the nearest beach from here? Please pay attention to the distance!"

We arrived on the nearest beach and Jack told me, "Two miles Carl".

"This is very close to the beach Jack. This is good."

"How many acres is this land?"

"The land is 2,100 acres Carl. I will tell Adam that land is good for development and investment. He must give you the money."

"Do you have an idea, what kind houses we need to build on this land Carl?"

"The project is ready Jack. I will give you a phone number and a name. You need to negotiate for a price, because I created the project myself."

"Do you think that a project is good for development here Carl?" Peggy and I laughed.

"Of course honey, Carl told you that he created the project. I am so sorry Carl."

"It is OK Jack. You must ask, because you are investing the money." We went back to Jack's house and I called Joshua and asked for Adam. After ten minutes Adam called back. I told Adam that that he should provide the financing for this investment.

"Give me Jack, Carl."

"Which day are you coming to New York?", Adam asked Jack.

"I am flying tomorrow, Adam."

"When you arrive call me Jack." Jack called and bought two plane tickets after he hang up the phone.

"What do you think about Marko, Carl?"

"Peggy knows what to do with Marko, Jack. She is the boss now." Peggy and I laughed.

"I need to go to the office Peggy." Jack shook my hand and he left. Peggy picked up the phone and asked "Are you ready for six o'clock? I will drop my friend at the airport at 5:00 o'clock and then will come to see you."

Peggy drove and we spoke.

"I will miss you Carl. I will never forget that you saved mine and Jack's life."

We arrived at the airport. Peggy embraced me and told me, "Kill her in bed Carl. I want to have a smart grandson" and she kissed me. I saw tears in her eyes. I try to ask her why she was crying, but she left. After one hour, I was in Nassau Bahamas.

CHAPTER 6

I arrived at the Nassau airport in the early evening. I was looking for taxi and I saw a man, holding a sign with my name on it. I walked towards him and said "I am Carl Hope."

"I am your taxi driver Mr. Hope Follow me, please."

I sat on the back seat of the taxi and I tried to give him the address he needs to take me too, but the driver told me, that he knows where to take me. He said "I know Peggy and Jack. Peggy called me yesterday and told me that I need to pick you up this evening. About an hour ago she called again and she told me the time you will arrive. My name is Rico."

"How do you know Peggy, Rico?"

"After Jack and Peggy bought the house, I have been their driver for everything. They call and order food, water, beer, wine. I buy and then drop it in the house. Peggy pays me for delivery and she pays me good. She is good, but Jack is cheap. When Jack and Marko order I have a problem when they pay me. They try to negotiate the price. Becky is like Peggy. When I deliver something, I pray to God, that Peggy or Becky open the door." We laughed.

"Hey Carl, I was very happy when Peggy called and told me, that she will pay me two thousand for five days, but she expects very good service for you Mr. Hope."

"I understand Peggy" and I told myself "Thanks God, that Peggy called me, and not Jack". We laughed and I told Rico, "You are a funny man, I think that we will be good friends."

"Of course we will be Carl."

We arrived at the property of Jack and Peggy and we entered the house.

"Do you like to me to show you the house Carl?"

"No Rico, I am an architect. The refrigerator is full, but if you like something else call me. This is my phone number."

"Rico, can come tomorrow morning at 9:00?"

"Where do you want to go Carl, because I need to pick up a client from the airport at 10:00am?"

"I have business in City Hall. I need information for the Bahamas."

"What kind information do you need?"

"I want to invest in the Bahamas."

"I have a relative, who works there. His name is Young. I will tell him, that he needs to wait for you at 9:30 a.m."

"Thanks Rico."

"Hey Carl, I promised to provide a good service. Peggy told me two thousand, but I know, she will give me at least five hundred more if you are happy with your stay here."

"I like you Rico, I will give you too."

"How much are you going to give me Carl?"

"Three thousand and if myself or any my friends visit Nassau, they will ask for you too."

"Thanks Carl, you are just like Peggy. I will tell her, that you are a good man. Tomorrow at 9:00 a.m. I will be here", and Rico left. I opened a door and went on the terrace. The beach was clean and the sand was white. The water in the ocean was quiet. It was perfect for a swim. I went in the house and I put on a swimsuit. I returned to the beach and jumped in the water. When I stopped swimming, the sun was touching the water. It was so beautiful. I went back to the house. A phone was ringing. I found it and picked up. As I was expecting, it was Peggy.

"Hey boy, is everything OK?"

"I just came back from a swim in the ocean and getting ready to take a shower Peggy."

"Did you check the refrigerator? I hope it has everything you need for tonight."

"I didn't check, but if I need something, I will call Rico."

"I called you, because Lorenzo Falsone asked for you. Do you want me to tell him, where you are?"

"You can tell him. He is a good man. I know that well, Carl" and Peggy laughed. "Do you like the house?"

"The beach is perfect and the water too. The house is good and I like that it is on the beach. The terrace and the balcony are open to spectacular views. I have not looked yet inside the house. I will look inside now."

"Have a good evening and if you have any problem call me."

"I will Peggy."

I looked through the house just to get familiar with it, then I found some salad and cheese in the refrigerator and some chilled white wine. I had dinner on the balcony admiring the view. I felt tired and decided to go to bed early.

Rico arrived 9:00 in morning as we agreed.

"Is everything OK Carl?"

"Yes Rico. Everything is perfect. The house is good, the beach is clean, the sand is white and the water is good for swimming. The place is quite and the refrigerator is full."

"Do you know, what I need to make this vacation perfect Rico?"

"I am guessing that you may need a girl Carl." We laughed

"You are right Rico. I need a girl."

We arrived at City Hall. I saw a man waiting outside.

"Carl, this is Young. He is waiting for you."

"Here are three thousand for you, and three thousand for Young. You give him the money later."

"Why are you giving Young money Carl?"

"If I work with Young, I need him to provide me the correct information. I am honest and Young must be honest.

"How much time do you think you need to speak with Young, Carl?"

"Not more than one hour."

"I will drop my client and I will be back to pick you up from here in an hour. If I am late, Young will tell you, where you can wait for me in a coffee shop nearby. You will need to wait for me there."

"Young, this is Carl Hope. He is a businessman from New York. He paid for the information he needs. I will meet you later to give you the money. I told you last night how much he will give me. You will get the same money."

"Thanks Rico. You know how to do good business Carl",

Young told me. I entered City Hall with Young. We were walking when somebody asked me, "What are you doing here? I don't believe that you here Carl!"

I turned around. Oh my God. It was my college friend Josh from the New York University.

"What are you doing here Josh?"

"I work here Carl" and we shook hands.

"Boss, if Carl didn't give me money when we were in college, I would have never finished. He is rich, but he has a big heart and he is a very good man. He knows how to make and spend money. If you need something in City Hall, I will help you."

"Young will give me everything I need Josh, but I am so glad to see you. See you later."

"See you Carl."

"I like you man", Young told me. "You know what to do. You are smart. You took my heart. I want to work with you Carl." We entered Young's office and he asked me, "What do you want to know, Carl?"

"You need to tell me, where I need to invest in the Bahamas, since there are many islands. I would like to build houses and hotels. If I buy land, I need to know, what permits I have to obtain and how long I need to wait to get them. I don't like to buy land and wait for a long time for permits."

"What do you want to pay for the land Carl?"

"If I buy a lot of land, I am expecting to pay less, but I want a fair prices and legitimate business. I don't like criminal business. I know that everybody wants to pay less for land, but if you give me a cheap prices and I pay less, maybe, someday I will have a problem. It may rise questions in the future. How did I get the cheap land and who gave me those prices? At that point we will have problem Young. I will spend a lot money and time in court and you will be fired. Do you want that Young?"

"No. I don't want that."

"Me too Young. We will do business, but according to the laws in the Bahamas. If I invest a lot of money, this will good for the Bahamas. I will make a lot of money too. This way both sides will be happy."

"Do you need the information now Carl?"

"I don't need information now Young. I will be back in two months and we will start to work."

"Looks like you paid me for nothing Carl!"

"No Young, I paid you for the future. I like to start by paying forward." We laughed and Young told me, "This is a good investment for the future Carl."

"Do you want Josh to help you Carl, because he is your friend?"

"You are right Young. Josh is my friend, but you are my business partner Young. I will work with you. When only two people know, it is better for the business."

"You are right Carl. As said earlier, you are smart and I want to work with you. Call me anytime. I think we will become good friends. I know that Rico might become jealous" and we laughed. I left the building. Rico was waiting for me. I opened the door and I was surprised to see Becky sitting on the back seat of the taxi.

"What are you doing here,? Weren't you supposed to go to Dallas Becky"

"If you have Mom whose name is Peggy, you never know Carl."

"I am so happy to see you and I kissed her."

"This morning you told me that you need a girl Carl. I brought the girl."

"Thank you so much Rico. I will have a good vacation."

"What are you doing in City Hall? You said that you were coming here for a vacation."

"I had to take care of some business Becky."

"You know how to make money. You swim to keep your body in good shape and women in bed for exercise. Did I miss anything, Carl?"

"No Becky. I don't like to change my life. Maybe someday I will, but right now it is OK for me."

"Do you want to have a wife and children someday Carl?"

"First, I need to find a wife. Second, I must have sex with her to have children. I will need some time need to think about that Becky." Rico and I laughed. Before you know, we arrived in the property of Jack and Peggy. I tried to pay, but Rico told me, "You paid Carl. I wish you a good time with Becky. If you need something call me".

"I will Rico", and he left. I and Becky entered the house. She jumped and embraced me with her hands and legs. I kissed and asked her.

"Do you want to go bed Becky or we are going to the beach?"

"I have not had sex for nine days, you have not had sex for four days. Let's forget about the beach for now. I think that we need sex."

"What should I tell Marko about it, if he asks me Becky?"

"This is your problem Carl. I don't have a problem with Marko. Marko has many mamacitas. I have one cowboy. Hey, I forgot to tell you. Mom spoke with Ethan. You need to call Ethan at his home office. I will take a shower and wait for you in bed."

I called. Ethan picked up the phone. "Ethan, this is Carl."

"Hey Carl. What are you doing? How is your life? Are you busy with business or you are spending most of your time in bed? Not for sleeping I am sure."

We laughed and I told him. "You are correct Ethan. She is waiting for me in bed."

"Carl, I spoke with Kate and she told me, that Scott Colman was in Midland and he took two very young men with him. Don't kill them. Kate told me that you must save those lives. Emmy called me and she said that Scott has a trip to New York tomorrow. That is it Carl."

"How is yours, Michelle's, Robert's and Mom's life?"

"I am busy in the office and at home. Now I have three women in the house."

"Do you have a girlfriend Ethan?"

"I know that Michelle and Mom are in your house. Who is the third woman?"

"I don't know what I need to tell you, but Kate moved in the house too. She is trying to sale her condo and buy another house or a condo around SMU. Michelle invited her to live in my house. Kate sleeps in Michelle's bedroom. I asked Michelle, why Kate is sleeping in her bedroom, because we have many rooms. She told me "Kate is my teacher. Please don't ask me what she is teaching me."

"Is Kate is teaching you how to have sex, because you want to be Carl?"

"If Carl doesn't have sex with me, I will find other boys father."

"Do you like to work on the street Michelle?"

"Who knows father, I need to be ready for everything?"

"Maybe I will be to sale something on the street father." Ethan and I laughed.

"Robert told me "Ethan, if Carl was here we will be laughing twenty four hours. Your mom and Robert are here Carl. Robert says Hi to you. He is busy in the kitchen. Robert and Julia are cooking for me, Michelle and Kate. Julia likes to speak with you Carl" and he gave her the phone.

"Hi, Mom."

"Why didn't you call me for four days Carl? I have been worried about you?"

"I am busy Mom and you know that they are listening to Ethan's phone. If they didn't I would have called every day."

"What are you doing in the office Mom?"

"I am the new boss. You don't know this business Mom."

"Don't tell me what I know."

"You are right Julia. You are my darling and I am honey for you. What are you doing darling?"

"This is hard for me Carl. You know that my life is simple and I want to stay in New York. I spoke with Jerry and he told me that you will change my life when we start to live again together in New York."

"He is right Mom."

"How many women are going to be with in the next four days Carl?"

"One is waiting in bed right now, maybe she will leave, if I continue to talk to you Mom. How is Michelle? Are you getting her ready for me or for other boys?"

We laughed and I heard the voice of Michelle.

"Can I talk to Carl, please?"

"You sound tired dear, you need to go to bed" and Mom hung up the phone. Julia knows that Michelle isn't ready to talk to me. She needs some time to change her life. It might be a short time, or a long time, but I think that with Kate's help Michelle can change her life faster. Kate was right when she told me that Michelle loves me and she is willing to try anything to be my wife. When I see Mom, I will ask her about Michelle, but right now I have Becky waiting for me in bed. I think that I will need to thank Peggy for that. I was laughing when I entered the bedroom.

"I want you naked Carl, I don't like to lose precious time taking off your clothes." I felt Becky's voice full of lust and my blood went straight into my groin. I took off my clothes, throwing them on the floor. Becky was following every move I made. I was set on her eyes. She was under the bedsheet. She took the corner and unfolded her naked body. That move made him spring up as I moved closer to the side of the bed.

"Do you like my body Carl?" Becky asked me.

"Isn't that obvious?"

"You know well that I love your body Becky."

"That sounds good, but I want to see some action. I am not interested in talking Carl."

I leaned over her and started kissing her neck going down toward her breasts. She closed her eyes. I jumped in the bed.

"O boy, you scared me" and she opened her eyes to look at me.

"Now I will really start to scare you" and I kissed her lips then and started to suck her tongue. We plaid with our tongues. After that I kissed her neck. I positioned myself between her legs. I sucked and played with her nipples. She was ready to take my cook inside her. Her pussy was wet. She sucked him in. She put her legs around my waist. She moved her hip up and down I was trying to get in sync with her movement. As we were synchronizing our movements became faster, our breathing heavier and heavier loosing ourselves in each other until we reached our climax together. As I was trying to catch my breath I continued to kiss her mouth lying on top of her. She was stroking gently my back. We were sweaty. When our breathing came to normal I rolled to the empty side of the bed and took her head and placed it on my chest. We were happy, enjoying this special moment in silence.

"Do you want to talk Carl?"

"I am listening Becky."

"You are a bad boy."

"I am Becky."

"You almost killed me."

"I know understand what Peggy told me at the airport."

"What did my mom tell you?"

"Kill her in bed Carl!"

"I was wondering what she was talking about."

"I hope that I fulfilled Peggy's wish!"

"I think that I can report back that you did good." I looked at her and we laughed.

"I wanted to tell you, what happened on Wednesday. I was sleeping in my mom's bed and asked her, if I have a chance to marry you. She told me that I have a zero chance. I was surprised Carl."

"Is it true, that I have a zero chance to live with you Carl?"

"I am so sorry, but it is the truth Becky."

She was not happy to hear that, but I didn't want to lie to her.

"I need to take shower Carl."

"Are you sure that you want to take a shower? Peggy is waiting for a grandchild, you need to keep my sperm inside you, if you want to make your mother happy."

"Don't worry about that, Carl. I know what to do."

"I am not worried" and I smiled.

"Why did you smile Carl?"

"I am happy that you are here. I didn't know what I was going to do if I was alone. Now I know that I will be with you and we will have a good time together as we did before."

I stayed in the bed, thinking of her beautiful body while she was taking a shower. She came back with wet hair and a towel wrapped around her torso. I was looking at her imaging that the towel is not there. She was looking intently at my eyes and I think that she read my thoughts.

"What do you want to do Carl?" she asked me teasingly.

"I think that you can guess?"

"Not really! Tell me!" I was certain that she knew what I mean but she wanted me to say it out loud. She wanted to hear from me that I want her.

"I am waiting for you to have sex again Becky."

"We just finished few minutes ago Carl!"

"May be you did Becky." She walked toward me and picked up the bedsheet uncovering me.

"Oh my! You are really ready to have sex again! I am glad that I have that effect on you."

She looked at me and I felt that words I said to hear earlier were still in her mind. She was still trying to process them and she was confused about her feelings at the moment.

"I am not ready to have sex again Carl."

"Make French love with me then."

"I don't like that, because I don't want to waste your sperm. I need your sperm. I think that after two or three hours I will be ready to have sex again ."

Looking down at my groin I said "I am so sorry. She isn't ready. You must wait boy."

"Are you talking to your cock Carl?"

I jumped out of the bed and kissed her.

"I am kidding Becky, we will have sex, when you are ready."

I embraced her tightly and kissed her. She put a robe on and I put some jeans and a T-shirt. We left the bedroom and we went to the living room.

"Do you like glass of wine Carl?"

"I don't Becky, because I am planning to go for a swim after 4:00 o'clock. Can you pour a glass of juice for me please?"

We sat on the terrace. She had a glass of wine in her hand, I was had orange juice and we were enjoying the view.

"Life is good. I feel good right now Becky."

"Are you feeling good, because I am with you Carl?"

"You are right Becky." She looked at me confused.

"I spoke with Peggy and she told me that I need to help you. I will try. I have many questions, but I don't know where to start, because it depends on what you want to do."

"I know that you don't want to hurt me, but you must tell me the truth Carl."

"OK then. You are jealous and greedy Becky."

"Oh my God. I can't believe what I am hearing! You just had sex with me. I saw that you were happy to see me. You came to my room, and now you are telling me that I am jealous and greedy!" She was upset.

"That is correct. I was happy to see you, but I didn't have any idea that I will be in bed with Becky when I saw you. It was your decision to go to bed with me. I don't want to fight with you. You asked me to tell you the truth, but you don't like what I have to say. I will call Peggy and I will tell her, that you need to go back to Miami."

She looked at me contrite. "Don't call her. I like to be with you" and Beaky kissed me.

She looked at my eyes and asked me "Why did you say that I am jealous and greedy?"

"I will tell you Becky, because I want to help you. You were jealous of your mom when you came to the house and asked her about the jewels. I am certain that Marco told you about them because he saw them in Jack's office, and he told you that I bought them for her. He told you about them because he knows that you will be jealous. Marko told you that I am your mom's lover and you believed him. He wants you to hate your mom. This is his goal. Can't you see that?" Becky was processing what I said for few minutes. I sat quietly.

"Why did you say that I am greedy, Carl?"

"When we were in the restaurant, Marko said that he is the vice president of the company and after one year he will take control of the it and Jack will have to listen to him. I think that Marko must listen to Jack. How many times Marko told you, that he will be rich some day?"

"Marko has told me that many times Carl. I don't think that there is anything wrong with that!"

"You are correct Becky, there is nothing wrong with having the goal of being rich. Have you ever asked him how is planning to accomplish that?"

"Not really. I assumed working hard."

"Well this is where the problem is. Marko will be rich when he kills Peggy and takes over the control of the company."

"Are you crazy Carl? Marko will never kill anybody!"

"I am telling you, Marko will kill Peggy."

"Mom never told me, that Marko wants to kill her."

"Would you believe, if Peggy tells you that Marko will kill her and so that he can take control of the company?"

"I will not believe her, because she hates him."

"This is the big issue Becky. You don't believe to your mom, you believe Marko. Of course, Marko is your future husband and you love him, but I will tell you what happened four months ago, maybe, this information will open your eyes. Four months ago Jack had sex with Marko's relative and Jack paid her five hundred dollars. Somebody told Peggy and she decided to divorce him. If Peggy and Jack divorce and you marry Marko, then Marko has two people on his side. You and Jack. Nobody is on Peggy's side. If somebody kills Peggy, everybody will believe that Jack killed her, because Jack has two reasons to kill her. First, Jack will be owner of the company one hundred percent. Now Jack has fifty, Peggy has fifty. Second, Jack wants to marry a young woman. This woman is a relative of Marko. If Peggy is death, Jack will be in jail. That means, that Marko is the boss and owner of the company and Marko is rich Becky. Marko told you many times, that he will be rich. You are supporting him blindly."

"Is it true that you want to be rich Becky?"

"Yes Carl. I want to be rich."

"So that explains why you are greedy."

"Who told you that Marko will kill my mom?"

"If Mom told you that, I won't believe it, but you spoke with Lorenzo, did he tell you that?"

"Lorenzo told me that if you don't marry Marko, he will kill you. But if do marry him, he will kill Peggy."

"I shared this information with Peggy and she asked me to help you Becky."

"Now I believe it Carl, because Mom told me the same story. If Peggy didn't ask me I would never gotten involved in your family's affairs Becky."

"What do I need to do now, because I don't have any idea Carl?"

"You must speak with Peggy and Jack. This is a family problem, but you also must think how to save your life. Honestly! Marko is dangerous. Lorenzo told me that. I believe him, because he is a detective."

"Why did Lorenzo tell you? He should have told Mom, because he is a good friends with my mom?"

"I didn't know that Lorenzo is a good friend of Peggy's! Maybe he was concerned that Peggy will not believe him. You and Jack need to support Peggy, because you sleep with Marko and Jack works with him."

"Are you jealous that I am sleeping with Marko?"

"I am not jealous Becky, because I like having good sex with you. That is all."

"You like the sex with me, but you don't love me Carl. That is why you are not jealous."

"It is true, I don't, but you are perfect in bed Becky." I smiled, she didn't.

"Do you think that it is polite to tell me that Carl?"

"This isn't polite, but is true and I am happy to be in bed with you Becky." I took her head with my hands and kissed her.

"I think that I love you Carl. I was stupid when I chose Marko. Many women want to sleep with him."

"They have sex with Marko, they don't just want Becky. They are succeeding."

"I have a question, is Marko better in bed than me Becky?"

"No Carl. He finishes very fast and often for his own pleasure."

"Every woman wants more sex and a rich man Becky."

"In Miami women want Marko, because they think that Marko

is rich. They use Marko to get money."

"You are right Carl. Mom told me that Marko has bought jewels for women."

"Where did you meet Marko?"

"I met him at a night club. After that we met several times. I invited Marko to the house. He was surprised, that I am rich. I am not rich Carl. My mom and dad are rich. Jack took Marko to work in the company. Honestly, Mom never says anything good about him, but Marko has good relationship with Jack. Now I know why Carl. I am so stupid. Marko used me. He uses Jack too."

"Finally, you understood Becky. This is good for you, Peggy and Jack."

"May I sit in your lap, I need to feel your body?"

"That is a great idea!"

As she made herself comfortable in my lap sidewise, I embraced her and I told her "You are a very sweet girl Becky" and I kissed her. She started sucking my tongue I responded back. She turned to the right facing me and her legs went up and around my waist holding me tightly. I was not sure where she was going with that move, so I looked at her and asked "Do you want to go to back bed?"

"I am not sure Carl, I just want you to hold me right now. There is too much in my head to process. I think that I will be OK in few hours."

"Do you want us to take a walk on the beach?"

"This is a good idea Carl."

We were walking and talking. My mom told me "Becky, Carl is a good, but a dangerous man. He is a gentleman, but sometimes he comes across as arrogant." I told her "Mom I think that there are two sides to him".

"You are right Becky. Carl is good and a gentleman for good people, but is dangerous and arrogant for bad people. Which side do you want to be on, Becky?"

"Of course, I like to be on his good side Mom. You are a good daughter" and Mom kissed me.

"Mom has not kissed me in a long time. You were in Miami for three days and you know who is who. Lorenzo told you everything, Mom too. I forgot to tell you that my boss said that you are a good man, and he likes you."

"Peggy told me that Carl will open business in Miami and in the

Caribbean. We are company that works with businessmen. I think that someday Carl will use my company and we will make good money Becky"."

"Is it true, that you will business with the company I work for, Carl?"

"Who knows Becky! The future will tell us."

"I am glad that your boss wants to work with me and if I open a business in Miami and the Caribbean, I will use him. Your mom and your boss are very good friends. I think that I have become a very good friends with Peggy and I know that I can trust her. She will tell me, if your boss is trying to do something wrong. You must have honest people, you work with Becky."

"I understand Carl. Marko is the wrong man for my father. Marko isn't honest."

"Marko is the wrong man for your family Becky, but you must decide what to do. Hey, Marko is your future husband. I must be careful talking like that about him with you ." I laughed. She didn't.

"Are you trying to hurt me Carl?"

"I didn't mean to Becky. I just told you the truth."

"You are the same as my mom Carl. She told me many times "When you live with a stupid man, it means that you are a stupid too my daughter."

"Now I know that she is right. Mom tried to open my eyes, I finally got it Carl. Do you believe in God, Carl?"

"Of course, I believe. I was seven years old when my grandmother told me "You must believe in God". I asked her "Why I must believe in God, Grandmother?"

She told me "Good people believe in God and they are Angels. Bad people don't believe in God and they are Devils".

"What is difference, between them Grandmother?"

"Angels help people. If somebody has problem and needs help, people should help. The Devil on the other hand tries to destroy the life of the people, who believe in God. He tempts them to do bad things to each other, makes them kill each other."

"Who do you want to be Carl?"

"I want to be an Angel, Grandmother."

"That is the right choice. You are a good boy. Your life will continue in Heaven. You should wear a cross Carl. It will remind you of God when you are tempted by the Devil and help you resist him."

"Who give you this cross?"

"When I was fourteen years old, my grandmother gave it to me. She said "You must carry this cross all the time Carl. God will protect your live"."

"Do you believe that God exist Carl?"

"Of course Becky. I believe that after I die, my spirit will be in Heaven."

"But you will be death Carl."

"My body will be death Becky, but the spirit never dies."

"How do you know, that your spirit will be in Heaven?"

"Grandmother told me that and I believe her, because she never lies. When I was in the University, I completed a very challenging project. My professor told me that I have succeeded only because God must have helped me." I remembered my professor for a minute, then I continued.

"Hey Becky, I am twenty six years old and I have millions. I will make hundred million, because I believe in God and he supports me. I told you how I think and feel about God. Now I have a question for you Becky do you believe in God?"

"Mom believes in God. She goes to Church and she prays to God. My dad and I believe in God, but we don't understand, why we need to pray to him."

"This is simple. You pray to God, because you believe in him Becky."

"I know that right now you love me and you want to live with me, but you are engaged and you are planning to marry Marko. If I knew that you were engaged, I wouldn't have had sex with you in Dallas."

"Why did you have sex with me now Carl, after you know?"

"I was here, you came here and you took me in bed. I was for three days in Miami and I didn't have sex with you, but now I want to have sex with you many times, because I want to put many antlers on Marko's head."

"Don't you think that by doing that you will be putting many antlers on the head of your girlfriend Carl or while you are here with me she may be putting many antlers on your head?"

"I am not engaged to anybody Becky, so there I is no danger of that. I am a free man or as my friend Michelle told me, that I am a horse in the bed." We laughed.

"O boy, you are so funny, but now I think that I need to go to

Church and pray to God." A phone ringing was coming from somewhere. I stood up and was ready to look for the phone, but Becky said "Carl you sit down. I will pick up the phone in case Marko is calling. Doesn't matter if Marko is calling or somebody else. You play your game, I will play my game Carl." She picked up the phone.

"It is my mom Carl, I would like to have a talk with her. It will be a while." I understood that Becky wanted to speak with her mom alone.

"I will go to swim then." I went to my room and put on my swimsuit. I went in the water. It was warm and relaxing. I was thinking about Kate, Vicky, Michelle and Becky. They are all beautiful and smart girls, but they have problems. They have different problems. Maybe I will help them, but they need to believe in God and pray. He could help them the more than anybody else. Now I know that Peggy goes to Church and she prays to God. I am certain that she prays for Becky.

I finished swimming and I went back to the house. I heard a noise in the kitchen. I entered, but I couldn't see Becky. The noise was coming behind the kitchen island. I walked around and asked "What are you doing Becky?"

"I am trying to find a frying pan. I cooked last time, but I don't remember where I put it." I saw Becky's ass and I was surprised. She had a shirt, but she didn't have bikini. She bended in a way that I saw her pussy. I couldn't resist that. I walked to her, when I came close I squatted and I kissed her pussy.

"O boy. What are you doing?"

"I just kissed your pussy Becky."

"After two hours of swimming you still have an energy for sex?" she said with a surprise.

"Of course, I am ready for sex any time. You should know that by now." I continued to kiss her and play with my tongue inside her. She started to move her ass and with a lusty voice she told me "I want to fill you inside me!". Her hands were in my hair. I stood up facing her and pulled her up on the kitchen counter, looking at her eyes. She wrapped her legs around my hips and pulled me towards her. I dropped my swim trunks on the floor, grabbed her hips and was inside her with one swift move. I started to move slowly forward and back. Her breathing became faster. She leaned back facing the ceiling. I picked up the speed filling her. I felt touching something deep inside her. She pulled her head forward to look at me and that was the carnal signal for our climax together. She whispered "I want you to stay inside me." I was holding her in my arms.

"How long, will we be staying in this position?"

"I want to be like that forever Carl. I felt you so deep inside me." Becky asked me to take her to bed. I picked her in my arms and I carried he in the bedroom. I laid her on the bed and I asked her, how long she will stay in bed and what she wanted for dinner.

"Not more than thirty minutes, and if you prepare some fish and green salad it will be great. I would like to rest for a little bit" and she closed her eyes.

I left the bedroom and went straight to the kitchen. I marinated the fish. I decided to cook on the grill that I saw earlier on the terrace. I started prepping some red peppers, corns, asparagus, onion, tomatoes, red potatoes, eggplants and squashes. I lighted the grill and I started to cook. I just finished with the grilling when Becky came to the terrace.

"Something is smelling very good Carl. What did you cook?"

"Could you sit on the table? I will be your waiter tonight Becky."

She came to me and kissed me. Looking intently at me she said "I love you Carl. You are the perfect man. You know how to cook, you know how to have good sex."

"You forgot to say, that I will make good money for you Becky."

"I need to ask you Carl, do you love me? It will make me very happy, if you say yes."

"Don't push me to say something you may not like Becky. I have the same question for you. Do you love Marko? I will be happy if you say yes Becky."

"Why did you ask me that, I am with you here now, Carl? Why are you bringing Marco in this conversation?"

"Because, Marko is your future husband and I need to help him to have a baby boy Becky. Maybe, someday Marko will tell me "I am so happy that we were partners for this boy Carl. I will never forget that". I will tell him that it is my pleasure to be a part of it."

"I can't believe that you are so arrogant Carl."

"I am not Becky. You asked me, if I love you and I told you how much I love Marko. I would never have said that, if you didn't ask me that question, expecting me to say I love you Becky, because I don't."

"Is it because you love somebody else Carl?"

"I love my mom, my grandparents, Mark and many of my friends."

"You don't love any of the girls you have sex with?"

"I never say that any of them that I love them."

"But you have many girls Carl? I can't believe that none of them has asked you if you love her!"

"Michelle told me many times that she loves me and she asked me if I love her."

"What did you tell her?"

"I never have sex with Michelle and I never told her that I love her."

"What are you going to do, if I want to leave now Carl?"

"I will ask Riko to pick you up and drop you at the airport Becky. I will be happy to be alone."

"I don't understand you. You cooked for me and you had sex with me. That was so sweet. All of a sudden you want to kick me out of my house?"

"This house belongs to Peggy and Jack. When your future husband kills Peggy and Jack is in jail, then you and Marko will own it Becky. Right now I am on vacation in Peggy's and Jack's house. Do you understand or you need more explanation?"

"Could you open a bottle of white wine? We should eat Carl."

"This is a good idea. You are a good girl."

"You will be good boy, if you tell me that you love me."

"Hey Becky, maybe someday if we have a boy I may tell you want you want to hear."

"I know that you will never say, that you love me."

"You are right Becky", and we started to eat.

"Who taught you how to cook, Carl?"

"My grandmother and my mom taught me. Sometimes I like to cook for myself. I don't like to cook for somebody else. I cooked for you tonight, because you needed to rest."

"Is this the same Grandmother that told you about God? Could you tell more about her?"

"I grew up in the Smoky Mountains with my grandparents. Grandfather taught me, how to be safe in the mountains. Grandmother taught me how to cook. I enjoyed spending time with her while she was cooking and I couldn't just watch, so I was helping her. It was our time together and I used to talk to her about anything that came to my mind. One time I asked her who is better, the men or the women? She immediately guessed that I may have asked my grandfather the same question, so she asked me "What did your grandfather tell you Carl?"

"He told me that the men are better."

"Do you believe that Carl?"

"I don't know Grandmother, but I would like to know?"

"Who is pregnant for nine months and gives birth to a child Carl?"

"Women are pregnant and deliver children Grandmother."

"Have you seen a man pregnant and delivering a child?"

"I never have seen or heard that Grandmother."

"If there are no women in the world, how will the world go forward? So, who do you think is better now Carl?"

"Women are better Grandmother."

"Could you promise me Carl, that you will never beat or hurt a woman and that you never lie to a woman."

"I promised her and I never hit or lie to a woman or anybody else. So I hope that now you understand why I can't tell you that I love you Becky, I will be lying. Do you want me to lie to you?"

"I don't want that Carl. I am so sorry that I was pushing you to tell me that you love me."

"I had a good life with my grandparents, full with fun. I like to tell you a funny story. I was thirteen years old. There was a political election in the small city we lived in. Grandfather asked Grandmother why she voted for a man who is from the other party."

"I voted for a person, I didn't vote for a party" she replied.

"Grandfather turn to me and told me that when I start to vote, I need to ask him who I need to vote for."

"Don't listen to him Carl. You need to vote for a person. John, if you push Carl to vote for the person, you want, I will kill you. This is a free country."

"Later that day, when me and my grandfather were alone I asked him "Do you think that Grandmother will kill you?"

"I don't doubt that Carl."

"Two days later I told this story to my Uncle Mark and asked him if he thinks that Grandmother will kill Grandfather?"

"She will kill him Carl."

"After I heard that my grandmother became my hero. She was my Jeanne d' Arc."

"Who is Jeanne d' Arc Carl?"

"A French woman who fought for freedom for her nation in the fourteen century."

"How do you know that?"

"From books. I love to read. I have been reading since I was a child. I read everything in the small library we had. I was number one in school. I helped my friends, with math and physics."

"Are you finished with dinner Carl?"

"Yes, Becky."

"I will clean the table and wash the dishes, since you cooked."

"You need to relax and enjoy Becky. I will do that." When I finished I went back to the table.

"Did your grandmother and mom taught you to help women?"

"Yes, they told me that I should help."

"If I ask Marko, he will tell me he is a man and that this is a job for a woman."

"I laughed and told her that Marko is a special man for her". We laughed and Becky asked me.

"Do you think that Marko will be a big problem for me and my family?"

"Marko isn't problem for me, but I don't know for you Becky. After one month you will marry him, you need to think very carefully before you that. Do you like more wine Becky?"

"Of course. Hey, I remembered last time when we were in Dallas you asked me if like more wine and "I told you no, I like more sex." She was gazing at me.

"After one more glass of wine, I will be like a lioness in bed."

We didn't speak for a while just enjoying the atmosphere of the quite evening. Becky finished the wine. She stood up and told me "I am going to get ready for bed. I will be waiting for you" and she left the terrace.

I took the dishes to the dishwasher and went straight to the shower. I wrapped a towel around my waist and went to her bedroom. She was in bed. She looked at me full of desire. "I want to do with you everything I know." I leaned towards her. She kissed my mouth, our tongs mingled. I laid next to her, giving her the access to my body. She leaned over me and started kissing my chest and moved south to my stomach then to my arousing erection. She started sucking hard. Without stopping she moved her left leg over me and my head was between her legs. Her pussy was above my head. That was very hot. I kissed her pussy and my tongue was on her clitoris. She picked up a rhythm and her body started shivering. She raised her body moving away from my head and turned around facing me with her legs around my waist. She slid over my full erection and started riding me.

"Carl grab my ass. I like to feel you deep inside me."

I grabbed her. She was moving up and down, I was meeting her movement with my hips. I was filling her. I felt that I was touching something inside her, just like earlier. I asked her "Do you feel this?"

"I feel it Carl, just keep up with me, I feel so good." I don't know how long we plaid. My hands were on her breasts tucking her nipples. They were hard. She was shaking her ass. I looked in her eyes, her pupils were dilated. She reached her climax I followed her. She stopped and she laid her body on mine. We laid like that, as our breathing was retuning back to normal.

"I am so tired, I need a rest Carl" and she kissed my chest. "I would like to stay like that until it shrinks and slides out."

When it slid out, she put her shirt between her legs and laid beside me. "I don't want to take a shower now. I just want to lay next to you. I like to feel your warmth."

"Do you like to talk Becky?"

"No Carl. I would like to sleep." I laid next to her and I thought for my life. I have many beautiful women. They say that they love me, but I only like them. I don't know how many I will have in the future. But there is one think I know, when I decide to marry, I must love one woman and that is the woman I will marry. I don't know which one will be. I need to ask my mom and grandmother. They have more experience in life. If I have married Edit, I wouldn't have this problem now. I think that she was the only one I loved. I will tell Mom, that she is the reason I have this problem and I now don't know what to do. I know what she will tell me that I don't have a problem, I should marry Michelle. I laughed. Oh my God. I am joking with myself again, but Mom will be right. Michelle is a good girl. I was at looking at Becky in her sleep. She looked peaceful and happy.

I woke up in the morning. Becky was steel asleep and she was in the same position I last saw her last night next to me. She didn't move the whole night. I kissed her cheek and left the house for a swim. I swam for almost two hours. When I went back in the house Becky was on the terrace.

"Good morning Becky" and I was leaning to kiss her, but Becky grab my head pulling me to her and kissed me passionately. Then she said "I love you Carl".

"I love our baby Becky".

"Boy, you will never tell me, I love you Becky."

I took a shower and wrapped a towel around my waist.

"Come to me Carl." I walked towards Becky.

"Stay still, don't move."

She grabbed the corner of the towel and pulled it away from me. I was standing naked on front of her. She went down on her knees and took a hold of my erection and squeezed tightly then she stared to kiss it. She stared talking to it "You are a bad. You tried to kill me last night, but I love you, because you are helping me a to make a boy. She kissed it again and wrapped the towel back around my waist. I was ready to take her again and I asked her "Why did you stop Becky, that felt good?"

"Of course, it felt good, but I am a human being, I am not an iron machine Carl."

I kissed and told her "You need to relax Becky. I will put on my shorts and shirt".

"What do you like for breakfast Carl?"

"I would like a light breakfast. Could you prepare fruit salad, yogurt and coffee for me, please?"

"It will be my pleasure Carl."

I dressed and went back on the terrace and sat on a chair. She brought the food on the table and we started to eat.

"Do you have problem with your Mom, Carl?"

"I had a big problem, when I decided to move to Dallas. Mom didn't approve that."

"If you go to Dallas, I will throw myself under the subway."

"I will stop the subway Mom."

"I will go on front of the bus then."

"I will tell the Mayor to arrest you Mom."

"Why are going to call the Mayor to arrest me Carl?"

"Because, you will be safe in jail." She laughed and told me "I know that you love me Carl."

"Everybody loves you Mom."

"Jerry told Mom that I am not a little boy anymore, but a twenty four year old man. Mom was disappointed, but she listens to Jerry. He is my brother, but I regard him as my father."

"Why did you choose Dallas?"

"I got a good offer from them assuring me the creative freedom I was looking for. They were curious why that was so important for me. I told them that one of the professors I worked with at the university advised me to ask for it and since I respected him a lot. I trusted him. They asked me, who my professor was. I think that they spoke to him, because they called me two days later and I started the job right away."

"Hey Becky, if I didn't take that job in Dallas, I would never have met you." Becky kissed me and said "Are you going to love your future son with me Carl? He will be half mine and half yours. If you love your future son, then you love me too, because he will be half of me."

"You are correct Becky." We got interrupted by a ringing phone. Becky picked up. "For you Carl" and Becky put the phone on a speaker.

"Hi Carl, I know that you are in the Bahamas."

"Who told you that Michelle? Nobody knows that I am in the Bahamas."

"Marko from New York called and asked for you. He said that since I am your girlfriend I should know where you are. I told Marko that I am dreaming to be your girlfriend, but you don't care for that. I taught that you were in Seattle. Marko told me that you are in the Bahamas with Becky. He told me that Becky will marry him next month. I asked Marko. Why did he throw Becky in your arms? Carl is a horse. He know how to have a good time in bed and for many hours. I told him to call Becky and tell her to change the entry door of their house. They will need a big door so that Marco can go through it, because Carl will have sex with Becky many times and Marko will have big antlers on his head. Do you love me Carl? I think that I know your answer, but I need to ask you in case it has changed since the last time we spoke."

"You know my answer Michelle, I am not ready to tell you, that I love you."

"I know that someday you will tell me that Carl. Hey Carl, Kate is teaching me about sex. I am getting ready to surprise you."

"That sounds good Michelle. I will wait and when you are ready, you need to take me to bed to show me."

"I will Carl, but now you need to take Becky in bed. I don't want to waste more of your time and she hung up the phone."

"Did you have sex with Michelle?"

"I slept one night with her, but we slept. We didn't have sex. I am not ready to have sex with her."

"You don't like Michelle or she has some kind of problem?"

"She is a virgin and I don't know, what will happen after sex with her."

"Every woman is virgin before the first time she has sex Carl."

"Honestly, I don't know what I to tell you Becky. You heard that Kate is teaching Michelle about sex and I am afraid that she may kill me in bed."

I laughed, but Becky didn't. She took my words seriously.

I tried to lighten the mood and said "I was kidding, come to bed with me."

"I am not ready Carl, maybe later." The phone was ringing again. It was Peggy. "Lorenzo called and told me that two people arrived in Miami from Texas."

"Where are they Peggy?"

"They are in a hotel" and Peggy gave me name of the hotel and the room number.

"Peggy, please call Kate and give her this information. Kate knows what to do" and I gave her Kate's phone number. "Kate is a good friend and tell her that I am staying in your house."

"Could you tell Lorenzo to keep these boys alive? I promised Kate to keep them alive. If you have problem, call me Peggy" and I hung up the phone.

"Why did you hung up the phone, I wanted to speak with my mom?"

"I am so sorry, but you need to speak to her later Becky. She is doing something for me now."

"Do you like to go for a walk Carl?"

"Not now Becky. I need to stay close to the phone. I think that I have a problem."

"How does Marko know Michelle's phone number and who gave it to him?"

"Don't touch the phone Becky. If the phone rings, I will pick up."

"Do you remember your first love Carl?"

"Of course, I remember. My first love was Edit. She is from France. Mom was scared that I will marry her. She told me that Edit is old for me. I asked my mom why she thinks that the fact that Edit is older than me is a problem."

"There is not a problem now, but after fifteen years, you will have a problem with her."

"I met Edit when I was in the University. She taught me what to do in bed. She was a good teacher and I was a good student. I had a good time with her. I went to Europe twice with her. She was an amazing woman and I loved her, but I left her, because Mom didn't approve of this relationship. One month after I came back from Europe the second time, Edit called and told me that she is getting married in three weeks and that she is pregnant, and she hung up the phone. She called me after eight months and she told me "We have a boy Carl". I congratulated her, but her husband took the phone and told me "I am so happy for our son Carl".

"What happened after that Carl?"

"Edit calls me from France and we speak sometimes. They had a daughter two years after they had the son. When I moved to Dallas Mom spoke with Edit several times. She didn't give her my phone in Dallas, but for Christmas I called Edit. She was so happy and she told me that the boy is growing very fast."

"Do you know the boy's name Carl?"

"No. I never asked Edit and she never told me."

"Is this is your boy Carl?"

"Are you crazy Becky? Edit never told me that I am the father of her boy!"

"You are stupid Carl? Edit didn't tell you, because she is married to another man."

"I think my mom knows something Becky, because she used to tell me all the time that Edit is old for me and she needs to marry an older man. I have not seen Edit for more than four years."

"You need to call and ask Edit for the boy."

"Hey, I think that you are going too far Becky. If Edit likes to tell me, she needs to tell me."

"This is your son Carl, trust me."

"But she has a husband and they have a second child. Who am I to get between Edit and her husband, Becky? Edit had sex with me, but she had sex with another man and she married him. If you have a child, but you have sex with me and Marko how would you know, who is the father?"

Out of nowhere to my surprise Becky told me "I am ready, come to bed with me Carl."

I relied teasingly "I don't like sex Becky."

"I don't need your sex, I need your sperm Carl" and she pulled me in the bed. She was in playful mood again.

"I don't need long sex but I need more sperm."

"How many liters do you need Becky?"

"Oh boy, stop talking and start working."

"Hey, I am an architect. I am not a miner that has a drill ready for your hole. I need to get ready for sex."

She started kissing my mouth then she moved down to my nipples, her hands were on my growing erection. Then she slipped into me and started going up and down at her own pace. After fifteen minutes, Becky pushed me to finish. I tried but I couldn't. I remembered the solution Dino shared with me having the same problem when having sex with Marisa. He told me that he thinks for another attractive woman. I imagined Vicky but no result, then Kate, still nothing. I imagined Michelle, the way she moves her ass when I saw her at the pool, how she slid her hand in my swimsuit and touch me, and I finished. I said you were right Dino.

"What did you say Carl?"

"Nothing Becky" and I pulled away from her.

"I need to take a shower Becky" and I tried to leave, but she told me, "You forgot something Carl".

"Of course, I forgot" and I kissed her.

I felt uneasy for some reason. I took a quick shower and went on the terrace wandering what does Becky wants and expects from me? I never promised anything to her! Why does she want me to tell her, that I love her or that I will marry her? Becky has Marko. Maybe he told her many times, "I love you Becky". Of course, he is planning to marry her.

I was laughing, when she came to the terrace and asked me, "Why are you laughing? What is so funny Carl?"

"I was thinking that you will marry Marko in a month and you will have a very happy family. I am so happy for you Becky."

"Do you think that Marko is a good choice for me?"

"I think that Marko is a good choice for you, because he told you many times "I love you and you will be my wife forever

Becky." I never said that. I am a bad man. Hey Becky, you have two men. One who loves you and wants to marry you, but he is not good in bed. One who doesn't love you and doesn't want to marry you, but he is good in bed."

"This isn't funny Carl."

"Are you jealous, because I will marry Marko?"

"I am so happy for you Becky and I need to ask you what present do you like for the wedding?"

"I am not planning to invite you to the wedding."

"I think that Marko will invite me."

"Marko hates you."

"Maybe your mom will invite me."

"Mom loves you and she will do that, because she wants to hurt me and Marko." The phone started ringing again. I picked up. "They left from Miami. They flew to Dallas, Carl."

"This is perfect. I am happy to hear that Peggy."

"Carl, when I spoke with Kate, she told me that if I want to have good time and sex, you are the perfect choice, because you know what to do in bed, but I shouldn't push you to do something fast. She said that you will disappear and will never call me. How does Kate know that? I think she loves you."

"Did you tell her that?"

"I didn't Peggy, but my mom is in Dallas. Kate and Mom are staying together in the house of Ethan Dreyfus. I think that Mom told Kate, what kind of a man I am. I have been with Kate one night only and I didn't tell her anything about my past. We spoke, but for our plans in the future. I have spoken to Michelle and now Becky about my past, because they asked me."

"Hey Carl, I told Kate that Becky is spending time with you in bed and that you will have problem with her, because she will push him to marry her. Kate asked me who Becky is. I told her that she is my daughter and she will marry Marko in one month, but Carl is a good choice for a grandchild. We bought giggled."

"Marko called and asked where you are Carl. I told him that I don't know. May I speak with Becky?"

"Of course Peggy." I gave Becky the phone and went for a walk on a beach. When I returned, Becky was still speaking with Peggy. When she saw me she said "Carl is here Mom. Do you like to speak with him?" Becky hung up the phone.

"I had very difficult conversation with Mom, Carl. She said that she will kick me out of her hose and she will never speak with me. Do you believe that she will do that?"

The phone was ringing. I put the phone on the speaker and said "Carl speaking."

"Hey cowboy. What are you doing in this house? Do you know who owns this house? Peggy told me that she doesn't know where you are, she is a bitch."

"She isn't Marko. Peggy loves you and she told you the truth. Jack knows where I am."

"How is your life with Becky cowboy, where is she?"

"I don't know Marko. You must know, because Becky is your future wife."

"Hey cowboy, are you kidding? Do you know how many girls I have in Miami?"

"I don't know, because I thought that you love Becky. You have sex with Becky and you will marry her."

"I sleep with many girls cowboy."

"It is easy to sleep with girls Marko, but do you have sex with them? Which one is it? Are you sleeping or having sex with them?"

"I have sex cowboy, but the reason I called you is, to tell you that I will take twenty five percent from the diamonds. This is your share cowboy. The shark takes fifty percent, Scott Colman takes twenty five and I will take the last twenty five percent, because the shark and Scott will kill you cowboy."

"You will receive one bullet in your stupid head Marko."

"Are you going to marry Becky, Marko?"

"When I have hundred million dollars, I will have hundred different girls. You need to know, that Becky Hodler is stupid, greedy and jealous woman cowboy."

"Hey Marko, I would like to speak with the shark or Scott." Somebody hung up the phone. Becky was angry. I need to think what to do. The shark and Scott know where I am. If something is wrong Lorenzo or Peggy will call me, but I don't know what to do with Becky. I know that she is disappointed, because I pushed Marko and he told me what he thinks of Becky. She needs to decide what to do for her future. Even though I don't like Marko I was surprised that he knows Becky pretty well and he is right about her. The phone was ringing again. I picked up.

"Carl, this is Peggy. Marko called again and he told me very nasty words about Becky, but she deserves that. Don't push and give Becky advice about Marco. She needs to decide what to do with him. Lorenzo will be in the Bahamas at the house after five or six hours. You are a good boy" and Peggy hung up the phone.

I sat on the terrace and looked at the ocean. Becky came back on the terrace. "Who called Carl?"

"Your mom called and told me that Marko told her nasty thinks about you."

"I will call Mom." Becky called several times, but Peggy didn't pick up a phone.

"Maybe she isn't at home Becky."

"I am so sorry that I pushed you to finish Carl."

"Don't worry Becky. I am OK."

"Why did you say, you are right Dino when we were in bed? I need to know, because you had sex with me, but you said something about Dino. Is he your boyfriend?" I laughed and told her "Dino is my brother, and Dino told me, what to do, when I have problem to finish. This is not polite, but since you are asking I will tell you that I thought about Michelle and I finished."

"You had sex with me, but you imagined being with another woman Carl. I can't believe it! Why did you do that Carl?"

"Because, you pushed me to finish fast. Hey Becky, I am happy now. I know that Michelle has a fantastic ass and when I have problem I will think how Michelle's ass moves up and down my erection."

"So, you don't love me, because you love Michelle?"

"I don't love Michelle, Becky."

"Do you want to go for a swim Carl?"

"I am sorry but I expecting some phone calls, but you should go."

"You are right. I will go for a swim." She went back to the house to change. After ten minutes she came to the terrace in her swimsuit.

"You look beautiful Becky, I stood up and kissed her. You are a good girl."

"I am, but you are bad boy" and she left for her swim. The phone was ringing and I picked up. I was surprised to hear Simon's voice.

"Who gave you this phone number Simon?"

"Adam gave it to me and he told that they know where you are. I spoke with Tony Capaci and he asked me where is Roger.

Somebody told Tony that the shark killed Roger."

"The shark doesn't know Roger, because Roger is at a low level of the shark's business. They are nervous Simon. I don't believe that the shark has killed Roger"

"Do you need people to help you Carl?"

"No Simon. If I have more people here, I will have more problems."

"I will give you a phone number to call if you need help", and Simon gave me the number. When you call, tell them "Carl needs help". See you next Tuesday" and Simon hung up the phone. I picked up the phone and called my grandfather's house.

"Grandmother, Carl is calling."

"Hey Carl, I am cleaning the jewels you gave me. Keeping them ready for your wedding."

"I think in a year I will be ready Grandmother, but first I need to choose a girl."

"Carl, I know you have many girls. I might be old, but I am not stupid. I see how they look at you. You just need to ask one of them to a marry you, to make your grandmother happy."

"May I ask you something Grandmother? Can I pick two girls to marry?"

We laughed and she told me, "Yes, if the girls like that".

"Do you need to speak with Roger, Carl?"

"Yes, please."

"Hey Roger, Carl likes to speak with you."

"Is everything is OK Carl?"

"I need to ask you Roger. I am waiting for a person who is a detective. If he asks me to stay with him in a house, knowing that people are coming to kill me, should I listen to him?"

"Do you trust him and how old is he?"

"I trust him and he is between fifty to fifty-five. I think that you should listen to him."

"Do you think that two people are enough?"

"He is detective and he knows what to do. If they come to kill you, they will kill him too, because he is a witness."

"Do you need my help Carl?"

"No Roger." Roger started telling stories about my grandparents, but I saw that Becky was coming back, so I told him that we will speak later and I hung up the phone.

"Were you speaking with my Mom?"

"No Becky."

"But I saw you speaking with somebody."

"It was a friend from New York."

"How does he know the phone number here?"

"Marko told him."

"You are laying to me."

"I will go to take a shower."

"I will be waiting in bed for you Becky."

"I don't want any more sex with you Carl."

"Thank God! I am so happy Becky!".

"Why are you happy?"

"Because I don't like you pushing me to finish so I have to imagine being with Michelle again." I laughed.

"This isn't funny Carl." I continued to laugh. Becky entered the house and she slammed the door behind her. I was still laughing when the door opened and Peggy walked in. I jumped and embraced her. I kissed her and said "I am so happy to see you Peggy! I was expecting Lorenzo, but you came instead!"

"Lorenzo is come from this side and Peggy pointed at the water. I must take Becky with me, because Lorenzo doesn't want Becky to stay here. I know that Becky will not leave before Monday. Two people from Colombia are coming to kill here, either tonight or tomorrow night."

"Do you trust Lorenzo, Carl?"

"I trust him, because if they kill me, they will kill him too."

"Do you think that Lorenzo knows that?"

"I am pretty sure that he knows that Peggy."

"I spoke with Kate and she thanked me that I sent off the boys from Miami alive. She is planning to go back to school to become a lawyer."

"I helped Kate and she changed her life. We will be friends forever, I think." Becky came on the terrace and she asked "Mom what are you doing here?"

"I came to see Carl, Becky. I love you Carl."

"But you are too old for Carl and you are married to Jack!"

"You will marry Marko, Becky and I am here for that. We must speak about your future, because Marko is out of control. We must stop Marko before he does something bad, but I don't want to speak here. I don't like Carl to be part of it. It is a family matter."

"You are right Mom."

"Where should we go to speak Mom?"

"We will go to a hotel Becky."

"I will prepare my things Mom", and Becky went in the house.

"I will be praying for you and Lorenzo. He is honest and good man. You need to listen to him Carl. I have known Lorenzo for more than thirty years. Once Jack and I had problem with a criminal. I spoke with Lorenzo and the man disappeared."

Becky was ready and they left the house. Rico was waiting for Peggy and Becky. I tried to kiss Becky on her lips, but she turned her head and I kissed her on the cheek. Peggy kissed me on the mouth."

"What are you doing Mom? Kissing Carl like that! Do you want him?" She sounded jealous.

"This time I only kissed Carl, next time we will have sex with him daughter" and Peggy winked at me. Peggy sat in the car. Becky looked at me and told me, "Maybe someday I will tell you what I think about you Carl".

"I will be waiting Becky." They left and I went back in the house to wait for Lorenzo. I was alone.

I thought to myself, I hope that he comes to help me stay alive, because I have no idea what to do."

CHAPTER 7

I was sitting on the terrace waiting for Lorenzo. I was thinking over what happened in the last few days. Becky was so happy when she saw me at the airport. She found Lorenzo easy and I spoke with him. Now I know one hundred percent, that the shark and Scott killed Louis and Louis's wife. The shark and Scott were trying to find out where the diamonds are. But I still don't understand why Louis Dreyfus's father didn't know where the diamonds are!

Maybe Louis didn't believe his father. But who would have given the diamonds to Louis? I don't believe that the diamonds are in the USA. The joker and I know that Louis was in Switzerland in the spring of 1950 and in the summer of 1951. The shark killed the joker. I think that the joker knew something, because he knew that Louis was in Switzerland in 1950 and in 1951. The shark is stupid. He could have taken the information from Louis and the joker, he didn't need to kill them. Konev was right when he told Scott that they should have kept Louis alive, because Louis knew where the diamonds are. I think that the diamonds are in Switzerland. Simon and Ethan didn't know about the diamonds, because they didn't tell me that Dreyfus's family has diamonds in a bank somewhere and the shark didn't kill Simon and Ethan after he killed Louis and his wife. I don't think that, Louis moved the diamonds from Switzerland to the USA. This would have been a long and dangerous trip for Louis. I suspect that Louis moved the diamonds somewhere in Switzerland, but not in Zurich. I think that the key to the diamonds is in Europe. I know three people in Europe:

Bruno, Hans and Konev. Bruno Corso was in Sicily. I will fly on Tuesday to Sicily. I know. Bruno doesn't have information for the diamonds. But I think that he will give me information for Hans and Konev. I think that Hans and Konev know more for the diamonds, because they worked with the shark. The shark must have collected a lot of information too over the years from many people. He doesn't want me to learn what he knows, so he wants to kill me. I am not interested in the diamonds, but I don't have a choice. If I find them then I have a chance to go back to my life before I got involved in this mess. Forty eight hours from now I might be dead, so right now I need to focus on saving my life. After that I can think for the diamonds. I saw a small boat approaching the house. Somebody stood up and waived his hand. I heard my name. "Carl, it's me, Lorenzo." I walked on beach and waited for the boat to come closer.

"Hi my friend."

"Can you help me to move the boat Carl?"

We move the boat on the beach.

"We don't have much time Carl. I need to tell you what you need to do." Lorenzo took cardboard target and he stuck it in the sand. He gave me a pistol. He walked and measured. He stopped and told me, "Carl come here. You must hit the cardboard. This is the head of the enemy." I raised my hand and fired. Lorenzo walked and looked at the cardboard.

"You hit the enemy in the head between the eyes. You are ready to face them. We need to prepare for them." Lorenzo explained to me what I have to do. He had a plan. We started working on it. Two hours later we finished. We were ready.

"You are a very strong man, Carl. I can't believe that you are not working for the CIA." I laughed and told Lorenzo.

"Tomorrow when your friends open the newspaper, they will read, "Carl Hope who works for the CIA arrested Lorenzo Falsone who works for the FBI."

"Don't arrest me now, because the I here to help you."

"You are right Lorenzo." We sat on the terrace and spoke. The phone was ringing. I picked up ,"May I speak with Lorenzo, Carl?"

"Of course Peggy." I gave the phone to Lorenzo.

"I know, I will remember Peggy. Could you give me a pen a paper, Carl?"

Lorenzo wrote something on the paper then he said

"Everything is OK Peggy. Carl is a strong man. Of course will be alive. I am kissing you Peggy" and he hung up the phone.

"Do you like a beer Carl?"

"No Lorenzo. I don't drink when I have an important job to do."

"Are you scared Carl?"

"I have never been scared Lorenzo. This is new for me. I am little disappointed that I have to do this. It is good that you are with me Lorenzo."

"Who thought you how to use a pistol?"

"My grandfather thought me when I was thirteen years old. He thought me, what I have to do to save my life in the mountains."

"You handle the pistol like a professional!"

"Do you have a driver's license?"

I entered in the house and took my driver's license. I gave it to Lorenzo.

"Why is your driver's license is from Texas, when you are from New York?"

"I worked in Dallas, Texas for two years, but I quit the job recently and I returned to New York." Lorenzo put the driver's license in his pocket.

"I am surprised that you are not asking me anything Carl!"

"Peggy told me, that you know what to do and I need to listen to you. I trust her."

"I am hungry Carl. We need to eat."

"I am not hungry."

"This is your decision Carl. I need to eat and we need to make a watch schedule."

"I don't need to sleep Lorenzo."

When Lorenzo finished dinner, he told me "I am going to sleep. If you hear a sound, you wake me up otherwise you must wake me up at one o'clock" and Lorenzo told me good night. I woke up Lorenzo at one o'clock. We drank coffee.

"After the coffee we need to move to the beach. We must stay there. Are you ready for the killers Carl?"

"I am ready Lorenzo."

As we were walking to the beach Lorenzo continued with his instructions to me.

"Don't forget. You must shoot in the head. You need to remember everything what I told you Carl."

"I remember what I have to do Lorenzo. When the beach is lit, I must fire in the heads of the killer." Now we will lay on the sand and wait for them. I heard a sound. Somebody spoke. I pulled the rope two times. Lorenzo pulled it one time. This was our signal that they have arrived. I was ready to fire. The beach was lit by large lamps. Two cardboard figures rose up. Two people from the ocean stared to fire with machine guns at the two cardboards. I saw a man who was coming towards me and I fired one shot. Lorenzo fired one shot too. Two bodies dropped in the water. Lorenzo walked to them and he held his pistol ready to fire again. He checked the bodies. Lorenzo told me that we finished a good job. I stayed back and didn't know what to do. I didn't feel like a human being. I felt like a machine.

"Come here Carl."

"Can you help me to pull the bodies from the water to the sand?"

We pull the bodies on the sand and Lorenzo took the passports, money, jewels and papers from the death bodies.

"Good shot. As we discussed. In the head Carl. I think that you will never miss when you need to kill." I didn't answer.

"Hey boy, Are you feeling sorry for them? They came here to kill you. They fired first and tried to kill you. Why are you feeling sorry for them? Believe me Carl, they would not been sorry for your, if they killed you. You killed them to save your live. They came here to kill you for money."

"I know Lorenzo, but this is the first time in my life I killed a person."

"You don't know how many you may have to kill, if you and I work in the Caribbean. Carl." Lorenzo put my driver's license in pocket of the man, who I killed. We need to take our things from the house Carl.

We went back to the house. Lorenzo held in hands the papers he took from the death men. Then he picked up the phone and called. Lorenzo was speaking, but I didn't understand, because he spoke in Spanish. He hung up the phone. Then he dialed another number and I heard him say "Peggy everything is OK. You must come back to the house tomorrow. We are going to New York" and Lorenzo hung up the phone.

"Come on boy, we don't have time." He checked the house and turned off the lights. We walked to Lorenzo's boat.

"Carl, help me to move the boat in the water." Lorenzo tied the enemy boat to his boat. We moved the two death bodies in their boat.

"You stay in the boat Carl. I need to check the beach and clean any evidence of what happen here."

Few minutes later Lorenzo returned and we left.

"That was a good job Carl."

"We killed two people Lorenzo. Do you think that this was a good job?"

"If they killed me and you, the killers would say that they finished a good job and deserve the money. Which job would you like to hear about Carl, the killer's job or our job?"

"I would like to hear about our job."

"You are good boy Carl and Lorenzo laughed. You should be happy, because you are alive."

"You are right Lorenzo."

"When I met you, you told me that you will kill the shark. Can you kill the shark, if you are scared Carl?"

"I am not scared Lorenzo, but my life has changed. You are correct Lorenzo. I must think positively. I killed people that came to kill me. They are my enemies. This is it, it's either them or me."

"You have understood very fast the rules this game Carl. The winner of this game is the one that acts first. You must be first. If you are second, you never have chance to be first, because you will be death." I saw a light and I looked at Lorenzo.

"Don't worry Carl. This is my fishing boat." Lorenzo stopped our boat.

"Give me the pistol Carl." He took and cleaned it with a cloth. Then he went to the body of the man I killed and he put the pistol in the hand of the death man. He turned to me and said "I think that he committed suicide Carl. What do you think? Does he look like he committed suicide or not?"

"He looks that he committed suicide Lorenzo. I think that he did that, because he loves the other death man." We laughed.

Then Lorenzo cleaned his pistol and put it in the hand of second death body.

"Now they look like they both committed suicide Carl. Some journalists will write in the newspapers that they loved each other so much that they committed suicide." We lifted the bodies from the beach and put them in the fishing boat. Lorenzo untied and pushed the boat with the two death bodies further in the sea. We pushed our boat into the sea too.

"You need to sleep Carl, because early in the morning, you will drive and I will sleep." I stepped into the boat. I was feeling very tired, so I laid down and closed my eyes. I don't know how long I slept, but I felt that somebody shook my hand and told me, "Carl wake up, we arrived". I opened my eyes and I saw Lorenzo. You must get up fast, because we don't have a lot of time. Lorenzo told me that I need to leave the boat and wait for him. I did as he asked. Few minutes later Lorenzo left the boat too and started to walk fast away from the marina. I followed him. We stopped on a parking and Lorenzo gave me a car key.

"You will drive."

We got in the car. I drove. Lorenzo told me that I need to take interstate highway 95. There were no cars on the highway, because it was early Saturday morning.

"I will sleep now Carl. When you see the exit to Orlando, you need to wake me up" and Lorenzo went to sleep. He started to snore. I drove and thought about what happened last night. I knew that my life has changed forever. I had to decide if I am killer or not. Of course, I killed a man last night, but in self-defense. On other hand I could have called the police. Maybe the police would have saved my life. I need to ask Lorenzo why didn't we call the police. But Lorenzo is a detective. He knows, what the police would have done, if we have called them. I couldn't help wondering if my life has changing for good, or bad. Only the future will tell. I told myself that I am alive and that is important. I know that Lorenzo saved my life. He did everything and we killed easy the killers that came to kill us. Lorenzo cleaned the pistols and staged the bodies to look like a suicide. Lorenzo is a professional. He was able to make everyone believe for twenty five years, that Louis killed his wife and committed suicide. Simon and Ethan spent millions of dollars for nothing. He will make everyone believe for another one hounded years that I am not a killer. I realized that I was driving Peggy's car. Looks like Peggy and Lorenzo are good friends. Maybe Lorenzo is Peggy's lover, but this isn't my business, because I am Becky's lover or maybe not. I realized that even after everything that happen I am still able to joke with myself. That made me feel optimistic about my future. I saw the exit to Orlando and I woke up Lorenzo.

"Is this Peggy's car, Lorenzo?"

"How do you know that?"

"Peggy drove the same car when we went to visit Becky's and Jack's offices. You were in the hotel with Peggy four months ago Lorenzo. Are you Peggy's lover?"

"If you tell Jack that I am Peggy's lover, I will tell Marko, that you are Becky's."

"I will never tell Jack, because if you marry Peggy and I marry Becky, then you will be my father in law."

Lorenzo smiled and said "Hi my future son in law." We laughed.

"Hey Carl, Peggy told me that for the first time in her life she saw a man who is confident in himself and knows what to do when she met you. She told me that she fell in love with you immediately and she will love you forever but you are too young to be her lover."

"Carl you must promise me that if I marry Peggy and if you marry Becky, that you will never sleep with your mom in law." We laughed a lot.

"I think that we will have a fun time in New York Carl." We stopped at a gas station. I filled up the car with the gas and we used the restroom.

"I need to make a call, Lorenzo."

"I will wait outside Carl."

I called Dino, but Marisa picked up the phone. "Hi Marisa, this is Carl." She laughed. I asked her, why was she laughing.

"Because Dino told me that you aren't Dino's brother because you were in New York and but you didn't call him."

"He told his grandfather, that you aren't Dino's brother anymore. Grandfather was angry with Dino and told him to stop saying stupid things like that!"

I laughed when Dino asked me "What do you want my brother?"

"Hey Dino, I am so sorry, but I was busy when I was in New York."

"Doesn't matter Carl. How can I help you?"

"I need to speak with Simon. You must go to Simon's apartment and tell him that I must speak with him. Simon needs to give you a phone number, I can call him on." I gave Dino, Simon's address.

"Could you tell Simon that I will call on the phone number he gives you three hours from now? I will call you again after one hour and thirty minutes."

"I understood Carl", and Dino hung up the phone. I was outside and Lorenzo asked me "Do you want to have breakfast Carl?"

"This is a good idea Lorenzo. I am starving."

We finished the breakfast fast, not saying much.

"I need to sleep for at least two more hours Carl."

"I have to stop after an hour and half Lorenzo, but you can sleep."

I was driving Lorenzo was sleeping. I started thinking for Tony Capaci. Nobody knows what kind of a man he is. Dino told me that he didn't know why the Italians in New York have a great respect for him. Roger thinks that I saved his life, because the Italians killed Roger's partner but they didn't kill him. I never have discussed with Tony, why he saved Roger's life. If Tony flies with me to Sicily, I will ask him.

I looked out the window. It was green and beautiful. Lorenzo was moving in the seat and yawning. It looked like he was waking up. He asked me "Where we are now Carl?"

"Almost in Georgia."

"You are driving very fast. If we keep with this speed, we will be in New York around eleven or twelve Carl. After lunch I will drive, but after 7:00 p.m., you need to drive again, because there will be traffic on the highway and I don't like to drive in the traffic."

"OK boss. You need to tell me what I need to do and I will do it." Lorenzo asked me what happened between Becky and me, because Peggy told him that I had problem with Becky.

"She pushed me to finish Lorenzo, but I couldn't. I had to imagine being with another girl, so I could. I told her about it and she got mad with me. "

I saw a gas station and I exited. I called Dino and he gave me a phone number and told me that Simon is waiting for me.

"I will call you later Dino. Thank you." I called and Vicky picked up the phone.

"Hey boy, where are you?"

"Far away from New York, Vicky."

"I will give you Simon."

"Simon, I will arrive in New York between 11:00 p.m. and 1:00 a.m. tonight. I need to stay in a quiet hotel, with as fewer guests as possible. I need the name, phone and the address of the hotel."

"Do you like to stay in my apartment Carl? I am alone."

"Where is your family?"

"They are in Long beach at the moment, I have a house there. They will back two months from now."

"I am with a friend. No problem Carl, I have two guest rooms."

"Ok. We will come to stay at your apartment." Simon asked me.

"Do you like to speak with Vicky, Carl?"

"I don't have time much time, but give would like to speak with her."

"How long are you staying in New York?"

"Three days."

"Thanks Carl", and she hung up the phone.

"Is everything OK, Carl?"

"Yes Lorenzo. We will stay in Simon's apartment."

"Who is Simon?"

"Simon is Louis Dreyfus's brother."

"Oh my God. Carl, are you sure that this is a good idea? Simon would like to kill me!"

"Don't worry about that. You are with me Lorenzo."

We left the gas station and Lorenzo told me that he will go back to sleep. I will wake him up for lunch. Lorenzo slept and I was thinking about Vicky. She is an interesting woman. Vicky never asks me what I do, when I am not with her. I never ask her too. I don't like to ask people. I wondering why my mom loves Vicky so much! I need to ask her, but Mom is Dallas now. She is spending a lot of time with Michelle. I think that Mom loves Michelle, because she is from the Dreyfus family. I will ask her who she thinks will better to be my wife, Vicky or Michelle? I suspect that Mom likes more the Dreyfus's family. If she doesn't want to tell me I will tell her that I will marry Vicky. I know that if I marry Vicky, she will never ask me, if I had other women, because Vicky will keep me busy in bed and we won't have time to speak for our past. I have known Vicky for almost four years now. I know Michelle for three weeks only. I don't know how is Michelle in bed. I am thinking about women, but I must be thinking for the shark instead. Before the shark kills me, I need to ask him if I should marry Vicky or Michelle. I think that the shark will tell me to marry Michelle, so that the Dreyfus family will tell me, where the diamonds are. I think that Michelle will give the shark the diamonds, because she tells me all the time, "I love you Carl". But when Michelle learns about the diamonds, maybe she will tell the shark to kill me, and will never give him the diamonds. I was laughing when Lorenzo woke up and asked me.

"Why are you laughing, what is funny?"

I told Lorenzo that Michelle Dreyfus will save my life, because she will give the diamonds to the shark.

"Are you joking all the time with yourself Carl?"

"Yes, I am not scared Lorenzo" and I continued to laugh.

"You know that you have three weeks to kill the shark. If you don't, the shark will say "I killed the Carl, the joker". Your relatives will cry and say that Carl was a good joker, but the shark killed him."

"How do you know that I have three weeks and why did you put my driver's license in the poked of death man?"

"When somebody finds the death bodies, the police will be called. The policemen will search them and they will find your driver's license. The police tell your relatives, that you committed a suicide and you are death. Your relatives will cry, but the shark will be happy. Nobody will know that you are alive and you will have three weeks to kill the shark Carl. It will take three weeks for the shark to find out that you are alive and he will send new killers. More experienced than the ones we dealt with and they will most probably kill you. Do you think it will be funny, if the shark kills you Carl? You must kill the shark in three weeks, but right now I am hungry and you need to stop somewhere for lunch."

"Why did you tell me that the shark will kill me Lorenzo?"

"Because after the shark kills you, he will kill me and my family Carl. Do you think that this is funny too? You are young and you don't understand this wolfish life. I am a detective and I know what will happen, after the shark kills you."

"You are right Lorenzo. I promised you that I will kill the shark. I need to figure this out fast."

"Do you like Mc Donald's Lorenzo? I see that there is one at the next exit. We don't have time, so fast food should do."

We stopped and after twenty minutes we were done with lunch. Lorenzo got behind the wheel and I went to sleep. When I woke up, it was 6:15 p.m.

"You are quiet in your sleep Carl. I snore. My wife pushes me when I start to snore, so I stop."

Lorenzo took the next exit because we had fill up the car. We stopped at a gas station and he told me "You fill up with gas, I will buy something for dinner. What do would you like Carl?"

"I am not hungry. Don't buy any food for me, only water and juice?"

When Lorenzo returned I told him that I need to use the restroom. When I came back Lorenzo has eaten his dinner.

"You finished your dinner fast", I said with a surprise.

"I don't like to eat in the car Carl."

We left the gas station. Lorenzo started speaking, while I was driving.

"You never asked me about the men who came to kill us Carl."

"Why talk about the past? But since we are talking about it I was wondering why we didn't call the police and tell them, that two people from Colombia wanted to kill us? I know that you are a detective and you know very well, what the police will do."

"You are right Carl. If we called the police and told them, that two people from Colombia want to kill us, they will ask who are they and why they want to kill us."

"Are you selling narcotics and that is why the Colombian Mafia wants to kill you?"

"What are going to tell the police Carl?"

"I will tell them, that people hired by the shark and Scott Colman are trying to kill me."

"The police will ask you who are the shark and Scott Colman and if they work with you and the Colombian Mafia. They will ask you to tell them the name of the shark, and they would have told you that the shark lives in the water."

"Boy, you must go to speak with a doctor about your problem. You are talking to the wrong people here. This is the police we have nothing to do with sharks" and Lorenzo laughed.

"I will tell the police to ask Scott Colman."

"Scott will never talk against the shark, because he knows that the shark will kill him. Scott is a businessman and everyone will confirm to the policemen that Scott is a good businessman."

"Who are you Carl? You are a low level architect. The people don't know you in Dallas."

"Many people know me in New York Lorenzo."

"Of course, they know that you are a good man who goes out with a lot of women and you have a reputation of a good lover." Lorenzo laughed and told me "Another problem is that you are young, but you have money. Everybody will think that you are making easy money with narcotics and you will need to explain how you made your money. You will spend a lot of time explaining to the police, going to court and paying a lot of money for a good lawyer. Do you want that Carl?"

"You are right Lorenzo. We killed them and we and the police don't have a problem. The police will tell us. You are hero, because you killed two crime people. I must be happy, because I am alive and police must be happy, because they didn't have to do anything." We laughed. This is a very logical argument Carl.

"Why did you get involved in this dangerous game Carl?"

"My live was quiet and good Lorenzo. I had to work in Dallas for two more months, when I met Ethan Dreyfus. He spoke with my mom. You know her too Lorenzo. Julia is my mom. You met her in Miami twenty five years ago and you tried to flirt with her. I laughed when she told me that. Do you flirt with every woman you meet Lorenzo?"

"Hey boy, I asked you first."

"Ok that is fare. I will continue Lorenzo. Mom told me that she had a sexual relationship with Louis Dreyfus years ago and I she asked me to look at the painting of Louis."

"What did you see?"

"I saw that Louis didn't kill his wife and committed suicide. I told Ethan and I he spoke with Simon. This happened on Sunday, and by Tuesday they tried to kill me."

"Who were they Carl, and why they wanted to kill you?"

"I know that Scott Colman's people tried to kill me, because I told Ethan that somebody killed his parents."

"Now I understand Carl. Scott Colman and the shark are scared, because Ethan and Simon will start to investigate again the deaths of Louis and his wife. Ethan and Simon are using you to do the investigation. But how did the shark and Scott found about you?"

"My friend Roger found a bug in Simon's phone. He told Simon and me, that they are listening to Simon's phone."

"Are they continuing to listen Carl?"

"Yes Lorenzo."

"This is good. I will tell Simon what he needs to do."

"My friend Roger told Simon what to do, but you are a detective. I am sure you know better. I think that, after I fly to Europe, Simon needs to remove the listening device from his phone."

"Where in Europe are you going to?"

"I am going to Sicily, Lorenzo."

"Peggy told me that you are a very dangerous man. Now I believe that she is right. Why are you going to Sicily? Are you going to look for Bruno Corso? I told you that my friend disappeared in Sicily."

"You are right Lorenzo, but I have a good friend in New York. He is from Sicily. I think that he knows Bruno Corso."

"Who is your good friend?"

"Tony Capaci is a good friend of mine. I saved Dino's life. He is Tony's grandson. I am Dino's brother."

"I am detective, but I don't understand what kind of man you are. I believe that Scott and the shark never understood that you are different. I have a feeling that you have planned every step you are going to take. I am certain that you will kill the shark."

"We will know that after three weeks Lorenzo."

"You must say, we will know that the shark is death Carl."

"I don't want to say that now Lorenzo, but that means that you don't have to be afraid of the shark anymore." I laughed, Lorenzo didn't.

"Oh my God. I am a Catholic and I believe in God. Do you believe in God, Carl?"

"Of course, I believe Lorenzo. God will help us to stay alive. You need to go to Church and pray to God, that I am not the first to die, because you will be the second after me. The shark has to be first."

"Do you ever stop joking Carl?"

"I like to joke. I find life amusing this way and right now I am happy, because you saved my life. I will save yours Lorenzo. I want to ask you a question about Peggy."

"Ok. Go ahead."

"Why didn't you marry Peggy? She is beautiful and smart?"

"Your question is wrong Carl. You need to ask me why didn't Peggy marry me?" Lorenzo took a deep breath and started talking again.

"The answer is very simple. Peggy was serious woman and she needed a serious man. Jack was a good choice. He loves and supports Peggy. I was a man who was chasing women on the beach, in restaurants or anywhere. I don't know why my wife has been living with me for twenty five years. I bought a house and we have two children. My grandfather told me that if I lived in Italy the family of the girl would have killed me. All my friends think that being a detective is a good job. When I started I was a very aggressive detective. I tried to arrest people who sale drugs and stopped crimes in my jurisdiction. But, when four bullets missed my body, I changed my job very fast. I understood that I will never stop crime and the sale of drugs. Crime people tried to give me money, but I never took any. I told them that I don't want to have problems."

"Why did you take money from Scott?"

"I didn't want to take the money Carl, but Scott told me that if don't take them the shark will kill me, so I took the money. The crime people never stop. They don't know how to leave a life without crime."

"Do you think that someday the shark or Scott will stop?"

"They will never stop Carl. They started again after twenty five years. You are an innocent person, but they don't care."

"You are right Lorenzo. Scott and the shark killed Ethan's wife for nothing. Did you know that Lorenzo?"

"I didn't know Carl. I have not seen Scott since he gave me the money. He called me sometimes, but I was surprised when he sent the two stupid young men to Miami. I gave them weapons. I told them, that they need to kill you. They told me, that they will never use the weapons but I must kill you. I decided to kill them instead, but Peggy told me that you wanted them alive. I understood that the game has started again. A friend called and told me, that two people from Colombia were asking for Carl Hope and Lorenzo Falsone. I don't understand why did Scott sent two young stupid people and why two people from Colombia asked for you and me Carl?"

"I will tell you Lorenzo. Scott and the shark want to know where you are every moment of the day. The two people from Colombia were sent to kill you. After that they will kill me Lorenzo. Everybody will think that the two young stupid boys from Dallas killed you but since you are an experienced detective you managed to kill them too."

"You are right Carl, but when Peggy took and dropped the two stupid young people at the airport, she called me and said, that Marko knows where you are and Marko told her that the shark will kill you. She told me to help you and that Becky is in the Bahamas with you. I told her that she must take Becky away from the house if I am going to help you. She said she will do what I asked and then she said that I have to do it if I love her a little. I told her that I love her and that I will get ready. I know that I have a chance to be alive, if I save your life. I told the office that I have business in Orlando and I came to Peggy's house in the Bahamas."

"Why did you save the lives of the young stupid people Carl?"

"They are from Midland Lorenzo. My friend Kate was born in Midland and she asked me to save their lives."

"You told me that Julia is your mom. When I met her she was fifty years old. What happened between her and Louis and when?"

"This is a long story Lorenzo, maybe someday I will tell you, but not now."

"Why were you speaking in Spanish last night?"

"I found a phone number in the death men's pockets. I knew that they must call after they kill us to report what happened. I called and said, "Boss we killed them, but we have problem and we need to disappear for two to three weeks". I know that tomorrow the boss that send them will call Peggy and ask for you. Peggy will tell him that you have disappeared and she doesn't know where you are."

"Now I understand why you told me that I have two or three weeks" and Lorenzo laughed.

"What will happen with me Lorenzo, if I don't kill the shark in the next two or three weeks?"

"It is very simple Carl. The shark will kill you. The shark will send more experienced people and they will kill you. But if you kill the shark, nobody will be after you to kill you, because you don't work with narcotics. You are nobody for them. When we killed those two men, we got rid of a trash Carl. I told you that you must shoot in the head, because if you injured them, they would have asked you to spare them. They would have pleaded with you not to kill them because they don't have anything against you, they were told to do it and promise not to come back. But that would have been a lie. Since you have not dealt with that kind of scam before I dint want you to give them a chance to leave alive, because they would have come back and try to kill you. I have the experience, you don't."

"I believe you Lorenzo. You how know crime people think very well."

"I will help you with anything I can Carl. You must succeed in this dangerous game. Hey Carl, you told me that when you are done with this issue, you would like me to work with you in the Caribbean."

"Yes, I would like you to work with me, but first I will send you to bed with Peggy. If you alive after that, we will work together."

"That sounds good Carl, even though it is dangerous."

We were in New Jersey. "We are close to New York Lorenzo."

"Can you believe that this morning we were in Miami, and tonight we are in New York, Carl?"

When we arrived on front of the building of Simon's apartment, he was outside speaking with the doorman. I stopped the car. We got out and Simon came towards us.

"Oh my God. I can't believe it. You must be Lorenzo. I thought that I will never meet you." Simon embraced him. Lorenzo was little surprised, but said "me too Simon". Then he turned to me and said "I am so happy to see you again, Carl, give me the keys for the car". Simon took the keys and gave them to the doorman and told him, "Please park this car in my parking spot. If anyone from my family ask you about the car, you tell them, that they must ask me, why the car is my parking spot. You don't know who parked the car and how long the car will stay in the parking. You must tell every doorman, what I told you."

"You know that me and the other doormen will have problem with your family."

"You just tell them to call me if they are very persistent."

"Come in boys" and we entered the building and took the elevator not saying anything.

We were in Simon's apartment.

"Come with me Lorenzo, I need to show you your bedroom."

After that Simon asked me and Lorenzo, if we were hungry.

"I am not hungry but I feel tired, I need to sleep Simon" and Lorenzo entered his bedroom.

"What news do you have Carl?"

"The news are good Simon. Me and Lorenzo are alive. The shark tried to kill us."

"I have good news too Carl. Tony will come with you to Sicily. Tony knows Bruno. When you told me that you are going to Sicily, I was afraid for you. Sicily is a dangerous place. I know that very well, but after I spoke with Tony, I am not anymore. Tony told me that he will never take you to a dangerous place."

"It is possible that Carl and I end up having a problem Simon, because we are going to Sicily, but I was born there and Bruno is my best friend. Bruno and I are like brothers and Carl is my grandson."

"I can't understand that Carl. You are Julia's son and you are Tony's grandson? How is that possible? Does Julia know that?"

"Of course, she knows Simon. We aren't related by blood. Dino is Tony's grandson. I saved Dino's life. After that I became a grandson of Tony's too."

"Is that the same Dino that works in Julia's store?"

"Yes."

"So let me try to get this straight. You are a Jew and Italian."

"There is more. I am a Hill Billy and little Irish too."

"When Ethan told me, Carl Hope is from New York, I was wondering how come I don't know you, but when he told me that you are Julia's son, I remembered seen you with Julia. I have seen you with Julia at the Jewish community Center, but we never spoke. You are an international boy" and Simon laughed. "I don't understand, why the shark wants to kill you" and Simon continue to laugh.

"I know why, because I will take the Dreyfus' family diamonds" and we laughed.

"If you marry Michelle, the diamonds will be essentially yours Carl."

"Can I ask you what do you think about Michelle, Carl? She called and asked for you? I didn't know what to say."

"Nothing Simon. Why do I need to think about Michell? If the shark kills me she will need to look for another boy" and I laughed. On a serious note I want you to know that I have a safe deposit box at Bank of America. I have very important letters there. Nobody except you now knows that I am keeping those letters there. I must see you on Tuesday morning at 9:30 at the bank. I need to give you a permission to be able to open the box in the event that something bad happens to me. I am going to Europe. The letters contain the names of the people I am going to Europe to find."

"You told me that you are going to Sicily. I must meet two more people Simon. One who lives in West Berlin or Switzerland and one, who lives in Russia."

"Could you give me the names of these people?"

"Not now Simon. If they kill me, you need to open the letters and decide what to do. You have to promise me that you won't open the box, if I am alive. Even Julia doesn't know about the box."

"I am guessing that the letters contain something about Julia."

"Yes Simon. I don't want anybody else to know, I trust you. There is one more thing I have to do. I need to see Adam at 10:00 a.m. in the bank. Can you call Adam and ask him to come there? You need to call him early in the morning on Tuesday."

"I will him Carl. I need to ask you, if you find the diamonds what are going to do with them?"

"The diamonds belong to Dreyfus' family. The family will have to decide."

"You are part of our family now Carl."

"Are you saying that because you think that I will marry Michelle, Simon?"

"No Carl. You will have to decide if you want to marry Michelle. You are part of our family because you cleared my brother's name. For the last twenty five years I thought that my brother was killer that killed his wife. Now I know that somebody killed him and his wife. The diamonds are important, but my brother's name is more important. I have enough money for me and my family. When you find the diamonds you will need to think what to do with them. You are young and aggressive. I am confidents that you will put them to good use and find a way to make more money with them. If you had them right now what would you do with them?"

"I think that I would like to open an international investment corporation. Me, you, Julia and Ethan will be partners. We will invest anywhere in the world. We will borrow money from the bank using the diamonds as our guarantee for the credit."

"Do you think that someday, we may have problem with credit?"

"Never Simon. I will calculate carefully the risk, before we invest. We will not invest in anything that we have to pay a lot of interest to the bank. If we have problem with credit, we must sale a property and cover the credit."

"You are smart Carl. We will invest the diamonds, but we will still own them."

"You are correct Simon."

"I will speak with Ethan. You need to speak with Julia, Carl."

"Mom will tell me that she will do it if I marry Michelle."

"Hey Carl, you will be one hundred percent Jew then."

"If Michelle marries me, maybe she will become fifty percent Jew and fifty percent Hill Billy, Simon."

"Who knows Carl?", and we laughed.

"I have a friend in Europe, Carl. He watches my back, when I am go there. I will call and ask him to watch your back while you are there."

"It will be good, if somebody watches my back. Thank you, Simon."

"Are you going to need more people to help you in Europe?"

"One is enough, but I don't need him to watch my back in Sicily. When I leave Sicily I will call him, where I am and he can start helping me then. Sicily is a dangerous place Simon. They will kill him."

"I have to agree with you on that Carl."

"What should I do with the listening device in my phone, Carl?"

"You need to remove it from the phone on Tuesday after 2:00 p.m. You call Ethan and tell him, that he needs to remove the one from his phone too. You know Julia's son Jerry. Call him to check Julia's phone too, because nobody lives now in Julia's apartment, so I am positive that they have installed one in her phone. Jerry needs to remove that one too."

"I will do as you ask. When you call me where you are in Europe, my friend will start to watch your back. He will find you a tell you "Simon sent me to watch your back". Now you need to sleep Carl." Simon told me "Good night" and he left.

I woke up and I didn't look at my watch. I took a shower and went in the kitchen. Simon and Lorenzo were on the table. They were talking and having coffee.

"Good morning gentleman", I told them.

"Good morning Carl", they replied.

"Did you sleep good Carl?", Simon asked me.

"Yes, I am feeling better and rested."

"You need more energy boy." Simon and Lorenzo laughed.

"Why do I need more energy Simon?"

"He is joking", Lorenzo told me.

"Why are you laughing?"

"Because we are happy for you boy" and they continued to laugh.

"Carl, please sit on the table, I prepared breakfast for you and Simon" and he gave me the breakfast. I finished with the food very quickly and I took a cup of coffee.

"Which city do you like more Carl, New York or Miami?", Simon asked me.

"I like then both. New York is a big city, I grew up here and I love New York. Miami is good for vacation. If I was living in Miami, I will swim a lot of miles between May and October."

"Which women are better?", Simon asked me.

"For sex the women in both places a good, Simon, but I didn't have time to try many of them in Miami." We laughed when bell rang.

"I looked at Simon. And he asked me, "Could you open the door Carl?"

I opened the door and Vicky was on front of me. I was surprised. She was carrying two shopping bags.

"Can you take the bags Carl? Don't stay and stare at me?"

"I am so sorry Vicky", and I took the bags. Vicky embraced and kissed me long claiming my mouth .

"We are together again after a week Carl. I can't believe it." She walked in and closed the door. We went to the kitchen. Simon stood up and kissed Vicky on the chic and introduced her to Lorenzo. She said "Hi" to him. Lorenzo was staring at her with an open mouth unable to speak.

"Hey Lorenzo say "Hi" to Vicky", Simon told him. Simon walked to Lorenzo and asked him "What happen with you Lorenzo?"

"I have never seen more beautiful woman in my life." Lorenzo walked and took Vicky's hand. "You are so beautiful Vicky", and he kissed her hand. She kissed him on the cheek.

"May I kiss your cheek?" Lorenzo asked Vicky.

"Of course Lorenzo." Lorenzo kissed Vicky on the cheek.

Simon and I laughed.

"Why did you laugh?", Vicky asked me and Simon.

"You may have a new lover Vicky", Simon told her and I, Simon and Vicky laughed, but Lorenzo didn't. "We need to move to the living room", Simon told us.

"Do you like coffee Vicky?"

"No Simon, I prefer tea."

"I will make some tea for you Vicky."

"I would like Carl to prepare the tea for me Simon. He knows the tea I like. Could you make the tea for me Carl?"

"I will Vicky", and I went in the kitchen. I know that she likes green tea with honey and lemon. I remembered that Vicky told me. The honey is better from sugar for tea and she told me that many products have sugar. "People don't understand that they are eating more sugar a day than they should. I check the sugar content of every product I buy." After Vicky told me, I am checking now the sugar content too.

They were laughing when I entered the living room. Vicky tried the tea and she said "You made a very good tea. I will hire you to make tea in my boutique Carl."

"You will need to build bedroom in your boutique Vicky. Carl will spend more time with your customers in the bedroom than making tea for them."

"You are right Simon, but I think, that if I hire a manager in the boutique, then I will spend more time in the bedroom with Carl."

"Speaking of the boutique, let me tell you what happened on Friday. I had four workers. On Friday morning I opened the door and told them, that they must demolish one of the walls. I left to buy coffee and when I returned I saw, that they were staying and looking at the wall. They didn't do any work. I was very angry. I took off my shirt and jeans. I took a hammer and started to hit the wall. When I finished, I turned my head and told them that they need to work, not to look at me. The boss told me. "You are so beautiful lady." I looked at myself and realized that that I was almost naked. I had on me only tiny bikini and a bra. I told them, "Don't look at me, you will never touch me. You must demolish the wall and you must touch it. They started to work and when they finished, I gave them additional two hundred dollars each and told them, "Don't use your hands tonight. You need to have sex with girls." Simon, I and Vicky laughed. Lorenzo asked Vicky "Can

I work for you Vicky?"

"You need to have a permission from Carl." Then Vicky turned to Simon and said "May I ask you something Simon? But you need to come with me!" Vicky and Simon left the living room.

I asked Lorenzo, "Why are your undressing women with your eyes?" Peggy was right to marry Jack. If she married you, Peggy had to follow your eyes all the time or make you blind." We laughed and Lorenzo told me.

"Do you know how many women I have seen on the beach and at the bars in Miami?"

"I have seen at least a hundred thousand, but I never saw one like Vicky. She is so beautiful. She is an alien Carl." We laughed when Simon and Vicky returned.

"Why are you laughing Carl?", Vicky asked.

"Because Lorenzo thinks that, you are an alien woman." Vicky laughed and she asked.

"Do you love me Lorenzo?"

"Of course, I love you Vicky."

"You are an old man, you don't have enough energy for me. I don't want to go to a funeral after I have sex with you." We laughed and we had tears in our eyes.

"You are right Vicky, I like to live longer." Vicky went close to Lorenzo and kissed him.

"You are a good and a smart man Lorenzo."

"Hey Lorenzo are you ready to leave?", Simon asked.

"I am ready Simon. I don't want to waste more of Vicky's and Carl's time. I hope to see you alive two days from now Carl."

"I hope too Lorenzo. If you have problem, this is an address of the house in Long Beach." Simon and Lorenzo left the apartment.

Vicky came to me and kissed my mouth then she sucked my tongue. I grabbed her hips and pulled her body towards me. I was ready and Vicky told me, that she felt how happy I was to see her.

"You are already hard Carl."

Vicky jumped in the bed. I was trying to put a condom, but she took and threw the condom.

"We don't need a condom Carl. I want you to finish inside me." She pulled me down the bed on top of her. My erection was on her belly. I was ready, but I was not sure about her. I started kissing and sucking her breasts. My tongue started to play with her nipples. Vicky was ready. "Give it to me Carl. I want you!" I moved between her legs. She moved her hips up and her pussy took and sucked it. I started moving my hips forward and back. I took her legs one after the other and put them on my shoulders as I was inside her. It was deep inside her. She closed her eyes and I heard quite groan. I started to move faster and her voice was going higher and higher. "Faster Carl." I knew that she was ready and she wanted us to finish together. I started to throw my sperm. I heard that Vicky said something, but I didn't understand. She was speaking in Russian. Vicky moved her legs and told me that she wanted me to lay my body on her body. She took my head and she kissed my eyes several times. "I love you so much Carl" and her hands embraced my shoulders. I laid on her, but I didn't press her, because I was supporting my body with my elbows.

"Do you feel good Carl?"

"Of course I am feeling good, but you tried to take all my energy at once."

"I need your body, because I need to use it for two more days Carl."

"Are you planning to throw my body in the trash after that Vicky?"

"No Carl. Two days from now you will be with another woman, She will use your body."

"Why are you saying that Vicky?"

"Are you scared that another woman will use your body?"

"Of course I am."

"What did you say in Russian, I didn't understand?"

"I am was praying for two boys Carl. I want my uterus to catch two boys. Are you happy that you know now?"

"Of course I am happy."

"I don't like to have you for two more days only. I would like to have you forever. I know that you love me, but you never tell me that. Of course, I never asked you and I don't like to ask you now either. I know that you have rule and I don't like to change your rule and hurt you. I am happy that I am with you and I know that you will be my friend forever, but I know that we will never live together."

"Why did you say friend? I will be your husband?"

"You never will be my husband. I want to have children and you will be the father of our children, but something has changed in my life Carl."

"Are you afraid of something Vicky?"

"I am Carl, but I don't like to talk about that now. I will tell you later."

"Can you get moving and go to take a shower Carl?"

I took a shower and I entered Simon's library. The shelves on the wall were full of books. I noticed that they were very well organized. Each shelf with books form different countries. One with USA books, then German, French, English, Russian…etc. The books were for geography, history, politics, science….etc. I took a book from the Russian shelf. It was "War and Peace". It is from Lev Nikolayevich Tolstoy. I was reading the book when Vicky entered the library. She took my book.

"You are reading a Russian book. This is good for you. Tolstoy was the best Russian writer." I heard a noise behind the open door and I asked Vicky, "What are you doing Vicky?"

"I am doing laundry. I cleaned the bedroom Lorenzo slept in last night."

"You have been many times with me in Julia's apartment, but you never cleaned my room."

"You never asked me to clean your room Carl."

"I am going to take a shower. After that I need to speak with you." Vicky left. I took "Faust", a German book, written by Johann Wolfgang van Goethe. I read that Faust sold his soul to the Devil. Oh my God. Faust sold his soul to the Devil. Why did Faust sell his soul, for money, power or something else? I will ask Simon to read this book.

I returned the book and I remember that Vicky wanted me to wait for her in the living room. When entered Vicky was sitting on the sofa. I asked her

"What should I do, if the Devil tells me that we will live together, but I need to sale my soul to him?" and I laughed.

"This isn't funny Carl. This is a very stupid question. Never ever ask anybody else. They will think that you have a mental problem. Can you sit down and listen to me?"

I sat next to her and Vicky took my hand. She was looking into my eyes, then she took a deep breath and started to talk.

"Carl, I had two wonderful days recently. First, on Sunday night I was with you. Second, on Monday morning I met Simon and we found a place for my business. I was going home that night feeling like the happiest woman in the world. When I went to the living room my mom was waiting for me with a worry on her face and asked that we speak."

"Are you alone Mom and where do you like to for us to speak? In the living room or the kitchen?"

"Let's go out to dinner Vicky, we have not done this in a while. Just you and me."

"We sat in the restaurant and Mom asked me if I was with you on Sunday night. I asked her if she was spying on me. She said that she is not, but she said that KGB is. Then she asked me if my father is pushing me to marry you. I told her that Father told me that you are rich and will have hundred million dollars in the future and if I am smart, I must marry you."

"Do you want to marry Carl for the money Vicky?"

"I don't Mom. You know that I love Carl."

"If you marry Carl, you will have a big problem with KGB. You must work for them and you will have to convince Carl to work for them too."

"I laughed and told her that this is impossible, because you love America and you are a patriot. You will never ever spy for the KGB. If KGB agents try to make you spy for them, you will kill them. He is a hard headed, I know that very well Mom."

"I know that too my daughter, but if you and Carl have children. They will tell you Vicky that if you and Carl don't spy for them, they will kill the children and you. May be they will kill Carl later too."

"Who told you that Mom?"

"I never planned to tell you, what happened in my past, but now I have no choice Vicky. When I married your father, we had a good life. You were born, your father rose in the KGB. After five years your father changed. He had a mistress. There was a party in Kremlin. Your father told me that he has a job to do and he left the party. I knew that he was with his mistress. I was alone and I didn't know what to do, when your father's boss invited me to dance with him. I drank and danced with your father's boss, and later that night we were in bed. After that your father raised faster in the KGB. I was the mistress of his boss. I was his mistress for four years. We didn't have a second child, because he had a mistress, and I was a mistress. One night after I had sex with the boss, he told me that your father and I were approved and to move to New York. He told me that he had a good time with me and wanted to keep a good relationship between us. He said that if I ever have a problem in New York, he will tell me. Two months ago he was in New York and he told me that KGB is spying on you and they will push you to marry Carl. They will kill Vicky, if she doesn't listen. They used your father Vicky and he is pushing you to marry Carl. Carl is a smart and someday he will have a political career."

"Carl, I remember that you told me a joke about the Devil. KGB is the Devil . You will have a chance to sale your soul to the KGB. Do you want sale your soul to the Devil, Carl? Honestly, I don't want you do that. You are so lucky, because you were born in America. I was born in Russia, but I am so lucky to grow up in America. I will never spy for Russia. I love America. Mom told me that when she was young, she was thinking with her pussy not her brain. When she became forty she was thinking more with her brain and less with her pussy. After fifty she is thinking one hundred percent with her brain, her pussy smiles when she sees a young boy with a good athletic body. I am young and I think with my brain one hundred percent. My brain allows my pussy to have sex. Mom told me that I need to tell you this. She said that you are smart and will tell me what to do. I know that you have problem right now, but I am certain that you will kill the shark."

"How did you know that I will kill the shark and who told you that?"

"Mom told me Carl. Initially she didn't want to tell me, but I told her, that I will not speak with you unless she tells me. Mom has a lot of information, but she never talks about that. I think my mom's lover tells her, what happens in KGB. This is dangerous for Mom, but she is a grown woman. I am her daughter, but I am not the person to tell her what to do. She must decide for herself. Mom told me that she wants me to be alive, so I shouldn't marry you."

"What do you think Carl? Should I marry you?"

"The shark tried to kill me, but I am alive. Your mom told you the truth. You are from Russia. Now KGB thinks that your father has control and you will do, what your father tells you. But not long from now, KGB will understand that your father doesn't have control and you do what you want to do. If we separate, KGB will wait and spy on you Vicky. You have time to get a green card. If you have a green card, KGB will have problem to take you back to Russia. We must separate. I agree with your mom. I want to see you alive Vicky."

"Thanks Carl" and Vicky kissed me.

"Can I ask you something?"

"Anything Carl."

"Why didn't you pursue your modeling career more aggressively? I think that you have a big future in the high fashion?"

"I want children Carl. It is very hard to be a model. You need to keep your body in a perfect shape and the same weight. Mom told me that she wants grandchildren. I love my mom. I am who I am, because my mom has always been supportive of me. She told me many harsh words, but she was right. I love her and I listen to her. I am a big girl, but I love my mom and you Carl. Hey boy, may be eight months from now when I see you my belly will be two feet on front of my body. You will look at me and wonder if that is me. I will say, "don't look so confused, it's me Vicky and you had something to do with the way I look. I am carrying two of your boys."

"Are you going to be happy, if you have two boys Carl?"

"Of course I will be happy, if you deliver two boys Vicky."

"I don't think that you and I will have ever a problem, but my mom saw that. I am divided Carl. I have the Devil on one of my shoulders. He tells me that I must marry you, but I know that the Devil is KGB. On my other shoulder I have an Angel. He tells me that I love you but I shouldn't marry you. The Angel is my mom. What should I do Carl?"

"I think that you must listen to your mom. She wants to save your life."

Vicky took my head and kissed me. She had tears in her eyes, but I know that she was happy and sad to hear my advice. She stood up and said "I will go in the kitchen to cook something for lunch Carl". She left the living room, but I heard that she was crying. I felt broken and sad. I promised myself, that I will kill anybody that hurts Vicky. I already killed one, why not more? After thirty minutes Vicky called that lunch was ready and I need to come to the kitchen.

"The kitchen smells good. Did you cook Russian food? So, Vicky, what language will my children speak?"

"Boy, first I need to be pregnant. I can tell you, after six or seven weeks. I have been with you for almost four years."

"Six or seven weeks are nothing Vicky."

"Do you know how long you have been with me Carl?"

"Of course I know. I have spent many beautiful days and nights with you Vicky. I will never forget that." We finished lunch and I told Vicky that I want to paint her.

"Why not Carl?"

"I met you when you were painting in the park. I will get ready Carl." When Vicky returned she had jean shorts and a bra.

"Could you take off the shorts? You need to have only bikini and a bra on."

"I like to show this painting to our children someday. I think that it will better if keep the shorts on. What do you think Carl?"

"You are right Vicky, but honestly, you look very sexy. I am ready to go to bed right now."

"Boy, you need to concentrate on the painting. We have two more days for sex." I started drawing and Vicky started to talk.

"I want to tell you what happened last week. Simon showed me one place and asked what I think. There is a lot of traffic of people on that street. I told Simon that the place is good and that I would to speak with the owner about the rent."

"I am the owner Vicky. If you sign a contract for two years, you don't have to pay rent for two years. You need to pay the property tax only. After two years, you will pay rent, but you don't pay property tax. Do you accept this contract?"

"We made a deal and on Tuesday morning I signed the contract. In the afternoon, I had contractors that started to work in the place. Simon was surprised and asked me when I plan to open. I told him in one month. That afternoon, I told Simon that I need an immigration lawyer. On Wednesday morning at 9:00 o'clock I was working with the contractors at the boutique when the phone rang. I thought that Simon was calling, because nobody else knows the phone number. An Immigration lawyer called me. She asked my, if I have time and to meet her in the afternoon at 2:00 o'clock. Could you believe that Carl? She already has all the information she needed. Simon gave her everything she needed from the contract. Simon is a smart man. She told me that with the business it will be easier to get the green cart fast. I asked her how much money I need to invest in the business, but she told me that the money isn't important because I have enough money behind me. It is Simon's backing. I had little problem with her, when she asked me who is

Carl and if I will marry him. I told her that I don't know, if Carl will marry me, because he is a strange man. You never know what he thinks."

"You have sex with him, why don't you ask him Vicky?"

"This isn't my place to tell you, since you are a married woman, but If you spend one night with Carl, the next day you will get a divorce and you will want to marry him too. But you never know if Carl wants to marry you lady. I sign the documents and she told me that I need to wait fifteen minutes. She returned and she was laughing."

"Simon told me that you are telling the truth Vicky. I am intrigued. I would like to meet this Carl and see for myself."

"You must be ready for a divorce if you meet him." We laughed. She is a good lawyer, because she told me that I have to keep my immigration a secret and I shouldn't tell Mom and Dad. They must think that I am working and building a boutique."

"Your father works for KGB and your mom sleeps with KGB", she said.

"I think that she is funny Carl, and she is right."

"Why did you tell her that I am a strange man?"

"Three months ago, Julia and I went for lunch. Julia told me that I need to call and ask you to come back to New York."

"Carl loves you Vicky and he will come back for you."

"I told Julia that if I call you, you will never want to see me again. Was I right Carl?"

"You were right Vicky. Julia told me about this conversation."

"What else does Carl need Vicky? He has you, me and money. I don't understand why he doesn't want to live in New York anymore? Every man dreams to have what Carl has. I know that he is a strange man. I think that Carl doesn't love you, and he doesn't love me Vicky."

"This isn't true Julia. I am positive that Carl has a very good reason to be in Dallas. I think it is a necessary step in his career. I believe that someday, he will return to New York forever Julia."

"I love you for that Vicky. You know Carl well, maybe I don't."

"We are different Julia. You are a Mom, I am girlfriend. You worry for Carl, I don't , because he is a man and he must decide for his life. Julia kissed me and told me" You are right Vicky".

"I am a little tiered from posing Carl. I would like to exercise with you. Are you ready for an exercise Carl?"

I was waiting for that Vicky. Sit on the sofa and wait for me Carl. I will go to take a shower. I was on the sofa when Vicky came back.

"I want to try something new. You will be good boy and you don't move your body." Vicky kissed my mouth and she moved her head. She kissed my chest then my belly. Then she unzipped my pants and pulled them with my boxers. I was trying to read her moves so I moved my hips up. He sprang free. She kissed the top and liked it then she sucked him. Her tongue was playing with it. I knew that Vicky was doing that, because it was arousing for her to see me melting. Vicky didn't want me to touch her. She stud up with her back facing me and she slowly eased into me just a little, only the head of my erection was inside her. She started to make slow circular moves. I felt how her inner mussels tightening around me. This was amazing. I didn't understand how the mussels of her pussy could do that. She became very wet and started to lose the head. Vicky pushed down and my full length was inside her. She picked up a rhythm up and down then a circular motion. I felt her inner muscles tightening, she stared convulsing that was my sign and we finished together. Vicky laid on my chest as we were calming down together. She laughed and told me "This is first and the last time I am doing that."

"Did you like it Carl?"

"It was amazing. You know that you make me very happy. You are an amazing woman Vicky. I will have hard time knowing, that two days from now I will never touch your body and he will never play with your pussy again."

"Hey boy, but that is the only way I will be alive."

"Who is more important?"

"Your it and my pussy or my life?"

"Your life is more important Vicky."

"I will turn around Carl. Don't move." I did as I was told. She moved her left leg little to the right. She raised her right leg up and moved and pushed her body with her left leg turning to the right. She was sitting in my lap facing me now. Her pussy didn't lose it. It was still inside her.

"How did you do that?"

"I was an acrobat, but I grew too tall, so I stopped."

"You never talk about your past that is why I never told you. I am obeying your rules Carl. I am looking into the future. What happened to you Carl? You look so different from last week."

"What is different Vicky?"

"I feel that your soul has changed." Vicky laughed, but I think that she was trying try to find words to explained it.

"For example Carl, you are more sensitive and more aggressive when you have sex."

"You are right for the first, but not me, you are more aggressive when we have sex. Are you afraid for my life Vicky?"

"Of course I am Carl. If you lived with parents who talk constantly about who was killed and who had disappeared, you will understand me better. Tomorrow morning I will leave at 7:30. I will be back at 10:00 a.m. I ordered something for the boutique. I need to be there to sign for the delivery."

"OK. Let's sleep. I am tired." We embraced and went to sleep.

I opened my eyes and I heard that Vicky was taking a shower. I went in the kitchen and decided to make breakfast.

"Why did you wake up?"

"I wanted to make breakfast and I then start drawing you holding the hummer while the construction workers are looking at your body."

"I think that this is a great idea, Carl" and she came and kissed the corner of my mouth.

Vicky left and I went back to my drawing.

Vicky came back at 11:30am with some bags.

"Did you buy lunch? It smells good!"

"Mom gave me something for you. I will prepare the table for lunch, because the food is hot. When I arrived in the boutique, the workers were waiting for me outside. I opened the door and they started to work. After thirty minutes a truck arrived and the workers unloaded the packages in the boutique. When they finished, I noticed a car and two people looking at me. I walked and asked them if they were looking for me or waiting for somebody else."

"We are looking for Carl. Our boss sent us to kill him."

"Are you from Russia?"

"Of course, sister."

"I told them that I am not their sister", and I went back in the boutique. KGB is looking for you. I called Mom and told her to bring me some clothes to your place. I tried to tell her your address, but she said that she knows where you live. She said that she will bring them at the back street of your building. I took taxi and I went there. The people I spoke with followed me there. They stopped behind a car with two people. The car was parked on front of your building. I gave the taxi driver one hundred and told him that If I don't come back after twenty minutes, he is free. I looked at them and I heard that they were speaking Russian. I entered the building, but I used the service door to exit. Mom picked me up at back of the building and she told me, that KGB has been watching your apartment twenty four hours. What do you think Carl?"

"Nothing Vicky."

"But they are looking to kill you. You don't have experience dealing with such people. You have never killed anyone before and you have professional killers after you."

"How can you be so certain that I have not killed a person before? You know that I am a wild man. When it comes down to it somebody will be first Vicky. I can't believe that they are trying to scare me in New York. Nobody knows who I am Vicky. My live has changed. You were right, that I look different, but after we have lunch I want to continue with the drawing."

"I think that you forgot to say, that we need to have sex Carl."

"You are right Vicky. Let's schedule three hours of drawing, then sex."

"I like this schedule Carl", and we laughed. The rest of the day wen as scheduled. By 10:00 p.m. Vicky was tired.

"I need to sleep Carl, I am tired." I picked her up from the sofa. She put her hands around my neck. I took her to the bed in the bedroom and put her to sleep. I went back to the drawing. I checked on her at 12:30 a.m. She was in a deep sleep. I took the keys of Peggy's car and left the apartment. I stopped the car behind the building where I live. I walked around the building hidden by the corner of the structure and looked at the parked cars on front of it. I noticed only one car with two people parked on street on front of the central door. The driver was smoking and the window was open. The other windows were closed. I knocked on the window of the passenger sitting next to the driver and the man opened the window with his left hand. He was holding a pistol in his right hand. He opened the window and pointed the pistol at me. I grabbed his hand and pointed the gun at the driver. I fired one shot in the head of the driver. Then I turned his hand and put the pistol under his chin and fired. I kept his hand and I cleaned the trigger. I came back to Simon's apartment. Vicky was sleeping. I tried to sleep, but I it took a while before I felt asleep.

I woke up in morning. Vicky wasn't in the bed. I took a shower and entered the kitchen. I found her in the kitchen and breakfast was on the table. We drunk coffee and watched the news. The reporter said that the Coast Guard in Miami found a boat with two death bodies. One of the bodies was Carl Hope from Dallas. The police found his driver's license in his pocket. They didn't find an ID in the other body. Vicky looked to me and said "What is going on Carl? They said that you death, but you are very alive and here with me." I tried to tell her, but the reporter said that thy had more breaking news. The police has found two death bodies in a car in Manhattan. The police said that two death men were from Russia and they think that this is a love story, because one of the man killed the driver, then he shot himself.

"Are you scared Vicky?"

"After this news I am not scared for you anymore Carl. I am beginning to understand now why you said that nobody knows you. I am sure that you will kill anybody that tries to harm me. I don't know what game are you playing, but make sure that come out alive. I will pray for you." She kissed my forehead, holding my head in her hands. She said, "May God be with you!"

"Could you promise me to stay alive?"

"I promise that I will come back alive Vicky."

"One more thing, you should marry Michelle!"

"Oh my God. I don't understand you Vicky. Why should I marry Michelle?"

"She will be good a wife and a mom. She will be very supportive of you. She will never be against you and will never hurt you. I will be good friends with her. If something happens with me, I know that you will take of our child. Michelle will be a good mom for it."

"Do you know that you have a son in Paris, Carl?"

"Who told you that?"

"Julia told me one year ago. She was scared that you will marry Edit, if you knew that you have a son with her."

"Why are you telling me this now? You should have told me a year ago!"

"After nine months, you may have another boy or boys Carl. You will be an international father in France and Russia. You are a good boy, that is why every woman wants to have a child with you. We need to leave this apartment soon Carl. We need to gather our belongings and go." After we packed up she checked everywhere making sure we didn't forget anything.

"Everything is OK, we can go."

We left the apartment using the service exit of the building. I stopped a taxi. Vicky kissed me and told me, "When you come back you must call me". I opened the door and she sat in the taxi. She sent me an air kiss. I took the air kiss with my hand and closed the door. I stopped another taxi and I gave the Bank of America address to the taxi driver. As I was sitting in the taxi I thought about Edit. Four years ago I broke up one of the best relationships I had with the biggest love in my life. Now I broke up another great love relationship with Vicky. Edit and Vicky will stay in my heart forever. I love them and they love me. I don't understand why everyone wants me to marry Michelle.

"Who is Michelle? Why is she in my life?"

I know Edit and Vicky very well. I don't know Michelle. I don't know what is in my future or if I have a future, because the shark, may kill me. I was smiling when the taxi stopped on front of Bank of America feeling good being alive.

CHAPTER 8

I entered the building of Bank of America at 9:30 a.m. I saw Simon, speaking with Greg. I walked to them.

"May I help you Mr. Hope?", Greg asked me.

"Yes. I would like to add the name of my friend, Simon Dreyfus to have access my safe box. Could you give him the application and explain to him, what he needs to do?"

"Of course I will give him the application, but I need to get one from my office." Greg left and Simon asked me.

"Do you know why Lorenzo was happy this morning Carl, when we heard about the love story of the two Russian people in the news? Lorenzo said that they were waiting for you, but you were first. I didn't understand him!"

"I don't know Simon. You need to ask Lorenzo. He is a detective, I am not." Greg came back and gave the application to Simon.

"Mr. Dreyfus you need to fill and sign this." Then he turned to me and asked me "Do you need to visit your box Mr. Hope?'

"I need to Greg", and we walked to my box. I took the Irish passport. I asked Greg if I can make a call, but I don't want anybody to hear me.

"Follow me Mr. Hope." We entered a room and Greg told me that he will close the door and he will stay outside and will not allow anybody to come in. I called my grandfather. He picked up the phone.

"I need to speak with Roger."

"You are alive Carl! Your grandmother and I were afraid for you, but Roger told us that this must be a joke."

"I am sorry, but I don't have time to talk about this now Grandfather."

"Roger, Carl needs to speak with you."

"I am listening Carl."

"If somebody ask me anything about Ireland, what I need to tell them?"

"You tell them that your family came to America, when you were four years old. You never have been in Ireland, but you have a dual citizenship. Where are you going?"

"To Sicily. I am going with Dino's Grandfather, Tony Capaci. I am sure that you will be OK. If Sicily was dangerous for you, Tony would never take you there. I know that you don't have time. Have a good trip Carl."

When I opened the door, Greg was waiting outside.

"Is everything OK Mr. Hope?"

"Yes Greg." and we walked towards Simon. Simon was ready with the application and he gave it to Greg.

"You have to sign too Mr. Hope." I signed and gave it to Greg.

"Thanks Mr. Hope. That is it."

"Why do you call him Mr. Hope, Greg? His name is Carl."

"For you, Mr. Hope is Carl, Mr. Dreyfus. For me he is Mr. Hope, because I want Mr. Hope to remember me. Someday Mr. Hope will ask me to work for him. He will be my boss in the future."

"You are right Greg. After three or four months Carl will be mine and your boss. I should to call him Mr. Hope too." We laughed when Adam entered the Bank at 10:00 o'clock. Adam had a newspaper in his hand.

"Oh my God! You are alive! I am so happy to see you Carl!" Simon laughed and told him that everybody is happy, except one person, the shark.

"What are we going to do now Simon?", Adam asked.

Simon gave Greg a Polaroid camera and told him, "You want you to take a picture of Carl and the newspaper, but make sure you get the date of the newspaper on the picture". Greg gave the picture to Simon. Simon looked at picture and said "That is a very good picture".

"Could you take one more Greg?"

Greg made a second picture and gave it to Simon. Simon gave the second picture to Adam and told him, "If the shark asks for Carl, you show him this picture Adam". Somebody asked Greg, why is he taking pictures in the bank, but when he saw Simon and Adam, he told him, that it is ok. Then he said to Simon "I am glad to see you Mr. Dreyfus."

"Me too", Simon told him.

"What is next Simon?"

"Do I need to stay any longer in the bank, because I want to leave?", Adam asked Simon.

"You don't need to stay. Go back to work Adam." Adam shook my hand then Simon's and left the bank. Simon and I left too. Simon asked me, "What do you think about Lorenzo, Carl?"

"Lorenzo will be working for our future company. He is a good man and a very professional detective. I trust him. You need to help me kill the shark, Simon."

"Do you have a plan Carl?"

"Yes, Simon. I need to know in which restaurant he goes for dinner and what wine he drinks."

"I am guessing that you are planning to poison him."

"Yes Simon."

"I need to know, in which restaurant the shark goes for dinner on Friday and Saturday."

"The person that will follow the shark and gives you this information must be somebody your trust with your life. Do you have the person that will poison the shark?"

"I have Simon and he is prepared to do it."

"Who is the person Carl?"

"I will not tell you, before we are ready to poison the shark. Why do you need to know who will do it? You need to help Vicky, if something happens with me."

"Are you going to marry Vicky?"

"I won't Simon, but you have to ask Vicky, why I can't marry her. She will tell you, because you are helping her and she trusts you. Vicky told me that I need to marry Michelle, but I haven't had a chance to think about it. I know that Michelle loves me, but right now I must save my life."

"You are right Carl. Don't worry about Vicky. I will be behind her, I promise you that. About Michelle, she is my niece. I love her, but you must love her too Carl."

"I saw in your library many interesting books. When I am done with the shark and find the diamonds, I like to spent time in your library."

"My home is your home Carl. You are welcome any time you wish to do that. How are you feeling today Carl?"

"I am feeling very good Simon, after two days with Vicky."

"You need to leave Carl, a limousine is waiting for you."

"Hey I am rich, because I use a limousine and a private jet, but you are the one paying for it Simon. You are richer." I saw Lorenzo, he was standing next to the limousine.

"Where will Lorenzo be staying?"

"He will stay in my house. You are right about him. He is a good man."

"How is your life Lorenzo, are you feeling good?"

"You need to worry about your life Carl, because if you don't kill the shark, he will kill you, and I may days will be numbered after that." We laughed.

"This isn't funny boys!", Simon told us.

"I know that, but it will be funny if Carl kills the shark, Simon.

"Hey Boy, if you have problem overseas, you need to call Simon."

"Thanks Lorenzo. I will" and I opened the door of the limousine. Tony Capaci was inside comfortable on the back seat. He looked like a boss of the Mafia. I sat next to Tony and I told the driver that he needs to go the Newark Liberty airport.

"Do you know why we are going to Sicily, Carl?"

"Because you need to see your friend Bruno Corso, Tony. Bruno needs to tell me what happened in Miami twenty five years ago."

"If he remembers what happened twenty five years ago in Miami, Carl!" and we laughed. "It is good that we are starting with a joke Tony. I know and you know that Bruno remembers."

"You are right Carl. Bruno will never forget this. This morning I met Lorenzo and he asked me if I was traveling with you to Sicily. I told him that we are going together. Lorenzo told me that Sicily is dangerous place. He asked me if I can keep you safe there. I asked Lorenzo, how he knows that Sicily is a dangerous place. Lorenzo told me that he lost a very good friend there."

"Do you know how Lorenzo lost his friend?"

"I know that Lorenzo sent his friend to find Bruno, and he

disappeared in Sicily."

"Why did Lorenzo's friend go to find Bruno?"

"They thought that Bruno knew where the diamonds are."

"Bruno never spoke about diamonds Carl. He disappeared, because somebody tried to kill him."

"This somebody is the shark Tony. The shark tried to kill me too. Right now Bruno and I have the same enemy, the shark. I need Bruno to give me information for two people. They worked for the shark twenty five years ago. Bruno and two other people killed Louis Dreyfus and his wife trying to get from them the location of the diamonds. The man that ordered this limousine is Simon Dreyfus. He is the brother of Louis. Lorenzo was the detective who investigated, the murders of Louis and his wife."

I noticed that we arrived at the airport so I told Tony that we will continue this conversation in the plane.

We were flying on our way to Europe when Tony asked me, "Carl, how long have you known Simon and Lorenzo?"

"I have known Simon now for two weeks and Lorenzo for one week."

"I got the impression that they know you very well and you have been their friend for many years."

"You have been my friend for many years Tony. You know me very well, because Dino told you everything that Dino and I have done. And I know that Dino doesn't have a zip on his mouth."

"You are right Carl. Every time Dino came to my house, he told me what you did together. I will tell you all I know that happened with Bruno twenty five years ago. I think that you should know what Bruno told me so you can compare with what he tells you when you meet him. If there is a difference you need to tell Bruno that."

Tony looked up and started telling me the story. "I was working when Bruno called me and asked me to help him. He said that he had a big problem."

"What is the problem Bruno?"

"They killed my partners and now they are looking for me Tony. If they find me, they will kill me".

"Where are you now?"

"I am in the Miami airport. In the morning I will be in New York."

"When you arrive in New York, take taxi and come at my work

place. I will be waiting for you in my office."

"Bruno came and he told me what happened. Bruno and two other men were in Miami. They had to get information from Louis Dreyfus. When Louis refused to give it to them, Bruno's partners killed the wife of Louis. They dropped her from a terrace. Louis started to fight with them. They threw Louis from the terrace too. The shark told them that he wants Louis alive, but Scot told them to kill him if he gives them any trouble and gave them $90,000. He also promised them an additional $90,000 after they finish the job. Bruno had the money. Bruno and his partners left the hotel room of Louis Dreyfus and decided to use the emergency exit to leave the hotel. They were in the corridor, when a man asked Bruno for a light. The man had a cigarette in his mouth. Bruno tried several times, but the lighter didn't work. Finally, Bruno's lighter worked and the man lighted his cigarette. Bruno was still on the fourth floor and he saw his partners walking outside the hotel across the street. Bruno saw two people walked behind them and shot them in the head. They killed Bruno's partners and checked the packets of Bruno's partners. Bruno took the elevator and used the main door to leave the hotel. He walked on the street and looked for a taxi. He saw a car that stopped and a lady got out of it. Bruno approached the driver and offered him two hundred to drop him at the airport. The driver asked for three hundred. Bruno gave him three hundred and he dropped him at the airport. When Bruno saw me, he was scared. "

"I believe in God Tony. God saved my life".

"Bruno asked what to do. I told Bruno that if he stays in New York, they will find and kill him. He must disappear in Sicily."

"I will never see my family and you Tony, if I disappear in Sicily!"

"But you will be alive Bruno", I told him.

"You are right Tony""

"Bruno disappeared in Sicily. Bruno has been living there for twenty five years now. We speak every month."

"What happened with Bruno's family?"

"Five years later, Bruno's wife left to Sicily, but Bruno has a son, daughter and grandchildren in New York. He dreams to come back to New York. He wants to die in New York."

"My family lives in New York too, Tony. I must come back to

New York".

"I spoke with Bruno and I told him that I will be in Palermo on Wednesday morning. Bruno was happy."

"How many people are coming with you Tony?"

"I told Bruno that I will be with my adopted grandson."

"Why is he coming with you Tony?"

"I don't know Bruno, but if you don't want to meet him, we won't come to Sicily."

"You must come with him Tony. I will be waiting on Wednesday morning for you at the airport."

"Do you want to know what time we are arriving Bruno?"

"I live in Sicily Tony. I will have this information."

"Why are you looking like a boss of the Mafia Tony?"

"Bruno told me that when we arrive I need to look like the boss of the Mafia in New York and introduce you as my bodyguard, Carl."

"How many people I will have to kill in Sicily, Boss?"

"We must leave Sicily alive, bodyguard." We laughed.

"Do you need to sleep Tony?"

"No Carl. I would like to continue our conversation. I was happy when Dino told me that you are back in New York. My wife joked with me."

"You are lonely Tony, because your grandson left to Dallas."

"Of course I am."

"Dino is your grandson too Tony."

"Dino is my blood but he isn't as smart as Carl. I can speak with Carl about what is happening in the world. With Dino I speak about what is happening in New York. You are a very different boy. I will never forget, when I asked you what you wanted for a present, when you saved Dino life."

"Dino finishing high school, will be the best present for me, Mr. Capaci."

"Dino finishing high school was my dream Carl. But you encouraged Dino and he finished a two year college. Now Dino works for your mom Julia. Julia loves him and helps him all the time. My family loves your family very much. Love and help, this is what the bond between mine and your family. When I tell the Italian families about that, they don't understand me. I had a good relationship with my father. I grew up when Al Capone and Lucky Luciano were heroes. Every Italian boy wanted to be Al Capone or

Lucky Luciano. My father told me that it is easy to be a criminal, but you will never know how and when your life will end. You will end up in jail or die young shot on the street. If you get an education, your life will be better Tony. I finished high school. I was in the military. After military I started to work and retired from the New York Post Office. Italian people respect me and they listen when I give them advice. I never had a criminal record and I never had a problem with the police. Do you think that Dino has a brain to finish a four year college?"

"Do you want me to speak with Dino about that, Tony? I know that Dino can do it but he is a lazy man. He listens to me. I will tell Marisa to tell Dino needs to finish four year college. If he doesn't, she will divorce him and marry a man who has more education."

"This is good idea Carl."

"Did you speak with Roger, Carl?"

"This morning."

"I laughed a lot, when an Italian man said that somebody killed Roger. I know that if something had happened with Roger, you will call me Carl."

"Why did you save Roger's life Tony? Roger thinks that I told you to save his life."

"When we found Roger and his friend, I knew that Roger's friend told his Irish friends that Roger is a stupid and a soft man, because he didn't kill you and Dino. Now the stupid and the soft man is alive. The smart and hard man passed away" and Tony laughed.

"Now you, Dino and Roger are good friends. I know that Dino and Roger will die for you Carl. I am feeling a little tired. It will be good to get some sleep."

"I will get some sleep too Tony."

The pilot woke up me and he told me that in thirty minutes we will arrive in Palermo and he asked me, how long he needs to wait for us and where we are going next. I told him that he will stay in Palermo for five hours and that we will go to Zurich, West Berlin or back to the USA.

I woke up Tony. Tony and I left the plane and we entered the airport. Somebody spoke to Tony. Tony told me to follow him. Outside the airport a limousine was waiting for me and Tony. Tony opened the door and entered the limousine. When I entered the, I saw Tony embraced and kissed another old guy. They were crying.

That was Bruno. I sat and the limousine left the airport. Bruno looked at me and said "You are a young man why do you want to lose your life? Nobody knows where the diamonds are. The last person who knew was Louis Dreyfus, but he died twenty five years ago."

"You and your partners killed Louis Dreyfus and his wife Bruno. I am in Palermo so that you can tell me, what happened."

"What do you want to know?"

"I need information for two people. Hans from West Germany and Konev from Russia."

"Why do you need this information?"

"Because I must kill the shark." Bruno laughed and told me, "You are too young to kill the shark boy. Can you tell me your name or show me your passport?"

Bruno looked my passport.

"Your name is Barry More and you are from Ireland?"

"I am Bruno." Tony looked at Bruno and me, but he didn't speak.

"I know your name boy, but it is good for you to have another name in Sicily."

"You think that I am here to ask you for the diamonds Bruno. I know that you don't where the diamonds are, because if you did, you and your friends would have taken them many years ago and you would have been back in New York. You have family in New York that you love. I know that you have information for Hans and Konev."

"You are right boy or Mr. More or Carl Hope. Which name do you like me to call you?"

"I prefer that you call me Barry More in Italy."

"Tony, I like this boy."

"You can go and see you family Tony, while I speak with Barry."

"Do you want me to stay with you Carl?"

"No Tony. You need to go and see your family. Don't worry about me, Bruno wants to go back to New York."

"Barry is right Tony, I have a chance to go back to New York." The limousine stopped.

"You must be back after three hours Tony."

"I will be here."

The limousine left and Bruno and I took a taxi and went to a big property. I looked at the house. It had three floors and I told Bruno, "This house is a Renaissance style".

"How do you know that Barry?"

"I am an architect and I have been to Italy before to study that. I love the Renaissance architecture. The house has a soul."

"I don't know, what kind of boy you are, but Tony had only good words to say about you. I believe Tony. Before we talk, my boss wants to see you."

"The person we are meeting doesn't speak English, but he will record our conversation. I will be your translator. When the boss asks, you keep your answers short. The boss will look at your face, don't show fear. You need to keep your eyes in the boss's face. The boss will lose control." Bruno and I entered the house. The boss was in a big living room. Bruno kissed the boss's hand. Bruno gave my Irish passport to him. He looked at my passport and said, "You are from New York, but you have an Irish passport!". I told him that my family left Ireland when I was four years old and I have a dual citizenship, American and Irish. When I travel in Europe I use my Irish passport.

"How long have you lived in America?"

"Twenty three years."

"Why did your family moved to America?"

"I don't know, I never asked my mom and dad, but Mom told me that America is better for me. Now I am an architect. If my family stayed in Ireland, Dad and Mom didn't have money to support me."

"Why did you come to Sicily?"

"I want to help Bruno to come back to New York."

"Who asked you to help Bruno?"

"Tony Capaci and members of Bruno's family asked me."

"Do you think that Bruno is a crime person?"

"Bruno's partners killed two people, Bruno didn't."

"Are you Tony's grandson?"

"I saved the life of Tony's grandson, Dino. After that I became Tony's grandson."

"Are you a criminal?"

"I don't have a crime record and I never have had a problem with the police."

"Did you pay for the trip to Sicily?"

"No. My friend paid. I don't have enough money to pay for this trip."

"I am guessing that your friend is rich and he paid for the trip, because he needs to get some information from Bruno"

"You are right boss." The boss was nervous, because I looked at his face and I answered. The boss asked Bruno to follow him and they left. After ten minutes Bruno returned and said "Follow me Barry". We walked outside.

"I don't want to speak inside. Before we start to speak I need to give you this phone number in Milan. The man who lives in Milan has a lot of information. Everybody calls him the lawyer, but his name is Vito Lombardy. You must be careful with him he is a very dangerous, but you must meet him. My boss will try to get information for Hans and Konev. Mafia, KGB and Stasi sometimes work together. The boss likes you Carl. I am sorry, Barry" and we laughed.

"This is what happened between Hans and Konev in New York. Konev was nervous and told Hans that the shark wants to kill him."

"Was your father killed in New York, Hans?", he asked him.

"He was, but this was almost fifty years ago, Konev. I am in New York to find what happened with my father. I was a little boy when they killed my father."

"The shark thinks that you know where the diamonds are. He thinks that your mom knows and she told you."

"Mom has never spoken for diamonds with me Konev."

"Why do you speak English, this people can hear us?"

"They are Italian and they don't speak English, Hans. You must disappear. If you stay in West Berlin, the shark will find you easy."

"Where do you plan to disappear?"

"I will be in Zurich. You know that I have an apartment in there. But nobody knows that I have a house in Zug. I will give you my phone number in Zug."

"Hans disappeared and I never saw him again. Konev is different. I saw Konev in New York, Miami and Milan. I saw Konev in the lawyer's office in Milan too. My boss asked me to go to Milan, because Vito Lombardy, the lawyer, wanted to see me. When I entered the Vito's office I saw Konev. I was surprised. Konev was too. The lawyer was trying to tell Konev something, but the phone rang and the lawyer answered. Konev walked to me and told me. not to tell Vito Lombardy that I know where Hans is.

Hans is my best friend and I was stupid when I asked Hans, where he will disappear. Somebody told the shark that Hans is in Zurich. If the lawyer asks you, you must tell him that you don't know me. The lawyer will ask you for Hans. When we finish I need to see you. If you leave before me, you need to wait for me in the cafeteria on the corner. The lawyer finished speaking on the phone. He walked towards me.

"Bruno, you know Konev very well. Can you tell me what happened in New York and Miami?"

"I don't know who this man is Vito. I saw him today for the first time in my life. I was never in Miami."

"But the shark told me that you know well Konev."

"Who is the shark?"

"Don't you know the shark, Bruno?"

"I don't and this is the first time I heard this name." The lawyer lost control. The lawyer asked Konev, "Do you know Bruno, Konev?"

"I never saw this man before."

"The lawyer looked at me and Konev and told us that he doesn't understand why the shark wanted to arrange this meeting between me and Konev."

"Vito, I know very well the shark, but I don't know this man. Konev looked me and asked. Is your name Bruno?"

"Yes. My name is Bruno, I am from Sicily and I don't know who the shark is."

"This is big problem for you Vito. The shark is in a high position in the KGB. Do you want the shark to know that you told us the shark name in this meeting?"

"I don't want that, Konev. I don't like to have problem with the KGB and the shark. If you need to speak with Bruno, you need to go outside. I don't like to hear any more Konev."

"Konev and I left the office and Konev told me that I need to stay in Sicily, if I like to save my life, because the shark is trying to find Hans and the he is using Vito for that. I know that Konev knows where Hans is, but he will never tell me."

"Did you hear from Hans after last time you met him in New York, Konev?"

"We have spoken every month after that meeting in New York. He gave me the information Stasi has on me. I gave him KGB information about him. We are helping each other to stay alive,

Bruno."

"What do you think about me Konev?"

"You must try to stay alive too Bruno. Me, you and Hans, we are partners. We must help each other if we want to survive."

"That is the first time I saw Konev laughing Carl. I think that Hans lives in Zug. Konev is smart. He hates the shark. Konev told me that the shark killed a lot of his friends."

"They worked for KGB Bruno. Why does the shark give information for people who work for the KGB? The shark is a KGB agent, but the shark is a CIA too. Don't you get it? The shark is a double agent Bruno."

"Konev told me to ask my boss to kill Vito, because it will be good for our people in Sicily."

"I hate the shark and Vito, Bruno, but I work for the KGB. I don't have a permission to kill them."

"If Konev knows that you want to kill the shark, he will help you, Carl. You must use Vito for information. He has a lot of information, because he uses the Mafia, KGB, Stasi and crime people. Vito makes a lot of crime money. Many people pay him for nothing, but they are scared. My boss hates Vito, so if the Mafia kills him, my boss will be very happy. You will be a hero for my boss, if you help with that. I know that Vito will continue to look for Hans. If you meet Vito and tell him, that you know where Hans is, he will use you and he will tell you information for the shark and Konev. I know that Konev spends most of his time in Russia. My boss gave me this information Carl. That is it what I know for Hans and Konev."

"Have you ever seen the shark Bruno?"

"Many people told me that the shark is a big boss and he has a lot of power in New York, but I never saw him. I believe that the shark exists. If you kill him Carl, I can come back to New York. I will pray for you to succeed. You are too young to die. The shark must die, because he is old and he is responsible for the murder of many innocent people." We were laughing when the boss came back. He spoke with Bruno first and then he walked to me. He took my head in his hands, kissed my forehead and said, "God bless you". Then he left us.

"I told you Carl. The boss likes you. He knows that you will help him get rid of Vito. The boss told me that Hans disappeared from West Berlin one year ago and nobody knows where he is.

Many people think that Hans lives in West Germany, but I think that Hans lives in Switzerland. Konev lives in Russia, but he has a son, Sasha who lives in New York. No big news Barry."

"Can you send somebody tell the pilot that he will be flying to Milan, Bruno?"

"I will" and Bruno left. I was alone so I started to think what I have to say, when I meet Vito Lombardy. Bruno returned and said that everything is OK.

"The boss called the airport and they will tell the pilot that he must fly to Milan."

Tony came back with the limousine as we agreed and we left for the airport. We were ready to enter the plane, when a car stopped behind me and Bruno. Two people exited the car. They spoke with Bruno. I asked Bruno, what the people want.

"They want to take Tony with them."

"Tell them that I will go with them."

"They want to take Tony, Barry."

I was very close to them. They aimed their pistols at us and said something to Bruno.

"This is very dangerous situation, I don't know what to do Barry."

"I will go with them Barry, Tony told me."

"You must stay there and don't move Tony."

The driver exited from the limousine with a pistol and he asked them something in Italian. They started to speak with the driver of the limousine. Since I was close to them I caught the hand of one of them and I took the pistol. The second man looked me and the driver of the limousine. He threw his pistol. I told Bruno to take the pistol from the ground. Bruno and I pushed them in the trunk of the limousine.

"Can you tell your boss what happened and I want to know, who sent them Bruno?"

"I will Carl and I need to give you mine and my boss's a phone numbers. I wrote the phone numbers down in a piece of paper. Tony and I boarded the airplane. I told the pilot that after Milan he needs to fly back with Tony to America.

"I will stay in Milan."

The pilot told recommended that I stay in hotel Napoleon.

"If you have problem, you ask for Luigi and tell him, that your friend from America, who is a pilot told you to stay in this hotel."

We were flying and Tony asked me "Do you think that we are just losing time and money for this trip?"

"I don't think so Tony. Bruno gave me information and now I know what to do. I had information for some of these people, but Bruno told me how to find Hans and what person Konev is. I must find Hans. If I find Hans, he will help me to meet Konev. Hans will tell me where I need to meet Konev. I know that Konev will never speak with me and Konev will never meet with me, if he doesn't know that I want to kill the shark. Now I know that Konev hates the shark, but he will never kill the shark. I will kill the shark, because I need to save my life. KGB and Stasi have a secret way of communicating and meeting. I know that Konev will help me, if Hans tells him that I want to kill the shark."

"Carl, when I go back to New York I will go to see Simon. What should I tell him?"

"Simon can't help me Tony. My brain must work fast and make the right decisions, so I can make it."

We arrived in Milan and I left the plane. I was alone. I realized that didn't have anyone to help me if I have a problem in Milan. I know that I will meet people who will help me find Hans. I took a taxi and I told the driver to drop me in hotel Napoleon. After thirty minutes I was there.

"May I help you sir?"

"I am looking for Luigi."

"I am Luigi sir."

"My friend from America told me about hotel Napoleon and you Luigi."

"I am glad to hear that sir. I have a business in Milan and I will stay here for two nights."

"What do you like sir, a rooms or an apartment?'

"I would like an apartment Luigi" and I gave him my Irish passport.

"Which floor do you like to stay on Mr. Moore?"

"The third floor." I showed him my credit card, but I covered with my finger the name on it.

"I don't like to pay with a card. I would like to pay cash, because I don't like anybody to know that I am in Milan."

"I understand Mr. Moore, cash is good."

"You need to pay eight hundred dollars Mr. Moore." I gave Luigi one thousand.

"Two hundred for you Luigi."

"Thanks Mr. Moore." I signed the check in papers and Luigi gave me the key.

"I have a question Luigi. I am alone in Milan. Do you know a girl between twenty or twenty four years old that would like to be with me for two nights? She needs to speak English and be pretty. I don't want a street girl."

"I have a friend. She speaks English and she is pretty. She is studying to be an architect in the University and she is her third year. How much do you want to pay her for two nights?"

"I will pay her three thousand plus additional for a good service."

"What time does she need to come here Mr. Moore?"

"Five o'clock is good Luigi. Could you tell her to bring ten condoms?"

Luigi smiled and he told me "I am certain, that she will have a good time with you Mr. Moore."

I put my bag in the apartment and I left. I took a taxi to the Train Station. I bought a ticket to Bern, Switzerland.

I returned to the hotel and I called Simon, "I am calling from Milan, but on Friday I am going to Bern in Switzerland. I need to speak with your friend". I give Simon my phone number in Milan. "He must to ask for Barry Moore, Simon. I will be leaving the hotel at 6:00 p.m. tonight. I don't know when I will be back."

"He will call you after one hour Barry" and Simon hang up the phone. I called in Palermo and I asked to speak with Bruno. Bruno told me that the lawyer sent the guys to the airport for Tony. I called and I ask to speak with Vito Lombardy.

"Who are you and what do you want?"

"My name is Barry Moore. I need to meet you tomorrow morning at 9:00 o'clock. I know where Hans Weber is."

"Do you want to know where the diamonds are?"

I didn't reply.

"I will see you tomorrow at 9:00 o'clock Moore. Come to my office" and he gave me the address. I was getting ready to take a shower when the phone started ringing. I picked up.

"Barry Moore speaking."

"Simon asked me to watch your back. I will be in Bern on Friday night."

"Where should I stay in Bern? Can you recommend a five star

hotel?"

"You need to stay in hotel Bellevue-Palace" and he gave me the phone number. I called and made a reservation. Then I took a shower and I was watching TV when the phone rang again. I picked up. It was Luigi.

"She is here Mr. Moore. Could tell her how to get to my room? I will unlock the door Luigi?"

I unlocked the door and I sat on the sofa. About ten minutes later there was a knock on the door. I said "Come in".

She entered and asked, if she needs to close the door.

"Yes, please." I stood up, walked to her and kissed her hand.

"My name is Barry Moore."

"I am Lilli Mr. Moore."

"Call me Barry. Do you like something to drink Lilli?"

"A glass of water will be fine Mr. Moore." I took water from refrigerator and gave her a glass of water.

"Luigi gave me this package for you Mr. Moore."

"What is your relationship with Luigi?"

"He is my second cousin." I saw that Lilli was feeling uncomfortable and I asked her.

"Do you like to stay here or would like to go out?"

"I will feel better if we go out, Mr. Moore."

"Hey Lilli, I have been in Italy several times, but I never been in Milan. Could you show me the city?"

Lilli smiled and she told me. "I will be very happy to show you around t Barry." I sensed that she was relieved that we were going out.

We left the apartment. I saw Luigi in the lobby. He was surprised. Thanks for the package Luigi. Lilli and I left the hotel.

"Where do you want to go Barry?"

"I want to see La Scala and the Milan Cathedral. I am an architect and I have read for the Milan cathedral when I was in the University of New York."

"May I kiss you Barry", and she kissed me on the cheek.

"I am studying to be an architect too. I am in my third year. It is great that we have something in common, the love of architecture."

"May I hold your hand Barry?"

"Of course Lilli." I looked for a taxi, but Lilli told me that the Milan Cathedral isn't far away from hotel Napoleon, so she suggested that we walk.

"Where have you been in Italy?"

"I have been in Rome, Venice and Florence."

"Do you like Italy, Barry?"

"I love the history of Italy. People are friendly and the food is good too."

"Were you in Italy alone?" I laughed and I told her.

"I have a friend in Paris. I met her in New York. We were very close friends for two years. I came with her to Italy."

We entered the Cathedral and Lilli told me that she will sit and pray.

"You look around Barry, I have been here many times. When I finish, I will wait outside for you."

I knew that people started to build the Milan Cathedral in 1387 and they finished in 1965. This is 700 years, but the Cathedral is a miracle. I was inside for one hour. Lilli was waiting outside. I walked to her. "Hey it is 7:15pm. Do you like to go for dinner somewhere Lilli?"

"I like to Barry, and I know a very good restaurant. They cook good fish there."

"I like to eat fish for dinner Lilli."

"We can walk there too Barry." While we were walking Lilli took my hand again.

"Do you like when a woman holds your hand?"

"I am OK, if she holds my hand to walk, but if she likes to hold my hand to marry me, I am not OK. Edit used to hold my hand when we walked. Vicky liked to me to put my arm around her shoulder."

"Could put your arm around my shoulder Barry?"

She let off my hand and I put my arm around her shoulder. I laughed.

"Why did you laugh?"

"Vicky likes me to put my arm around her shoulder and she is the best woman I have been in bed with."

"There might be something about that. You never know, I might be a lioness in bed."

"I know that you don't have experience with men and I know that you won't surprise me in bed, but I like you Lilli." We entered the restaurant. The hostess started talking to me in Italian and Lilli intervened telling her that I don't speak Italian. Lilli asked me, where I want to sit, outside or inside.

"I prefer outside Lilli." Lilli and the hostess spoke and laughed, I followed them. We sat on a table and Lilli told me, that they laughed, because the hostess likes to be our waitress and she wants to be in bed with me. "Why not Lilli? She is pretty and I think that she has experience with men and she will be a good partner in bed."

"Hey Barry, I am with you. You need to be with me for two nights first."

"But, you aren't ready to be with me in bed Lilli."

"Now I am not, but later who knows? I am happy to be with you Barry."

"You were scared three hours ago when you entered the apartment."

"I was Barry, but you know why I was scared?"

"Could you tell me, why you were scared?"

"Luigi called me and he asked, if I like to have a good time with a good man. He said that you want a girl to be with you for two nights. I told Luigi that I am not a prostitute."

"Barry wants a woman who speaks English and is pretty", Luigi told me.

"Do you think that I am pretty Barry?"

"If you were not, I wouldn't have gone out with you Lilli."

"Thanks Barry. Everything was OK, but when I arrived in the hotel, Luigi called you and gave me a small package."

"What is this Luigi?", I asked him.

"Mr. Moore asked for ten condoms Lilli, but you shouldn't tell Mr. Moore that I bought the condoms. He gave me a good tip. Don't be scared, he is a good looking businessman. I think that you will have good time with him."

"Ok Luigi, I will go to see Mr. Moore."

"Barry, you are right. I don't have experience with men and I never have been in this situation. I never have sex with a man who paid me. Luigi told me that you will pay me three thousand dollars. That is why I was so happy when you told me that we were going out."

"How do you feel now Lilli?"

"I am OK now Barry. Luigi was right when he told me that you are a handsome man." A waiter came interrupting us asking what we want for an appetizer. "I am in your hands Lilli, you decide what to order." She ordered calamari, crab legs and Greek salad.

Then she turned to me and said "Barry, you order the wine."

"Could you give one bottle of white wine Pinot Grigio, please?"

"What do you like for dinner?", the waiter asked us.

"The white fish is better Barry."

"I agree Lilli."

"We like two white with fish with pasta, please."

"I think that everybody knows you in this restaurant Lilli."

"Of course, they know me Barry. I am from Milan. I want to talk to you about sex Barry."

"Hey Lilli you need to have sex, you don't need to talk about it."

"Now we will talk, but later we will have Barry."

"How much time do you have sex Barry?"

"I have sex with girls between forty minutes to one hour. Depends on how attractive the woman is." Lilli laughed and she told me "I never have sex for more than ten minutes."

The waiter brought us the appetizers and the wine, so we paused our conversation.

"Cheers Lilli. I think that we will have a good time."

"Cheers Barry. I hope so. What do you do for forty minutes to one hour of sex?"

"Hey Lilli, I am an architect. I am not a porn producer, who tells people how to have sex. It comes to me natural. Me and the woman I am with do what we like to do. When I have sex, I never think how long I need to have sex, but I read the woman and finish when the woman is ready to finish. This is very important when you have sex."

"How do you know that woman is ready to finish Barry?"

"My body feels that. Her body feels that too. Two bodies make sex Lilli and bodies need to play and enjoy when they have sex."

"It is hard for me to understand that Barry, but I will try. Now I am not ready for that."

"Somebody started to speak with Lilli in Italian."

"Barry, this is Flavio. You can sit here. We are talking for sex." Flavio sat and Lilli told me, that Flavio was her ex- boyfriend.

"Do you like to speak with him Lilli?"

"I am with you Barry."

"Don't worry about that Lilli, speak to him if you like."

"What would you while I am speaking with Flavio?"

"I will call my friend in Paris."

"Give me ten minutes Barry. Please come back after ten minutes."

"I will Lilli" and I asked waiter where the phone is.

I called Paris. Edit picked up the phone. "Oh my God. Where are you?"

"I am in Milan for three days."

"Do you have a problem?"

"Are you my mom?" and Edit and I laughed.

"You know that I never have problems."

"I know Carl. I am so glad to talk to you. Are you coming to Paris?"

"I will be in Bern on Saturday. Then I will go in Geneva. After that I will come to Paris. But I don't know which day right now, Edit. I am sure that next week I will be in Paris."

"Do you like to stay in my apartment?"

"No Edit. You have a husband and children, but I need to see you."

"When you finish your business call me."

"I will call."

"See you Carl" and she hung up the phone. I returned on the table. Flavio looked at me and laughed. He said something in Italian and left.

"Cheers Lilli."

"Cheers Barry."

"Do you know why Flavio laughed?"

"I didn't understand what he said. I don't know Italian."

"When I told Flavio that you had sex with me for one hour, he started to laugh."

"Why did you tell Flavio that you had sex with me? I never had sex with you Lilli."

"Flavio tried to hurt me, so I said that, because I wanted to hurt him. Flavio is a jealous man. He will think that I am with you and I have sex with you."

The rest of the evening we talked about architecture. We finished dinner and we left the restaurant. We were outside when I said "We need to get a taxi Lilli."

"For who Barry, the hotel isn't far away."

"Do you like to stay in the hotel with me?"

"I would like come to the hotel to check, if you can have sex with me for one hour."

"Are you ready to have sex with me Lilli?"

"Don't speak for sex. You need to have sex with me Barry, these were your words."

We were in the hotel apartment and I asked "Are you sure that you want sex Lilli?"

"I am sure and I am going to the bathroom to get ready. You need to be naked in bed waiting for me."

"You are a good girl and I like you, Lilli. I would like to have sex with you."

I was naked in bed. Lilli came in the bedroom. I look at her. She had a perfect body. She laid next to me and she tried to touch my erection. I took her hand and put it on my shoulder. Lilli took my hand and placed it between her legs. I kissed her and tried to suck her tongue. We kissed and played with our tongues. I was getting very aroused and Lilli was breading fast. I moved on top of her holding myself on my elbows. My erection was on her stomach. She moved up I put it between her legs touching her pussy. Lilli told me that she wants to feel me inside her.

"You need to push it, don't be afraid, Barry." I did as she asked. I was inside her. I started moving forward and back, but she didn't move. She didn't have experience. I raised her legs. I felt it deep in her. I started to move faster.

"Don't finish Barry. I am feeling so good." She tried to move her hips, but she was out of rhythm. I understood that I need to teach her.

"Do you like to be on top of me Lilli?"

"I like too, but I don't know what to do."

"I will teach you."

I moved her on top of me. She tried to take him in her hand.

"Lilli don't use your hand. Use your pussy. Take it with your pussy." She looked at me then she started sliding into me.

"Barry, this is so new for me. I took a hold of her ass and started to move her forward and back.

"Let me do it." I took off my hands and Lilli moved her ass forward and back. She moved in a circle then forward and back several times. Her body started to shiver. I knew that she was ready and that was my signal to finish to. She called my name and we finished one after each other. She was kissing my chest.

"Oh my God! I don't believe it! I had sex for forty two minutes!"

"How did you know that we had sex forty two minutes Lilli?"

"I looked at the watch when we started and then when we finished."

I laughed and said "The right thing to say will be that we had sex for forty two minutes."

"You are right Barry. I need to figure out how to be more attractive, if I want to have sex for longer than that."

"You need to know that sex is a feeling, Lilli. You don't need to watch the time."

"You told me that you have sex between forty minutes and one hour. Now I believe you. You didn't lie, but next time we need to have sex for one hour" and she laughed. You are a good teacher Barry" and Lilli kissed me.

"I have a meeting tomorrow morning, but since I don't know the city I am not sure what time I have to leave the hotel, to be on time."

"I might be able to help you. Do you have the address?"

"Yes, here it is."

Lilli looked at the address and she said that this isn't far away from the hotel.

"You will need to leave at 8:30 a.m. I will let you know how to find the place", and she gave the directions.

"Before I leave in the morning I will order breakfast. Do you want anything special Lilli?

"No. Order for me the same you are ordering for yourself. You must be here when they deliver the breakfast Barry."

"I will be here Lilli."

"You need to sleep Barry. I am so excited, but I will try to sleep."

I kissed Lilli and I closed my eyes.

I woke up at 6:50 a.m. Lilli was sleeping. I took a shower and ordered breakfast for 8:00 o'clock. At 8:00 a.m. somebody knocked. I opened the door. A male server was delivering. He tried to enter. I told him that I will take the breakfast and gave him a tip. I took the trey and closed the door. I entered the bedroom and Lilli asked me "Who was at the door? I heard the knock and you spoke to somebody."

"They delivered the breakfast."

"Are you afraid to stay alone here?"

"No. When you leave, I will lock the door from the inside.

Thanks for breakfast Barry. You are a true gentleman."

"I am, and I am sorry but I need to leave now for the meeting."

"Good lack Barry and Lilli sent me an air kiss."

I made it to meeting location on time. I knocked on the lawyer's office door at 9:00 a.m. A man opened the door. He was about sixty or sixty five years old and about five feet and six inches tall.

"Come in Mr. Moore. Would you like some coffee, tea or water?"

"No thanks."

"You were in Sicily and you arrested my people Mr. Moor."

"Your people tried to take my boss and the Mafia arrested your people."

"Where are you staying in Milan?"

"In hotel Napoleon."

"How many days are you staying in hotel Napoleon?"

"I don't know, but if you tell me where Hans is, I will leave Milan. "

"Who is Hans Mr. Moore?"

"Hans Weber. He works for Stasi."

"Who told you that Hans Weber works for Stasi?"

"The shark told me and he also told me that I need to speak with Bruno Corso."

"Why did you meet with Bruno, Sicily is a dangerous place?"

"I need to know where the diamonds are. Otto Weber knew where the diamonds were, but they killed him. Louis Dreyfus knew, but the shark and Konev killed him too. Now the only person that knows where the diamonds are is Hans. If I want to find the diamonds, I need to find Hans. If you help me, I will take fifty percent and you will take fifty."

"You forgot Hans and the shark."

"I will kill Hans and KGB will kill the shark."

"Why will KGB kill the shark?"

"The shark has been trying to find the diamonds for the last thirty years. Finally you and I will have the diamonds. KGB has spent a lot money and time for nothing. They will kill the shark for that."

"What do you think about Konev?"

"Konev is almost retired and he stays in Russia. He knows that he will never get the diamonds. Konev hates the shark and he will never help him."

"What do you think about Bruno Corso?"

"He is happy in Sicily and he doesn't think for the diamonds."

"What if the Mafia wants to take the diamonds?"

"You are the boss of the Mafia Vito, but I want to call you the lawyer. You control many people and they work for you. I think that, we don't have a problem with the Mafia."

"How do you know this?"

"The people in Sicily told me."

"What if I decide to kill you Mr. Moore?"

"I am not scared Vito. Many people tried to kill me, but they are death. I am young and aggressive. I have the support of many people that love me. If somebody tries to kill me, they will kill him."

"What are you going to do after we get the diamonds?"

"I will disappear somewhere. Nobody will know where I am."

"What will happen with your friends that are supporting you and are behind you?"

"You don't have friends when you have hundred million dollars. You have enemies Vito."

"You are smart Mr. Moore. I will help you find Hans, but I will need some time."

"Could give me a call every day Mr. Moore?"

"I will tell you what I know about Hans. I know that Hans disappeared a year ago from West Berlin Mr. Moore. I think that he is in Switzerland." The phone was ringing and the lawyer picked up and listened for few minutes. Then he looked at me and said "I need to take this call in the other room of the office Mr. Moore."

He left. This gave me a chance to look at the items on his desk. I saw a business card. It had the phone number and the name of Peter Volak. The phone number was from New York. I took the business card and put it in my pocket. The lawyer returned in the office. He had something in his hand. He said "I am giving you this phone card Mr. Moore. You need to use it in Europe. If you have problem, I will send people to help you."

I took the phone card and left the office. I looked at my watch. It was 9:30 a.m. I started to walk back to the hotel I was there at 9:55 a.m. I was about to take the elevator, when Luigi approached me.

"I need to speak with you Mr. Moore. After 9:30 a.m. somebody called many times and asked for you."

"You need to tell them, that I am out and I will back after 5:00 p.m. "

"How is Lilli Mr. Moore? She is my second cousin. I love her very much. She is good and a beautiful girl, but she has problem. Can you help her? She tried to kill herself six months ago!"

"Why did she do that Luigi?"

"Lilli and Flavio were engaged, but Flavio left Lilli and he said that he will never marry her. This was very devastating for Lilli."

"Did she tell you about Flavio, Mr. Moore?"

"I met Flavio last night in the restaurant and Lilli spoke with him, I didn't, because Flavio doesn't speak English and I don't speak Italian."

"Lilli's mom was pushing her to marry Flavio, because she thinks that he has money. If Lilli's mom hears that you are with her and you are rich, she will push her to marry you. You are a strong and good looking man Mr. Moore."

"Thanks Luigi" and I kissed Luigi on the cheek.

"You are so sweet Luigi."

"Tanks Mr. Moore, I will never forget that you kissed me."

"Maybe someday I will love you Luigi."

"Who knows Mr. Moore" and Luigi kissed me on the cheek too.

"I have to go now Luigi. I will talk to you later." and I took the elevator. I knocked on the door.

"Could you open the door Lilli? This is Barry." I entered the apartment and I laughed.

"Why did you laugh Barry, what is funny?"

"I flirted with Luigi. I kissed Luigi and Luigi kissed me back."

"Oh my God. Do you love Luigi?"

"Hey Lilli, this is private."

I embraced Lilli and kissed her.

"I need to talk to you Lilli."

"I don't like to talk Barry. I want to make French love to you. Last night you spoke with a French woman. I am sure that she is better in French love than me, because she is from France. I am from Italy, but I will try to do my best." Lilli took off my clothes. I was naked. She pushed me, so I was laying on the bed. She took off her shirt and bikini and she jumped in the bed. She tried to grab my erection. I gently stoke her hand and said "I am not ready Lilli we don't need to rush this. We need some time to prepare our bodies for sex." I started kissing her breasts then moved down to her belly. Her nipples extended. I was getting aroused. I was ready for sex. She tried to grab me again, but I gently pushed her hand.

"Why did you move my hand? I want to do this."

"You told me that you will make French love to me Lilli. You don't use a hand for French love." She looked at me and smiled. She leaned on me and started kissing me. The she started sucking hard. She was moving her ass. She took my finger and tried to put it inside in her. "I don't like to use fingers when I have sex Lilli. I will move your left leg and placed it next to my left shoulder. This way her pussy was above my head. I started kissing her pussy and my tongue was a little inside her. Lilli took a condom and she place it on me with her mouth. She stared sliding her body towards erection. When her hips reached my erection she raised up, then down and she took it inside her. She started moving up, down and sideways. I felt good, but I asked Lilli, "Do you like me to teach you something else?"

"What do I need to do Barry?"

"Turn your body, but keep it inside." I was trying to help her, but she said that she didn't need my help. She turned around and kept it inside effortlessly. Now she was facing me. She was happy riding me, moving forward and back. She started to shiver making a high pitch sound. I enjoyed looking at her. After a while she stopped moving and laid on me. She was kissing my chest and throat.

"Barry, I am so happy. I felt her tears."

"Why are you crying Lilli, is something wrong?"

"Everything is perfect Barry. I am crying because I am feeling good. I have never felt like that before. Flavio used me to have sex, I didn't have sex."

"Did you check how long you had sex Lilli?"

"We had sex and for forty nine minutes. Next time we have to get to an hour Barry. I need to be ready for that, I know that you are."

"Why do you think that you need to have sex for one hour Lilli?"

"I don't know. Maybe something is wrong with me. Maybe for the first time I feel that I am woman who wants sex. When you left for your meeting, I looked at the watch the whole time, hoping that you come back soon. I wanted you. My body wanted sex. I am twenty two years old."

"How was your meeting with the lawyer?"

"How did you know that I met the lawyer?'

"Last night you asked me for directions. This is where the lawyer's office is. You forgot that I am from Milan. Many people from Northern Italy know the him. People are afraid of him, because he has a lot of political power and he is a big Mafia. Did you tell him that you stay in hotel Napoleon?"

"Yes, I did but this doesn't concern you Lilli."

"This isn't good for you Barry, because after 9:30am the phone rang two times. Somebody wanted to know where you were." The phone was ringing again. I tried to pick up, but Lilli told me not to. "I will go to speak with Luigi".

"Do you think that the lawyer will kill me?"

"Of course he will kill you. This is Italy." She left. Lilli returned and said that Luigi's friend called and told him that Luigi will have a problem. Luigi said "I think that they want to kill Mr. Moore Lilli. Can you help Mr. Moore?"

"How many days will you stay in Milan?"

"Tomorrow afternoon I will leave Milan and I will be out of Italy."

"You need to cancel your reservation and leave the hotel as soon as possible."

"I will not do that Lilli. The lawyer needs to think that I am in Milan."

"That is much better Barry, because we will be out from Milan." After ten minutes we were ready to leave.

"You got ready quickly like a soldier Lilli."

"Don't tell me, who I am. You need to move your ass faster, because if you don't I will kick your exactly like a soldier."

We were in the elevator and Lilli told me that I need to ask Luigi where the emergency door is.

"You never been here before Lilli?"

"I have been many times, but my client and I used the main door. I didn't need to use the emergency door."

"Are you happy now Barry?"

"I am sorry if I hurt you."

"You didn't hurt me, but you don't understand, that you are in big trouble. We will talk later about that Barry."

I asked Luigi where the emergency door is and I told him that tomorrow I will back to take my things.

"Don't worry about that Mr. Moore, I will collect your staff. Lilli should come and take them. It is for your safety."

"Thanks Luigi. Maybe I will see you, maybe not, but I will never forget what you did for me. Lilli is an amazing girl. Thank you for introducing me to her."

"You need to listen to Lilli, she might be young, but she is smart Mr. Moore? I am so happy for you and Lilli. Finally she was with a real man in bed" and Luigi kissed my two cheeks.

"One kiss for you and one kiss for Lilli." We laughed. We left the hotel and used public transportation to get to her car. She had a small Fiat. Lilli drove fast and well. She kept talking, I listened. She asked me, what happened to me, because I didn't say anything .

"I am ashamed Lilli."

"Are you ashamed, because we used the emergency door Barry?"

"No Lilli. Because I asked if you have been before in hotel Napoleon."

"I have never been, but don't worry about that right now Barry."

I took my American passport and gave it to Lilli. She looked and laughed. "You are not Barry Moore, you are Carl Hope. Now I am with Carl Hope, but I want to be with Barry Moore. If Carl Hope can have sex as well as Barry Moore, I will like him too", and she laughed. Lilli had tears in her eyes. "Last night and this morning I had good sex with Barry Moore. I wish to have more sex with Carl Hope in the afternoon and tonight."

"Is Carl Hope as good as Barry Moore in bed?"

"I will try to embarrass Barry Moore, Lilli. Carl Hope will have sex for one hour."

"That sounds good Carl Hope" and we laughed.

"I am happy. It doesn't matter to me if I am with Barry or Carl, because the name is different, but the body is the same. I would like to tell you what happened in the restaurant last night. When Flavio came and you left, I understood that you are a gentleman. You didn't know what the problem between me and Flavio is, because you knew me for three hours. Flavio asked who you are and what I am doing with you in the restaurant. I told him that you are my boyfriend. He told me that after him I will never have a man and a sex in my life, because he was the first man who had sex with me."

"Remember you tried to kill yourself, because you love me. You will never forget that I had good sex with you Lilli."

"Flavio had sex with me for five to ten minutes Carl, but I didn't understand that was not sex. Flavio was the first man who had sex with me. I didn't have others to compare. I told Flavio that you and I had sex for one hour and I you make me feel like a real woman. I felt good with you. When you returned, you saw that Flavio was laughing and he left. I told my self's, that I must have sex with you, and I had Carl. Now I know that some man have sex for more than ten minutes" and Lilli laughed.

"When you told me the address last night, I knew where you were going. I was there with Flavio ten months ago. Flavio carried a bag with something. I asked Flavio what was in the bag, but he didn't tell me. I knew that he carried money. Honestly, this isn't my business, what you did with the lawyer, but I want to spend more time with you. If somebody has told me before I met you that I will have sex for forty minutes, I would have thought that this person is kidding, but not anymore. You changed my life. Now I am a different person Carl."

"Hey, you started very fast to use my new name." We arrived in Como. Lilli stopped and we went to a hotel. Of course, they knew Lilli.

"Hi Lilli."

"Hi Simona. This is my friend Carl Hope. He is an architect from New York. He would like to see Como's historic center and Lake Como. Mr. Hope is rich and maybe someday will buy a house on Lake Como. I and Mr. Hope will stay one night."

"You know, we have different rooms Lilli. If you want to stay together I recommend that you get the Quadruple room."

"Would you like to stay in the Quadruple room Mr. Hope?"

"I like it" and I gave her my passport and credit card. I signed and Simona gave me the key. Simona said something to Lilli then she turn to me and said "You will have a good time in Como Mr. Hope".

"Thanks Simona" and we walked to the elevator. We entered the room and Lilli told me that Simona likes me and if Lilli doesn't use me tonight, she will be more than happy to come to bed with me.

"Do you want to have sex now Lilli?"

"We have time Carl. I want to show you Lake Como and the downtown. There are many historic houses. If you have three, four millions, you won't have a problem to buy a house here."

"I have more Lilli, but I will buy in New York."

"I have a friend in Switzerland. We are in the same class in the University. He likes more Lugano, because he is from Switzerland. I like more Como, because I am from Italy. He has been many times in my house and he never has tried to kiss me, but I know that he loves me."

"What is his name Lilli?"

"Denis. He lives in Bern. I like Denis, but now I am with you."

"Do you like to see Denis in Bern?"

"I don't know Carl. Now my life is going so fast with you. When you leave I will have to think what to do with my life."

"Where do you want to live in a small city or a big city Carl?"

"I love New York and I will stay in New York, Lilli."

"I love Milan, Carl."

We left the hotel. She showed me many different properties and houses. Lilli knew who lives in the properties.

"Are you working for the Italian secret service, because you know everyone who owns the properties?"

"I have been watching TV and reading the newspapers. They talk and write all the time for the people that live in these properties."

"Do you like your live to be shown every day on TV, Lilli?"

"I won't like that Carl. I know who I am. But many people who have a show on TV or are an actress or an actor need that. This is a free advertisement for them. They like to stay twenty four hours in the public eye. They are crazy and they like somebody to watch their life all the time. They make money from that.

"May I ask you, a personal question? You don't have to give me an answer if you don't want to,"

"What are you going to do when you finish your mission?"

"I will start to build hotels and houses everywhere in the world. I am an architect and I worked two years very hard to get the experience I need."

"You must have a lot of money, to do that Carl."

"I will have the money, but I need to finish this mission and I must stay alive Lilli."

"I will help you Carl."

"I am happy that I am with you Lilli" and I kissed her.

"We need to go back to the hotel Carl.:"

"Why Lilli, we are having a good time outside and I am happy to walk and talk with you?"

"If you are tiered, after two hours we will be ready for dinner and we will sit in a restaurant. We will have dinner. Hey Carl, I can use you for one more day. You must teach me more new things in bed. You aren't a porn producer, but you are a good teacher." We went back to the hotel. I took a shower and I sat on the sofa and waited. She came naked and she asked me "Why are you sitting on the sofa, you need to be in bed?"

"I will teach you something new. Come and sit on my lap." Lilli sat and I kissed her. I thought her what Vicky did in bed the last time we were in Simon's apartment.

"Oh my God! We had sex for one hour and five minutes. I love you Carl. I don't need to love Barry. Life is fun with Carl" and she kissed my body everywhere. We were locked in a long kiss, our tongues giving and taking. We were enjoying our time together. "Hey Lilli, do you like to go out or you want to stay in bed?"

"It will be better if we go out Carl. After dinner we will continue in bed. Are you scared to go back to bed after dinner?"

"Not at all. I want you Lilli" and I rubbed my erection at her side. "He really likes your pussy. We will continue in bed after dinner." We left the hotel. After dinner we had long sex. When we finished we both were happy and tired.

"Now I know what I need to do Carl. I need to use my body when I have sex, not mine or your hand. I am really sleepy" and she closed her eyes.

In the morning when I opened my eyes, my brain went back to work on my mission. The lawyer gave me a phone card to call him. I know that he wants to know where I am. If I was in America, I won't have a problem with the lawyer, but in Europe I do. What should I do? Somebody needs to kill him. Bruno told me that the Sicilian Mafia hates the lawyer. Lilli told me that many people in Northern Italy and Milan are afraid of him and they pay him because of that. As a result the lawyer has a lot of enemies. I must do something and somebody will kill the lawyer, because he has a lot of information. Think, Carl think, I told myself.

I took a shower and I was in the living room when Lilli came. She kissed me and asked "How are you feeling Carl?"

"I am feeling good Lilli, but is it going to be OK if I speak with your friend Dennis?"

"No at all Carl, if you think he can help."

"Could you give me his phone number?"

"Sure" and she wrote it on a piece of paper

"If you have problem with Denis, you need to tell him that you are with me."

I called and asked to speak with Denis.

"This is Denis. Denis, my name is Carl Hope. I am calling you because I am coming to Bern tomorrow. I am in Italy right now. I have business in Bern and I need to invite people to a restaurant. I don't know the city, so I am looking for you to recommend a quiet place."

"I am sorry Mr. Hope, but I don't know you. Who gave you my phone number?"

"Lilli gave me your phone number. Would like to speak with her?"

"Are you her boyfriend?"

"No Denis, I am Luigi's boyfriend."

"Luigi told me that you and Lilli have a good relationship. I never asked Luigi, if Lilli is your girlfriend. This isn't my job to ask people, what kind of relationship they have. I recommend that you go to Schwellenmatteli. The restaurant is quite and the food is good. Write down their phone number." As I was writing down the phone number Denis asked me if he can speak to Lilli now.

"Of course", and I gave the phone to Lilli. I left the living room.

I was in the bedroom getting ready for my trip, when Lilli came and kissed me.

"You know how to have good sex, but you also know very well how to communicate with people Carl. You know what to tell them. Denis invited me to go to Bern and I said yes. He was so happy that am I going to Bern to see him. He thinks that Luigi is a good friend of yours."

"This is true. He is Lilli."

"I don't get you Carl. All I care right now is that you are a mystery lover and I am with you."

We left the hotel and I told her that she needs to stop at a gas station, because I need to make a call.

"I need to call too Carl. I need to speak with Luigi, then go to take your things from hotel Napoleon." Then Lilli went quiet for a while looking at me like she wanted to ask something. I encouraged her. "What is in your mind Lilli? You can ask me anything. I thought you figured that out by now."

"OK, how many girls have you been with this year?"

"In the last three weeks I have been with four girls in bed."

"Am I the fifth one in the last four weeks?"

"Yes, you are correct Lilli."

"Do you love all of them?"

"I love only one of them. She is a special woman. I love her very much, but why are you asking me that Lilli?"

"I am sorry Carl" and she turned the other way not saying anything else. It looked like she was trying to hide her feelings. I decided to let her be and don't ask. We didn't speak until Lilli stopped at a gas station. I called Vito.

"I have a meeting with Hans on Saturday night at 8:00 in restaurant Schwellenmatteli in Bern" and I hung up the phone. Lilli called Luigi and told him what he had to do. We left the gas station and I gave Lilli an envelope.

"What is this Carl?"

"Could you open and see Lilli?" She did as I asked.

"I know that you are rich. I see money. Why are you giving me money Carl? I am with you because I like to be with you. I don't need money. I am not your lover. Luigi is your lover" and Lilli laughed.

"Could you tell me what to do with the money?"

"Give the money to my lover, Lilli."

"Sure, I will do that" and she continued to laugh.

"You are so crazy Carl. If I didn't have a good time with you, I would have kick your ass out of my car right now."

"Hey Lilli, if you throw me when you drive, you will kill me. I want to be your teacher for one more night."

"I think it will be a good idea to keep you alive for one more night then. Life is so much fun with you Carl."

We were at the train station and Lilli told me that I need to buy a ticket for her and I wait for her where the train to Bern leaves. Lilli returned after one hour. We got on the train and soon after it left the station. Lilli was nervous, but I didn't ask her why. I knew that Luigi told her something that made her feel that way. I assumed that when the train passes the border she will tell me.

"I feel tired Carl, I will take a nap. Can I lay may head on your Lap?"

"Absolutely, make yourself comfortable." She laid down and closed her eyes. I was happy that Lilli was with me.

CHAPTER 9

Lilli was sleeping. She moved her head. I looked at her face. A muscle around her mouth was flickering. She was so sweet. I turned away from her and I looked outside through the window. I remembered that Edit enjoyed looking through the train windows when we traveled in Europe. She was sweet too, but this was four years ago when I was in love with her very much. I am a lucky guy, I have had good time with girls. I don't know why, but I remember many things about Edit and Vicky. I guess, it is because they have spent more time with me than the rest of the girls I have known. Life is a joke. I love Edit and Vicky, but I left Edit, Vicky left me. I have a son with Edit. I might have one with Vicky too after the last few days we spent together. We will see. I am the father of Edit's son and I may be the father of Vicky's child, but I didn't marry Edit or Vicky. When Lilli woke up, I need to ask her if she wants to marry me. We had sex, but what will I tell her if she wants to have a child too? How many children am I going to have? Mom will tell me, that it will be a big problem for her to see her grandchildren.

"I need to travel to Paris, Miami and Milan. I am an old woman. You need to bring them to New York. When you decide to buy an apartment, you need to count how many rooms you need for all the women and children you will bring there." I will tell her that she must be happy, because she will have many grandchildren. Mom needs to prepare the children to go to school. She will not have time to think that she is an old woman, because she will be busy. I will tell Mom, that she must stay alive for two hundred years, because she needs to take care of great-grandchildren. I was laughing to myself when a conductor entered the cabin and he asked me for our Lilli's tickets and passports. Lilli woke up. When Lilli tried to take her passport from her bag, I looked at her ass and legs. The conductor saw me and he asked "Are you traveling together?"

"Of course we are together", Lilli told the conductor. "We are going on vacation in Bern."

"Where are going to stay in Bern?", the conductor asked.

"We have reservation in hotel Bellevue-Palace", I told the conductor.

He look at me and said "You are a lucky man, she is beautiful and I wish you a good time in Bern". The conductor left and closed the door.

"Why did he say that I am beautiful Carl?"

"The conductor saw me looking at your ass and legs. He was right Lilli. You have a sexy ass and beautiful legs, but we don't have a room, so I don't have a chance to touch your ass and legs here."

"Do you love my body Carl?"

"Of course I love your body Lilli. You have an amazing body. I am little jealous that Denis will have your body in bed, but I will wish you and Denis a good sex."

"Don't cry about that Carl. Denis is a very shy man. He will never kiss my pussy. You did that. I was so happy when you kissed my pussy and your tongue plied inside. I felt so good. When my pussy took it, I wanted to suck your whole body inside me."

"If you did that, you will kill me Lilli."

"I won't kill you Carl, I will save your life. The lawyer wants to kill you. If you stay inside me, you will be safe. The lawyer won't know where you are." She laughed, then she looked worried.

"The lawyer tried to kill Luigi, Carl, but he has many friends and they saved him. When the lawyer henchmen went to check your apartment in hotel Napoleon, Luigi took your things and moved them in my house. Luigi put someone else's things in your apartment and the henchmen thought that you are in Milan. Luigi loves you Carl and he will never tell them where you are. I was scared when I returned from the apartment, because we were in Milan. I am not scared anymore, because we are in Switzerland. Do you want to know what else Luigi told me?"

"Carl will kill the lawyer Lilli. He will create a big problem for the lawyer and the Mafia will kill him, because he has a lot of information for many people. If police arrests the lawyer, it will be a big trouble for the Mafia, Stasi, KGB and many crime people. They must kill him before the police arrests him."

"I think that Luigi was scared when he told me that."

"He is correct Lilli. I have been thinking of how to create a big problem for the lawyer, so that the police tries to arrest him. I know that the Mafia has informers in the police and it will kill the lawyer before the police arrests him."

"Did you take a business card with name of Peter Volak from the lawyer's office Carl?"

"Yes Lilli, but what is the problem for taking one business card?"

"The henchmen told Luigi that they will kill him and you for that. I think that Peter Volak is the boss of the lawyer or the lawyer depends a lot on him."

"Thank you so much Lilli! Now I know what to do. The police must know and I took the business card with the phone number of Peter Volak. I suspect that he is the person who ordered the attempt in my life in America."

"Who are you Carl, and why do they want to kill you?"

"It is a long story Lilli, but yesterday you saved my life. You were right when you took me away from Milan."

"Do you want me to stay with you Carl?"

"No Lilli. It is not safe to be with me right now. One life is enough. You are young and beautiful. You must look after yourself. I want Denis to marry you. After one year you and Denis will graduate from the University. You have a promising future on front of you. You are both young and educated."

"I am so glad that you are concerned about me, but I don't want to overthink since last night. I want to have sex now. That is what my body is telling me."

"Do you want to have sex here in the cabin?"

"No Carl, but I know a place where we can have sex." Lilli took condoms and told me "Follow me Carl". She opened the restroom door. We went in and she told me "This is the best place we have right now" and she claimed my mouth. I responded. The tight space was not comfortable but we wanted this. All the adrenalin from the morning excitement was in the air. She unbuttoned her shirt and pulled up her skirt. I pulled down my pants and briefs together. I picked her up and she hugged her legs around my waist. She was ready as well as I. I was inside her, moving forward and back. We were breading heavy enjoying our time together in this moment. Nothing mattered, except the two of us. We were entangled in each other. It felt like the time has stopped. At some point we finished. We tight up our clothes and were ready to leave the restroom. I opened the door. A man was waiting outside.

"Oh man what happened? You were the restroom for forty six minutes!" When he saw Lilli he laughed and said, "She is happy that you were there that long" and gave me a conspiratorial wink. Lilli smiled and told him, "Thank you sir. You are right, I am happy". We went back to the cabin. It was comical what just happen, because Sisi wanted to have sex in the plane's restroom and I didn't want to do it, but I now I sex with Lilli in the train restroom. I guess the circumstances are very different.

"If I call you and I ask you to fly with me somewhere, would come?"

"I will fly Carl, but why are you asking this question?"

"Sisi is air-hostess and when we flew together she talks about us having sex in the plane's restroom, but she didn't take me there. If we are in the plane together, I know that you will do it."

"Why not Carl?" We laughed when the door opened. Lady between forty to forty five years old told us, "My husband told me what happened in the restroom and I told him that I want to go to see this boy. I want you in my bed boy, but I see that you are in the company of a young and beautiful lady. I wish you a good trip" and she closed the door.

"Do you prefer me and for how long Carl?"

"Tomorrow you will be in Denis's arms, Lilli. You need to ask Denis, but if I decide to fly, I will call Denis and ask him if I can take you to fly with me so that you help me find the restroom in the plane. Do you think that Denis will tell you that you need to fly with me Lilli?"

"I think that Denis will ask you why do you need Lilli to help you find the restroom Carl?"

"I know that you are joking, but you need to tell me what to do when I see Denis tomorrow."

"You need to listen to him. Don't say anything."

"I don't know Denis, but I think that he will ask about your relationship with me. You said that he is shy. When Denis sees you tomorrow, he will be happy that you are there, but next day he will ask you if I am your friend or your lover. You must know that shy people don't trust. They need time and when they are sure that you are not lying, they will believe you. When you speak with Denis you must think before you say something. If Denis doesn't believe you, you need to ask him why should you be with him, if he doesn't believe you."

"You should leave Denis, if he asks you to leave. If he calls you later and apologizes telling you that he regrets not trusting you, don't speak with him. He must understand that he needs to think before he decides to punish you. You aren't his property. You are a human being. Your life with me is in the past Lilli. You told me that you have spent a lot of time with Denis. Why Denis didn't he take you to bed to have sex? Past is in the past Lilli. Denis doesn't need to ask you for me and your past. Denis needs to look in the future. If someday I decide to marry and the woman asks me for my past, I will never marry her. If I was married I will divorce her."

"How long have known Denis?"

"I met him three years ago in the University."

"Why did you choose to get involved with Flavio?"

"My mom likes Flavio, because he is Italian and she thinks that he is rich. Denis is from Switzerland. Don't ask me why I am with you Carl. I am so happy that I met a man who gave me back my life and gave me a good advice. You changed my life two days ago. I know that tomorrow I will have difficult day, because we will go in our separate ways and I will meet Denis. You need to understand me Carl. I am on Everest with you today. Tomorrow I will be in the ocean with Denis. Tomorrow my body will drop from 8,848 meters, but I need to survive. You gave me a lot of power and advice. I understand what you are saying to me. I must fight for my life. I don't need somebody to decide for me."

"You are right Lilli. You are so beautiful, smart and educated. If you love Denis, you go with him. But if you have a problem with him, you should go and meet another man. You need to choose somebody."

"You forgot to say that now I have more experience in bed too Carl. I can teach others a thing or two."

"Don't say that, because I am jealous" and we laughed.

"Life is good and a lot of fun with you Carl, but if you are lonely, Luigi will be there waiting for you."

"Hey Lilli, do you know that Luigi and I kissed on the cheeks?"

"Oh my God! Looks like you will have lover, no matter who." We laughed and we had terse in our eyes.

"If Denis gives you hard time tomorrow, to go back to Milan, but call Luigi to make sure that you don't have problem to go back. If you do, you need to call this number in Paris. This is the phone number of Edit. Call Edit and tell her that you need to stay in Paris."

"Who is Edit?"

"Just tell her that you were with me in Milan and you have a problem. Edit will never ask you, what your problem is."

"Is that the same Edit you spoke with, when we were in the restaurant?"

"Yes. Edit and I have a son."

"Oh my Gog, you have a son?"

"How old is he? Do you know his name?"

"He is three years old, but I don't know his name. I didn't know about him until last week, when I was with Becky on vacation in the Bahamas. She told me that I have a son, but Edit never told me. Last Monday I was with Vicky and she told me too. Mom told Vicky that I have a son in Paris, but she never told me, because she doesn't like Edit. My mom thinks that Edit is old for me. I am planning to see my son next week, but I don't know which day. I will call Edit before I go to Pairs, and I will know then. You have a good time with Denis Lilli, but you need to think. I am having a very good time with you Lilli. I love Luigi, because Luigi introduced us and I am happy, that we spend time together." Lilli kissed me.

"I am happy too Carl. You are right and I need to listen to you, because the lawyer's henchmen tried to kill Luigi. If they know that I was with you, they will try to get information from me about your ware bouts and they will kill me. If I have a problem to go back to Milan, I will call Edit."

"Could you tell me more about what to do with Denis?"

"If Denis invites you in his home or apartment and you are alone with him, don't take Denis in bed and push him to have sex. You must wait for him to take you in bed. Don't show him that you have experience in bed. Denis needs to show you, what he knows in bed. Denis is a shy boy. You may be his first woman. You need to encourage Denis, but you don't try to teach him. If

Denis loves you and he likes to marry you, then you teach him slowly in bed. It will be better if you and Denis drink wine before sex. Alcohol makes man to be more aggressive in bed. When Denis is aggressive, then you can teach him. You need to tell him that you are very happy with him in bed. If Denis asks how Flavio was, you tell Denis that Flavio made sex for ten minutes, but he was your first man in bed and you didn't understand. You tell Denis's, that he needs to have sex longer than ten minutes, if he wants to be different."

"Do you think that I need to tell him that?"

"You tell Denis, but you don't mention my name. If he tells you, that he knows that I was your lover, you tell him that I am your friend and that I am Luigi's lover."

"You are Carl." We laughed. We arrived in Bern. We took a taxi to the hotel. I checked my reservation. Everything was OK. I paid for two nights and we took the elevator. We entered the room and I asked Lilli, where she likes to have dinner, in the room or out.

"I prefer that we go to a restaurant Carl. I will be ready to go out in twenty minutes."

I took a shower and changed. I was ready. I sat on the sofa waiting for Lilli. She came from the bathroom. She looked so different. I couldn't move.

"What happened with you Carl, I am ready?"

"You look so hot and sexy Lilli. I changed my hair style on my clothes. My body is the same."

"Your body is the same, but your hair and clothes changed your body."

"You have been looking at my body for three days. Finally you discovered that I am hot and sexy? Come on Carl. We don't have time for bed now. We were in the lobby when somebody said "You look hot and sexy lady".

"May I take picture of both of you?"

"Why not? I like to have picture with you Carl."

The gentleman who took the picture asked me "Are you Carl from New York?"

"He is from New York sir", Lilli told him. My friend Simon lives in New York. Every time when Simon travels to Europe I watch Simon's back. When you have the picture ready, you send it to my room and I told him the room number."

"I will." He kissed Lilli's hand.

"Have a good evening" and he left.

"Why didn't you ask for his name Carl?"

"When he gives me the picture I will ask him." We entered the restaurant. Many people turned and looked at us. Lilli took my hand and she asked me "Why are they looking at us Carl?"

"I told you that you look hot and sexy, but I am with you. I will not give a chance for somebody else to touch you. I am a jealous man" and I laughed.

"How many people are in your party sir?", the hostess asked me.

"Two lady."

"Follow me." She took us to a table for two close to a window with. I pulled the chair and helped Lilli to sit down.

"The restaurant looks pompous Carl."

"You need to open your heart Lilli. This is the last night, we will be together."

"I would like to see you again someday Carl."

"If you have a permission from Denis, Lilli."

"Why, do you think that I will marry Denis?"

"I am joking Lilli, but you need to think for the man that might be your future husband. You had one disaster in your life. Don't do that again. You must hear your heart and think with your brain. You don't need to listen to other people."

"May I ask, why you didn't marry Edit?"

"I told you. My mom didn't like her. I had two choices. Mom or Edit. I let Edit go."

"You are right Carl. I need to do what I want, because my mom pushed me to marry Flavio and this was so bad."

"Could you give me your hand Carl? This is our last night. I feel good with you" and she kissed my hand.

I kissed her hand too. After dinner we came back to the hotel room. We had a wonderful night. Lilli did everything I taught her in bed. I didn't say anything about it, but it looked like Lilli read my mind and she said "I did that, because I wanted to remember this night forever Carl." Lilli kissed me and she closed her eyes with her head on my shoulder. We feel asleep like that. When I woke up, Lilli wasn't in bed.

I took a shower. When I came back, she walked in the bedroom.

"I spoke with Denis, Carl. I will meet him at 10:00 a.m. You need to come with me."

At 10:00 a.m. we meet Denis. He was not able to take his eyes from Lilli.

"Carl this is Denis." We shook hands, but he looked at Lilli. Denis' mouth was open.

"You are so beautiful. You look different than the last time I saw you in Milan."

"I am the same Denis."

"I am happy that you came to Bern."

"Carl insisted that I come."

"How long do you plan to stay in Bern and where are you staying Lilli?"

"I wanted to see you this morning, because in the afternoon I am going back to Milan. Carl has a business to attend to and I will have to be alone."

"You can stay with me Lilli. We can get a hotel or If you like you can stay in my house."

"What are you going to tell your parents?"

"Don't worry Lilli. I told them that I have a friend, Lilli, from Milan and they asked me to invite you to Bern. I promised to invite you, but you know, I am shy. Now you are in Bern and I like you to meet them. They are on vacation right now. They will be back in four days, so if you stay, you can meet them. They will be happy to meet you."

"Do you love Lilli?" I asked Denis.

"Of course I love Lilli. Now I am not scared to tell her, but a year ago I was. Flavio asked her to marry him. He left Lilli and now I have a chance to ask her. If Lilli decides to live with me, we need to decide what to do in the future."

"You are right Denis."

"I need your help Dennis. I have a name of a person, but I don't know where he lives in Switzerland. How can I find that?"

"You have two choices. The police or the banks. My father works in a bank, but he will ask you to go to the police."

"I will ask the police Denis, but if I need to meet your father I will call you. Where do you want to work after you graduate from the University?"

"I want to work in Bern, but if somebody offers me good money and freedom in my work, I will go to work anywhere. Look at this building, Carl. It looks OK for most people, but you see, on the right side of the third floor three windows are missing. I think that they have built inside a secret or a dark room or something that few people know about. They are hiding something there. The building doesn't look right."

"Dallas."

"What did you say Carl?"

"Nothing Denis, but if you decide to marry Lilli, I will give you money to buy a ring for her." I gave Denis a check for three thousand dollars.

"This is a lot of money Carl."

"I have money Denise and I will be happy if you marry Lilli."

"You will have to come to the wedding, for sure"

"I will do my best to be there Denis. Maybe I will marry too."

"I need to leave now. You take care of Lilli." I kissed Lilli's hand then I shook Denis's hand and I left. I was in the hotel room, when I heard a knock on the door. I opened.

"Come in, I was waiting for you. I am alone."

"You are Carl Hope. My name is Aaron Vogel. I told you my original name, because Simon told me that you will find it. I have known Simon for many years and I trust him. Where is the girl?"

"She went to see some relatives and she decided to stay with them."

"I told Simon that you were with a beautiful girl. Simon laughed and he told me that he is not surprised, because you are always in the company of a beautiful girl."

"Can you tell me what happened in Sicily, Carl?"

I told Aaron and he asked me "Why did you tell Vito where you were staying?"

"I wanted to provoke him."

"If you stayed any longer in Milan, Vito would have killed you Carl."

"Why does he want to kill me?"

"You were in Sicily. Vito didn't know what you did there."

"I told Vito that I was in Sicily to meet with Bruno Corso."

"That sound very suspicious, because you arrived with a private jet and a man who is your boss. Where is your boss now?"

"My boss never tells me where he goes. Do you think that Vito will try to kill me in Bern?"

"Vito already sent two people to kill you tonight in Bern."

"How do you know that?'

"I have been in this business for thirty years. I have people everywhere. I need to save your life, because if somebody kills you, your mom will kill Simon. I need to take your Irish passport Barry."

"Do you have any information on Hans, Aaron?"

"I tried to find Hans. A man offered me a lot of money to find Hans, but nobody knows where he is. I spoke with Lorenzo. He told me that you are a good man and you can handle a pistol well Carl."

"I told Vito that I have a dinner with Hans in restaurant Schwellermatteli. I need a man that looks fifty five, sixty years old."

"Why did you tell Vito, that you have a dinner with Hans?"

"You told me that Vito send two people to kill me. I will kill them. I will need a pistol Aaron. Can you give me yours?"

"I don't have a pistol now. I carry one only when I need to use it. I will kill Vito's people when they come to kill you in the restaurant."

"I don't think that they will try to kill me in the restaurant. Too many witnesses. I am pretty sure that they will be waiting outside. If that doesn't work they will look for another chance later somewhere in Bern. Do you have a friend who so fifty five, sixty years old?"

"Why do you need that Carl?"

"He will be Hans. The people that will come to kill me need to see me with another man. They will think that this man is Hans."

"They will kill you and my friend too, because he is with you."

"Do you think that I am stupid Aaron?"

"I must kill them. I need to know where Vito's people will be waiting for me."

"Who will give you that information?"

"I was expecting that you will find that information for me Aaron. I need you to watch my back."

"I need to make a call Carl."

Aaron called and spoke with somebody, but I didn't understand, because Aaron he was speaking German. When he hang up, he told me that his friend will be in the restaurant at 8:00 o'clock tonight.

"Who will kill Vito's people Aaron, I need to know that now?"

"Why do you need to know now?"

"If you don't want to kill them, I must have a plan, how I will kill them and I need a pistol for that."

"I will kill them Carl, you don't need a pistol."

"I prefer to have a pistol Aaron."

"Can you give a pistol to your friend? When he arrives at the restaurant can give it to me. He isn't a professional Carl."

"What do you want me to do after I kill Vito's people, Carl?"

"I will give you this business card. You need to put the business card in the pocket of one of death bodies."

"Why do I need to do that?"

"The business card has the name of a person who lives and works in New York, but he works for the KGB. The police will find the business card with the name of the person who works for the KGB."

"I don't understand you Carl?"

"You need to read the name on the business card. The printed name is Vito Lombardy. The handwritten name with a pencil is Peter Volak. Vito is the Mafia. Peter is the KGB."

"Who has a bigger power Aaron, the Mafia or the KGB?"

"KGB has a bigger power and they keep control everywhere."

"You are right Aaron. Peter will kill Vito, because Vito has a lot of information. Vito uses KGB, Stasi and many crime people. Everybody closes their eyes because Vito helps them in Italy, but he uses them to make money. The moment the police decides to pay Vito a visit he will be dead."

"You want Vito dead? Vito likes to kill you and find Hans. You will kill Vito and find Hans."

"Exactly Aaron. You got it."

"My friend's name is Ben, Carl. I need to speak with Simon and I will be around the restaurant tonight. When you finish your dinner with Ben, take a taxi and go back to the hotel. Ben knows what to do. See you tomorrow morning at 10:00 o'clock, Carl" and Aaron left my room. I picked up the phone and I called Jerry Shapiro.

"Jerry this is Carl."

"Oh my God! Where are you? I have a big problem with Julia. She told me that I am your brother, but I do not care for you. She told me that I need to speak with Simon and he must tell me where you are. Simon and he told me, that Julia needs to zip her mouth. I called and asked Ethan and Michelle and pushed them to ask Simon. They told me that if they knew, they would have told Julia."

"Simon is right Jerry. Mom must zip her mouth and stay in Dallas. When everything is OK, I will call and tell her when she can return to New York."

"I will tell her that Carl."

"Where is Max, I need to speak with him?"

"He is in Geneva. Max loves it there."

"Could you give me his phone numbers in Geneva?"

"Give me a moment. Are you ready to write it down Carl?" He gave me Max's phone numbers at the home and at work.

"Do you need anything else Carl?"

"When you speak with Mom, tell her that I am sending her a kiss."

"I will Carl", and Jerry hung up the phone. I know that Jerry didn't tell me everything that Mom told him, but she knows that I am fighting to save my life and she is scared for me. I know that if they kill me, Mom will not forgive herself. I must stay alive. I called Max's. He was at home.

"Where are you Carl?"

"Grandmother called and asked about you."

"I am in Bern, Max. Tomorrow I will be in Geneva. I will call you, when I make it to Geneva."

"Come to my house Carl."

"Thank you Max, but I will stay in a hotel. I can't tell you why right now. We will talk when we meet."

"See you tomorrow Carl."

"I ordered a taxi for 7:30 p.m. I was at the restaurant at 7:55. The hostess asked me how many people will be for dinner, but I saw that somebody was waving at me.

"My friend is waiting for me lady" and I walked to table where Ben was.

"Nice to see you Ben. Me too Carl" and we shook hands.

"You should call me Hans and I will call you Barry, because we don't know who can hear us. What do you like to drink Barry?"

"White wine Hans and I prefer fish for dinner." The waiter came and we ordered Chardonnay from the Burgundy wine region of eastern France and rainbow trout for dinner.

The waiter brought the wine and poured into our glasses. "Cheers Barry!"

"Cheers Hans." I asked Hans if he has a pistol for me.

"I have one for me Barry."

"Didn't Aaron tell you to bring one for me too?"

"He didn't."

We ate. The waiter arrived and gave a piece of paper to Ben. Ben told me that two people were waiting outside for us.

"You aren't a professional Barry."

"I am not Hans."

"Why are you doing this? You are too young to risk your life? Aaron told me that you have experience with women, but you don't have the experience to save your life. Aaron thinks that if they don't kill you tonight, they will kill you in the next two or three days."

"Why did Aaron tell Simon, that he will watch my back?"

"I think, when Vito's try to kill me, Aaron will watch and he will be happy Ben."

"Who knows Barry?"

"Maybe you are right" and he laughed.

"Don't worry. I am with you Barry. I spoke with Simon too. I know who you are."

"Do you know Vito, Ben?"

"Vito works with the KGB and the Mafia."

"He is the Mafia, Hans".

"Do you think that Aaron will help me kill Vito?"

"He will, because Aaron hates him. I don't know why. Aaron has been in this business for more than thirty years."

"Do you trust Aaron, Hans?"

"I trust him Barry, but who is who in this business. Nobody knows anybody. Many of my friends were killed, because somebody gave information for them, but I am alive. Aaron is too."

"Cheers Barry."

"Cheers Hans. You must be happy to say cheers, because you are alive Hans"

"You are right about that Barry" and we laughed.

"Simon was right when he told me that you like to joke all the time, but you have a logical argument, because Aaron must keep you alive, but you don't trust him. You are sensitive and you are feeling that Aaron isn't honest with you. This will save your life Barry."

"Why does Simon uses Aaron to watch his back?"

"I don't know that Barry. Simon is my best friend, but he chose

Aaron to watch his back for the last thirty years."

"How did Aaron meet Simon? Are they old friends?"

"I introduced them. Aaron told me that he wants to watch Simon's back when Simon travels in Europe for his safety."

"Why does Aaron think that Simon isn't safe in Europe?"

"After the Olympic Games in Munich, many things changed Barry."

"Do you know how long I have known Simon, Hans?"

"I spoke with Simon for you, but I didn't ask him how long he knew you Barry. I thought that Simon knew you for many years."

"You are right Hans. He knows me for many years, because my mom is Jewish, but I spoke to Simon for the first time two weeks ago."

"Do you trust Simon, Barry?"

"I do Hans. I think that Simon loves me, but I don't know why."

"This is my phone number Barry. Don't tell Aaron that you have it. I think that Aaron likes to keep you close to him. I don't know why. Maybe Simon told him, that Aaron needs to stay very close to you."

"Did you know Louis Dreyfus, Hans?"

"I knew Louis before I met Simon. I had been with Louis in Paris and Zurich many times. When somebody killed Louis and his wife, I met Aaron and I asked him about it. Aaron told me that Louis killed his wife and he committed suicide. I didn't believe that Barry. Louis had a big heard and he loved life."

"Did you tell Simon that Louis didn't kill his wife and committed suicide?"

"Simon, Aaron and I were together when I tried to tell Simon, but Aaron told me that I was wrong. Simon didn't take a side and I never spoke again with Simon for Louis. Louis was Simon's brother. Simon needed to know what kind of a man Louis was."

"You are right Hans." The waiter brought another piece of paper.

"Every think is OK Barry. When you are ready we will leave."

"I need to order a taxi Hans."

"I will drop you at the hotel. I am with a car."

"Aaron told me that I need to get a taxi."

"Aaron knows very well that I am with a car. I know that you need to get a taxi, if Aaron told you, but I will change Aaron's plan."

We were walking when Ben told me that I need to lie on the ground. I threw my body on the ground and I heard that bullet missed my head. Ben opened the car with the remote control and he told me that we need to run fast to the car. We jumped in the car and Ben started the engine. Ben pushed the gas and we left the parking very fast.

"You are lucky Carl. God saved your life. This was Aaron's mistake Carl."

"Do you think that we need to go back and see what happened with Aaron?"

"If we go back the police will ask us, what we saw. Tomorrow morning we will have the news Carl."

"Where do you want me to drop you?"

"In the hotel ", and I told Ben where the hotel was.

"Why did you change the hotel Carl, because Aaron told me a different name for your hotel?"

"If I have problem in future, may I call you to help me?"

"Of course Carl. You call me any time if you have problem and me or my people will help you."

"Thanks Ben" and I left the car. I entered the hotel and took the elevator. I took a shower and lay in bed. The phone rang. I didn't know what time it was. I picked up.

"Good morning Carl. This is Denis. I am sorry to call you so early in the morning, but Lilli asked me to."

"Don't worry Denis, I woke up thirty minutes ago."

"What is going on?"

"Lilli wanted to know if you have a preference for the ring for her, because you gave me the money."

"I don't have anything in mind, Denis."

"Could you tell her that she needs to choose the ring?"

"If you need more money I will send you a check, but I don't have your address Denis."

"This is OK Carl. We will choose a ring and if the ring costs more I have money in the bank. You know, my father is banker."

"How was your dinner last night Carl?"

"It was OK Denis. The people wanted to know where they need to invest. I told them that the Caribbean is a good place to invest, but they need to have a lot of money, because the land is expensive there."

"What time did you leave the restaurant?"

"I think that we left around 10:30 p.m., but I didn't look at my watch. I was in the hotel by 11:00. Why are you asking?"

"The police found two bodies in a trunk of car. The car was parked in the parking at restaurant Schwellenmatteli. Many people are wondering what happened, because Bern is a quite city."

"I don't know Denis, but there are crime people everywhere nowadays."

"Did you watch the TV news this morning?"

"No. I was in bed when you called me, but I don't care what happened on parking at restaurant Schwellenmatteli. This is the job of the police. I didn't stay in the parking to see what happened there."

"Why did you ask me what happened on parking at restaurant? Do you think that I have something to do with it? If you think that, you need to call the police and tell them."

"I have a personal question Carl, do you love Lilli?"

"Why did you ask me that Denis when you are with Lilli?"

"Because when the police said that one of the men that was killed was Barry Moore, Lilli started to cry and she told me that you were killed."

"I am Carl Hope Denise, and I am alive."

"Could you ask Lilli, who Barry Moore is?"

"Maybe Barry Moore loves Lilli, but he was killed. You need to be happy that somebody killed her ex- lover. If you think that, I am her lover, I am alive. Could you ask Lilli, if she loves me or not? I will be happy, if Lilli loves me, but I think that she doesn't. I don't love her either. If Lilli hears this conversation, I don't think that she will be happy."

"She heard it Carl. I don't like to talk behind her back."

"Did you ask her what she thinks when you asked me if I loved her?"

"Lilli told me that if I don't want her, she will leave, but she doesn't love you Carl."

"Let me give an advise Denis. You need to spend time in bed with a woman if you want to keep her happy. Follow my advice."

"Two women left me, because I spent more time to asking them questions, but I didn't spend any time in bed with them."

"If you continue to investigate, what happened on the parking of the restaurant, somebody will jump in bed with Lilli. Do you want that Denis?"

"I love Lilli and I don't want that."

"Somebody is knocking at my door Denis. I have to go now. I am sorry, but maybe someday we will continue this conversation" and I hung up the phone. I opened the door. "Come in Aaron. I was waiting for you."

"Did you watch the TV news this morning Carl?"

"I don't like to watch news Aaron."

"Do you like to know what happened last night?"

"Did you kill the people who tried to kill me last night Aaron?"

"I killed them and I put your Irish passport in the pocket of one of them. I put the business card you gave in the pocket of the other. Now Vito must answer to the police, why the dead man had his business card and what kind of business they are in. Many people in Milan know that Barry Moore was in Milan. Vito must answer why Barry Moore was killed and who did it. I think that by Monday somebody will kill Vito, Carl, because the police from Bern will send people to Milan to ask Vito or the Milan police will ask him."

"Do you hate Vito, Aaron?"

"I had a problem with Vito many years ago and I hate him. We must be happy, because we are alive. Where are going from here Carl?"

"I am going to Paris, but I will stop in Geneva first."

"I can droop you in Geneva with my car."

"I will be ready in an hour. Wait for me in the lobby." Aaron left the room. I picked up the phone and called Hotel de la Cigogne in Geneva. "My name is Carl Hope. I have been in your hotel four years ago. I like to stay again in your hotel and I in the same room" and I told them the number of the room. "I have business in Geneva and I will stay four nights." I gave them the information of my credit card.

"You have a reservation for the same room for four nights."

"Thanks lady.'

"My name is Clara."

"Thanks Clara."

I called Max and told him that I will stay in Hotel de la Cigogne. "I will be in Geneva between three and four in the afternoon. You need to wait outside and when I enter the hotel, you follow me."

"I will be there at three o'clock Carl." I left the room and checked out. Aaron was in the lobby waiting for me. We left Bern with Aaron's car. We didn't speak. I was happy that we didn't speak, but Aaron was nervous.

"Where are you staying in Geneva?"

"I am staying in Hotel President. It is close to the lake and has a beautiful view."

"Don't you have relatives in Geneva?"

"I don't have Aaron."

"What do you think about Hans, Carl?"

"Nothing Aaron."

"You wanted to find Hans, but now you don't. Why did you change your mind? Yesterday you were positive. Today you are negative."

"Yesterday I thought that somebody was watching my back, but today I think that somebody wants to kill me."

"Who is this somebody Carl?"

"I don't know, but last night a bullet came near my head. I think that next time, he won't miss me, but you were right Aaron, we are alive. I need to think what I am going to do next time when he tries to kill me."

"You are lucky Carl."

"I am Aaron."

"Do you think that Hans has another name?"

"How many names do you have Aaron?"

"Five or ten."

"How many passports you have Aaron Vogel?"

"Everybody who works for any inelegant service has many names and passports."

"You have two Carl."

"Of course Aaron, I have two, but I work for Simon. Why are you asking me for Hans?"

"I tried to find Hans in the past, Carl. And I was not successful. I have a friend that works in a bank. I told him to check, if Hans Weber has a bank account."

"Why did you do that?"

"I was trying to find where Hans lives in Switzerland."

"Who told you to do that?"

"Simon, but this was many years ago."

"Do you know that Dreyfus's family has diamonds in a Swiss Bank, Carl?"

"I don't Aaron. Simon and I have never spoken about family diamonds."

"Why is Simon paying you? You came with a private jet to Sicily and you have credit card that is used by the very rich people. It looks to me you can afford it yourself."

"Because I will marry Michelle. She is his niece. Michelle is Ethan Dreyfus's daughter. The Dreyfus family pays me to meet and have sex with beautiful women who teach me how to have good sex with Michelle. If I don't know how to please her in bed, Michelle won't marry me. The Dreyfus family will cancel the marriage. Now I have sex with many women and they are teaching me. I want to marry Michelle, because she has hundred million dollars in the bank. When I get the money, I will disappear. Do you think that I am stupid Aaron? I may not get Michelle's money after all the trouble I am going through."

Aaron stopped talking. We arrived and he dropped me at hotel President.

"Good luck Carl. I wish you to find the diamonds of the Dreyfus family."

"I will find them Aaron and I will be rich. You will stay poor and stupid. Next time when you shoot at me, don't miss my head, because I will not miss yours. If you don't believe me, ask Lorenzo. He knows very well who I am. Now you know that you and I are enemies. I am happy to kill an enemy. Good luck Aaron and you need to stay away from me." I entered the hotel. The lady at the front desk asked me "May I help you sir?"

"I am looking for my friend Aaron Vogel. He stays in this hotel and he will pay if I stay here. My name is Carl Hope."

"I will check sir."

"Call me Carl, lady."

"We don't have a person with the name Aaron Vogel, Carl."

"I have to call and ask Aaron, why he isn't in the hotel."

"You my use the hotel phone Carl."

"Thanks. I will use the public phone." I walked to the public phone. I called and I told Max that I will be in hotel de la Cigogne after thirty minutes.

"I will be waiting for you, Carl."

I returned at the front desk.

"My friend has a problem and he will come to Geneva four days from now. I don't have the money to stay in this hotel. Could you recommend to me some hotels where I can pay one hundred per night?"

She wrote on a paper several hotels. I took the paper, thanked her and left. I took a taxi and it dropped me nearby Hotel de la Cigogne. I saw Max. I entered the hotel and Max followed me. I checked in and took the key. We went to my room.

"What are you doing Carl? Where have you been? Everybody is concerned for you! I am getting calls from everyone in the family, but now seeing you I don't understand why. You look great! Julia has been calling more than everyone else. I told her that I don't know your ware bouts. She got pretty upset with me."

"You are the same as your father. Jerry told me that he doesn't know where my son Carl is. Jerry is lying, you are too Max."

"Don't worry about Julia, she is worried like any mom is. I will call her. I am in Geneva, because I need your help. I must find a man who lives in Switzerland, but I don't know where he lives. If I give you a name, can you see if your bank has that information?"

"If he has a bank account, the bank must have this information, but remember there are many banks and cities in Switzerland. I need you to check first in Zug. If you don't find a person with this name, you need to check for people with the same last name."

"Give me the name Carl."

"Hans Weber, but he has second name Hans Wabern."

"So, you don't want anybody to know the other name, Hans Wabern."

"You are right Max. I don't want that."

"Do you know how many people know about Hans Wabern today?"

"Only two people, me and you. The third was Julia's husband, but somebody killed him twenty five years ago. I don't know how many people in Zug know Hans Wabern, they may know Hans Weber. How many days will you need to get this information?"

"Call me on Tuesday afternoon Carl. May I ask you something?"

"I am listening Max."

"Could you tell me the name of the last woman who was in bed with you?"

"Her name is Lilli, Max. She is from Milan, but this is in the past. She left me, because she met another man. Lilli will see how he does in bed and after that she will decide who is better."

"Where is she now?"

"Lilli is with Denis in Bern. She may marry him."

"I love you for that Carl. You know what to do with women. I don't."

"Hey Max, I need to ask you, what do I buy for a three year old boy?"

"I don't know Carl. You need to ask the sales people at a toy store, or you can ask the lady on the front desk of the hotel. Who's boy are buying these toys for?"

"My son. Edit and I have a son. I am going to Paris to see Edit. It will be her decision, if I can see my son."

"Oh my God. You are a father?"

"Hey Max, looks like a I am big daddy."

"Do you like to have dinner with me tonight?"

"No Max. I don't like anybody to see us together tonight. We will have dinner after Tuesday."

"Is your life at risk Carl?"

"Yes, it is. I have only two or three weeks to figure this out Max."

"I will find what you need Carl, because if I don't Grandmother will kill me." We laughed.

"I will have the information by Tuesday, you can count on me. Call me in the afternoon Carl" and Max left.

I turn on the TV. They were continuing to talk about the story in Bern. The good news was that they talked about Vito Lombardy from Milan and Peter Volak from New York. Now I know that Aaron Vogel wants to eliminate them. He wants to take the diamonds of the Dreyfus family. Aaron was watching Simon's back for many years. He wanted to be close to him because he thinks that Simon knows where the diamonds are. Simon will be very angry when he understands that Aaron used him as bait to find the diamonds. I will joke a lot with Simon about that. I will tell him that he is a small fish for the shark Aaron. As a result now we need to kill two sharks. I picked up the phone and I asked, what is the schedule of the train from Geneva to Paris. I had two choices, the morning or the afternoon. If I take the train in the morning I won't have time to buy toys. I need to ask the lady on the front desk, what at time the toy store opens. I was in the lobby to ask her. When I approached her she asked me "Do you remember me Mr. Hope? I spoke with you this morning."

"Yes. You are Clara. Tomorrow I am going to Paris, but I need to buy toys for a three year old boy and a one year old girl. There is one train in the morning and one in the afternoon. I prefer to go to Paris the morning, but I need to buy the toys before I leave."

"I have a friend. She works in a toy store Mr. Hope, but today is Sunday. The store is closed. Do you like me to call and ask her to help you?"

"Please Clara, that will be great." Clara spoke and she told me, that her friend has toys in her house and if I want she will wrap them and bring the them to the hotel.

Clara hung up the phone and told me, that her friend will be in the hotel after one hour and a half.

"Thanks Clara."

"You are young, good looking and are rich Mr. Hope."

"How do you know that I am rich Clara?"

"I have seen only few people having the credit card you have in this hotel Mr. Hope. I am a married woman with two kids, but my friend is beautiful and single."

"Do you think that she would like to go to bed with me Clara?"

"You need to ask her Mr. Hope. I know you for a short time Mr. Hope, but it is easy to talk to you for everything. I work for many years in this branch, but I never met the someone like you."

"Call me Carl, Clara. When my friend is here, I will call you Carl."

"Thank you so much Clara."

"My pleasure, Carl." I returned in the room and I called Edit.

"Where are you?"

"I am in Geneva. I am staying in the same room we stayed four years ago."

"You will never forget me."

"You are right Edit. I will never forget you."

"When are you coming to Paris?"

"Tomorrow morning I will get the train from Geneva to Paris. I will be waiting for you at train station."

"Are you traveling alone, Carl?"

"I had a women companion until yesterday, but I let her go, so she can marry another man."

"It was the same with me Carl."

"No Edit. I was with her for three days. I was with you for two years. I will never forget that you were my teacher. Now I am the teacher" and we laughed.

"You will never change Carl. You are joking all the time, but nobody knows that you are telling the truth. I love you for that."

"Do you still love me Carl?"

"Hey, you are a married woman. Your husband will kill me if he hears that I love you, but I am ready to die. I love you Edit."

"Oh boy, you are funny."

"Do you want me to bring my son with me?"

"Our son Edit. I will be very happy to see him."

"I will bring him with me Carl" and Edit hung up the phone. Few minutes later the phone rang. I picked up. "She is here Mr. Hope."

"Could you tell her to come to my room, Clara?"

Clara laughed and she told me "You need to come down to the lobby Mr. Hope". I headed down the lobby. There was a woman talking to Clara. I assumed that is whom I had to meet. She was tall and slender built.

"This is Veronica Mr. Hope."

"Nice to meet you Miss. Veronica."

She extended her hand for a handshake, but Instead I took and kissed her hand. Clara laughed and told me "You are young Mr. Hope, but you know how to take the heart of a woman."

"It will be better if I take her in bed Clara." We laughed, but Veronica's cheeks were red.

"I am so sorry for making you uncomfortable with my sexual infused joke Veronica. I just met you. Please accept my apologies if that is offensive to you."

"It is OK Mr. Hope. Could you take the gifts?" She didn't have the courage to look at me. She was still uncomfortable.

I took the gifts and I tried to give her three hundred.

"You don't need to pay Mr. Hope. I will be happy if the children like them."

"I wanted to give you money, because you saved me a lot of time Veronica. Now I can leave for Paris tomorrow morning. If you didn't give me the gifts, I had to take the train in the afternoon."

"I don't want to take money your Mr. Hope."

"Call me Carl, Veronica."

"How many days are you staying in Paris?, Clara asked me.

"I need to be back in Geneva on Tuesday afternoon."

"You paid for four nights. When you made the reservation, you told me that you have been in this hotel with your girlfriend four years ago."

"That is correct Clara."

"Do you like to cancel the reservation for Monday, Carl?"

"No Clara. I think that everything is OK. I like to keep the reservation for four nights."

"You decide Carl. This is your money."

"For whom are these toys?" Veronica asked me.

"Edit lives in Paris. She was my ex- girlfriend. When I left her, I didn't know that she was pregnant. I just recently learned that I have a son."

"Maybe Edit doesn't want to see you Carl."

"I spoke with her half an hour ago. She was happy, that I want to see my son Veronica. Edit will be waiting with my son at the train station."

"Why did you leave her?", Veronica asked me.

"I was twenty two years old and didn't understand many things. Now I know that I should have stayed and married Edit, but you cannot return the time back. My mom came between me and Edit. I love them both, but Mom won."

"I am, so sorry Carl."

"This is OK Veronica, but you need to take the money."

"I won't Carl. Hey I have an idea, Clara. Since Veronica doesn't want to take the money for the toys, can I take you all to dinner at least? Me, you, your husband and you Veronica."

"I don't want to go out Carl. I left my boyfriend and I am not a good company right now."

"Don't worry Carl, my husband and I will go. I like your company and I am sure my husband will enjoy it too. I am sure we will have a good time and a lot of laughs."

"Could you invite your boyfriend Veronica?"

"I am not speaking with him right now."

"Why are not you speaking with him?"

"I saw him kissing another woman."

"Maybe the woman was kissing your boyfriend. I think that she was teaching your boyfriend, how to kiss you better. I think that next time, she will take your boyfriend in bed and show him how he needs to have better sex with you. You need to be happy about that. But you need to tell your boyfriend that it isn't good if he is paying for a teacher in bed. If you marry him, he will spend the family money on women teachers." That made Veronica laugh too and she told me that she will join us for dinner, because I am a very funny man. Clara suggested a restaurant we should go to and she gave me the directions. We will meet at the restaurant at 7:00 p.m.

I went back to my room, took a shower, watched some TV and got ready for diner. I made it there at 7:00 p.m. Clara, Veronica and Clara's husband were already there.

"Carl this is my husband, Chris." Chris had already reserved a table, so we were taken there.

We sat and Clara asked Chris "Why did you ask for a table for six people?"

"This way we will have more room, because we will order a lot of food."

"Do you think that I am stupid Chris?"

"I know that you are Patrik's friend and you want Veronica to sit far away from Carl. Carl will sit next to Veronica."

"This is OK Clara. I don't need to sit close to Veronica in the restaurant. I need to be close to her in bed."

"Hey Carl, this is the girlfriend of my friend."

"I heard that your friend is taking classes how to be better in bed. It is only fair that I teach Veronica too."

"Clara told me that you are funny. Now I believe her" and Chris laughed. "I will tell Patrik that Veronica will be better next time in bed."

"He is here Chris", Clara announced. Patrik came to our table.

"Did you tell Patrik that we are here Chris?"

"Patrik is my friend Clara."

"You should have sked me before you decided to invite him."

"No problem Clara."

"Yes, it is Carl, but I will deal with Chris later."

"Hi Veronica."

"Hi Patrik."

"May I sit Carl?"

"Of course, Patrik."

"How did you know Carl's name Patrik?"

"Chris told me that Carl invited me to the restaurant."

"That is right Patrik. I invited you."

The waiter arrived and asked us for the order.

"Clara you decide for me. I am in your hands", I told her.

"I would have loved to here that, if were in bed."

"Hey Clara, you are my wife and we have two children."

"If I divorce you, I will be free Chris and Carl will be the father of the children."

Clara ordered white wine and fish for me Veronica and her. "Chris, you decide for you and Patrik", she told Chris. He ordered the same for him and Patrik.

"Come and sit next to Veronica, Patrik. I will sit between you and Clara."

"Thank you Carl." The waiter brought the wine and the food. We ate and talked.

"Carl, can you give me your credit card?", Clara asked me. I gave it to her and she asked Patrik "Do you know who has a credit card like this Patrik, since you work in bank?"

"Very rich people have this credit card Clara. They have hundred million dollars."

"Now you know that next to me sits a very rich person, Chris"

"This person is Carl Hope. If you want to stay on this table, you need to tell me, where you were last week Patrik. I called you, but you didn't pick up the phone."

"I went to Zurich with my boss."

"I called you yesterday. It was Saturday."

"My boss met a woman in Zurich and she invited us to Zug. She has a big house there."

"So are saying that your boss was with her? Were you with another woman."

"I spent a lot of time with her uncle. He plays the piano very well."

"What is her name?"

"I told you that he is a man Clara."

"Can you tell me his name?"

"His name is Hans, but he didn't tell me his last name. Hans didn't give me a business card."

"Can you tell me the name of the woman who invited you and your boss in her house?"

"Her name is Greta Wabern Renner. She gave me a business card."

"The man who plays the piano very well is Hans Weber. I met him in Paris four years ago when I was with Edit. He is from West Berlin. He is around fifty five years old, isn't he Patrik?"

"You are correct Carl. Hans looked around fifty five."

"What do you do Carl?"

"I am an architect, but I build hotels and houses everywhere in the world."

"So, you make millions of dollars a year."

"Yes."

"What do you do when you have a free time Carl?", Chris asked me.

"I like to listen to music and paint. I like to travel too. So If I have time I am planning to go to Zurich and Zug."

"Can you draw me Carl?", Chris asked me.

"Why not Chris? I need to ask the waiter for a some paper and a pencil." Clara whispered something to Chris, but I told her "Don't worry Clara. I will eat, drink, speak and draw. I have done that many times." We drank, ate and spoke. When I finished, Chris asked me to see the drawing. I showed him.

'You draw very well Carl. I am surprised, you didn't lie."

"Can you draw me too, but naked Carl?", Clara asked me.

"I will Clara. I will draw you when we are in bed and you can show the drawing to Chris. I think that he will be surprised to see that his wife is beautiful. Chris will discover that when he sees the drawing. He has been in bed with you Clara, but Chris was thinking of other women. When I am in bed with you, I will be thinking of you." We laughed and Patrik asked me "Can you draw me next time Carl?"

"I hope that you don't want me to draw you naked. I will draw Veronica naked and if she will give you my drawing. When you see Veronica naked, you will never kiss another woman. You will kiss only Veronica after that. Hey Veronica can you love Patrik again?"

"I still love him Carl. Thank you for your help. We will be together again."

"I saved your relationship with Patrik. You saved my time when you gave me the gifts for the children.'

"Carl has a son in Paris", Veronica told Patrik.

"How old is your son Carl?", Patrik asked me.

"He is three years old, but I will see him for the first time."

We left the restaurant and Chris told us that next time, he will take us to a restaurant. I was surprised when Veronica kisses me on the mouth. Patrik laughed and said that he is not jealous. Chris asked me if I want a taxi.

"I would like to take a walk Chris, thank you."

I walked and I thought about Clara, Chris Veronica and Patrik when a car stopped next to me and two people jumped out from the car. They were pointing guns at me. One of them told me that I need to enter the car.

"Volodia, help Carl to get in the car." Volodia tried to push me to enter the car, but he lost control. I caught Volodia's hand and took the gun from him. I put Volodia's on from of me and said to his companion "If you don't throw your gun, I will kill you and Volodia." The car window opened and I saw Aaron. Aaron told the second man to give him the gun. He gave gun to Aaron. I saw a light on the corner behind the car.

"Come in the car Carl."

"Thank you, but I prefer to walk Aaron."

"In that case, I will join you." Aaron came out of the car and I gave him the gun. We walked and Aaron asked me "Why did you change the hotel?"

"Somebody was supposed to meet with me in Hotel President. I told the front desk, that I lost my credit card and my friend will come to pay for me, but nobody came. I took a taxi and the taxi dropped me in Hotel de la Cigogne. I was in my hotel room. A man called me and said that because you were with me, he didn't want to speak with me. I am going to Paris tomorrow to see him."

"Do you think that I believe you?"

"This is your problem Aaron, if you believe me or not."

"I will kill you Carl."

"After the incident on Saturday night, your people know that you tried to kill me. If you kill me, they will tell Simon and he will kill you and your family, if you do that."

"How do you know that I have a family?"

"I know everything about you and your family Aaron. Simon too, but now Simon knows that you used him for thirty years to find the diamonds. If I am alive you have a chance to be alive. If I die your chance to be alive is zero. Your choice Aaron. You will never touch the diamonds. Anybody who tried to touch them has died. You need to tell your family, that you have decided to die."

We were on front of the hotel and I asked Aaron "If you want to sleep with me, I will call to tell of Simon that you are good at French love and he needs to pay you for the service."

Aaron left saying nothing. I walked to the hotel room, when

Ben came behind me.

"Come in Ben. I finished with Aaron, now I will start with you."

"Hey boy why did you say that? I want to help you.'

"I know, you are a good man Ben. You saved my live on Saturday night. Aaron tried to kill me, but he missed."

"Why do you think that Aaron was the man that tried to kill you?"

"Because, Aaron fired one shot. If it was someone else they would have fired at least two shots. One shoot for me and one shot for you. Aaron didn't want to have problem with your secret service."

"I think that you are right Carl. My people found one cartridge. Aaron uses the same bullets."

"Don't kill Aaron, Ben. Use me to catch Aaron's people. They will give you a lot of information. Finally you can catch Aaron and send him to your secret service. Aaron works with many secret services from different countries. Tomorrow morning I will go to Paris. Aaron knows that. Can you send people to watch me and Aaron's people, while I am in Paris?"

"I will. You need to look for somebody waiving at you, this will be the person watching your back. Good night Carl" and Ben left.

CHAPTER 10

I was sitting in the train looking at the people saying good bye to friends and loved ones. The train started moving. We were leaving Geneva. I was going to see my son in Paris. Becky was the first person who told me that I have a son. Vicky knew that one year ago, but I think that Vicky was afraid to tell me, because she didn't want to have problem with Mom. I know that Vicky loves me. I love her too. When Vicky understood that she will not marry me, she told me that I have a son. Maybe after nine months she will have a child and I will be the father of that child too. I don't understand why Vicky wants to have a child with me. Honestly, I don't understand women when it comes to their decisions to have children. I am happy with them. I am in bed with women, because they take a lot of my energy, then I have to recharge my battery. I need to have more exercise and keep my body strong. Women are keeping my body healthy. I have thank women for that. If I marry, I will have to remember to thank my wife for keeping my body strong. I think that I will have a wife one day. Becky and Michelle want to marry me. Michelle is OK, because she is single and a virgin, but what if I marry Becky? I will have to sleep with Becky and Marko in the same bed. I think that I can count on Peggy to kick Marko out. If somebody ever reads my thoughts, he or she will laugh a lot, because I am joking with myself. Enough about all the women. I need to think for my son. Maybe my son won't be interested to speak with me. I have not spoken to my father for nine years. My son may tell me "Who are you mother fucker?" He will be right, because I haven't seen him for three years, since he has been born. But knowing Edit I think that she will tell him "Carl is good man and he will be a good father, you need to speak with him". Edit loves me and she will never be between me and my son. I forgot that my son has a father and he lives with his him. Why am I going to Paris to see my son who has a father?...

Maybe I am going to see Edit. But she is married to a man who is the father of my son. I need to stop with my imaginations about my son now. I will know, what kind boy he is, after I meet him and Edit. Edit was happy that I wanted to see him, because she knows that I love her and I will love my son. She knows that if her husband doesn't like me, I will never try to see my son, because I don't want her to have a problem with him. Edit knows me very well and she is right. My thoughts were interrupted by two people that approached me. One of them said "We need to speak with you but we don't want to do it here. We suggest that you follow us". I followed them to another cabin on the train, I sat down and one of them gave me a letter. I opened the letter. Aaron had written instructions for me.

"Are you kidnapping me?", I asked them.

"If you don't listen and stay with us, we will kill you."

"What if I need to use the restroom?"

"One of us will come with you."

I was wandering where Ben's people were. I looked for them. I saw a man who waived his hand, while the two men were facing me. I knew that Ben's people followed Aaron's people. After twenty minutes I told them that I need to use the restroom. I stood up and I saw that the man who waived earlier stood up too. I walked towards the restroom and one of my kidnappers followed me. I opened the door of the restroom and asked "Do you want to come inside with me?"

"I will stay outside." I was in the restroom and thought what I should I do now, when a heard a knock on the door and a man asked me "Can you open the door Carl? Ben sent me to watch your back."

I opened the door. Ben's man was holding Aaron's guy.

"Take him inside Carl." I pulled the kidnapper inside the restroom.

"What do I do now?"

"You have to return back and tell to other person that his

friend has stomach problem and he is in the restroom." I went back and sat down. The other kidnapper looked at me surprised and asked me "Where is my partner?"

"He has a stomach problem and he is the restroom."

"I will go to check on him. You need to come with me." We walked to the restroom. The kidnapper walked behind me. I saw that the same man that helped me was outside the restroom. He looked at us and said "I don't understand, the restroom door is open, but somebody is inside."

"This is my partner. Let me check." He opened the door. Ben's person kicked the kidnapper in the head and pushed him inside the restroom.

"Carl, you need to return to your sit." I did as I was told. Nobody followed me.

I arrived in Paris. I was looking out the window while the train was slowing down to a stop. I saw Edit. She was holding the hand of a little boy with her right hand. I took my bag and started walking towards the exit door. Once I stepped out I walked to them. I dropped the bag and took the boy in my arms. I kissed him and said "He is big boy Edit".

"Now he is little boy, but someday he will be big a boy like his father." She hugged me . Her arms were around my neck and we kissed for a long time. I carried the little boy in my arm. My son kissed first mine and then Edit's mouth. Somebody took a picture of the tree of us kissing. It was so funny. Edit said "God blessed us Carl".

"I want to carry him Edit."

"I will ask him if he wants to you to do that." Edit started explaining something to him in French. He replied back.

"He likes you Carl. Your son's name is Julian Jr. We need to get my car." We walked to the parking lot. I was carrying Julian Jr. We found the car. I put my bag in the truck and we were in the car.

"Would like to go to my husband's apartment or to a coffee shop?"

"I think that I need some time Edit. It will be better if we go to a coffee shop, but one where children can play."

"You will never stop thinking for other people Carl."

"He is not just anybody, he is our son Edit. I must think for him." We stopped and entered a coffee shop that Edit picked. Edit and I sat on a table. Julian Jr. started to play with the other children there.

"So how do I look since the last time you saw me and the fact that I have delivered two children?"

"You look great Edit and your face is beautiful."

"O boy, nobody tells me that. Everyone says to me that I have two children and I am not in my first youth."

"They say that because they are jealous. You look sexy."

"I bet many man have asked you to go in bed with them?"

"When they asked me I thought that they were joking with me."

"They weren't joking Edit. I know that you are a serious woman and you think for your children and your husband. You love them."

"You are right Carl. After you left and I married Julian, I didn't think for other man. Julian isn't perfect, but he saved the life of Julian Jr. I will never forget that. I will never divorce him or go with another man."

"Could you tell me what happened after I left you Edit?"

"You never ask me for my past before. I was with you for two years."

"Why did you change?"

"We have a son Edit. I need to know, why Julian had to save the life of Julian Jr., but if you don't want to remember the past, you don't have to tell me."

"I will tell you, because you need to know, what kind of a man Julian is."

"When you left me I was in deep depression. I cried for two weeks. I called Julian and I asked him for advice. Julian was my lover before I met you, but we had problem and we separated for political differences. After my call, I met with Julian. He was single and I asked him why he didn't marry."

"I still love you, Edit."

"It has been two years Julian. You need to meet another woman."

"I meet them to have sex Edit, but I don't love them."

"Julian asked me to move in his apartment, but I wasn't ready to do that. I worked and sometimes we met for a coffee. The big disaster happen when my menstruate didn't come. I was pregnant. I was happy, because the baby was yours, but I was in panic. I didn't know what to do Carl. I called Julian and we met. I told him that I am pregnant. Do you know what Julian told me?"

"I love you Edit and I want to spend my life with you. Can you marry me?"

"Oh my Gog! I didn't believe it Carl. I told Julian that you are the father of the child."

"Carl isn't here Edit, so I will be the father of the child."

I asked Julian to give me twenty four hours to think about it. The next day we met and I asked him. "Why did you do that Julian? I didn't believe what he told me."

"Children need to have a father. If someday I marry, but I and my wife don't have a child, we will adopt one. What difference does it make, if I am the biological father of this child? If we marry, we will have another child. Mine and your friends will think that I am the father of the children. Nobody will know that the first child has another father. I will love my children."

"We married and we have a second child, Michelle. Everybody knows that Julian is the father of Julian Jr. and Michelle. We live together for four years now. Julian Jr. came and asked Edit something. He wants his father to comes here Carl."

"I would like to meet Julian. Call him."

"I will call, but you need to watch Julian Jr., while I do that."

"I will watch him, Edit."

Edit came back and told me, that Julian will come after thirty minutes.

"Can you tell me what have you been doing? I haven't seen you for four years Carl?"

I laughed and told her. "I have a schedule. Job and women. Women and job. Now I saw Julian Jr. and I will try to change my life, but this will be hard for me Edit. I need some time. Grandmother asked me, when I will marry and I told her that I need one year."

"How is Julia? I know that she was very afraid that you will marry me!"

"She is still afraid that I may marry you. She knows that we have a son, but she doesn't know that you are married."

Julian Jr. came and asked me something in French. Edit took him in her lap. She told me, that Julian Jr. was asking where you live. Edit told him something and Julian Jr. left to play with the children again.

"My husband and I have decided to teach Julian Jr. English. He is a little boy, but Julian told me that he needs to speak English."

Julian Jr. came and told us that his father is here. I saw a man who was carrying a little girl. He came to our table. I stood up and we shook hands. Julian told me that I reminded him of Hercules. Edit said that she will go to get more coffee.

"You need to watch the children Julian. Go ahead Edit, I will watch them." After she left, Julian asked me "How are you feeling after you saw your son, Carl?"

"Good Julian, I didn't know I have a son until very recently."

"Your mom and Edit didn't tell you?"

"No. They didn't."

"How did you find out that you have son?"

"I was on vacation on the Bahamas two weeks ago. I was with Becky and she asked me, if I loved a woman in my past. I told Becky that I had a girlfriend in Paris and I loved her, but I left her four years ago. I haven't see her since, but I have spoken with her and her husband. I told Becky's that you and Edit told me "our son". Becky told me that this is my son. I thought that Becky was crazy, because she loves me and she wanted to have a child with me. But last week Vicky told me that I have a son from Edit too. I was surprised, because I love Vicky and she loves me too. I asked Vicky who told her that I have son in Paris."

"Your mom told me about a year ago."

"I know that Mom loves Vicky and wants me to marry her. I don't know what to tell you Julian. I love Edit as my best friend. Now I saw and I love Julian Jr., but I will never stay between you, Edit and Julian Jr. You and Edit must decide for Julian Jr. You are his parents. I will happy if you allow me help you with money."

I looked at Julian. He looked at me. Edit took a picture. She laughed and she said "Julian loves Carl. I like that. If I need to get a divorce I will show in court this picture and I will tell the Judge that you two are lovers. I need to get a divorce, because they want to marry". This was so funny. We laughed and Julian told me " Carl marry me".

"You need to get a divorce first Julian." We laughed and I felt that Edit was happy. She knew that me and Julian are becoming friends. She was right. We were.

"How old are you Carl?"

"Carl is almost twenty seven Julian", Edit answered.

"How did you know that Edit?"

"Carl was my first love Julian."

"But you were with me before you met Carl."

"You are right Julian."

"I was."

"Where am I Edit?"

"You are my second love Julian."

"Why am I your second love, Edit?"

"Because, you are thirty seven years old."

"Who is your first love Julian? A woman who is twenty four years or thirty four years old?"

"The woman that is twenty four. That is why I am choosing Carl to be my first love" and we laughed again. Julian Jr. came and spoke with Edit. Julian told me that the son likes to go back home.

"Carl, come with us. It will be great if you stay with us tonight. My apartment isn't big, but is paid off. I am happy that i don't have mortgage."

"Thank you very much. I will be happy to." I wanted to spend more time with Edit and Julian Jr.

"Can you take the children to the apartment Edit? Carl and I will go to buy some food and will come a bit later."

The store was conveniently nearby so it didn't take a lot of time. We went to the apartment. When Edit saw us, she asked Julian, why he bought so much food.

"Carl bought it Edit. I told him that this is too much, but he didn't listen."

"It is OK Edit. It is my first time with you, Michelle, Julian Jr. and Julian. We are a family now."

"OK Carl, you know what to do."

She started to prepare the table. Julian showed me the bedrooms, a bath and a living room. "I love this apartment Carl. What do you think?"

"Everything is OK Julian. I like the apartment." Edit laughed and she said "Carl is being polite. He is an architect Julian. If you need to use the bathroom, you need to get in early in the morning Carl, because if you don't you need to wait for two hours" and Edit laughed.

"Carl lives in an apartment with four bathrooms."

"Really!"

"She is right, but I like your apartment." We sat to eat. I spoke with Julian about sports and world events. Edit was busy with the children.

"Do you like France Carl?"

"My love was from France. Julian Jr. is French. I love France." Edit laughed and told Julian "Carl has an answer for every question and he doesn't have a zip on his moth Julian. You need to think before you ask him anything. He never lies."

"Do you love America Carl?"

"Of course I love America."

"Let me tell you what is the difference between Julian and you Carl. If America is attacked, Carl will fight and die for America, because he loves America and freedom. He believes in God. Julian's boss is a conservative and he will fight and die for France. He believes in God too. Julian doesn't believe in God, because he is a Socialist. He will wait somebody to fight for his freedom. Socialists point fingers at capitalists all the time. They wants to take money from the capitalists, because they are rich. The socialist will never say that the capitalists work very hard to make money. The socialists use the system to manipulate the people and take the power. The capitalists don't. They believe that people are free and they need to fight for their freedom. Did you understand what man Julian is, Carl? I need to put the children to the bed", and Edit left with them.

"She is right Carl. I need to change my political views. Edit is a close friend of my boss's wife. Edit, my boss and his wife go to church. I don't. My boss hasn't given me a raise."

"Do you think that Edit said that, because I am here?"

"She didn't. That is the reason she left me seven years ago, for my political views. She told me that she didn't like to marry a man, who spends a lot of time to protest on the streets. She wants to marry a man, who works hard and spends his time with his wife and children. When I married her I promised to change my life, but I have friends, who are socialists. After I married Edit, I stop going to protests on the streets, but I spend considerable time with my friends. The children are growing. Edit works and she need to care of them when I go to meet with my socialist friends, who like to take money from the government. Edit is right Carl. Instead I need to spend time with the children and help her. I need to buy a bigger apartment, because the children are growing. Now Michelle and Julian Jr. sleep together in one room. It will be nice to have one more bedroom., so each of them will have their own room, especially since they are a boy and a girl."

"How much do you need to buy a bigger apartment?"

"If I sale this apartment, I will need three hundred thousand more Carl." Edit returned to the table and we spoke about French wine. She looked tired, so I told them that I need to sleep. I didn't want her to stay late to keep me company.

"Could you show Carl where he will sleep? I will clean the table Julian."

We entered the bedroom where Michelle and Julian Jr. sleep. I closed my eyes and went to sleep.

When I woke up in the morning I remembered that Edit told me that I need to use the bathroom first, because otherwise I have to wait for two hours. I immediately went to the bathroom. When I was done I went to the kitchen. Nobody was there. I looked thought the window. It was still early in the morning, when Edit entered. I went back to the room and got the presents I had for the children. I gave them to Edit. She had tears in eyes.

"How did you sleep Carl?"

"Good Edit, but I need to ask you if Julian will be upset if I offer to help him to buy a bigger apartment?"

"I told you that Julian is socialist. He will have no problem taking money from a capitalist, because you are a capitalist. You should not do that Carl. This is mine and Julian's problem."

"I have money, I want to help Julian, because he is a good father. I think that if Julian buy a new apartment, his socialist friends will tell him that he is rich capitalist. If Julian will distance himself from them, he will spend more time with you and the children."

"What do you like for breakfast?"

"Last night we ate a lot of food. I would like to have only fruit salad and yogurt."

"Can you go to the living room Carl?"

"I will call you when the coffee and the breakfast is ready." I was in the living room looking thought some magazines when Julian came. "Good morning Carl."

"How did you sleep?"

"I slept good Julian, but I woke up early."

"Did you wake up early, so that you are the first one to use the bathroom?", and Julian laughed.

"Edit was right last night when she told you that. We use the bathroom two or three people at the same time. It will be better, if

I have two bathrooms."

"Can I make a phone call to New York, Julian?"

"No problem Carl." I called and told Joshua, that I need three hundred thousand and how long I have to wait to get them.

"Where are you Carl?"

"I am in Paris, Joshua."

"If I start the paperwork today, after two days the money will be in Paris, but I need the name of the Bank and the account in Paris."

"You will speak with Julian. He will give you this information, because the money is for him. "

Then I turned to Julian and told him "Julian, you need to speak with Joshua, he is my broker." They started to speak when Edit announced form the kitchen that the breakfast is ready.

"Come to the kitchen Carl." I ate and spoke with Edit. Julian came to the kitchen and said that Joshua wants to speak with me.

"Carl, Julian said three hundred thousand French francs."

"You need to transfer three hundred thousand dollars Joshua" and I returned to the kitchen. I finished with the breakfast. Then played with Julian Jr. Edit was translating for us. It was so funny. We were happy. Julian came in the kitchen and Edit told him, that he needs to get ready to go to work.

"I spoke with my boss and I am off today. We will meet a Real Estate agent at 10:00 a.m. She will show us three apartments. Carl is an architect and I like him to see them. We are going to buy an apartment for two million French francs Edit. I told Joshua that I will need three hundred thousand francs, but Carl told him to give me dollars. I am a rich man Edit."

"What are you going to do with your socialist friends Julian?"

"They will hate me, because I am becoming capitalist Edit, but I want to be a capitalist. Doesn't matter if I have friends or not." We left Julian's apartment and we met the agent at 10:00 o'clock. I chose the second apartment. Julian told the agent that he needs to prepare the contract for the second apartment. I walked to Julian's car, but he told me that he will take the children and return with them to the apartment.

"Edit will drop you at the train station Carl. I kissed Julian Jr. and Michelle. Julian embraced and kissed me. They left. Edit was driving and talking. I didn't.

"I know that you are busy and you don't have time Carl. I am so happy that you came and saw Julian Jr."

"I came to see Julian Jr. and you Edit."

"Boy, I know that, but now me, Julian and you know what to do in the future. I knew that you will help Julian Jr., if you knew that he is your son. Now Julian knows that too."

"Do you think that Julian will change and he will leave his socialist friends?"

"I think that Julian will do that Edit. He loves the children and you very much. But don't push him. He needs time. After six months you will not recognize him. He will be a new person."

"Carl, you are always positive. I think that this is why you have the power to change people."

"I don't have that power Edit. I couldn't change Mom to love you."

"You are right Carl" and we laughed.

"Are you going to tell her that you have a son and his name is Julian Jr.?"

"Believe me Edit. She will know that I know about my son and she will ask me about him."

"How is your son Carl? You will have to help him if he has a problem."

"I love Julia for that. She forgets the past very fast and she wants to speak for the future, but I will find a way to punish Mom. She likes me to marry Michelle."

"Michelle is one year old Carl." I laughed and told Edit that I am speaking about Michelle that lives in Dallas.

"Why don't you want to marry her?"

"I don't know why Edit. Michelle is a good girl. She is pretty, rich and educated. She has everything and she loves me. She likes to marry me. Oh, and she is a virgin."

"Oh my Gog. This is good Carl. If she has sex with you, she will remember her first night forever. Michelle will be the a perfect mom and a wife for you Carl. What more do you want? Don't overthink this Carl. You must marry this girl."

"I have one problem, I don't want to make Mom happy Edit." We laughed.

"Then do it to make me happy. It's about time that you marry and have children."

"You know that I am a strange man, but you are right Edit. I will consider seriously to marry Michelle, if she still likes to marry me after she learns that I have a son. When I saw Julian Jr. something changed in me. Isn't easy to be a father Edit. I wasn't ready to be a father, but now I feel that I will be a good father and a husband. This morning when I decided to give money to Julian, I didn't think for Julian Jr. only. I thought about you, Julian, Michelle and Julian Jr. You are a family Edit."

"We have fifty more minutes until the train lives, Carl. Do you like to have some coffee?"

"Yes, Edit." She bought coffee and we sat.

"Sometimes I think about you. This was four years ago, but I feel as if it was yesterday Carl. Julian wanted me to tell him about you. I told him that he is my husband and I don't understand."

"I am your husband, but you love Carl. We need to speak about him, because he is the father of Julian Jr."

"I felt disappointed with myself, because but I didn't tell you that I was pregnant Carl. I know that Julian and I will talk a lot about you after he met you. Now Julian knows you. He understood that you are a good man. You are responsible, because you found out that you have a son two weeks ago and you came to see him. When you are ready and you like to take Julian Jr. for a visit, you call and ask Julian. I would like him to spend time with you Carl."

"You are right Edit. I must be ready when I decide do that. I need to marry and my wife must know that Julian Jr. is my son. I know that Julian will not have a problem with that. Edit, would you excuse me, I need to make a call?"

"The phone is there Carl" and she pointed me to it. I called Max. He said "I found one person in Zug with the name Wabern. This is Greta Wabern-Renner. There are four people in Zurich with the name Wabern, but I didn't find any named Hans Wabern."

"Thank you Max. I will see you tomorrow night."

"Call me at the hotel."

"See you tomorrow Carl."

When I returned Edit asked me "Is everything OK Carl?"

"Of course, Edit." I was getting ready to leave for the train. Edit kissed me and said, "Next time we meet, I would love to meet Michelle too".

"I will see what I can do to make that happen Edit. I know that Michelle loves me, but I don't love her at this point. I need to spend more time with her to get to know her better. The time will tell if my feelings for her will change. Take care of yourself and your beautiful family Edit, until next time."

I boarded the train to Geneva. My return trip was uneventful. When I arrived I decided to eat something before I go back to the hotel. I found a small place and asked for something quick. I had a grilled chicken salad. I was trying to figure out if anybody was following me. I didn't notice anybody in the train or when I was walking on the way to the hotel. I entered my room. I was tired. I decided to go to bed. I wanted to sleep. I closed my eyes and felt asleep.

I woke up at 7:00 in the morning. At 8:00am I was ready to go for breakfast. I was in the lobby.

"Good morning Mr. Hope."

"Good morning Clara."

"How was your trip to Paris?"

"I am happy that I saw my son Clara."

"Was your son happy when you gave him the gifts?"

"I don't know Clara. I remembered that I took and kissed Julian Jr."

"Could you call and ask Edit, Clara?"

Clara called and she spoke with Edit. They spoke in French.

"He is here Edit. I will speak in English. You gave the gifts to Edit, Carl. Oh my God. New apartment in Paris! Carl bought for your family Edit!..."

"Do you like to speak with Edit, Carl?"

"Tell her that I am kissing everybody."

Clara continue to speak with her, I went for breakfast. When I finished I came back to the lobby.

"Do you want to know what Edit told me Carl?"

"I know that everybody is happy."

"They love you so much."

"I love them too Clara."

The phone rang. I tried to leave, but Clara told me, " it is for you Carl." It was Patrik.

"I need to see you Carl. I have lunch break between 12:00 p.m. and 1:00 p.m. I will tell Clara where I will be waiting for you."

They spoke shortly then Clara said "I will give you a map so you can find the restaurant".

"Are you leaving tomorrow Carl?"

"Yes, at 10:00 a.m. Clara" and I asked her to give me a paper and pen. I wrote my phone number in New York.

"If you and Chris decide to come to New York, call me."

"I will call you Carl."

I was in the restaurant at 12:00 o'clock. Patrik was there. He asked me how my son was.

"He is great. I saw my son after three years and my first love after four years Patrik."

"Veronica is so happy that she met you and we are back together Carl. I am planning to buy a ring and ask Veronica to marry me."

"I am happy for you and Veronica, Patrik."

"I wanted meet with you, because Greta asked for you. She called me to ask, what happened between me and Veronica. When I was in Zug, I told her that I have a problem with Veronica. I told Greta that you helped me and we are back together. I told Greta that you are a smart, handsome and rich. She laughed and asked me to give her the phone number and your name."

"I would like to meet him and persuade him to come to bed with me. Every woman wants a man like him Patrik."

"I don't feel comfortable giving you Carl's phone number, Greta."

"I am just kidding Patrik."

"But on Tuesday Greta called me again and asked for you. I told her that you are in Paris. She asked me if you are coming back to Switzerland. I told her that I don't know, but I will ask my friend Clara. Clara told me that you were coming back on Tuesday night. I called and told Greta that. This morning Greta told me that Hans wants to see you. I knew that you met Hans in Paris and I told her that after lunch you will come to my office and she can speak with you. Do you have time Carl? I promised Greta that you will."

"I have time Patrik. I will come to your office and speak with Greta." On the way to Patrik's office I saw a jewelry shop. I stopped and said "I need to see something in here Patrik. Can you join me?". We walked in an I asked him, "Can you choose an engagement ring for Veronica, Patrik?"

We looked for about 10 minutes when Patrik said "I like this one, but I don't have enough money to buy it Carl. I will go outside and wait for you." I told the salesmen to put the ring in a gift box and I paid. I took the box, found Patrik and we continued our journey to his office.

We were in Patrik's office. "This is Greta's number, Carl." Patrik left and closed the door.

I called and asked for Greta. "This is Greta."

"Hi Greta, my name is Carl Hope."

"Patrik told me that you like to speak with me."

"Hi Carl, Patrik told me that you are handsome and rich."

"I am not sure how much money I need to have in the bank, so you that you will consider me to be rich Greta."

"How old are you Carl?"

"I am almost twenty seven. Every woman thinks that I am too young to be with her in bed."

"Why do they say that? Maybe you need to tell them that you are young and you don't have experience?"

"I tell them Greta, but they need to find out for themselves. If I am young and I don't have experience in bed, then they have to teach me. I will be a good student."

"Would you like to be in bed with me Carl?"

"If you are going to teach me, then I will be happy to."

"Are you coming to Zug?"

"I will be in your bank tomorrow afternoon Greta. How many condoms do I need to bring with me?"

"Oh my God. You are a serious man."

"I am Greta."

"You decide, how many condoms you will need." We laughed.

"Patrik told me that you are a funny man. Now I believe it. I am sending you a kiss Carl."

"Me too Greta."

"See you tomorrow Carl."

"See you Greta." Since I was done with the conversation I opened the door to see where Patrik was. He was walking back to the office.

"Come in Patrik. Looks like I need to buy condoms. Can you tell me where the shop is?" We laughed and Patrik told me where the go.

"I need to warn you that she is a little heavy and has big breasts. Actually, she has huge breasts."

"Thanks Patrik. Are you trying to tell me that I have to be with a strong woman or a little heavy woman?"

"A little bit of both, Carl."

I took the jewelry box from my pocket and told Patrik, "I am giving you this ring because you need to ask Veronica to marry you. I will be happy, if you marry her".

"Why did you buy the ring for Veronica, this is my job Carl?"

"My son was happy when he saw the gift Veronica prepared for him. I want Veronica to be happy, when she sees the ring."

"I need to tell her that you bought the ring."

"It isn't important who bought the ring Patrik."

"Thanks Carl. Now I can ask Veronica to marry me."

"You are right Patrik."

"I need your advice Patrik. My grandfather is death, but he has money in several swiss banks. What do I need to do, if I decide to check how much money are in the accounts?"

"If the accounts are under your grandfather's name it is easy, but many people use code numbers. You must know the codes."

"Thanks Patrik." We walked in the corridor and we met an old man.

"Boss, this is Carl Hope. The man I was telling you about."

"Mr. Hope, I was told that you are young and rich. I will be happy, if you deposit your money in my bank."

"I will consider your offer sir. Next time when I meet you I will bring some money to deposit."

"I will be waiting for you boy."

I left the bank and I saw a phone and I called Max.

"Carl, I will come to your hotel at 6:00 p.m."

I bought condoms and I returned to the hotel. I was wandering why Hans wanted to see me. Maybe something happened in Milan. I haven't watched TV in the last three days. I picked up the phone.

"May I speak with Luigi, Please.?"

"Just a moment."

"This is Luigi."

"Hey Luigi, this is Barry Moore."

"Oh my God. I can't believe that you are calling me."

"I will be calling you all the time Luigi. I will keep surprising you."

"You are succeeding Mr. Moore. I am surprised. I need to tell you that the Mafia killed Vito with one bullet in the head. No more Vito Mr. Moore or no more the lawyer" and Luigi laughed.

"I told Lilli that you will kill Vito. You did that Mr. Moore. Lilli called me and she asked if I know where you were. I will give you her phone number" and Luigi gave the phone number.

"You shouldn't be coming to Milan or anywhere in Italy now, Mr. Moore, because Vito's people will kill you. If you plan to come to Italy, plan to come at least a year from now. Nobody will know who Vito is after one year. There will be new Vito by then."

"Thank you very much Luigi. I am kissing you."

"Me too Mr. Moore." I hung up the phone and then called Lilli.

"Hey Carl."

"Where are you? I was scared for you!"

"Do you know the big news in Milan?"

"I spoke with Luigi and he told me. Luigi is your big love, but he doesn't know that you are Carl Hope. Luigi knows that you are Barry Moore."

"If I spend time with Luigi, he will know Lilli. You know that I am Carl Hope, because you spent time with me."

"You didn't say the correct words Carl. You must say that you had the best time and sex with me."

"Is that true Carl?"

"It is true Lilli. I had the best time and sex with you."

"I will not forget this time Carl. But now I need to think for Denis."

"How is he?"

"He is OK. You were right. Denis needs time to change his life. I will help him. Denis loves me very much Carl. I know that he will be a good husband."

"Do you love him Lilli?"

"I need some time too Carl to be sure, but I think that I love Denis. Denis does everything I want. Tomorrow is big day for me. Denis's parents will come back from their vacation. I was looking for you, because I need you to tell me what to do with Dennis's parents."

"Denis's mom is very important for your future with Denis, Lilli. If you get her heart she will support you. I know that Denis loves his mom and he will listen to her. I was the same as Denis when I decided to marry Edit. Now I regret that I listened to my mom. I saw Edit and my son and I love them, but you cannot go back in time Lilli. Denis's mom knows him very well. If she sees that you are a good girl for him and you will be a good wife, she will encourage Denis to marry you. You were with Denis for five days, but Denis didn't speak with you for your and Denis's future. Denis is waiting to ask his mom."

"What should I do with Denis's father?"

"He listens to his wife. Denis is shy, because he listens to his mom. If Denis's father was the head in the household, Denis would have been different. Denis would have been an aggressive man. But I think that Denis's father will support you. Parents want grandchildren. Lilli, I told you before, you need to listen to your heart. This is your life."

"Did Luigi tell you what happened in Milan?"

"Yes Lilli. I hear Denis."

"He is here Carl. Do you like to speak with him?"

"I have to go Lilli, another time." I didn't want Denis to ask me stupid questions. He needs to ask Lilli. Somebody knocked on the door. I looked at my watch. It was 6:00 p.m.

"Come in Max." He gave me a paper.

"I don't like to tell you what to do Carl, but if you need more information, I will try again."

"Everything is OK Max. I spoke with Greta. She found me and Greta wants to speak with me in Zug. I think that I will finish with this business next week."

"I spoke with Grandmother. Julia knew that you were in Paris."

"Can you tell me about Edit and your son?"

"I need to tell you that I was stupid when I listened to Mom, Max. If you are in the same situation, you need to listen to your heart. Don't listen to other people. I know that I need to look for my future, but I need to take care of Edit and Julian Jr. The good news is that Julian is a good father and I will never have problem to see Julian Jr. I will punish Mom for not telling me that I have a son. She is my mom, but I am the person who has to decide what to do."

"Jerry told me that you are the only person who can scare Grandmother. I asked him why did he thinks that you will scare her?"

"Father, Julia is your yours and Carl's mom. Why are you afraid of her?"

"I am a soft man Max. I was strong father for you and your sister, but I will never say anything against my mom. Carl does that, because he is a strong and an aggressive man. Mom is always scared when Carl decides to do something, because she knows how aggressive he is. It doesn't mean that Carl doesn't love Mom. He loves Mom very much, Max."

"I remember when Julia came in my father's apartment and spoke with him about Edit."

"Can you tell Carl that Edit is old for him?"

"Mom, you need to be happy, because you will have more grandchildren."

"Can you tell Carl to use condoms?"

"Carl is a big man, Mom. He needs to know what to do. He is twenty two years old. He isn't a child. Did your Mom tell you what to do in bed with Louis Dreyfus?"

"This was different Jerry. I loved Louis Dreyfus."

"Carl is in love with Edit too, Mom. Don't you understand that?"

"Jerry, you are a bad son, I don't love you. I came here to ask for you to help me but you don't want to."

"Of course, you love Louis, but he is death. You leave Carl alone, you take care of your life."

"Julia left the apartment Carl. I looked at my father and told him that he is my hero."

"Why didn't Jerry ever tell me about Louis Dreyfus, Max?"

"Honestly, nobody in the family wanted to speak about him, because it hurt Julia deeply. This was a taboo in your family. I was surprised to hear his name mentioned by my father. Julia was angry with my father and didn't speak with him until you left Edit. One weekend she came to my father's apartment and said that you have a new girlfriend."

"Her name is Victoria but Carl calls her Vicky".

"Jerry was disappointed and tasked her if she was happy that you have a new girlfriend?"

"Of course I am happy Jerry. Edit was old for Carl."

"I am not happy Mom, but remember someday Carl will punish you for that."

"Carl loves me Jerry and he will never punish me."

"Jerry is right Max, I will punish Mom, believe me. But I don't know how."

"Hey Carl, I think that I can help with that. When Grandmother calls me, I will tell her congratulations, you have a fifth grandson".

"Let's not speak about the past anymore Max."

"Where is your girlfriend?"

"She wanted to come to see you, but I didn't want her to see the papers." After we reviewed the papers I asked Max to call his girlfriend to join us for dinner.

"Carl, do you have a preference for the restaurant for dinner?"

"No Max. You decide, because you live in Geneva." Max told her where we will meet her.

I changed and we left the hotel. It was a walking distance from the hotel. We got a table for four and were sitting down when Max's girlfriend arrived. Max introduced me to her. Her name was Sofia. She sat down, we spoke. Sofia was listening and looking at me. Max laughed and told her.

"Sofia, I have seen many women looking at Carl like you. You aren't the first one."

I asked Sofia, "If Max asks you to marry him, but somebody told you that Max has a son, will you marry him?"

"If I love him, I will. I won't care that Max has a son, because this in his past."

"Will you accept Max's son as your son?"

"Absolutely."

"You are a good girl Sofia."

"Do you have a son Max?"

"I am the one that has a son Sofia."

"Max told me that you were in Paris, but he didn't tell me why."

"I went to see my son."

"What is his name Carl?"

"Julian Jr.. I had many women in my past, but I think that is time to change my life."

"You need to marry Carl."

"I will plan to merry next year."

"Do you want to marry Sofia, Max?"

Sofia laughed and told me, "Thinking is nothing. Taking an action will be better Carl."

"Oh my God. You think the same way as me Sofia."

"Do you like New York, Sofia?"

"I have never been to New York, but I know that everybody wants to live there. I think that I have little chance to live in New York."

"Why don't you come back to New York, Max?"

"My bank pays my rent in Geneva."

"If I come back to New York, I will have to pay Carl."

"Why do say that Max? You have an apartment in New York."

"I don't have an apartment in New York, my father does. I know that Mom wants me to return to New York and live with my parents, but I don't like that Carl."

"Max, Julia's apartment will be free after three or four months."

"Where are you and Julia going to live Carl?"

"I have decided to buy a bigger apartment and I will ask Mom to live with me."

"Julia will never move Carl."

"If I tell her, she will Max. I moved out for two years. It was hard for me and Mom. You know how much I love her. When I return to New York I will tell her that we will never live separately. This is my punishment for Julia. I will ask her to give you her apartment."

"What do I need to do Carl?"

"When your contract with the bank end, you and Sofia should move to New York."

"Do you like to come with me to New York, Sofia?"

"Of course I like that Max. I love you."

"I love you too Sofia. Thank you so much uncle."

"Who is your Uncle Max, Carl is too young?"

"Carl is my father's brother. My grandmother, Julia is my father's and Carl's mom. Since I am Julia's grandson, Carl is my uncle."

"You are a good man Carl."

"He is Sofia. Carl has a lot friends Jewish, Italian, Irish and Russian."

"Hey Carl, how is Vicky?"

"She is very busy working on opening a boutique for clothes."

"Vicky is very beautiful Sofia."

"Am I not beautiful Max?"

"You are beautiful Sofia" and I kicked Max's leg. "He is kidding. Max likes to know how much you love him."

"What did she do before Carl?"

"She was a model Sofia", Max told her. I kicked Max again.

"Max, you are right. Vicky is beautiful, because every model is beautiful." Max laughed and he kicked my leg.

"Where are you going tomorrow Carl? Max told me that you are travelling a lot."

"I need to meet a friend in Zug, Sofia. I haven't seen him in four years."

"Where have you been this month Carl?" Sofia asked me.

"I was in Dallas, New York, Miami, Bahamas, Milan, Bern, Paris and Geneva."

"Your question isn't correct Sofia. You need to ask how many women did you sleep with this month?"

"I have been with five women Max."

"Your past is good Carl, but I think that your present is bad. You need to change your present Carl", Sofia told me.

"You are right Sofia, but when I ask a woman to marry me, this time will become the past."

"You have an answer for every question Carl. How do you do that?"

"Honestly, Max knows that I don't like to talk too much. I like to listen. After I saw my son, I have decided to change. Edit was the first person who understood that. I am changing, because I need to be there for my son."

We finished dinner. We left the restaurant. We were talking outside waiting for a taxi for Max and Sofia. "After I visit Zug, my plan is to go back to New York, but I may have to return to Switzerland after two or three weeks Max. I will call you if I am coming back."

"That sounds great Carl. I am always happy to see you. Good night" and a taxi pulled up and they entered.

"God night Sofia and Max.".

I was walking back to the hotel thinking about Sofia and Max. Mom will have many questions for Max if he deices to marry Sofia. I know that Jerry will never ask Max. I will support Max's decision. He is a very good man. Sofia is a good girl too.

I returned to the hotel. Nobody was following me. Ben was working hard to keep my back clean. It will be good, if Ben is able to keep Aaron away from me, but if I have a problem tomorrow with Aaron, I will have to kill him. If I don't, he will become a big problem for me. I know that Konev will never meet with me, if I have people following me. Konev is right. Why does he have to risk his life? I know that Hans is a low level Stasi agent. He uses all his energy to stay alive. He doesn't have time to spy, if he knows the meaning of the word spy at all. I will ask Hans tomorrow, why does he work for Stasi? I needed a good night sleep before tomorrow. I went to bed. I felt that very important events were about to happen and I needed a well-rested mind. I stopped to think and went to sleep.

CHAPTER 11

I woke up in the morning feeling hopeful. If I meet Hans today, I will be very proud with myself, because many people have tried to find him for years but they haven't succeeded. Konev is the only person that knows where Hans is. Now, I am the second. He will be surprised, when I tell him, that my ultimate goal has been to find Konev. If Hans asks me why did I spend time and money to find him, when you want to meet Konev? I will tell him that I am counting on him to convince Konev to meet and speak with me. This should be simple for him, because he works for Stasi and Konev works for KGB. He knows how to arrange a meeting between two secret service agents. I don't, because I work for Simon. Simon is a rich man, but he doesn't work for CIA. Simon didn't tell me, what to do to find Stasi's and KGB's agents.

The phone rang and interrupted my thoughts. I picked up. Clara asked me "Do you want the breakfast in your room Mr. Hope?"

"That will be great Clara! It will be even better, if beautiful a girl brings the breakfast to my room."

"Do you think that I am beautiful girl, Carl?"

"I think that you are a beautiful woman Clara, but I am afraid that Chris will kill me talking about that. I am still a young boy and deserve to live longer. I don't want Chris to kill me."

"I will choose the breakfast for you then."

"Of course Clara. The breakfast will be ready in thirty minutes Mr. Hope."

About 40 minutes later a man delivered the breakfast. He gave me a small box and told me, "A gift for you Mr. Hope".

I gave him a tip and I opened the box. It was a wrist watch. In back side of the watch I read. Clara, Veronica, Chris, Patrik and Carl. Now I know that I have friends in Geneva forever. I was in the lobby at 9:30 a.m. Clara was at the front desk.

"Are you ready to check out Carl?"

"I am ready Clara" and I gave her my old watch.

"My grandmother bought this watch for me when I was fifteen years old. I thought that I will wear this watch forever. But from now on I have decided to wear this watch forever" and I showed her my new watch on my wrist.

"Thank you so much Clara!"

"What should I do with your old wrist watch Carl?"

"Keep it as a souvenir. The new wrist watch will remind me that I have friends in Geneva. The old wrist watch will remind you that you, Veronica, Chris and Patrik have a friend in New York."

"I will call for a taxi Carl."

"I will take Carl, lady."

I turned around and I saw Aaron Vogel.

"Is it OK Carl?"

"It is OK." Clara kissed me and told me that they will never forget me.

"Me too Clara."

Aaron and I left the hotel.

"Where are we going Carl?"

"You drove me from Bern to Geneva. You are pick up me from Geneva, so logically you need to drop me in Bern, Aaron."

"Are you afraid Carl?"

"Why do I need to be afraid Aaron?"

"You need to be afraid for your life Aaron, not me."

We went to the car and drove off. We didn't speak. I watched outside through the car windows the nice scenery of houses, mountains and pastures. After we passed Lausanne I started to think what I have to do. I need to kill Aaron before Bern, if Ben doesn't stop the car and take Aaron with him. I don't have a pistol. I need to stop at a gas station and when Aaron follows me in the restroom, I will have to kill him with my hands in the restroom or when we return in the car. I need to choose a quite gas station. Aaron is short and I won't have a problem to break his neck. I saw in the car mirror that a car was pretty close behind us for a while now. I will watch how long this car follows us. If the car continues to drive behind us, I will ask Aaron to stop at a gas station. The car was behind us for twenty minutes. I was pretty sure that the Ben's people were following us.

"Can you stop at the first gas station Aaron? I need to use the restroom?"

"If you create a problem for me, I will kill you Carl."

"If you want me to use your car for a restroom, then don't stop Aaron."

Aaron stopped and the other car stopped too. A man walked and knocked on Aaron's window. It was Ben. Aaron and I exited the car.

"I am taking Carl with me, Aaron. Carl is a dangerous for our country. He is a spy for the KGB."

"Can you tell me where I need to drop Carl, Ben?"

"Come to my car Aaron, I will give you a map, where you need to drop him." Ben and Aaron walked and entered the other car.

In the meantime another man came and sat on the driver's seat of Aaron's car and he told me "Carl come in the car, I will drive." I sat and he asked me, where he had to drop me.

"In Bern."

We didn't speak during the drive to Bern. When we entered the city, I told him where he needs to drop me. I was in the downtown of Bern. I walked down a street and looked to see if somebody was following me. I didn't not notice anybody.

I went to the train station and took the train from Bern to Zug. Nobody followed me in the train. I was in the bank where Greta works. I asked for Greta and a man told me that I need to follow him. We entered Greta's office.

"This man asked for you Greta" and he left.

"Nice to see you Mr. Hope." Greta was trying to shake my hand, but I took and kissed her hand.

"Sit down Carl. I need to call Hans. He is waiting for you. Hans is teaching my son to play the piano. Maybe someday my son will be a good pianist."

"What time are they scheduled to finish the lesson?"

"At 5:30 p.m."

"Don't call Greta. I don't like to interrupt your son's class."

"If you don't mind I would like to go to a coffee shop and wait there for you. Could you tell me how to get to one that is close by?" Greta told me where the coffee shop was.

"See you there Carl."

I left and found to coffee shop. I sat on an outside table. I was drawing the building to right of me, when Greta came.

"May I see the drawing Carl? You draw well!"

"I am an architect Greta. Do you like something to drink?"

"I will buy, because I like something different Carl."

"Can you write what you like? I will order it."

She wrote down and I went inside the coffee shop to make the order. I told them that they need to bring order outside on the table. I gave them a good tip. I came back to the table.

"Why are you coming to Zug, Carl?"

"Did you forget that you invited me to Zug, Greta?"

"You want to see Hans."

"I never mentioned to you Hans, when we spoke yesterday."

"Do you know Hans, Carl?"

"I don't know Hans."

"But you told Patrik that you know Hans and that you met him in Paris."

"Four years ago I spoke with Hans from West Berlin. I met him in Paris. Do you know how many people in Germany have the name Hans?"

"You are right Carl. Do you think that Hans will have problem with you?"

"Why did you ask me that Greta?"

"If you think that I am a dangerous man, I don't want to speak with you. You should leave this table, if that is what you think about me, Greta! There are plenty available tables around us."

"I am so sorry Carl. I am afraid, because Hans is my uncle. After you left the my office Hans called me. He told me that I need to figure out who you are in the coffee shop. I came and saw that you were drawing. I was surprised that you were sitting and drawing calmly. I don't know why Hans was afraid."

"Do you think that Hans has something in his past that he might be concerned about, Greta?"

"I haven't heard anything. He lived in West Berlin, but in the last one year and half he has been living in Zug. Hans is a quiet person and he is a good pianist."

"Why do think that Hans is scared about something then

Greta? I suggest that you call and ask him, if he wants me in your house."

"That is not necessary Carl. You will meet with Hans, because he told me, that he likes to speak with you. If you have an argument with him, please stay calm and don't raise your voice. He is a quiet man."

"I am not an aggressive man Greta. Many women told me that I am arrogant, but I told them the truth. I know that many women didn't like to hear the truth."

"Patrik was right. You are a good man Carl. I like you and I want to be in bed with you. I will prepare a bedroom for you. I am making assumptions here and as I told you I have a son… Hum, where would you like to have sex with me, in my room or your room Carl?

"I think that it will be better if you come to my room, in case your son wakes up. He will not come and knock on the door of my bedroom."

"I will come to your bedroom Carl." We arrived at Greta's property. The house was huge. It looked like a castle. I was surprised.

"You have a castle Greta. How many people live here?"

"Sven, me and Hans. Only three people live in the house. Hans doesn't want other people and he is angry when I invite anybody. That is why I was surprised that he invited you. When I married I thought that my husband and I will have two or three children, but he died four years ago. I don't like to speak about that." We entered the house and I saw Hans. He was nervous and he asked, "Where were you Greta, you were supposed to call me an hour ago?"

"We went for a coffee Hans. This is Carl. Do you want to speak with him now? He is here."

Hans came towards us and we shook hands. "Nice to meet you Carl."

"Me too Hans."

"Greta, the dinner is ready."

"You cooked for us Hans!"

"Of course Greta. You know that I have two hobbies. I like to play the piano and cook."

"Could you play the piano for us after dinner Hans?"

"I will be very happy to play for you Carl, because Sven and

Greta are tired of it. I am playing every day for them." Greta smiled. I think that she was surprised, that Hans was trying to joke, but I was happy, because I felt that he was getting comfortable with me. That gave me a hope that he may open his heart for me, so I can ask for Konev.

"This is my son Sven, Carl.'

"Hi Sven." We shook hands.

"Mom, Carl looks like my father!"

"Your father was a little heavier, but you are correct, he does look like him. I need to show you your bedroom Carl. Can you follow me?" We were in the bedroom and Greta asked me.

"Do you like me to show, where the bathroom is and where you need to put your thing?"

"I don't need that Greta." I took her in my arms and kissed her.

"I will never forget what you are doing for me."

"You must ask Hans what you need to know, Carl."

"I don't have to ask. He must tell me and help me. Hans needs to speak with his best friend, but don't tell him that Greta." I kissed Greta again.

"Is this very important to you Carl?"

"I am fighting to save my life, but this is a long story and we will speak about it after Hans helps me. I know that we will have a wonderful night together. I don't like you to ask me after we sex either. I don't like you to be afraid for my life", and I kissed her.

"I need to return to the kitchen Carl. When you are ready come there or if you prefer wait in the living room for the dinner to get served."

I took a quick shower and decide to wait in the living room. There was Sven.

"I was waiting for you Carl."

Sven took my hand and told me, "I will show you where the dining room is". Hans and Greta were already there. They looked at Sven and me.

"I will sit next to Carl, Mom. I prefer that he sits between me and you Mom."

"Can you let the hand of Carl go before you and Carl sit?"

"I will Mom."

"I am, so sorry Carl."

"Sven is OK."

"I cooked meat. I hope you like it."

"Which beer do you like Carl?"

"Actually I would prefer red wine If you have."

"What kind of wine do you like to drink Carl. I have French, Italian, Spanish, and German?"

"I prefer French wine. My first love was from France. She taught me a lot about wine. She told me that when I eat fish I should drink white wine. When I eat red meat I should drink red wine."

"Where is she now Carl?"

"She lives in Paris and her name is Edit, Greta."

"I heard that you were in Paris, before you came here."

"Did you see her in Paris?"

"Yes, I did. We have a son from her, but I didn't know that Greta."

"How old is your son Carl?" Greta asked me.

"Julian Jr. is three years old. He changed my life. When I saw him, something happened to me. Honestly, in the last eight years my life has been my job, exercise and women. I love to work, because I make money. I like exercise to keep my body in shape. I like to be with women. Actually, women like to be with me, and I have a good time in bed with them too."

"Well, that explains why you have a son, because you enjoyed being in bed with women."

"You are right Greta. This is as a result of my enjoyment with women in bed." Everybody laughed.

"Do you love Edit?" Sven asked me.

I tried to answer, but Greta told him "I don't want you to ask Carl any more personal questions Sven. This is Carl's life. We need to have dinner now." Greta raised her glass and said "A toast for Carl and his son" and Greta looked at her son. Sven raised his glass with water.

"Cheers Carl." Greta took control of the conversation on the table. We spoke mostly for sport. Sven told me, that his father was a good skier and started teaching him skiing when he was two years old. After his father died, Sven likes to play piano. Sven asked me, what kind of sport I like. I told him that I like to swim and run. Hans told us that when he was growing up in Switzerland he skied, but when he moved to West Berlin, he spent more time playing piano. Greta looked at me, but I didn't have any reaction. When Hans said that he grew up in Switzerland and moved to West

Berlin, I knew that Hans was going to help me. After dinner Hans played the piano. When he stopped playing, Greta told us that we all need to get ready for bed.

"May I sleep in Uncle Hans's bedroom Mom?"

"You need to ask Uncle Hans, Sven."

"Of course Sven, you can sleep in my bedroom." Hans' bedroom was on the first floor. Sven's, Greta's and my bedroom were on the second floor. Greta looked at me and she smiled. Like a good boy I went to my room, took off my clothes and jumped in bed waiting for her. She entered and told me "Could you turn off the light? I am feeling shy for some reason. If you see me naked you may want to jump through the window."

"You don't need to be concerned about that Greta. I like to see you naked. I want to look at your body when we have sex and the way it responds to my touch. I believe that you need to feel when you have sex. You don't need to think, how your body looks." Greta took off her pajamas and I saw a big and beautiful bosoms. I wanted to touch and kiss them. I wanted my tongue to play with her nipples. I haven't seen bosoms like that before."

"Please join me in the bead. She laid next to me. I turned towards her and started kissed her mouth. We played with our tongues, while my right hand was touching her breasts. I moved to her bosom kissing every inch on the way. My tongue was playing with her nipples. They were extending and becoming hard. It was very arousing. I continued moving down kissing and sucking her stomach and then her inner tights, but my fascination was with her breasts. I went back kissing them and this time I was sucking her nipples. At this point I was ready to feel more of her. I capped her sex with my hand and she was very wet. She was ready too, but she didn't like to me to stop. She was holding my head there so I continued to kiss and play with her bosoms. Greta laughed and told me " I like this foreplay a lot, but don't forget that I have a pussy that is dying to play with it" and she gently squeezed my grown erection. I put it between her legs and started to tease her pussy. She grabbed my hips and pulled hard towards her kissing my mouth hard. That was the my signal to go inside her. I wanted to go slow, so I had only the head inside her. She moved her hips and tried to get more inside her, but I pulled back and didn't let her. She asked me "How long are going to play Carl? You are making me crazy." She grabbed and pulled my ass really hard this time. I felt her desire for me and this time went along with her. My whole erection was inside her going deeper and deeper as she started to moved faster. I was surprised at how fast she moved, because she looked a little heavy.

"Do you want to be on top of me Greta?"

"Aren't you scared, to let me be on top of you Carl?"

"I am not scared Greta."

"Why do you want me to move on top of you?"

"I was trying to distract you, because you were ready to finish, but I am not. I need more sex to be finish. It is better if we finish together. Both of our bodies need be ready for that. We need to be in synch. We need to have sex longer, to get there since this is our first time together and we are learning about each other."

We changed the position. Greta was a top of me. She tried to keep her body a little above mine. I know that this was hard for her, but she was trying her best to continue.

"I want to stay more on top of you Carl, but this is hard for me." We changed position, so I was behind her. She was building again, so I changed again. I was on top of her and we were in sync with our movements, feeling each other intimately. We finished together. She took my head in her arms and kissed my eyes and mouth many times.

"Oh boy, you made me feel so good. I felt the same when I had sex with my husband."

"Since you ae honest Carl, you need to tell me how many kilograms do I need to lose?"

"I think about fourteen, fifteen pounds."

"This is seven kilograms Carl. If you stay in my house for a month and we have sex, I know that I will lose ten kilograms very fast." We laughed and Greta asked me "Are you in Zug for the diamonds? Hans told me that if you are, you will be the next dead man."

"I don't want somebody kill you Carl. Do you want me to check the banks for you Carl?"

"No Greta. I have a name, but I don't have the code number."

"How do you know that you need a code number?"

"Patrik told me, that I need to have a code number."

"You told me that you need to speak with Hans, because you are trying to save your life. Why are you afraid for your life?"

"I am not afraid Greta. They tried to kill me, but I am still alive."

"Who wants to kill you and why?"

"You need to ask Hans. He knows who they are. The same people are looking to kill Hans too. If he helps me, I will help him. If he doesn't like to help me, I will leave on Saturday to New York. Who told you about the diamonds Greta?"

"You are honest with me and I will be honest with you. I will tell you my story Carl. Four and half years ago, my husband gave me a name, Louis Dreyfus. He told me that I need to check if Louis has a safe box in any of the banks. I told him, that this is a criminal. He told me that if I love him, I need to do that. Since I loved him I did as he asked, but I didn't find the name Louis Dreyfus in the banks register. Louis didn't have a safe box either. One day I felts sick and I left from work earlier. I came back at home. I entered the house and I heard that Hans and my husband were yelling at each other. When I entered the living room they were almost ready to fight. They saw me. Hans left the house. He didn't say anything. He left Carl. I know that Hans love me very much. I love him too. After three weeks my husband died in a ski accident. Hans's family didn't attended, my husband's funeral. The first six months were very hard for me. I ate a lot of food. I didn't sleep. My boss took me for dinner and he spoke to me about my son."

"Greta, you have son. You need to be strong for him. He lost his father now you have to fulfil the gap."

"I went home and thought a lot about that. The next day I took control of my life, but I picked up these kilograms. I never thought that I need to lose the weight. I have to think for my son. I have men and they like to have sex with me. Doesn't matter that I am a little pig." Greta laughed.

"Now I am ashamed. I need to lose seven kilograms. I will do that for me and my son. Sven will be very happy if I lose seven kilograms. Next time when you see me I will be a sexy woman." We laughed. I took and I kissed her.

"This is your life Greta, you need to fight for your life. I am happy that you decided to lose the weight. This is for your health and of course for your son. You must keep your son happy."

"Don't worry about Hans, Carl. He is a good man. He will help you. Hans came back to Zug one year and five months ago. He didn't call me, the whole time. My friend saw Hans and spoke with him, but he didn't ask for me and Sven. This was so sad for me. I called Hans and met with him. I asked him to teach Sven to play piano. Hans came and he spends a lot of time with Sven. We never speak for the past and my husband. Do you think that my husband was killed for the diamonds Carl?"

"I don't know Greta, but many people have been killed for these diamonds. The fact is that many people are killed for diamonds every day."

"Do you know the names of people who were killed for the diamonds, Carl?"

"Hans's father, Otto. He was the first and this was in 1942. Somebody killed Otto in New York. I don't know how many people were killed in the last fifty years. I got involved in this game four weeks ago and they tried to kill me, but they missed. Next time they won't miss Greta. I need to kill them before they kill me. I have ten days to finish this job. I have to strike first in order to survive, this is what I have learned so far about this game. Everything has a price. Human life doesn't seem to be of any value in this game. Your husband risked Sven's and your life. I will never do that."

"May I stay in your bed tonight Carl?"

"You can stay tomorrow too Greta" and we laughed.

"I like your head on my chest Carl."

"Do you think that if I didn't look to find the safe box for Louis Dreyfus they wouldn't have killed my husband?"

"They didn't kill your husband. They didn't know that your husband knows about the diamonds."

"If Hans didn't tell my husband for the diamonds, he wouldn't have asked me to look for the safe box of Louis Dreyfus."

"Your husband was greedy Greta. Hans didn't do anything wrong, because he lost his father. I think that Hans' mom told him what happened with her husband. I think that when Hans and your husband started to fight, Hans told your husband that this is a game, where somebody will die. Hans wanted to save the life of your husband. But I don't like to speak more for the diamonds Greta. The diamonds belong to the Dreyfus family. They need to find them and decide what to do with them."

I kissed Greta. "Oh boy, you are ready."

"I am Greta."

"I need to use the bathroom. I will be back shortly. I don't remember how long it has been since I had sex two times in one night." We had sex for a long time. When we finished Greta laughed.

"I told you Carl, I will lose ten kilograms with sex." We held each other and I fell asleep.

I opened my eyes in the morning. Greta wasn't in bed. When I went to the living room, she was ready to leave.

"How was last night Carl?" Sven asked me.

"You won or lost? My mom is heavy. I think that Mom won" and Sven laughed.

"What did you say that Sven?" Greta asked.

"Ignore Mom, I am so happy for you."

"You are right Sven. I need to lose seven kilograms."

"I was surprised that you didn't eat this morning, Mom. You had only one cup of milk. I will be very happy, if you lose seven kilograms, but you should use Carl for that."

"I promise Sven. I will use Carl." This was so funny. I was very surprised by the open relationship Greta had with Sven. We laughed a lot. Sven kissed Greta and went back in his room.

"Hey I need to leave to work, but if you come to have lunch at 12:00 with me I will be very happy very Carl."

"I will be at your office at noon, Greta. May I kiss you?"

"Of course Carl. I kissed her and she left the house.

"Do you love her Carl?" Hans asked me.

"I don't love Greta. I am enjoying her company, Hans."

Sven came in the living room and said that he is going outside to play soccer with some neighborhood children.

"It is good that Sven left the house Carl. Do you have any plans after breakfast?"

"I am planning to go downtown. I like to draw."

"Would you like to spend some time to speak with me?"

"I will listen Hans. I don't need to speak with you, because I know what happened with you and Konev in New York."

"Do you like to ask me?"

"Now, I don't need to ask you. I will ask you when I know that you will tell me the truth."

"You don't know me Carl."

"Is that what you think? You are Hans Weber or Hans Wabern. You were born in Germany, but you grew up in Switzerland. Before going to America your father, Otto Weber, moved you and your mom to Switzerland for security reasons. Otto was killed in 1942 in New York. I have a letter with a signature describing who killed Otto. You and your mom returned to West Berlin 1960. This was a big mistake for you. You work for Stasi, but I don't know why."

"You know a lot for my family Carl. I will tell you why I work for Stasi. We returned to West Berlin, because my mom has many properties there. I was in college when a man came and asked to speak with me He insisted that we go somewhere outside. We went to a park and he showed me a picture of me with a pistol in my hand, pointing it at a little boy. Otto was in SS uniform and he was next to me. The man told me that Stasi wants me to work for them. If I refuse, Stasi will give the picture to the newspapers and East Germany will want to sue me, because I killed a little boy. I was a little boy too Carl, but my father worked for the SS. I told him that I need twenty four hours. I spoke with Mom. She told me that if am going to work for Stasi, someday I have to ask them to help me find what happened with my father in New York…"

"I promised my mom that I will do that I never found information in Stasi. I traveled to New York and I met the shark and Konev. I asked them to help me, but they didn't know what happened with my father. When the shark understood that I am Otto Weber's son, he told Konev that I was in New York to get the diamonds. Konev told me that the shark was scared."

"Hans will get the diamond Konev. We need to kill him."

"Konev helped me and I disappeared from New York."

"Why did Konev help you Hans?"

"Konev and four Russian people were in West Berlin. They needed to move somebody to East Berlin. My boss from Stasi told me that this is trap and somebody will kill them. I told Konev, but he didn't believe me. I ask Konev to walk with me. Konev and I walked a little behind from the other Russian people. Somebody killed Konev's partners, but Konev was alive. I asked Konev to walk with me an d say nothing if ae are stopped and that I will speak. They stopped us. I showed them my West German passport and told them that Konev is my friend. They left us alone. After that Konev told me that I saved his life and I am his friend forever. He is Carl. Konev loves me. He will die for me. I met many people who work for Stasi and KGB, but they were killed. I never found out what happened with my father in New York, but I created a problem in my life. The shark has been trying to kill me for many years."

"Peter Volak is the shark, Hans."

"Peter Volak was born in Russia. He spies for KGB and CIA. "

"He doesn't spy for them Hans. Peter uses them to make money and he has power in New York. The shark or Peter Volak tried to kill me. You and I are in the same situation. I am here and you must help me to kill the shark."

"Oh my God. I don't believe that you will be able to kill the shark. On Monday, I spoke with Konev. He told me that you are a smart and dangerous."

"You must meet with Carl, before he decides to kill you Hans."

"This is the first time I heard that Konev was scared for my live. Are you going to kill me Carl?"

"Hans, I told you that I will kill the shark. You need you alive, because you need to help me."

"What do you need Carl?"

"You need to call Konev and tell him that I will kill the shark. Konev needs to give me a poison. The shark likes to drink wine with his dinner. After he goes to bed, he will never wake up. The shark must pass way. Konev needs to tell me the Russian name of the shark. I know that the shark was born in Russia."

"Do you think that Konev will help you Carl?"

"You have to convince him. He is KGB. Nobody knows what Konev thinks, but I know that he hates the shark. Konev stays in Russia, but you need to tell Konev that I know that he has a son, Sasha, who lives in New York."

"Do you want to scare Konev?"

"I don't want to scare Konev. I need you to send him the message that in this game people die."

"I don't like to die Hans. The Nazis started this game, but the KGB has continued it after World War II and they haven't stopped for forty five years. If I kill the shark, find the diamonds and bring the Dreyfus family to them. The game will stop."

"You don't want the diamonds?"

"I believe in God, Hans. Many people were kill for these diamonds. The diamonds have a lot of blood on them. Nobody will die after the Dreyfus family gets them. This will be the end of it. Now the Dreyfus family doesn't know if they really own the diamonds, because nobody has seen them. Now everybody wants to own them."

"You are right Carl. I will call Konev and ask him to speak with you."

"I don't need to speak with Konev, Hans. I must meet with him."

"You speak with Konev and tell him that I need a poison. I will get ready to go to Greta's office. You need to call Konev, Hans."

I walked to my bedroom to get dressed. When I returned to the living room, Hans was there.

"I am expecting Konev to call me, but I don't know when."

"You are looking good Carl."

"Thanks Hans. Greta told me, about your conversation in regards to her husband last night. You were right, when you told her that her husband was greedy."

"You and Greta shouldn't tell Sven what happened with his father, Hans. Sven must think that his father was the best father and husband. Sven is growing now and if he knows that his father was killed because he tried to get the diamonds, that isn't good news for Sven."

"I will tell Greta that Carl."

"You don't need to tell her. I think that she is smart enough to know that."

I left the house and I bought flowers. At 11:50 a.m. I was at the Bank. I entered Greta's office. I gave her the flowers and kissed her.

"Thank you Carl! I forgot when was the last time I received flowers. Could you sign here for me Carl?" I saw my drawing and I signed.

"I will hang the drawing on the wall behind my chair. When I enter my office, I would like to see it. It will make me happy every day when I am in here." Greta kissed me and she put the flowers in a vase. At noon we left for lunch. I took Greta's hand while we were walking to our lunch.

"Why did you do that Carl?"

"I just felt like doing that, Greta. I am so happy that I met you. You are different from the other girls I usually meet."

"You need to tell your other girls, that I am different from them." We laughed and entered the restaurant. Greta ordered vegetable soup and chicken salad. I ordered vegetable soup and grilled chicken.

"I told Hans about our conversation last night. I hope that you are not going to be angry with me about it."

"It is OK Greta. Hans will help me. I need him to call and speak with few people he knows."

"I need to know who ordered to kill my husband. You need to help me find that Carl. If I meet with Konev, I will ask him Greta."

"Do you think that Hans knows something?"

"I don't believe that Hans knows anything. If Hans knew, they wouldn't have killed your husband."

"Why are you defending Hans, Carl? Is it because you need his help?"

"No Greta. If Hans knew, he would have taken your husband with him. Hans loves Sven and he would have tried to save Sven's father."

"Why do you think that?"

"Hans grew up without a father, because he was killed when he was a little boy. Hans wouldn't like Sven to grow up without a father. Maybe Hans told your husband to stay away, but your husband was greedy and didn't listen. You shouldn't think that Hans is a bad man Greta. You need to think what kind a man your husband was. Do you think that your husband loved you after he found out that somewhere in a bank are diamonds worth hundred million dollars?"

"Why are you asking me that?"

"Because, after you didn't find the information he needed, he should have stop thinking for them. He didn't stop and they killed him."

"Why didn't they kill me Carl?"

"Why should they kill you Greta? You didn't find any information. If you did, they would have taken the information from you. After that they would have killed you."

"If you are going to meet somebody I will come with you Carl."

"This is dangerous Greta. I will take you with me if you insist, but you need to ask Hans. Don't forget that you have a son."

"You have too Carl."

"It is different for me Greta. I am fighting to save my life. You are placing your life in a dangerous situation, but you are a grown woman. I will never tell you what to do."

"Thanks Carl!"

"My pleasure Greta." I took her hand.

"I will be happy if you are with me."

"Why?"

"I will be with you for one more night Greta."

"Oh my God. You never stop joking."

"Sex isn't a joke Greta. The sex is feeling."

"You are right Carl. Maybe I will lose some kilograms." After lunch Greta returned to the bank. I went back to Greta's house. I heard music. Hans was playing the piano. I sat on a chair and listened. When he finished playing, I applauded him. He smiled.

"Finally I have a public who appreciates the music I play."

"Where is Sven, Hans?"

"He is playing with children. This is good for him. I like to teach Sven to play piano, but he needs to play soccer too. He loves the Winter, because Greta or the school takes him to ski in the mountains. He is very happy when the winter starts, because he likes to ski."

"Do you want some coffee Carl?"

"Of course."

We sat and had coffee.

"Greta asked me for her husband Hans. I knew that they killed him, but Greta wants to know more."

"Why didn't you tell Greta, what happened with her husband?"

"I will tell you what happened between me and Greta's husband Carl. We were sitting and dirking. I was drunk when I told him for the diamonds. Greta didn't tell me that she and her husband looked for Louis in the banks. My informant told me, that somebody will kill Greta, her husband and Sven and I need to leave Zug. I told Greta's husband that Greta needs to stop looking for Louis Dreyfus and I left Zug. After three weeks they killed Greta's husband."

"Why didn't they kill Greta, Hans?"

"They were waiting to see if Greta has found where the diamonds are. They wanted to get this information and they were planning to kill Greta too. But After Greta's husband died, Greta stopped. I didn't know who told her to stop, but this saved hers and Sven's life. They told me that it was an accident, but I knew that they killed him."

"…And you were sure that they killed Greta's husband, because

Konev told you that you must leave Zug."

"You are right Carl, but I will never tell Greta what Konev told me. He said that the Mafia killed Greta's husband."

"Did you believe that Hans?"

"I don't know Carl. Many people that have plaid this game are death."

"Can I make a phone call Hans?"

"Of course Carl. I will call Sicily and I ask if this is true."

"Ask, if you have reliable people in Sicily."

"I have Hans." I called and put the phone on a speaker. It was Bruno's boss. "This is Carl. May I speak with Bruno?"

"One moment,"

"Hey boy, my boss said Hi and thanks." He laughed and told me "Nobody believed, but you did a good job".

"Do you need something?"

"Can you ask your people if they ordered to kill a person who lived in Switzerland? His last name is Renner. Four years ago somebody killed Renner at a winter ski resort in Switzerland."

"We don't kill people outside of Italy. Somebody else ordered it, but call me after one hour. I will see what I can find out." Hans was looking at me with an open mouth.

"Who are you Carl? I can't believe that people from Sicily will give you information!"

"They will Hans. I must be sure, if Konev lied to you or he told you the truth. I don't understand one thing Hans, why are people saying that they don't know where you are? You have always been in West Berlin or in Zug."

"That is correct Carl. They have been waiting for me to get the diamonds, then they will kill me and get them. I disappeared from West Berlin, because Konev told me that no longer East and West Germany will be together and I need to leave West Berlin. Everybody knows my name Hans Weber, nobody knows that I have a second name Hans Wabern. You were the first person outside of Zug who knows my second name. When you told me that you have a letter in New York, I was sure that you told me the truth. Konev doesn't know my second name. Few people in Zug know that, because I didn't show my Swiss passport to anybody. My enemies are trying to find Hans Weber, Carl. I don't have a bank account with my name. I use a code. Greta asked me, but I thought that her husband pushed her to ask me, why I didn't have a bank account in Switzerland. I told them that I am West German citizen and I don't like to have problem with the government when I sign my tax form. I told them that West German government has been asking questions on my tax returns. Greta understood that I lied, but she was smart and she didn't take a side. I have enough money for my family, Carl. I don't want to show that I am rich, because I am just a piano teacher in a West Berlin University."

"You are smart Hans. Now I understand why people think that you don't have the diamonds. If you show that you are rich, they will think that you got them."

"You have very good logical argument Carl."

"Do you think that Konev lied to me?"

"Depends on the information I get from Sicily, I will tell you." I called Sicily and Bruno told me that KGB gave the order.

"Do you need more information?"

"No Bruno. This is enough. You must stay and wait in Sicily. When I am ready I will tell Tony."

"Tanks Carl. I will wait for Tony to call me."

"I can't believe it Carl. Why did Konev lie to me? I thought that he is my friend!"

"KGB doesn't have friends Hans. They use and kill people. Do you think that your mom knows something for the diamonds?"

"No Carl. She never spoke with me for diamonds."

"Many people think that your mom knows and someday she will tell you. Did Konev ask you every time you met, how your mom is."

"Yes, he did Carl, but I thought that he was asking to be polite. Konev saved Greta's life, because he knows that Greta works in a bank and someday she will find where the diamonds are located."

"Do you think that Konev keeps me alive to get the diamonds Carl?"

"Yes. It makes now why he wants to speak with me once a month."

"Now you know that Konev is your enemy, but we must use him to kill the shark. Konev will help us to eliminate the shark. Konev must give me the poison and the Russian name on Peter Volak."

Greta and Sven came back in the house and we seized our conversation. After dinner Greta and I were in bed. We had another wonderful night together. Early in the morning Hans knocked on the door.

"Carl, I am sorry to bother you so early, but we have news for you. I will be waiting for you in the living room."

I put on some pajama bottoms and a t-shirt and went to the living room. I sat on the sofa, Hans was standing pacing on the left side of the sofa. He looked intense.

"You will meet Konev in Helsinki on Sunday at 11:00 a.m. I was surprised that he wanted to meet with you in the morning, because when I met with Konev in Helsinki, it was always in a restaurant after 8:00 or 9:00 p.m. We never met in the morning. I think that somebody will be with Konev. Konev asked me which airport you will arriving from. I told him that you are flying from Zurich. Konev didn't ask me if you have direct flight or you will stop and change flights. He will give you the poison. Whoever drinks wine at night with that poison, will be death from heart attack next morning, but nobody will find the poison in the body. He will give you the shark's Russian name too. You and Greta will fly from Zurich to Stockholm, then to Helsinki."

Greta came to the living room and Hans said "Carl, Greta will be your boss. You and Greta will fly together and stay together in the hotel. Greta you need to check in and checkout from the hotel. You will pay the hotel with your credit card. This is the address where Carl and Konev have to meet at 11:00 o'clock. Greta, you need to be inside the coffee shop at 10:40 a.m. You need to check the restroom before Konev and Carl arrive. Carl, when Konev gives you the poison you must touch your head with your left hand. When Carl does that, you need to go in the restroom Greta. You need to open the door of the restroom a little and look for Carl."

Hans brought a hand bag and told Greta "You need to carry this handbag! When Carl walks towards the restroom, you need to leave the restroom. When you and Carl are closest to each other, you need to open the handbag and Carl will have to drop the poison in the handbag. You will return to your table. Five minutes after Carl comes back to his table, you need to leave the coffee shop Greta. You must be back in the hotel and you need to take yours and Carl's things and check out. You need to take a taxi and wait for Carl at the airport. If Carl doesn't come, you must leave Helsinki. This is a dangerous game Greta. You have a son and you must decide if you are going with Carl or staying in Zug."

"I am going with Carl, Hans. I must help him. After you give Greta the poison, if Konev gives you something else you must throw it away before you leave the coffee shop. Don't be afraid if somebody sees you throwing it. Greta and Carl, you need to get ready to leave in the morning."

"I need to make a phone call Hans." I called Ethan's house. Robert picked up the phone.

"Robert, I need to speak with mom…Mom, you need to go back to New York" and I hung up the phone.

After that, I called my grandfather. "Tomorrow, Mark needs to take Roger and they must go to New York and stay in Julia's apartment. Call Jonathan and tell him that I need a jet. The jet must arrive in Stockholm on Sunday at 4:00 p.m. The jet needs to wait for me. If I don't arrive by 8:00 p.m. the jet needs to return to America. If something is wrong, you need to pay Jonathan. I am sorry but I don't have time to explain anything right now Grandfather" and I hung up the phone.

Next, I called Simon. "If you have found which restaurant the shark goes for dinner regularly you need to employ some person who looks the same as Roger. If you have a problem, you need to ask Tony. He will help you. Tony knows well Roger. I will be ready and we will start next week."

"I will be ready too" and Simon hung up the phone.

"I am ready to go now Hans."

Greta and I got our luggage and left the house. We flew to Stockholm. I was happy that Greta was with me.

"How are you feeling Carl?"

"I am feeling great" and I kissed her. "Last night we were interrupted, but tonight I like to spend more time in bed with you Greta."

"Me too Carl."

We arrived at the Helsinki airport in the early evening. We took a taxi and Greta told the taxi driver where he needs to drop us. We were in downtown Helsinki. We entered hotel Kamp. Greta checked in as planned. She took the key and we entered the room.

"We need to prepare for tomorrow morning, so we need do it now Carl. Hans told me that we need to check the coffee shop, before you meet Konev." The coffee shop was close to the hotel.

"I will go inside first Carl. I will order coffee and check the restroom. You need to come after ten minutes and order coffee.

We need to sit on different tables. When I leave you need to leave after five minutes. I will wait outside, but a block away from the coffee shop. We checked the coffee shop. Greta told me that she is hungry and we entered the first restaurant we saw. We ordered dinner. I asked Greta.

"Why are you doing this Greta?"

"For two reasons. First, four years ago I was a very happy woman. I had a son and a husband. I love them. I have a good job. I had everything that a woman dreams. After my husband died, my life became a disaster. I loved my husband very much, so I decided that I will never marry again. I slept with men, but I didn't think that I will marry somebody. I also had a problem with Sven. He didn't want another man in the house. But that changed when you came to the house. Sven loves you and he wants us to live together in my house. I know that this is impossible, because you are young and I know that I am old for you, but I saw that Sven is happy. Now I know that if I meet a man who I love and he loves me and Sven, then Sven will like this man to marry me. I know that Hans will speak with Sven and tell him that I am old to marry you. Sven loves Hans and he will listen to him. You were in my house for two days and you changed Sven and me. Second, I am with you, because if something happens with you, I will call the police and tell them that my boyfriend has disappeared. I am a Swiss citizen, you are an American citizen. The police will try to find you. Honestly, I like to be with you one more night too, Carl." We laughed and Greta asked me "Do you want to be with me one more night Carl?"

"Yes, Greta." We left the restaurant and returned in the hotel.

We were in bed. I told Greta "You are my boss. You need to do, whatever you want with me. You will be my teacher, I will be your student. This is your night Greta. I like to remember this night." Greta was very happy to fulfill my request. She was a good teacher, I was a good student. She woke me up in middle night and we had sex again. In the morning we had sex again. I finished when I was behind her, but I didn't think for another woman. I looked at Greta's ass when I finished. It is a little big, but beautiful. Our voices were at high pitch, when we finished. We didn't speak. We were so happy. We knew that this was the last sex between us, but we didn't want to speak about that. We were savoring the experience we had together. Greta spoke first.

"We need to get ready Carl. We have to leave soon."

She walked to the bathroom. She was a little heavy, but her body looked sexy. I didn't want to look at her bosoms for too long, because I would wanted take her in bed again. I didn't have time to do that. I had to go to the meeting Konev. I asked myself, what is more important Carl? Do you want sex with Greta or you save your life? I will need to ask doctor, if I have a mental problem. Of course, women make me happy, but now I must think how I will save my life. If the shark kills me, I won't have a chance to be with another woman again. I have to get the poison and kill him. After that I can be with as many women as I want. Greta won't be the last woman. Greta walked back in the room. I couldn't recognize her. She was wearing a black wig over her blond hair.

"Do I look different Carl?"

"Yes, you look different Greta. I didn't recognize you at first." She came to me and kissed me.

"I will be waiting for you in the coffee shop, Carl."

She left the room at 10:10 a.m. I left the room at 10:30 a.m. When I entered the coffee shop, I saw Greta. She was sitting on a table and sipping coffee. Greta's table was on the corner and she had a good view of the coffee shop. It would be easy to go to the bathroom. I saw a man who waived his hand at me. This was Konev. I walked to his table. Konev stood up and we shook hands.

"I will get coffee Konev. Do you like me to get you something to drink?"

"I already got coffee Carl. Thank you!"

I got the coffee and returned to Konev's table. I noticed that there were no many people in the shop, but it was 11:00 a.m. on Sunday morning. I thought that somebody looked at me and Konev.

"What is Hans doing?"

"He is busy with Sven. Hans is teaching him to play the piano."

"Hans is a good teacher Carl. He told me that you need to kill the shark" waiting for me to respond.

"I must kill the shark Konev, or Peter Volak will kill me."

"Peter already tried to kill you Carl."

"He missed Konev and I am alive. Now I have a chance to kill Peter."

"Do you have people to do that?"

"This is my problem Konev."

"What is Ethan doing?"

"He went back to work. After I left the company, he had to go back, because he had nobody else to replace me with."

"Did you make good money at Ethan's company?"

"I made quarter a million a year, but I would like to make more in the future."

"How many times have you been in Ethan's house Konev?"

"I have been once with and Peter. Ethan's Grandfather invited us."

"I thought that Peter asked for help Ethan's Grandfather."

"Peter used Ethan's Grandfather to look in Ethan's house for the diamonds or information about them, Carl."

"Did you see anything unusual in the house Konev?"

"I think that the house has a hidden office. I am not sure about it, but if you want to find the diamonds, you need to look in the house, Carl"

"Are you going to marry Vicky?"

"I don't know, because I am young and I like to spend time with different women. Vicky is beautiful, but at this point in my life I am planning to wait one or two more years before I marry. What I am going to do, if Vicky decides to go back in Russia? Do you think that I will follow Vicky to Russia? I want to live in America. I love my country Konev. America is the best country in the world. America is number one. I will be polite with you Konev. Russia is number two." I laughed, but Konev didn't

"Who ordered to kill Greta's husband, Konev?"

"KGB, but Greta's husband was so aggressive. We thought that he will get the diamonds."

"Do you think that you will find the diamonds, Carl?"

"My first priority is to save my life. My life is more important than any diamonds. When I kill Peter then I will think for the diamonds."

"Did you speak with Hans's mom?"

"I was in Switzerland, she lives in Germany. I did not go Germany, Konev."

"Do you want to know what happened with Louis and his wife?"

"Lorenzo Falsone told me what happened. They are death Konev. We are alive.

"Do you think that you deserve that I give you the poison?"

"If you don't think that I deserve your help, then why did you tell Hans that you want to meet and give me the poison?"

"If you want to be my enemy, then this isn't my problem Konev."

"There is no problem for me too Carl. I will go back to Russia. You will never follow me there, because you know that my people will kill you very easy there."

"You have a son who lives in New York, Konev."

"What do you want Carl?"

"The poison."

He gave me a small box under the table. I took the box with my right hand and scratched my head with my left hand. Greta walked to the restroom. I looked at clock on the wall of the coffee shop.

"What is Vicky doing now, Carl?"

"She is a model Konev. When I left to work in Dallas, we spoke on the phone and we spent time together when I was in New York. We had two hard years, but now I left Dallas and I have decides to live to go back to New York."

"You need to excuse me for a moment, but I need to use the restroom Konev. Are you coming with me?"

"I don't need to use the restroom Carl."

I walked to the restroom. I saw Greta walking out. When I was close to her, she opened her handbag and I dropped the box inside. When I returned to the table, Greta was getting ready to leave. I sat on the chair and Konev told me "If somebody tries to get the box with the poison you must kill him. I will give you a pistol." Konev gave me a folded newspaper. The pistol was inside.

"Are you ready to leave Carl?"

"I need to make a phone call Konev."

I walked and asked who the manager is. "I am sir."

"I need to make a call, but I want to use your phone in the office."

"No problem sir, follow me." I walked and I saw an exit door for employees. I opened the door and I saw a big trash can. I threw the newspaper with the pistol and closed the door. I entered the office of the manager. I called the hotel and asked for Greta.

"What time did she leave? This is OK" and I hung up the phone.

"My girlfriend left the hotel. I had to meet her there", I told the manager. When I came back to the table Konev was gone. I left the coffee shop. I was walking on the street when two policemen told me that I need to stop. I stopped and they told me that they need to check what I have on me. I walked to the police car with the policemen. They asked me to put my hands on the hood of the car and one of them pad my body. He toke my passport, wallet and plane ticket. He said to the other policemen that I don't have a pistol. The policeman who checked me was young. The other policeman was older. The young policeman asked me where the pistol is.

"I don't know what you are talking about sir. I don't have a pistol. I am in Helsinki for business, but I after this unprovoked police padding I will have to reconsider my plans to do business in Helsinki." He opened my wallet and looked at the name of the credit card and the passport.

"You need to arrest me first then you can check my ID at the police station."

The older policeman took my credit card and laughed.

"Carl Hope is so rich. They will fire you from the police if he tells them what happened." Then he turned to me and asked me.

"Where do like to go Mr. Hope?"

"Could you drop me at airport sir?"

"I will, but I don't like anybody to know what happened."

"I will never tell sir." They dropped me at the airport.

"Thank you so much gentlemen. The police of Helsinki provided me with a good service. I will not forget this." The older policeman laughed "You are so funny boy."

I entered the airport and I saw Greta. She smiled and she walked and checked in. I followed her.

I was looking at her ass. It was so sexy. Then I thought to myself sorry Carl, somebody else will enjoy Greta's body in bed. You won't have chance to be with her anymore. Your time with her ended this morning. I didn't regret one minute of it, because I had a good time with her.

I checked in and found my gate. I saw Greta. She was sitting and reading a magazine. I sat in a distance from her and I looked around to see if somebody was looking at me or her. I didn't notice anyone. I went to sit next to Greta. She laughed and told me "When I heard the siren of the police car I thought that they come to arrest me, I was scared. But when I saw that you left the police car and you said something to the policemen and one of them laughed, I knew that you were joking with them. What did you tell them?"

"I thanked them for the good service Greta. They were my taxi." Greta laughed "Hans told me that he has never met a man, who is so funny and so dangerous."

"Hey Greta, I looked at your ass when you were checking in. I was behind you. It is so sexy. I was ready for bed."

"I love you for making me feel so sexy and wanton, Carl. I know that I am old for you. You must marry someone younger Carl."

"Why do I need to marry Greta?"

"You are making a women happy. When you have sex with a woman, she feels that you love her and you are so happy to be with her. You make women crazy in the bed. I know that, because I felt that last night. I had sex three times. I woke up you in middle of the night and we had sex. I have men in my life. I know what the word sex means. When a man and woman have sex for a long time, the two bodies become synchronized in bed. When a man and a woman finish together they are in sync and the two bodies become one. In the past when I had sex, when man finished, I didn't."

"What kind of sex in that Carl? I didn't have sex, because I didn't finish. Man had sex, because he finished. You know how to prepare a woman to have sex. It is very obvious they want to have sex again with you, but you tend to leave them Carl. Women know that they cant's stop you to leave them. They have two feelings about you. Good time when you are with them in the bed and bad time when you leave them."

"How did you figure this out Greta?"

"I feel that right now Carl. I had four wonderful days with you and I am so happy right now. Three hours from now when you leave, I will be sad."

"What will change if I marry Greta?"

"When you marry, you will have one woman. If someday she isn't happy, she will know that next day she will be happy, because you will never leave her."

"What if I divorce her?"

"This is different Carl. You and your wife will have a reason to divorce, if you aren't happy to live together. If you tell her that you will leave, she will tell you that she doesn't care for you, mother faker, so you can go and never come back. She will thank God that this stupid man is leaving. You won't hurt your wife. She will be happy that you are leaving." Greta laughed.

"Are you happy now Carl?"

"You are right Greta. I don't think much when I leave women. I thought that they were happy."

"How old are you Greta?'

"Thirty four Carl. You are almost twenty seven."

"How did you know that?"

"Hans looked at your passport, when he bought the tickets. He told me that I am old for you. "

"You need to think for that, if you try to keep Carl in your future."

"Hans was right Carl. You deserve a young woman that can keep up with you in bed for many years to come. I will try to meet a man too. If he loves me and Sven, I will marry him. I will try to have one more child. When I lose seven kilograms, I will be a sexier woman and many men will want to marry me." We laughed and I told her "You are sexy now Greta, but when you lose seven kilograms, you will be a model. I will see you in many magazines."

"I hope so Carl, but I need to lose the weight."

They started to board the plane. We entered the plane. Greta told me that she wants to move to Geneva. "Patrik's boss promised me that he will help me to move to there. He thinks that I will be his mistress, because he is married, but I will use him just to move."

"It will be good for you and Sven if you move to Geneva. It is an international city. You will meet many different people. You will have many man to choose from there, but I need to know you that you are the last woman in bed with me before am married."

"Why did you say that, Carl?"

"I am planning to get married when I return to America. I have a son and my life will be different if I have a wife."

"Oh my God. I am the last woman with you, before you marry! What should I tell your wife when I meet her and she asked me who am I? I will have to tell her that I was the last woman in bed with you and that I deserve a chance to check you have learned something new in the bed since the last time we were together." We laughed and we had tears in your eyes.

We arrived in Stockholm. I checked what my next gate is, Greta checked hers.

"I need to use the restroom Carl. Can you wait for me?" When she came back, she gave me the box with the poison.

"I may never see you again Carl."

"I am coming back to Geneva in two or three weeks Greta. I would like to see you, Sven and Hans."

She had to leave, because they were boarding Greta's flight. I gave her a long kiss.

"I know that you love me Carl. You need to remember that I was the last woman, before you married" and she laughed. After one hour I entered my jet and I left Stockholm.

CHAPTER 12

As I was flying I was wondering, why Konev left the coffee shop before I returned to my seat after the phone call. Hans was right when he told me that something was wrong. Now I know that Konev wasn't alone. Somebody was watching Konev and told him what to do. He was careful and he gave me the poison fast. He let me to go to the restroom. He must have suspected that I will give the poison to somebody. I think that Konev recognized Greta, but he didn't tell me that. Konev gave me the pistol after I returned from the restroom. When Konev gave me the newspaper with the pistol, he wasn't fast and careful, because somebody had to see that he did. This somebody must have been watching us from the outside. It was smart of me to make the call from the manager's phone, because the public phone was outside on the wall on the coffee shop. If I called from the public phone anybody would have seen me. I didn't need to call anybody. I needed to throw the pistol. Hans was right when he told me "Doesn't matter if somebody see you. I didn't touch the pistol." I touched the newspaper. I think that Hans told Konev's that I know for his son. Konev gave me the poison when I told him that Sasha lives in New York. But why didn't he tell me the Russian name of Peter Volak? Konev should have told me before he left the coffee shop. Something went wrong and Konev had to leave before I came back. Maybe KGB wanted the police to arrest me and Konev. I know that nobody knows that Konev gave me the poison. The police asked for a pistol they didn't ask for the box. I have the box, but I don't know what is inside. I need to open and see. I opened I saw three phials and two small pieces of paper. The first piece of paper described how I need to use the poison. The second piece of paper I read "Peter Volkov-Peter Volak-the shark and Boris Bromich- Los Angeles-Ethan's wife." What is that Konev? Who is Boris Bromich? I taught for few seconds and then it hit me. Oh my God! Ethan's wife was killed in the hospital. Konev gave me the name of the person that killed Ethan's wife. Why did Konev do that? I think that something happened in KGB. Vicky told me that the shark asked her father to go back to Russia. Why the shark needs to return to Russia? Vicky's father told the shark that they will kill him in Russia. The shark knows that they will kill him. This isn't good news for me, because the shark will fight for his life in America. He must kill me. I covered the box and I asked for scissors. I cut the paper and separated the two pieces. One with the name Peter Volkov-Peter Volak-the shark, the other with the name Boris Bromich- Los Angeles- Ethan's wife and I put this one in my wallet. I put the other piece back in the box. I put the box in my bag. Then I thought about Michelle. Poor girl, she lost her mom when she was only twelve years old. Why didn't Ethan marry again? Maybe Michelle didn't want another woman, the same way Sven didn't want another man. If I have a chance I will ask Michelle. She loves me and she will tell me, why Ethan didn't marry. It has been a long day. I was tired and I closed my eyes and feel asleep.

When I opened my eyes we were close to New York. I looked at a magazine for a while. I arrived in New York. I left the airport and looked for a taxi. A limousine stopped and a driver came out. He opened the door of the limousine.

"Come in Carl", Simon called me from the inside of the limo. I entered and Simon embraced and kissed me.

"Hey boy, you saved my life. Yesterday Julia called and asked to meet with me and she was not happy."

"Simon, if something happen with Carl, I will kill you."

"I am safe. You are alive and Julia won't kill me." We stopped on front of at the building where Simon lives. We went to his apartment.

"Do you want some coffee Carl?"

"I am OK Simon." I took my bag. I got the small box and gave it to Simon.

"What is this Carl?"

"I brought a small gift for the shark Simon" and I opened the box.

"What is inside the phials Carl?"

"A poison. The shark will be poisoned."

"Do you know who the shark is Simon?"

"I think that Peter Volak is the shark, Carl."

"You are right Simon." I gave Simon the second piece of paper. "Oh my God. The shark is Peter Volak or Peter Volkov who was born in Russia."

"Peter Volak or Peter Volkov is a double agent Simon. He uses KGB and CIA to make money on Wall Street and buy a power in New York. I don't know why, but your father invited two KGB agents Peter and Konev to look into Louis's house in Dallas. Peter ordered to kill Louis and his wife."

"Why did Peter kill them Carl?"

"Peter wanted to know where the diamonds are."

"I don't believe that the diamonds exist Carl. For twenty five years nobody has seen them."

"They are in Switzerland, Simon, but I don't know which bank has them."

"I will kill Peter, Carl."

"Roger must finish this job Simon. You must help him."

"Hey Carl, do you like to call Vicky and invite her to come here?"

"No Simon. I need to stay far away from Vicky, because if I continue to meet and have sex with Vicky, I will create a problem for her."

"What is the problem for you to meet Vicky?"

"KGB will kill Vicky if I marry her, but don't spy for them."

"Are you serious?"

"I am serious Simon. Many people don't know that KGB has a big power everywhere. Simon, I think that CIA will start to look for me after two or three days, so you must keep the poison with you. Me, you, Roger and Mark need to meet tomorrow morning in Julia's apartment. You need to come there at 9:00 a.m."

"What is Michelle doing Simon?"

"Are you going to marry Michelle, Carl?"

"I don't know. I have some concerns Simon."

"I know why you have concerns. She is an unusual girl. Michelle loves you so much and she likes to marry you. When you left for Europe she called me every day and asked for you. I told her that I don't know where you are. Do you know what Michelle told me?"

"Simon I know that you are lying to me. You know where Carl is, but I ask you, because I love him. He is a real man. I want a man to take my virginity and I will be waiting for Carl."

"Oh my God. This is so personal Carl. I am Uncle Simon. I am not her mom or father to tell me that she is a virgin. I am sorry, but I told her where you were."

"It is OK Simon. Now I am in New York. If Michelle calls what I should I tell her?"

"Don't worry. I will call her. I have been thinking about her, but I don't know what to do."

"Ask her to marry you Carl."

"It is easy for you to say that Simon. I don't know how to ask Michelle to marry me."

"Do you need the limousine?"

"No Simon. It is better if I take a taxi."

I took a taxi and went to Julia's apartment. When entered the living room I saw Mom, Roger and Mark. Julia raised her hands and said "Thank God, Carl is at home." She took my head in her arms and kissed my forehead. Roger and Mark laughed.

"Are you hungry Carl?"

"No Mom, I am OK.

"Do you want anything?"

"Mss. Shapiro give Carl a feeding bottle with milk. He is hungry and he needs to suck some milk." Mark and Roger laughed.

Mom turned towards them and told them "If you don't stop to joke, I will kick your ass out of my apartment." They stopped to laugh. I laughed and told her, "Hey Mom, you scared Mark and Roger". Everybody started to laugh. Roger asked me for my trip in Europe. I told them in general. I didn't want to tell them what happened in detail. Roger understood that I didn't want to speak about it.

Mom went in the kitchen and I asked Roger "Are you ready Roger?"

"If we have the poison, I am ready Carl."

"We have it Roger, but I don't like to speak when Mom is here." Mark knows me very well. He didn't ask me anything. He saw that I was nervous. Honestly, I was. I didn't know why, but I was. After dinner Mark told Roger that they need to go to bed. I was with Mom.

"For the first time in my life, I saw you nervous tonight Carl."

"I am Mom. Could you leave the apartment tomorrow morning at 8:00 o'clock?"

"What time I need to return Carl?"

"You need to come back for lunch Mom."

"After 12:00 o'clock?"

"Yes Mom. Good night Mom" and I went to my room. This was the first time I didn't kiss Mom on the cheek, before I went to the bed. I know that was hard for her and I am sure she didn't sleep that night. I know that before Mom leaves the apartment tomorrow morning she will ask me, why I didn't kiss her. I was in bed when Mom knocked on the door.

"Come in Mom." She came and sat on the bed.

"Something is wrong between us Carl. What is it?"

"Nothing Mom."

"Why didn't you kiss me last night?"

"I am so sorry that I hurt you. I know that I have everything. Money, education, women, freedom, but I have a hard time dealing with the fact that somebody is trying to kill me. You thought me how to help people. You didn't tell me that there are many dangerous people in this world. I saw many of them. For four weeks they have been trying to kill me: in Dallas. in the Bahamas. Then they waited to kill me in New York. They were looking for me to kill me in Milan and they tried to kill me in Bern! I don't get it!"

"Ethan told me that they started again Carl. Nobody believes that. I know that I need to listen to you."

"You are right Mom."

"I will do as you ask me to Carl."

"I need to speak with you after lunch Mom. I need to talk to you about Michelle. You need to marry here. She is a good girl Carl and she loves you very much. Why don't you marry her?"

"You will never change Mom. I am talking to you that somebody is trying to kill me, you are telling to me marry Michelle."

"You must think for your future Carl. You say all the time that the future is what is important to you. Isn't that true Carl?"

I laughed and said "You are right Mom". She kissed me and left my room. When I went to the kitchen she was leaving the apartment. Roger and Mark were having coffee there. The doorbell rang at 9:00 o'clock. I opened the door and I saw Simon and Ben. I couldn't believe it.

"I didn't think that I will ever see you Ben! I am so happy that you are here with Simon. Come in." We all sat in the living room. Roger asked me if I had a plan already.

"Carl did his part Roger. Me, you and my friend here will kill the shark." Simon didn't say Ben's name, and he continued to speak.

"I have a plan Roger. Friday night is very busy night for the restaurants, because many people go out to have dinner in a restaurant. The shark goes to the same restaurant on Friday night. Tomorrow me, you, and Roger, will go to that restaurant. I will ask the owner of the restaurant, if he needs addition people for Friday night and I will tell him that you are looking for a job. You are a friend of my relative. The owner will give you the job, because he knows who I am. The shark uses the same table. I have a friend who knows well the shark. My friend will come in the restaurant at 8:00 p.m. The shark drinks red wine. When my friend starts to speak with the shark, you must put the poison in the glass of the shark."

"What should I do if the shark holds his glass with red wine?"

"My friend will embrace the shark. When he puts the glass on the table, you must put the poison Roger. If we don't have chance to poison the shark, then somebody will have to kill the shark with one bullet in the head. If we kill him with the poison will be better. I will take you with me tomorrow morning at 11:00."

"Mark, you need to leave New York tomorrow. My friend likes to speak with you Carl. Follow me." Ben and I went to my bedroom. Ben showed me a photo of me taking the newspaper with the pistol.

"I had this picture after twenty four hours, Carl. I think that the CIA will receive the picture soon. KGB wants to create a problem for you with the CIA. That means that, you need to disappear from New York, before we move forward with the plan to kill the shark or Peter. I was surprised when Simon told me, that the shark, Peter Volak and Peter Volkov is the same person. I took the plane and came to New York. My friend who disappeared thirty six years ago told me that he and Peter Volkov had a mission in Syria. He told me that our boss was the only person that knew where they were going. He didn't understand why Peter Volkov didn't want somebody else to know that my friend was with him. My friend left and after three days somebody killed our boss. Nobody knew that I knew the name Peter Volkov. Now I know that Peter Volkov killed my friend and KGB sent him in New York to spy for them. I can't bring my friend back, but I have a chance to kill Peter Volkov. You were also right about Aaron. He spied for many secret services."

"I will leave New York on Thursday Ben."

"This is a good plan Carl. If someday you have problem Carl, you tell Simon."

"I will be back in Switzerland after two or three weeks, Ben. If I need your help, I will call you. When I met Aaron I thought that he was a good man, but you are the good man Ben, he is not."

"When you asked me for Aaron, I told you that nobody knows who is who in this business. Honestly, nobody knows how long he or she will live, but you are young and smart. You deserve to live long Carl and you need to marry Michelle."

"How do you know that I need to marry Michelle, Ben?"

"I work for the secret service and I don't need to tell you that Carl, but I am sure that Simon, Roger and I will poison Peter Volkov on Friday night. On Saturday morning Peter Volkov will die. You need to focus now to find the diamonds Carl."

"I will Ben." Simon and Ben left the apartment.

"What is next Carl?", Mark asked me.

"We need to have a party tonight Mark. You and Roger need to buy food and alcohol. I must stay home."

"We will gladly do that. You stay here." Mark and Roger left. I called and bought a ticket from New York to Dallas. Mom came back after 12:00 p.m. We sat in the living room and she asked me "Do you think that you and I should live separate Carl?"

"Are you planning to marry somebody Julia?"

"Oh boy, I am asking you a serious question and you are joking with me."

"Why do you think that I am joking?"

"Because you told your grandmother that you will marry. She told me that you think that you need one year to do it. Why didn't you tell me, that you have decided to marry?"

"When I told Grandmother I didn't think that I will marry soon. But now I think that I should."

"Where do you want to live after you marry?"

"I will buy a big apartment and me, you and my wife will live there."

"I have an apartment Carl and I don't want to move."

"Don't you love me anymore Mom?"

"Don't say that. I have one more question for you Carl. Can I see the letters that you found that were written by the joker?"

"They are in a safe box. I don't like anybody to read them Mom."

"Who knows where the safe box is?"

"Simon knows. If something happens to me Simon must to open the box. The letters have information about the people that killed Louis Dreyfus. If I am death, Simon needs to kill the person who ordered to kill Louis and his wife."

"Is Simon more important for you than me Carl?"

"Simon is the brother of Louis. He must decide what to do with the killer of Louis. Who are you Julia? An ex-lover or you are still dreaming of your love for Louis Dreyfus? Louis left you fifty years ago. He is death for twenty five years. I don't understand you. Where is your place in the Dreyfus family? Leave alone the Dreyfus family. They must decide what to do. It is not your place."

"You are right Carl. Who am I for the Dreyfus family? Jerry told me that one day you may have harsh words for me, and it is today. Do you love me Carl?"

"Of course, I love you Mom."

"Are you going to marry Michelle?"

"I need to ask Vicky, before I ask Michelle to marry me."

"Vicky won't marry you. I spoke with her."

"How is your son Julian Jr. doing Carl? Also how are Edit and Julian?"

"I think that Michelle won't marry me, because I have a son."

"Don't worry about that. Michelle spoke with Edit and Julian Jr."

"How did Michelle find Edit's phone number?"

"I gave it to her and I told Michelle that she needs to call and speak with Edit. I told her that Edit was your big love and I was wrong when I got between you and her. Michelle spoke with Edit and Julian Jr."

"Julian Jr. doesn't speak English, Mom. How did she speak with him?"

"Michelle speaks French. She was happy when she learned that you have a son. She told me that she is certain that someday you and her will have a son too. Are you going to marry her now, Carl?"

"I think that Ethan is not going to be happy that I have a son. He will tell Michelle to choose a better man."

"You are right about that. Ethan wasn't happy when he heard that you have a son, but Michelle doesn't listen to her father, because she loves you and she believes that you will save her life."

"Why do you want me to marry Michelle, Mom?"

"I love Michelle. I love Vicky too. Vicky loves Michelle too. She thinks that Michelle will be a good mom and a wife. I trust Vicky. She is sensitive and she never lies."

"You are right Mom. I love Vicky, but I in order to save her life I can't marry her."

"Vicky told me everything Carl. She loves you and she wants to be your friend forever."

"Do you think that Vicky will marry someday Mom?"

"She will marry Carl, but she will need time. I spoke with Vicky's mom. She is happy that you decided to separate. She told me that it is good for both of you. She told me what the problem is. She is a mom and she is right. I know that you will support Vicky. When you finish this job I expect you to tell me when you are ready to find a new apartment. I will be happy to live with you and Michelle."

"Thanks Mom" and I kissed her.

"I have five grandchildren. I like to have more Carl. If you marry it will be good for Julian Jr. Jerry told me that he isn't worried for you getting married. He worries for Max. You know what to do with women. Max doesn't. Did you see Max in Geneva?"

"I went to dinner with him and Sofia. She is Max's girlfriend."

"What is your impression of Sofia, Carl?"

"Jerry is right Mom. Max doesn't have experience with women. I think that she has the control in the relationship, but the good thing is she will push Max in the right direction."

"How do you know that?"

"I told Max that, if he comes back to New York, he and Sofia can live in your apartment. Sofia was so happy that she will come to New York and they will live in your apartment."

"Max doesn't have money to buy my apartment Carl!"

"Someday you will give the apartment to Max. When I buy a new apartment I will put your name on the contract."

"I will not sign the contract. You should be the sole owner of your new apartment. You have never asked me for money and I know that you will not ask me to put any money in the new apartment either. I spoke with Jerry and I told him that if someday I die, you, Jerry and Debby must divide my money. Jerry told me that you must be in control of the money."

"Mom, Carl know how to make money. I know that Debby and I will have more money if Carl manages them, we will never lose any of them."

"If that is what you want to do, I can promise you, that I will do my best to keep the money safe and look after Jerry and Debby."

Roger and Mark returned to the apartment.

"We will continue our conversation later Carl."

"What is this Mark?", Julia asked.

"We will have a party Julia."

"This is an excellent idea Mark. I will cook. Somebody needs to help me in the kitchen."

"I will help Mom."

"You need to call Michelle, Carl. Mark or Roger will help me."

I went to my bedroom and I called Michelle. "Hi Michelle, this is Carl."

"Hey boy, you miss you so much. Where are you now?"

"I am in Mom's apartment. Mom is in the kitchen. She is preparing to cook, so I decided to call you."

"Can I come to New York, Carl?"

"You don't need to come to New York Michelle."

"I know that you don't love me, but now I know that you don't want me at all."

"This isn't true Michelle."

"Why don't you want me in New York then?"

"Because, I will be coming to Dallas on Thursday afternoon. I bought the thicket this morning."

"Do you want to stay in my father's house?"

"If I have permission from Ethan, I will be glad stay in his house."

"Are you afraid of Ethan, Carl?"

"I am not Michelle, but I left Ethan's company. I don't know how he feels about me now."

"He is happy that he returned back to work Carl. Now he is different. Hey Carl, I think that Ethan has an affair, but I don't like to tell you with whom. If you have sex with me, Ethan will tell you to take me with you and both of us are not welcomed back in his house, because he has a woman in his life."

"Do you think that Ethan will want to shoot me if I have sex with you Michelle?"

"Hey boy, if my father kills you after you have sex with me, you will be a hero in Dallas. It will be written in the local newspaper that Carl died because he loves Michelle." We laughed.

"Do you love me Carl?"

"You know my answer Michelle."

"Oh boy, you will never change."

"I may change after we meet on Thursday Michelle."

"How many days are you planning to stay in Dallas?"

"If you get me in bed, maybe forever."

"That sounds so good Carl. Me and you in bed. I don't wat to talk about sex. I want to have sex. I had some education on the subject while you have been gone…"

"I spoke with Edit and your son. I was so happy when Edit told me, that you bought apartment for them. I told my father, but he told me that you are crazy."

"Do you want to marry Carl, Michelle?"

"If Carl asks me, I will marry him father."

"Carl will spend all your money on charity. He reminds me of my mother and father. Carl loves people and they love him. He has a big heart. You don't have a heart like his, but you are crazy like him. If that is what you want to do, I wish you good luck with him."

"I love you Carl, because you are like my mom. I know that I will never forget my mom. Sometimes I miss her so much. If I marry you I will have husband and a mom. Do you understand what I said?"

"I understood Michelle, but I have had many women before you. I don't know what you will think if you knew my past?"

"I have heard about your past and guessed some too, but this is your past. You can't change the that. I spoke with Vicky. She told me that you will be a good husband and a father. Kate told me the same. I spoke with Sue and Emmy as well. They all love you Carl.

They told me, that you are a good man. You know that I don't have experience in life and I asked people who I trust to tell me about you. Ethan told me that you like go get in bed every woman you see. I told him that maybe women are taking you." We laughed. I know you for five weeks only, but you had my heart, when I first saw you. I knew that someday I will be your wife. This is my dream Carl. You are an aggressive and strange man. One person that believes that you will marry me is Emmy Colman. I can't wait to see you on Thursday Carl" and Michelle hung up the phone. I was holding the receiver when Mom asked me.

"What did Michelle tell you Carl? You look like you can't believe something that you just heard."

"Mom, why did Michelle tell me, that took her heart when she first saw me?"

"Edit and Vicky told me that they felt the same way too about you. Many of my friends told me that I will have problem with you, when you become twenty, twenty two years old Carl. This is because you have personality and you are charismatic . Popole notice your presence in a room and are drawn to you."

"Did you ask her to marry you?"

"No mom. It is hard to ask her to marry me. I am not ready to that right now. Maybe when I am in Dallas I will ask Michelle to marry me."

"What I learned about Michelle is that she lives in her past. Michelle told me that she dreams of her mom every night. It has been a is a long time since her mom past away. I think that if you marry Michelle, her mom will leave her alone, because she knows that you will save Michelle's life. You need to trust me on this one Carl."

"I believe you, Mom."

We went to the dining room and we started to eat and drink. Me, Roger and Mark got dunk after few hours. Mom was talking to Roger. I was talking to Mark. I asked him "Did you have problems with my aunt after you married her?"

"Everybody has problems, but this is normal for married people Carl. I had sex with other women, but I didn't have a relationship with them. I just had sex. That is it. If any of them started speaking for future together. I stopped seeing them. Sex yes. Future no. Your father was stupid when he started his love affair with Larisa. Two years ago for Thanksgiving your father said that you don't deserve our family, because you haven't visited the family for seven years. Oh my God, Mom was so angry with him."

"If I had an abortion when I was pregnant with you, I would have been a happy women now stupid son. You are a traitor. You have sex with a teacher and you want your father death so you can sale the land of your father and marry her. You use Mark. Do you have property and any millions in the bank son? I don't think so. Carl and Mark have a Dealership and millions. Son, take your stupid wife and never come back to my house."

"My father tried to say something, but Mom told him that he should have spoken fifteen years ago. It is too late now, so he needs to shut up, because she will kick him out of the house too".

"After that Mom haven't seen your father. She pointed a finger to me and told me that if I don't stop, I will be next. I stopped. Now I am a loving husband." I and Mark laughed.

"What do you think about my brother Carl, he is your father?"

"I don't know Mark. I have not seen my mom and dad for nine years, but I haven't thought about it much. I am happy with Julia. She has been my mom and dad. I love her Mark."

"Are you going to invite your mom and dad to your wedding?"

"I will tell my wife that I have a Mom and a Dad. It will be her decision to invite them or not. I won't." Mark told me that I am the same as Grandmother. Julia told us that we are drunk and we should go to bed.

In the morning Mark left to Knoxville. At 11:00 a.m. Simon came.

"Are you ready Carl?", Simon asked me.

"I am little nervous Simon."

"Don't worry, Michelle doesn't eat people." Simon, Mom and Rorer laughed. Simon and Roger left. I was with mom. Mom asked me what I like for lunch. I asked her if she want to go out.

"This is a good idea Carl. Let's go." We left the apartment. We walked and I asked Mom, if she needs a taxi.

"I want to walk Carl." After lunch Mom told me that she likes to see Vicky's boutique. I tried to get a taxi, but Mom told me that she wants to walk.

"I am young Carl." Few blocks from the restaurant we reached the boutique. Vicky was there.

"I am so happy to see you Julia." Vicky embraced and kissed

Mom.

"Oh boy, I am so happy to see you back in New York" and Vicky kissed me. Vicky's mom entered the boutique too.

"Hi Mss. Shapiro." Mom kissed Vicky's mom.

"Hi Carl." I kissed the hand of Vicky's mom. My mom and Vicky's mom walked away from Vicky and me and she asked me "Are you ready Carl?"

"I don't know what to tell you Vicky. Honestly, I am little uneasy."

"I know Carl. You don't have problem to get women in bed, but now you need to get the hand of a woman. Oh boy, one woman forever" and Vicky laughed.

"I spoke with Michelle. You know that I love her, Carl. I am so happy that you will marry her."

"That can happen if she wants to marry me, Vicky."

"Michelle is waiting for you Carl. She is crazy for you, as I was crazy for you before, but she has a better chance than me. I had a chance to be with you, but I don't have a chance to marry you. I don't have any regrets about our relationship. I am happy that you have a chance to have a beautiful and a smart wife." I touched Vicky's belly and looked in her eyes.

"We need to wait four more weeks, Carl. How is your son in Paris?"

"Edit and Julian Jr. are well. Edit told me that I should marry. She was so happy that I went to see my son. Edit's husband Julian knows that I am the father of Julian Jr."

"This is good Carl, because if someday you like to take your son to visit or live with you, it will be easier. If I marry I will never tell my husband that you are the father of my child. I believe that this will good for me, you and the child. You will be my best friend forever Carl. If you want to see the child, I will be happy to arrange it. I am from Russia. Edit is from France. We think different."

"When do you plan to ask Michelle to marry you?"

"Either on Thursday or Friday. Vicky, you have contract with Simon for two years. I would like to buy the boutique for you. I will speak with Simon about it. Is that OK?"

"This property is very expensive Carl."

"You are more expensive to me Vicky. I will never forget you. You deserve it." I embraced Vicky. We embraced each other and kissed for a long time. We bought knew that that was our final good buy as lovers. From this moment forward we will be friends, not lovers. Mom and Vicky's mom came towards us. They were crying looking at us. We hold hands for few moments and Vicky walked away with tears on her eyes.

Mom walked towards me and said "Are you ready to go Carl?"

"I guess so." I was looking at Vicky.

She turn around and said "Carl, call me when you and Michelle come to New York. I will be happy to see, you and Michelle married."

Mom and I walked on the street. We passed by some jewelry stores.

"I want to buy the engagement ring for Michelle, Carl."

"I don't know Michelle's ring size."

"I know it."

"I will buy it Mom. I am not a cheap man."

"That is true Carl." We returned to the apartment. Mom opened a special wine for dinner.

"Cheers Carl!"

"Cheers Mom! This is your last night as a single man."

"I can't believe that every night, when I go to the bed and every morning when I wake up I will have the same woman next to me. Oh my God! I am scared of that Mom." We laughed.

After dinner I wanted to help Mom, but she told me that I need to go to bed.

In the morning I kissed Mom and told her, "I promise you that I will come back with Michelle".

"God bless you son, and good luck."

That afternoon I arrived in Dallas. I took a taxi and I told the driver to drop me in the Galleria shopping center. I went to Cristal's shop. I walked to him.

"I was waiting for you Carl."

"How did you know that I will come Cristal?"

"Your mom, Julia Shapiro, called me. I am ready with the engagement ring. Julia told me what to do." He gave me a small box.

"Open the box Carl?"

I opened and I couldn't believe it! The ring was so beautiful.

"Who chose the ring?"

"Your mom chose the ring. Julia Shapiro spent her whole live in the diamond business Carl. She knows what is perfect for

Michelle."

"How much do I need to pay Cristal?"

"Nothing Carl. Your mom paid."

"I don't understand Cristal. Do you think that Mom should buy the engagement ring?"

"Why not Carl? Your mom loves Michelle. Michelle will remember your mom forever."

"What should I do if I want Michelle to remember me forever?"

"After marriage, you buy her another ring. Michelle will be happy to wear the two rings. When she looks at them, she will know that two people love her very much."

"You are right Cristal. I will buy another ring for the wedding. I will come back in your store and I will buy the second ring.

"Do you want some coffee before you go Carl?"

"Why not Cristal?" We entered in the coffee shop. I bought the coffee. We sat and I told Cristal, that I need his help.

"This is so hard for me Cristal. What should I to do when I see Michelle?"

"Oh boy, you are scared."

"I had never been scared, but now I am."

"I know why you are scared Carl. You want to marry Michelle, but you haven't told her that you love her."

"You are right Cristal. I know that Michelle has everything. She is beautiful. She has education and she loves me very much. I know that she will listen to me and she will be a good mom and a wife. But I don't know how to ask her to marry me. She is a virgin too. I will be the first man for her."

"This is every man's dream Carl", and Cristal laughed.

"Do you like me to help you Carl?"

"Yes, Cristal. I will come with you and I will drop you outside Ethan's property."

Cristal drove and he told me what to do. "You will do great. Just be yourself and don't be scared Carl." We arrived. I walked to the door and pushed the bell on the gate.

"Carl, you are here!"

"I am Michelle."

"I will open the gate." As the gate was opening Cristal told me "Walk and don't listen to what Michelle is telling you. Don't answer. When you on front of her, knelt down on one knee, open the box with the ring and say, Michelle would you marry me?"

Cristal left. I walked. Michelle was talking as I was approaching her, but I didn't listen or say anything. When I was close to her I opened the box, knelt down and I asked her, "Michelle marry me". She looked at me and she didn't answer. I didn't know what to do. Robert was standing next to her and he told her say yes Michelle, Carl is asking you to marry him."

"Yes, yes Carl!" I put the engagement ring on her finger. I stood up. She jumped and embraced me. Her arms were around my neck. Her legs were on my waist. Michelle kissed me many times.

"Come in Carl", Robert told me. We went to the living room.

"Do you like something to eat or drink Carl?", Robert asked me.

"Can I have green tea with honey and lemon?" I was still holding Michelle. She took off her hands and legs from me and said " I will make the tea Robert."

"What do you like Robert?"

"Green tea for me too, Michelle".

"How many spoons with honey do you like Carl?"

"Three, thank you."

"I will put four, because you need more energy Carl." Robert and I laughed. Michelle went in the kitchen.

"Where have you been, boy?"

"Overseas."

"I asked you, because Julia and Michelle were afraid for you."

"How many years have you been working for the Dreyfus family, Robert?"

"More than thirty five years, but the last fifteen I am working and living here. Louis had a room for storage. Ethan remodeled that room for me."

"Would you like to see my room?"

"Of course Robert." We entered the room. It was eight feet wide and fourteen feet long. It had a window. There were shelfs with boxes on the left wide wall. On the right wide wall was a closet. The room had a bed, table and two chairs.

"The room is small, but it is good for me. I don't need to use a car to come to work and pay rent. Don't need to rent or buy a house."

"Hey boys, the tea is ready. Come to the living room." We sat and had tea.

"Do you want to go on vacation Robert?"

"For how long Michelle?"

"Do you want to go for ten days?"

"I will need to ask Mr. Dreyfus, Michelle."

"It would have been Mr. Dreyfus's decision one hour ago, Robert, now is mine."

"Where are you and Carl going to live?"

"We will be living in New York."

"Do you think that Mr. Dreyfus will fire me Michelle?"

"If he fires you, you can come to New York and you will live with me, Julia and Carl."

"What do you think Carl?"

"Michelle is right Robert."

"I grew up with you Robert. Sue and Emmy were my moms. You were my dad." We finished the tea and Robert told us that he will be cooking fish for dinner.

"Come with me Carl. I would like to show you the house." As Michelle was showing me around she asked me, "Which room do you like to have sex in, Carl?"

"I would like to be in bed with you Michelle."

"I took a shower an hour ago. Since you just came from the airport I assume you would like to take a shower. I will be waiting for you in my bed."

"Do you think that you are ready to be in bed with me?"

"Yes, Carl because I love you. I can wait to be with you."

I took a shower and walked in the bedroom, Michelle was under a sheet. I picked a corner and pulled it. Michelle was naked. Since she said "Yes" to my proposal I was not anymore the anxious men that arrived earlier. Being alone with her naked was a familiar territory for me. I felt good. I leaned over her and kissed her mouth, then every inch of her body. Michelle let me to do what I want. She was moving sensually in answer to my touch and kisses. I was getting aroused by her innocence and want for me. I was on top of her, my erection pressing on her belly. She told me that she wanted to feel me inside her. I wanted to be gentle with her since I knew that this was her first time with a man, so I was trying to read how she felt by her reactions. She had her eyes closed for the most, but she opened them and she said as if reading me, "Don't worry Carl, I am ready, I want you."

"Give me a moment to put a condom, Michelle."

"We don't need a condom Carl."

"Are you sure?"

"I am very sure Carl. I want to feel you."

I started going inside her very slowly. She was very tight. She encouraged me to go on and I did. I heard a grunt and she stopped breading. I saw tears on the side of her cheeks.

"Are you OK?" I sked her.

She said "I never been happier in my life. Please don't stop."

I continued going forward and back. She was moving in sync with me. I was happy that we were able to read each other so well. We finished together. I was kissing her face. Michelle laughed and she had tears. I looked at her and she answered my unspoken question.

"I laughed, because I was anxious and scared of this moment, but it was a wonderful experience. I had tears, because was overwhelmed with the emotion of being with you, because I love you." She kissed me many times. We were gazing at each other. There was a knock on the door. Ethan was talking from behind the door, not opening it.

"What are you doing Michelle?", Ethan asked.

"I am in bed with Carl. Get your pistol ready, because I am not a virgin anymore."

Ethan laughed and told Michelle. I have a special whisky for the occasion. I will be waiting you and Carl in the living room. Congratulations!"

When Ethan left Michelle told me "I want Robert go on vacation, so that he doesn't ask us all the time, what we like for breakfast, lunch or dinner. He will ask, because he loves us, but I want to be with you Carl. I don't want people around us. I don't like to hurt Robert's feeling, so it will be better if he is not here for few weeks."

"Where is Kate, Michelle?"

"When I told her that you are coming and staying here, she left. Don't talk about Kate. My father is unhappy, that she left."

"Are you going to leave me too someday Michelle?"

"Why do you think that I will have to leave you, Carl?"

"If I am not a good husband and a father."

"I know that you are going to be a wonderful father and a husband, so there won't be a reason for me to leave you. I know that you will take care of our family and make money even though I have money. We will never allow money to be between us. I will never be with another man. You were my first and you will be the last. The only reason I will separate with you is if you love another woman. If you want a divorce, I will divorce, but I will never ask you for one."

"Do you love me Carl?"

"I love you Michelle. It took me some time to realize it, but I have been thinking about you since the day I met you. I couldn't get you out of my mind. I think that will love you forever." She kissed my forehead.

Robert knocked on the door "Mr. Dreyfus is waiting for you both".

"Give us few minutes Robert. Tell Mr. Dreyfus that we will be there." We put some clothes on and went to the living room. Ethan shook my hand.

"I am happy to see you Carl." We sat and Ethan saw the engagement ring on Michelle's finger. He asked her "What is that Michelle?"

"Carl asked me to marry him and I said yes Ethan."

"I am surprised that Carl asked to marry you. I think that he has many women."

"He had Ethan. Now Carl has one."

"My dear daughter, Carl doesn't love you."

"Carl told me that he loves me Ethan and I believe him."

"Why are you calling me Ethan? I am your father Michelle!"

"Because, you aren't happy that I will marry Carl. You think that I must marry the boy of our friend that you like. You think that he must have control of me and my money."

"Of course Michelle. Carl doesn't know how to control your money. He just bought a house for his son. He spent three hundred thousand dollars for his ex- girlfriend. How many more children do you have Carl?"

"I don't know Ethan. I had many women, but now I know that I have one son. Maybe I have more, but I think this is between me and Michelle. If she doesn't want my son, she doesn't have to marry me. I think Michelle must decide. You are her father, but Michelle is a big girl."

"You forgot to say that I am not a virgin anymore Carl" and she laughed.

"This isn't funny Michelle."

"Of course Father. Now the boys of our friends can't tell make fun of the fact that I am a virgin."

"Did you tell Robert that he needs to take a vacation, Carl?"

"It wasn't Carl, I told Robert to take vacation Father."

"Why did you do that?"

"Michelle wants to be alone with Carl in the house Mr. Dreyfus. I will be in their way asking what they want. When Michelle asked me, I understood that I need to take a vacation. I was happy Mr. Dreyfus."

"You need to ask me before you decided Robert, but this is OK. You need a vacation. I will give you a check, so you can have a good time on your vacation."

Ethan left and Michelle told me, "Ethan is in love with Kate. You and Robert aren't the problem. It is Kate, because she left the house." Ethan returned and he gave Robert a check.

"How much did you give Robert Father?"

"Five thousand Michelle." Michelle left the living room.

"Did you speak with Kate, Carl?"

"I didn't Ethan?"

"The last time I spoke with her was when I was in Miami."

"Do you love Kate, Ethan?"

"I don't know what to tell you, but I think that I love her. I fully realized that when she left the house and how much I missed her. It is sad that we realize our feelings for someone when we miss them."

"Kate is a good girl Ethan."

"I know that Carl, but I worry that she is twenty three years younger than me." Michelle came back and gave Robert ten thousand dollars more.

"Five from me and five from Carl, Robert."

"Oh my God. I am rich. I will have a good vacation."

"You should to take a girl on your vacation Robert."

"You are right Mr. Dreyfus. I will prepare the table for dinner" and Robert left.

"I am so sorry Michelle that I said bad thinks to Carl."

"Doesn't matter Father. You must think for your life. You are young and you need to marry. Hey Father, when I have children and you have children, we will become a big family. That is what I always wanted."

"Do you think that I should marry Kate, Michelle?"

"Why not father? You are still good looking and rich. If Kate doesn't want to marry you, then I am sure another woman will."

"I love Kate, Michelle."

"I will talk to Kate, Father."

Robert announced that the table is ready and we moved to the dining room. We had a nice dinner and light conversation about wine and architecture. Michele saw that I was tired, so I was glad when she said that she was tired and wanted to go to sleep. We left the dining room and went to Michelle's bedroom. I was happy the she was able to read me so well. I took her an in my arms and kissed her then I said "Thank you for being so supportive and understanding." She replied "Carl, you seem to forget that earlier today I said yes. We will go thought live together as a team. You can always count on me to be by your side thought good times and bad times and I will be counting on you. You made me the happiest girl in the world when you asked me to marry you today and told me that you love me." She started kissing me with passion and love. I replied. We made love many times during the night. At some point we went to sleep holding each other. I felt happy.

I woke up in the morning. Michelle wasn't in bed. I found her in the kitchen.

"How are you feeling Carl after our first night together?"

"I am happy Michelle. If every night from now on is the same as last night, we will have a good life together."

"My father left early in the morning to drop Robert at the airport. I am going to SMU. I need to speak with the administration office to see what I have to do to transfer so I can transfer to an university in New York in order to complete my studies. Do you like to come with me Carl?"

"No Michelle I will go to the leasing office of my apartment to cancel my lease. Then I need to sale my car. I don't want to have to come back to Dallas to deal with this. I have some business plans that I am working on that will require me to travel elsewhere. Could you ask if somebody at SMU wants to buy my car? I will give them a good deal since I am trying to get this done today."

"Do you like to call my father and ask him to help with the sale of your car? He can ask in the office too."

"It will be better if you ask him Michelle. I think that he is jealous, because I was with Kate in past."

"You were with Kate, before my father knew her, but you might be right. I will call and ask him. You need to be quite for two, three days Carl. You don't need to get my father angry. I don't want to have problem with you and my father. I am so happy that I am marring you. Your breakfast is ready. Do you like to have lunch with me today?"

"Go and finish your job at SMU. We will have lunch together many time in the future."

"Thanks Carl!" Michelle kissed me and she left.

I finished my breakfast fast. I took a cup of coffee and walked outside. I looked at every side of the house. I didn't see anything unusual. I entered inside the house and went back to Robert's room. Robert told me that Louis used the room to store documents. I measured the distance between the kitchen door and Robert's room door. It was thirty two feet. I went inside the kitchen and measured between the kitchen door and the wall of Robert's room. It was twelve feet. Then went inside Robert's room and measured between the room door and the wall of the kitchen side. It was ten feet. I calculated that twelve plus ten was twenty two feet. Thirty two minus twenty two was ten. Ten feet of space between the kitchen and Robert's room was not visibly accessible to any ordinary person.

I entered the kitchen and I tapped on the wall. I went in Robert's room and I looked at the bookshelf. I sat on the chair and I looked at the first shelf. I stood up and I moved everything from all shelfs. I started to check the wall and the bookshelf. The shelfs were painted two or three times. That is why I couldn't see an opener. If there was an opener, it will be in the corners. I checked the corners. My finger touched something on the corner of the bottom shelf, but it was covered with paint. I returned to the kitchen and took a knife. I cleaned the paint where my finger touched something. I saw a metal button and I pushed it. The whole bookshelf moved a little. The air from inside was stuffy. I had to open the window of Robert's room, so I can breathe inside. I moved the shelf and I saw a dark room. I turned on the lamp in Robert's room. I went to the living room. I sat and I waited for ten minutes. I came back in Robert's room. I entered the dark room and looked for a lamp. My eyes adjusted and was able to see a desk lamp. I turned on. The room had a desk, chair and a bookshelf on the wall. There were carton boxes on the shelf. I opened the desk drawer. I saw an envelope. I opened it. Inside was a letter and a business card. The business card was of a bank in Geneva. The letter had numbers on a figure. I went back to the living room and I picked up the phone. I called Greta and I asked her, what I need to have if I want to open my safe box.

"I have the name of the bank and the code, Greta."

"The relatives need to show an ID, Carl."

"See you next week Greta."

"I am sending you a kiss Carl."

"I can't accept it Greta. I am engaged."

"When did you do it?"

"Yesterday, Greta."

"In that case I am taking my kiss back." She laughed and hung up the phone. I returned to the secret room and turned off the lamp. I pushed back the bookshelf. I had to paint the places of the shelf where I took the paint off, so that nobody will know what I found. I took the phone book and looked for Home Depot. I took a piece of the paint for a sample. I bought paint and came back to the house. I painted the shelf. I kept the window open. After one hour I entered Robert's room I looked at the shelf. You had to look very carefully to notice the difference in the color of the new paint. I put everything back on the bookshelf. I cleaned Robert's room and closed the window. I took everything that I bought from Home Depot and put it in the Home Depot bag. I closed the door of Robert's room. I took my car and left the house.

I went in the leasing office of my Dallas apartment. I told them that I will move to New York and I want to cancel the contract. I told them that I am not taking my furniture from the apartment. A man that was signing a lease in the office told them that he will take my furniture.

The leasing agent told him "If you move in Carl's apartment, you will get the furniture."

"Absolutely. I will take the apartment with the furniture. I am new to the town and had to look for furniture. Now am done. It is my lucky day to be here. "

"Do you need to take something from the apartment Carl?" the leasing agent asked me.

"I need to take my clothes only." I signed the papers for the cancellation. We went to the apartment with the leasing agent. I took my clothes and gave him the key.

I returned to Ethan's house. It was late in the afternoon Michelle was already there.

"Did you cancel the contract?"

"I did. I need to sale or give my car for free to somebody Michelle. I don't want my car to stay in Ethan's garage."

"When do we have go to New York?"

"When you ready with your paperwork from SMU we will go. I am ready, Carl."

"Did you talk with Julia?"

"I don't have to talk to Julia. She is waiting for us."

"But she doesn't know that we are engaged."

"Mom knows everything."

"I have a little problem with my father. I will speak with him in the afternoon.

"Could you stay quiet for me Carl?"

"I will do whatever I need to for you Michelle." Ethan arrived and told us that we will should get ready to go out for dinner.

"I invited my friends Michelle."

"What time do we have to be at the restaurant father?"

"At 7:00 p.m." and he told us the name.

"We will be ready" and we left the living room. We went to Michelle's bedroom. We didn't have much time, so we took shower together and changed.

We left the house at 6:30 p.m. At 7:00 p.m. we were at the restaurant. I knew Sue, Emmy, Jimmy, Frank and Cristal with a woman I assumed was his wife. There were more people on the table, but I didn't know them. Two of the men were around my age. Emmy wanted to sit next to Michelle, but Ethan asked one of the man that were my age to sit next to her. I asked the other man to sit next to Michelle and he did. Cristal said that this is a good idea, because Michelle needs to be protected. I sat between Sue and Emmy. Kate arrived and everybody looked at her. Michelle looked at me and she winked. We ate, drank and spoke. One of the man that was sitting to the right of Michelle asked me where I finished college.

"Carl finished high school", Emmy told him. The man that was sitting to the left asked me where I work. Emmy continued to answer.

"Carl works in a topless bar. He is bodyguard and as part of his job he has to evaluate personally every night how will the women do."

"You better believe it. Carl buys every week a lot jewelry from my store for the women", Cristal told him. After this exchanges the parents of the young man asked Ethan, why he approved of the engagement.

"Carl is good in bed and that is why I like to marry him", Michelle told them.

"I don't think that it will be necessary for my father to evaluate that. Now I am free, because I gave all my money to Carl. I am poor, he is rich." Emmy told Michelle that she is a smart girl.

"I would like to have a toast for Carl, who is a rich man now" and Michelle raised glass of wine. It was so funny. When we finished dinner, Ethan invited us to continue the party in his house, but nobody accepted. When we left the restaurant I saw that Cristal and Michelle were speaking and looking at me. Me, Michelle and Ethan returned to the house. Ethan told us good night and he went to his bedroom.

"Do you want to have sex Carl?"

"I don't want to have sex in this house Michelle. I am sorry. We will have many times in the future."

"I understand Carl. My father made a big mistake when he invited his friends for diner. He didn't respect our engagement. Do you think that Ethan is your enemy Carl?"

"I don't think so, he is your father. It was hard for Ethan tonight, because he lost two women." Michelle and I laughed. You forgot to tell the names of the women, but I know them. Kate and Michelle" and she kissed me.

I woke up in the morning. Michelle was not in bed or in the shower. I went to look for her the kitchen. Michelle and Ethan were talking. I left them alone and went to the living room. Michelle asked me to come back to the kitchen for breakfast.

Ethan was leaving.

"I want to see the killer of my mom Carl."

The phone was ringing. Michelle picked up.

"For you Carl." It was Mom.

"He is dead Carl. There is no more, the shark-Peter Volak-Peter Volkov. They found him dead in his bed this morning. In his hands he held two passports, American and Russian and a letter that he was born in Russia. Simon is smart Carl. First, he killed the shark, after that he showed who the shark was. Don't call Simon. Many people called and asked for you, but didn't say who was calling. If Roger and I have a problem we will go and stay in your grandmother's house. You need to stay far away from New York for two or three weeks. If you need to return to New York, you need to stay in Jerry's apartment. Cristal told me everything Carl. I am happy for you and Michelle. I am kissing you both", and Mom hung up the phone.

"I am sorry Carl, but I heard the shark. Who was he?"

"The person that killed your grandparents and ordered to kill your mom. He tried to kill me, but somebody got to him first. I am happy that the shark death and I am in Dallas with you Michelle."

"I know why Uncle Simon loves you Carl. You wanted to kill the shark, but Uncle Simon did it."

"Louis Dreyfus was Simon's brother, Michelle. Simon did what he thought he had to do. We need to think for our future. Do you really want to meet the killer of your mom?"

"Yes, I want to Carl. I need to know what happened to her." I picked up the phone and called.

"Vicky, his name is Boris Bromich. He lives in Los Angeles."

"I need the address. Give me two hours Carl."

Ethan called and told Michelle that somebody will come after one hour to look at my car.

I called and asked Emmy to come to Ethan's house after three hours. "I need you to drop me and Michelle at the DFW airport Emmy.

Vicky called and told me the address of Boris Bromich. "Good luck Carl. You finished a good job. Many people are happy now. Kiss Michelle for me."

"I will Vicky." I told Michelle that we need to get ready to leave. She prepared two bags.

A young man came to look at my car and he asked me how much I want for it.

"Make me an offer", I said to him. I accepted his offer and signed the title to him.

Emmy came and picked us up as we agreed. She dropped us at the airport. She said, "Scott is scared Carl. He told Frank that you killed the shark and that he is next. Frank was surprised, but I didn't tell Frank, why Scott is scared".

Emmy kissed Michelle and me. Then she said "Good luck Michelle, you deserve to have Carl for a husband. Your mom will leave you now. I know that you will stop dreaming about her." We bought two tickets to the first available flight to Los Angelis. The plane was leaving soon and there were available seats. We got to the plane and flew to Los Angeles.

CHAPTER 13

Michelle and I arrived in Los Angeles. We went to a hotel close to Boris Bromich's place. We were tired so we had dinner at the hotel's restaurant and went back to our room. We went to bed. I kissed her and told her good night. I knew that she was thinking about tomorrow, and what she will say to the man who killed her mom. I embraced her. We felt asleep with her head on my chest. I wanted to give her comfort. I wanted her to know that I am here for her.

When we woke up in the morning Michelle took a shower and said that she was not hungry. I had a quick breakfast and we left the hotel. Since we were close to Bromich's apartment we walked. We got there in ten minutes. I knocked on the door. A man opened and asked me "I was waiting only for you Carl! Who is this woman?"

"This is Michelle. You killed her mom. She wants to speak with you, not me."

"I thought that you are here to kill me Carl!"

"I don't have anything to do with you Boris. I finished my job with the shark or Peter Volkov. Peter was my enemy. You aren't. Why do you think that somebody wants to kill you?"

"This somebody is Konev, Carl. We are old enemies."

"Are you scared to speak alone with Boris, Michelle?"

"I don't want to hear what happened to your mom. I will be outside."

"I am not Carl."

I left the room and closed the door. I could hear Boris talking in a very low voice, but couldn't understand what he was saying. Michelle didn't say anything. I think that she was trying to hold it together. Then it became quite. I was wondering what was going on and was about to knock on the door, when it opened. Boris and Michelle were coming out of the apartment.

"We finished Carl. I told her what happened to her mom. I need to leave, because if I stay here, they will kill me. I will drop you and Michelle in the hotel with my car."

As Boris was dropping us at the hotel he said "Thank you for the money Michelle. Your money will save my life." He left immediately.

Michelle and I went in our hotel room. She told me "I don't want to go back to Dallas. You decide where we are going from here Carl."

"Do you like to go and meet my grandmother Michelle?"

"I would love to, Carl!"

"Then it is decided. Let's get ready. I don't like to stay here any longer either."

We left the hotel. We were at the airport. I bought two thickets to Knoxville. We had one stop, before arriving in Knoxville. I called Mark and told him that he needs to wait at the Knoxville airport at 8:30 p.m.

We arrived on time. Mark picked us up. At 9:30 p.m. we were in my grandmother's house. Julia and Roger were there.

I told Michelle "I am returning to the house of my grandmother after nine years. I grew up here."

"You are home Carl", and Grandmother took a hold of my head and kissed my forehead. "I am so glad that you came back with a woman. Julia told me that you will marry Michelle. I am happy that I will see a great grandchild before I die. God bless you and Michelle." Grandmother embraced Michelle too and gave her a kiss on the cheek. "Welcome to the family."

The dinner was ready and waiting for us. The main conversation was about Michelle. Gran mom wanted to know everything about her. Michelle seemed happy with all the attention she was getting. Later she told me that she was very happy to be in a big family like mine, because she grew up mostly with her father and always was jealous of the kids in school that had big families.

Gran mom told me that she had prepared my old room for us. I couldn't wait to get Michelle in the bed. The last time I slept in it was nine years ago. I was a teenager. It brought all those memories. I wanted to have sex. I felt like I couldn't get enough. I woke up Michelle in middle night and we had sex again. In the morning we had sex again.

"Oh boy, I am not for one day. I will be with you forever. We have many days on front of us to have sex Carl, but I am suspecting that you want me to get pregnant here and I like that."

"You are right Michelle. I grew up here and I love this house and the people who live in it." We were staying in bed holding each other. We were happy. After a while Michelle said "I think that we need to go and see everybody else. They are probably wondering what is going on with us."

"I think that they are guessing what is going on. We are young couple getting married" and I winked at her.

We got ready and went to the living room. Everybody look at us smiling.

Mark laughed and said "Mom, I told you that Carl and Michelle are alive. I heard them having sex in the middle of the night. You know you can hear through the walls of this house. Mom was concerned for Michelle and you."

Everybody laughed and Michelle told them "You are right Mark. Carl wanted to kill me in the bed, but he forgot that now I am a half Hill Billy."

Grandmother kissed Michelle and said proudly "You are Michelle."

After breakfast I told Mark that I need to go and see our Dealership, but I don't like anybody see us. When Grandmother said that she likes to show Michelle something, Mark and I left the house. "What should I say Carl, if somebody in Dealership ask who you are?"

"I am a client looking to buy a car. I don't like anybody to know that I am in Knoxville. I don't believe that anybody will recognize me after nine years." Mark drove. I told him that he needs to call Simon and ask him what happened with Simon's friend who wanted to buy a car. You need to tell Simon that car was ready on Friday, but his friend didn't come to buy the car. You called him Saturday, but he didn't pick up the phone. Mark, you need to tell Simon your phone number and you will be waiting for one hour. Simon's friend needs to call and tell you what he decided. If he doesn't call, you will sale the car. Mark called and Simon told him that he will tell his friend. Few minutes later the phone was ringing.

"This is Mark's Dealership." Nobody answered. Someone is listening to Simon's phone, Carl."

"I know Mark." The phone was ringing again. Mark picked up. "For you Carl."

"Congratulation boy!"

"Thanks Uncle. You and Ethan must be in Hotel de la Cigogne in Geneva on Wednesday. You both need to have documents proving that you are the brothers and that Ethan is the son of Louis."

"See you on Wednesday boy."

"See you Uncle."

"Oh my god. What kind people are you talking to?"

"Rich people Mark."

"Now is nine thirty Carl." We have to leave the Dealership before the salesman start coming if you don't want anybody to see you here.

We came back to my grandmother's house. She was still busy with Michelle. I went to my Grandfather's office and called Geneva.

"This is Clara, May I help you?"

"Of course you can Clara. How are you my friend.?"

"Where are you Carl?"

"I am in America right now, but on Wednesday I will be in Geneva. I need three rooms for four nights and one room for five nights."

"Do you need Veronica to prepare gifts for you and deliver them to your room?"

"If Veronica wants to sleep with me and my fiancé, I am OK with that Clara."

"Do you have a fiancé?"

"I am an engaged man Clara. You were free two week ago Carl."

"I was, but Veronica didn't take me to bed then. She missed her chance." we laughed.

"Carl, I will be happy to see you and meet your fiancé."

"Do you like the same room you stayed before in?"

"You decide Clara. I am in your hands."

"Carl, will you ever stop joking?"

"We have one life Clara. I am trying to go happy through it by joking as much as I can. I am happy that I am alive and I soon to be a married man."

"My boss is here Carl" and I heard him saying to her "Who are you speaking to? You have been on the phone for 20 minutes. You know that you have to keep personal conversations to a minimum?"

"Give me your boss Clara."

"Mr. Hope would like to speak with you sir."

He took the phone and the first thing he said was "I will fire Clara."

"Hey boss, I am Carl Hope. I stayed at your hotel two weeks ago and Clara is the reason I just made a reservation for three very rich people and myself. I think that you must her a raise, because she is bringing more business to the hotel and she is my friend. I will be telling all of my friends to stay in your hotel when they have business in Geneva. I will be coming on Wednesday. If you are not going to give her a raise, I will cancel the reservations I just made."

"Considered done Mr. Hope. I will give you Clara back."

"I am sending you a kiss Clara."

"Thank you. Me too" and I hung up the phone. I looked for Michelle. I asked her to come to the office.

"Do you have your passport with you Michelle?"

"Yes, Carl."

"Thanks Michelle."

"Do you have any more questions Carl, because I want to go back to be with Julia and Grandmother?"

"Could you ask Julia to come to the office Michelle?

"No problem."

Julia came in and I asked her if she had her passport with her.

"I do Carl. Why are you asking?"

"Would you like to come with me and Michelle to Geneva Mom?"

"Of course Carl. I like spending time with Michelle."

I laughed and asked Mom "What about me? Do you love Michelle more than me?"

"Of course. Michelle is a woman. She will delivery my grandchild. You won't Carl."

"Could you tell Roger and Grandfather to come to the office Mom?"

Roger came in first I asked him if he wanted to come with me, but he said that he wanted to go on vacation.

"Do you like to go to Miami or the Bahamas? I have a friend who has house there."

"This sounds good Carl."

I called Peggy. She told me that Lorenzo is the happiest man in the world because he is a free man now.

"I don't know what he is talking about. Do you Carl?"

"Maybe Lorenzo got a divorce Peggy. If that is the case he may ask you to marry him. You might be in trouble."

"Oh boy, that is a problem. I have a husband."

"Looks like you will have two husbands."

"You are right. This might not be a bad idea, Carl."

"Peggy, I called you because my friend is standing next to me here and he wants to go on vacation to Miami or the Bahamas…"

"My house is open for him Carl, because he is your friend, that means that he is my friend."

"His name is Roger and when he arrives in Miami, he will call you. If he wants, I can pick him up from the airport. We don't know what time he will arrive in Miami, but he will be flying tomorrow. Could you introduce Roger to Lorenzo? I will be working with both of them in the future and with you and Jack too."

"We will be happy to work with you all too. Jack doesn't have a partner anymore. I kicked Marko's ass out of the house and the company, but Marko and Becky are still together. This is good for everybody" and Peggy laughed.

"I am an engaged man now Peggy. Her name is Michelle."

"Congratulations!"

"Could you kiss and tell Michelle that she has a friend in Miami?"

"I will."

"Sending you kisses. I miss you so much."

"I am kissing you back, Peggy. "

Grandfather was at the office door looking at me. When I saw him I asked "Do you like to come with Grandmother to Geneva?"

"Me, Michelle and Julia are going tomorrow."

"No Carl. We are busy. We must get ready for a wedding. I will call Jonathan to be ready for you. What time tomorrow?"

"At 7:00 p.m."

Grandfather arranged the jet for us. Then he bought the ticket to Miami for Roger.

"How much do I owe you Roger? You risked your life for me!"

"I did that, because you are my brother Carl. Simon gave me enough money. If I need more I will ask you. If you decide to invite somebody, don't call. Peggy will make the call. You have to stay there, because Lorenzo is a detective and he knows what to do. He saved my life Roger. You can trust him as I do."

"Do you want to know what happened with the shark Carl?"

"Not now Roger. When I return from Europe I will come to Miami. We will start investing in the Caribbean and we will have time to speak."

"I have something else I want to tell you, Carl. I have a girlfriend. I didn't tell you, because you know my life. I will ask her to marry me. Simon gave me a lot of money. I will work with you and I will have money to support my wife and children. I will have a normal life."

"I am very happy for you Roger. You deserve it. You are a god man."

The next morning Roger left to Miami. Me, Michelle and Mom left the airport at 7:00 p.m. During the flight Michelle told me that she was happy with my family. They made her feel part of the family.

"Now I have a mom, a grandmother and you Carl. One week ago I had Robert, Emmy and Sue."

"You forgot your father Ethan, Michelle."

"Ethan will have big problem with me Carl. He didn't save my mom's life. She had a chance to be alive. Cristal told me that Mom had a chance to live. Boris too. My father is greedy Carl…"

"I couldn't believe when Cristal told me about Ethan is. Cristal was the one that pushed me on Friday to ask you, to arrange for me to meet the killer of my mom. He told me that it will be better for our future if I know what happened with my mom. He said that many people will try to tell you that I have a mental problem, including my father, so that he will have control of my money. Crystal said that you will never touch your money, because you are an honest man. I am so happy that you are marrying him."

"Cristal was the first person who told me about you Michelle. The first time I met Cristal when I bought the jewelry for Sue. Cristal told me that you are beautiful and smart. I didn't know who you were, but now I know that you are my future wife and I am happy Michelle."

"Do you love me Carl?"

"Of course I love you Michelle." Mom heard me and Michelle and she smiled. I know that Mom and Michelle were happy that I will be the husband of Michelle. They spoke for a while. It was late. They fell asleep. I was thinking for my life. I made a decision and changed my life really fast. One week ago I was a free man. Now I am engaged and not long from now I will be a married man. Michelle closed the door for other women, but I don't regret that. I have a son and want to see him and have a good relationship with him. I will have more children. I love Michelle. Mom will be happy to see Michelle, me and the children all the time. This will be good for her, because she will have a long life with us. I love Mom and I like her to live a long life. At some point I fell asleep too.

I heard Mom whispering to me, that we have arrived in Geneva. I woke up then I kissed Michelle on the cheek to wake her up. She smiled and said "I was dreaming about you my love and you kissed me. It's the perfect end to my dream."

"I am sorry to wake you up but we have arrived. Let's go, so we can make your dream a reality."

We took a taxi and went straight to the hotel. Clara was on the front deck. She came and embraced me. She gave a long kiss. Mom and Michelle were laughing.

"Clara this is my mom and this is Michelle, my fiancé."

"Nice to meet you ladies. I am so happy that you are here with Carl. So this is the lady that finally captured you hart. Michelle is your future wife."

"She is."

"No more spending time in the company of strange women, Carl."

"No more. You are a lucky man, she is beautiful."

"She is Clara."

"Hey Carl, now Veronica will be unhappy, but Patrik will be happy", and Clara and I laughed. I looked at my watch and Clara said "I am glad that you are wearing our gift. Well, I think that you must be tired form your long journey and need some rest. We can talk later when you had a chance to do that."

We got our keys from Clara and went to our rooms. I picked up the phone to call Patrik when Michelle asked me "Who is

Veronica, Carl?"

"I am calling her fiancé, Patrik. When I finish speaking with him you can ask him about Veronica."

"I am sorry Carl, I am just curios. It doesn't matter" and Michelle went to the bathroom.

"Hi Carl, where are you? Clara told me that you were coming to Geneva."

"I am in Geneva Patrik. I will be in your bank tomorrow morning at 9:00. Could you tell your boss that I must meet with him at 9:00 o'clock? If your boss wants to meet another time, please call at Hotel de la Cigogne and tell me what time is better for him."

"I will call you after five minutes Carl. "I sat on the sofa and took of my shoes and put my feet up. Patrik called and confirmed the meeting for 9:00 a.m.

Michelle was still in the , so I went toward it and I heard the shower . I took of my clothes and joined her. I embraced her while the water was falling on my shoulders. I started kissing her. She pulled me tighter to her body. Our bodies felt like one with the water falling on both of us. It was a great feeling. I pulled her up holding her ass and she wrapped her legs around me. I turned around and her back was against the tile wall behind the shower. I went inside her slowly savoring the moment. I looked at her eyes, they were full with love. Michelle was happy. I was happy too.

After we finished making love, Michelle said "You know that was a little stupid of me asking about Veronica".

"I know that you aren't jealous Michelle. You can ask me anything you want to know. You will be my wife and I have no intention to hide anything from you, unless I think that it may put you in danger. Tomorrow morning you will meet Patrik, so will have a chance to ask him."

"I will decide what to ask him when I meet him tomorrow."

"Hey, you will be my wife. You need to ask me, where I am all the time." We laughed.

"You are funny Carl. I don't know when you are serious and when you are joking."

"I am serious Michelle, when I have sex with you, because if I have children someday they will ask me who are I am and what I am doing in the house of their mom."

"Oh boy, you will never change. I need to stop asking you. I will try to be more observant. After a while I will figure many thinks out and I won't have to ask you so many questions."

"Ok. In one condition, if you want sex you will ask me Michelle."

"I will be happy to."

Clara called and told me that Simon and Ethan Dreyfus are in the hotel and they want to speak with me. "Tell them that I am busy with Michelle in the bed. When I finish, I will call them." Michelle laughed.

"I like that Carl. You are punishing my father. I know that Simon is happy for us."

After one hour I called end asked Ethan, if he wants to see me. "Ethan doesn't want to see me Michelle. He wants to speak with you in his room."

I called Simon and ask him what time he likes to go for dinner. I proposed 7:00 p.m. Simon agreed.

"You need to tell your father, if he wants to go to dinner with us, he needs to be in the lobby at 7:00 o'clock. Michelle left and I called mom and told her that to be in the lobby at 7:00 o'clock for dinner.

"Simon and Ethan are here mom. We are going together out for dinner."

Michelle came back from her talk with Ethan and she told me that he was crying for Kate. "This is Ethan's problem Michelle." At 7:00 p.m. we left the hotel. Ethan was holding Michelle's hand. Simon and mom were holding my hands. Me, Mom and Simon were walking behind Michelle and Ethan. Michelle turned and looked at us. I told her, "You have one person who loves you Michelle. I have two people who love me." Michelle laughed.

Ethan turned and he saw that Mom and Simon were holding my hands. He let go of Michelle's hand and said "You need to hold Carl's hand Michelle." Michelle came and tried to take my hand, but I told her that I need permission from my mom to hold her hand.

"Mom, can I hold Michelle's hand?"

"Of course Carl." I took Michelle's hand. Everybody laughed. Ethan didn't. We entered the restaurant. We ate, drank and spoke.

Michelle asked her father "Do you think that Carl is a good man father?"

"Why did you ask me that Michelle?"

"Because I think he is."

"How many men have you known before Carl, Michelle?"

"I spoke with many men father, but they always wanted to know how much money I had. They didn't want to have sex with me. Carl had sex with me. He didn't ask me for my money."

"You don't have control of your money Michelle."

"I have control of my money Ethan. You forgot that I have a document for that. You forgot that you and Mom signed a document, that after I am twenty three years old, I will have control of my money."

I tried to say something, but Michelle told me "Don't say anything Carl. I have to do this. I was eleven years old, when Mom gave me this document father. Mom told me that if something happened with her, when I am twenty three I need to give this document to Simon. You need to look at the document Simon. One month ago I turned twenty three" and she gave the document to Simon.

"You didn't even remember my birthday, but Uncle Simon called me and told me happy birthday Michelle. After Mom died Emmy, Sue and Simon always called me for my birthday. I dreamed about my mom every night Ethan. Did you know how that Ethan? You never asked me, because you and your friends were busy thinking how to keep control of my money. You never cared for me. I stopped to dream about my mom when I was in Carl's grandmother house. Mom smiled and she left. She knew that Carl will save my life. Mom was scared, that I will be killed like her. I met my mom's killer and he told me what happened."

"Could you read this document Simon?"

"The document says that now you control your money Michelle. Ethan had control of your money until one month ago."

"You and your friends must be very disappointed Ethan."

"Cheers everybody! Now I am rich and in control of my money. Carl will make enough money for me and my children. I will keep the money my mom eft me for my children and grandchildren. Could you call to your friends in Dallas to have one bullet for your head Ethan?" Then Michelle turned to me and said "Thank you so much Carl" and Michelle kissed me.

"I remember that my brother Louis told me that someday he will have grandchildren and that some of them will be smart. He was right. You are smart Michelle and I am proud of you."

Mom didn't say anything. It was unusual for her to be so quiet.

After dinner we walked back to the hotel. I had my arm around Michelle's waits. Mom was walking with Simon. Ethan was walking alone. We were in the lobby and I told Simon and Ethan that tomorrow morning at 9:00 we need to be at a bank.

"We need to leave the hotel at 8:30 a.m."

When we got in the room Michelle told me "Finally I told my father what I thought for him."

I didn't reply. I felt that that was something between the two of them that they had to resolve. She started to take her clothes off. "I want you. I want to have sex Carl. Now I am rich and free."

"Hey I am your future husband. Did you forget that?"

"Don't talk, just make love to me Carl" and we did with passion. I was happy that Michelle's mom finally left her alone. Now Michelle had a chance to have a normal life with the living.

When I woke up in the morning Michelle was sleeping. I woke her up and told her that we had to leave the hotel at 8:30 a.m.

"Where are we going Carl? I like to sleep late."

"Yesterday you wanted to know who Veronica is. I am taking you with me to meet Patrik. He is her fiancé."

"Are you kidding with me again?"

"I am not kidding Michelle. Please get ready so we can be on time for the meeting."

Me, Michelle, Simon and Ethan left the hotel at 8:30 a.m. At 9:00 a.m. we were in the bank. Patrik was waiting for us. He told us to follow him. We entered his boss office.

"How much money do you have with you Carl?"

"I don't know boss. This is Simon, Ethan and Michelle Dreyfus. Louis Dreyfus was killed twenty five years ago. He has a safe box in your bank. They want to access the box."

"I need an ID."

The boss checked the ID and called the safe box clerk. The safe box clerk said that Louis Dreyfus doesn't have a safe box.

"I am so sorry Dreyfus family" the boss said. I took from my pocket the paper with the code and gave it to the boss.

The boss called again the safe box clerk. He took the number and went to check it. When he returned he said "You are right Mr. Hope. Louis Dreyfus has a safe box in this bank."

"Do you want to see the box?"

"Yes, we would like to see the box", Simon told him. Follow

me. We followed the boss and I told Patrik that I need to make a phone call.

"You can use my office Carl. I will walk them to the safe." I entered Patrik's office. I called the hotel.

"What are you doing Mom?"

"Watching TV Carl."

"Do you like to go out to see the town with me?"

"Aren't you busy with the Dreyfus's family."

"I did what I had to do for them Mom. I am coming back to the hotel shortly. Can you please get ready to go out?"

"I will be waiting for you." I got Mom from the hotel.

"I want to buy you something Mom."

"I have everything Carl."

"I think that you need to buy some new clothes for the wedding."

"I think that you are right Carl."

We entered a shopping center and we choose many items for her. When we finished I called Max and told him, that I am with Mom in Geneva and we want to have lunch together. I told Max that we will be in the same restaurant where me, him and Sofia had dinner. I called the hotel and told Clara where we will be for lunch.

"Do you want me to tell your relatives Carl?"

"Yes Clara." Mom and I reached the restaurant first. They asked how many people will be for lunch. I told them that we will need a table for seven people.

"Do you think that Dreyfus's family will join us for lunch here Carl?"

"I am sure that Michelle and Simon will be here."

Max and Sofia arrived. Max introduced Sofia to Mom. Mom told Max that she wants Sofia to sit next to her. Max and I spoke, Mom was talking to Sofia asking rather personal questions. I winked at Max and told him that this is Sofia's first interview.

"What are you talking about Carl?"

"I think that Sofia will take mom's job. She will marry Max. Sofia didn't understand, why Max and I laughed.

"Could you stop joking Carl?"

"I will Mom, but you need to tell Max, if he has permission or not. If Max doesn't, he needs to look for another woman." Mom understood that I won't stop, if she doesn't stop asking Sofia so many personal questions.

"You are a good girl Sofia. I will be happy if you marry Max."

"What do you think Mom, if Michelle, I, Max and Sofia marry on the same day? We can have the weddings in the same restaurant, because the Shapiro family will be the same. We will save some money." Max and I laughed. Sofia didn't understand. Mom didn't know what to say, because I was right.

"I will think about that Carl, but I would like to ask Michelle, Sofia and your grandmother before I answer."

"Max, why should I and you marry, if the women will make the decisions for everything? Mom didn't say to us that she has to ask Jerry, Grandfather, me and you."

"You are right Carl" and me and Max were laughing when Michelle, Simon and Ethan came to the table.

"What are you laughing about Carl?"

Mom was trying to stop me, but I told Michelle.

"Who cares for you Carl? I will find another man. This morning Patrik told me that I am beautiful. I am a rich woman, many men will want to marry me."

"Are you going to do that Michelle?"

"Are you scared Carl?"

"I am not Michelle. I will be so happy, if you choose another man. I will be a free man again, if I don't marry you."

"You know that Carl is kidding Michelle."

"I am not Mom." Mom tried to change the subject. She stood up and introduced Sofia to Simon, Ethan, and Michelle. They sat on the table and Simon said that if I don't marry Michelle, Ethan will be happy, but he will not be.

"So what are you going to do Carl?"

"I thank that I will marry Michelle." It was so funny. Everybody laughed, Ethan didn't. Michelle kissed me and told me that she loves me very much. Sofia was looking at Michelle when Max asked her "Do you love me Sofia?"

"I love you, if we marry and we move to New York." Sofia made a big mistake saying that. Mom tried to ask her something, but I told Mom that I suggested to Sofia and Max to consider moving to New York.

"Sofia loves Max and they love Geneva. Sofia and Max want to live in Geneva, but I told them that New York will be better for them. Michelle understood that the situation for Sofia isn't good and she said "Hey Max, if you ask Sofia to marry you, we can marry the on same day in New York. Do you think that my idea is good Julia?"

Michelle killed Mom with one bullet. I told Mom and now Michelle told her the same thing without us ever discussing it. As if she read my mind.

"I think that this is good idea Michelle, but I will need to speak with Sofia first." I changed the subject and I told them that Mom and I went shopping for her this morning, so she will be ready for the wedding. Michelle was so smart. She asked Mom.

"May I see what you got Julia?"

Michelle and Mom started looking at the clothes. Sofia was trying to talk to Max, but he told her to keep her mount shut. Sofia asked me what happened.

"You must think before say something to Mom."

"Max should have told Sofi, what kind of a person Mom is. Don't be so hard on Sofia. She has no idea who she is dealing with."

"You are right Carl. I will explain to you later and you better listen to me Sofia, when it comes to Julia."

I told Max that tomorrow night we will have a party in a restaurant and that I will call him later about the details. Max and Sofia stood up. They had to go back to work. Sofia kissed Mom. Mom told Sofia that they need to meet again.

"I will be happy to meet with you again Mss. Shapiro." This was the perfect answer. Now Mom had mixed feeling about her. She was not sure if Sofia is good or bad for Max. We left the restaurant and Michelle said to Mom that Sofia is a good choice for Max.

"How do you know that Michelle?"

"I looked at Max and Sofia. She loves him Julia, but Max is a shy man. Carl will need to give him some lessons."

"What do you think Carl?"

"I agree with Michelle."

"I know that Mom likes Sofia."

"I will be happy if Max and Sofia marry Carl."

"Me too Mom."

"Where is my father?" Michelle asked Simon.

"He left for the airport. He is picking up Kate from there."

"What do you think about Kate, Carl?", Simon asked me.

"Kate is a good girl Simon, but Ethan needs to change his life. If Ethan likes to live with Kate, he needs to forget his friends, because Kate is young. Ethan and Kate are twenty three years apart."

"If my father has problem with Kate in bed, Carl will have to help him." Simon and Mom laughed.

"If Ethan has a child, do you think that Carl will be the father of the child Michelle?" Simon asked.

"I think so Simon, but my father will never let Kate be with Carl and Carl will be too busy with me in the bed."

"I am so happy that you are moving to New York and me, you, Julia and Carl will have a lot of fun together."

"You are right Simon. I have been with Carl for one week and my life has been so much fun, but I also know that when Carl is joking, he is telling the truth."

"Is it that true Carl?" Simon asked me.

"It is true Simon", Mom told him. We came back to the hotel. I told Michelle that I need to speak with Clara and I will stay back for a moment.

"Clara I need your recommendation for a restaurant for a party for tomorrow night. I like a restaurant with life music. Please tell Chris, Veronica and Patrik that they are invited to the party after 7:00 p.m. I gave her Max's phone number and I told her that she needs to call him and he has to be with Sofia. Clara, you are in charge of the party. I am counting on you."

"How many people are going to be there, Carl?"

"Fifteen."

"May I use your phone Clara?"

"Of course."

I called Greta's house. "Hans, this is Carl. I am in Geneva at Hotel de la Cigogne. Tomorrow I will have a party at 7:00 p.m. I am inviting you, Sven and Greta."

"I will be more than happy to be there. See you tomorrow Carl." I entered the hotel room. Michelle was speaking with someone on the phone. I heard "I will tell him Edit. I am kissing Julian Jr." and Michelle hung up.

"Carl, I saw the diamonds. They are so many and they are beautiful. Finally, the Dreyfus family saw them."

"Why did you leave?" You found them and you should have stayed to see them."

"You may be right Michelle, but I am not from the Dreyfus family. Simon had asked me before what I think about the diamonds. I told him that the they belong to the Dreyfus family. I didn't want your father to tell me, that my goal all along was to find the diamonds. My goal was to save my life. Now the Dreyfus family took the diamonds. They own them. I am alive."

"And I will be your wife and you need to know that me, Simon and Ethan voted. Simon and I voted for you. Ethan didn't believe that Simon voted for you. He asked Simon why he voted for you."

"Because Carl found the diamonds Ethan. Why didn't you find this information? How many years did you live in my brother's house and you never figure it out? My brother didn't tell you that he has the diamonds, because he didn't trust you Ethan. You must think. Why didn't Louis trust you. Louis didn't tell his wife either. I think that my brother lived in a house with people who hated him. Louis didn't deserve, for you and your mom to hate him. You are jealous and greedy Ethan. Before you hated Louis. Now you hate Carl, because he will marry Michelle. Did you ask Michelle, if she loves Carl and wants to live with him?"

"I didn't ask Michelle, but I am her father."

"You didn't ask, because you thought only about Michelle's money, you didn't think for her future. You don't care if she is happy or not. Do you love or hate Michelle, Ethan? You are a shame for the Dreyfus family. You need to improve your relationship with Carl, because if you don't you will have a big problem with me. I knew that if my brother dies, his grandchildren will take everything. You will lose everything. You will lose Kate too. Do you want that Ethan?"

"I don't want that Uncle Simon."

"Simon is a psychiatrist Carl. I understood that I have to be silent just by the way he looked at me. I didn't take a side Carl. Ethan agreed with Simon. I know that Simon fought for you and me."

"Do you want to make love now Carl?"

"Of course Michelle."

"Are you surprised?"

"It is your chance to surprise me in the bed Michelle" and we jumped in bed. She said that she wants to make French love to me.

"How did your learn to make French love, Michelle?"

"I watched a video Carl. I know that I may not be that good at it, but I want to try." I let her to do what she wants. Michelle was surprised when I kissed her pussy and my tongue played with her clitoris. I made her crazy. When we finished she told me that I need to teach her more thinks in the bed.

"I didn't know that having sex is so good Carl. After we have sex I feel like I am somewhere in the universe. Kate told me that I need to listen to you, because you know what to do and you will teach me."

"So, now Kate teaches your father."

"How did you know that?"

"I think that is why Ethan went to take Kate from the airport, so she can give him lessons in the bed." The phone was ringing. Michelle picked up.

"Yes Kate. I will be there."

"You are right Carl. Kate is here." When Michelle returned she told me that Ethan and Kate want to have lunch with us.

"Carl, do you think that Kate will change Ethan?"

"She lived one month in Ethan's house with you Michelle. You should have figured Kate during that time."

"I don't know her that well, I have been with her for one night."

"Julia loves Kate too Carl."

"If Julia loves her, I think that she is a good person and she will change Ethan."

"So, if Ethan marries Kate, she will be your mom or to be correct, your step mom."

"Don't go there Michelle. You know what you are about to say Michelle. You want to tell me that I slept with my step mom. Is that were you going Michelle?"

"You are right Carl." We laughed.

Michelle went to the bathroom. I was thinking about her. She will be my wife, my girlfriend and the mom of my children. I love her. Vicky, Cristal and Mom were right when they told me that I must marry her.

Michelle, I, mom, Simon, Kate and Ethan left the hotel for lunch. We were in the restaurant at noon. I zipped my mouth, because I didn't like to hurt Kate. She was very nice with me. Michelle and I have to be supportive of her. Mom and Simon were surprised that I was quite. Michelle knew why I was quite and I think that she appreciated it.

Michelle, I , Mom and Simon spent the whole afternoon together sightseeing. Simon told us that if he pushed Louis to stay in New York, maybe Louis he would have stayed, because he loved Simon.

"If Louis stayed in New York, you would have married him, Julia. When he was in New York and he told me that he made a big mistake not marrying you, but it was too late. If Louis married you Julia, now my brother would have been alive."

"I still love Louis, Simon. I know that Louis left me fifty years ago and he has been dead for twenty five. But I still love him. Doesn't matter if he is alive or dead."

Michelle was surprised when Mom said that she still loves Louis even though he has been dead for so long. Michelle took my hand and squeezed it hard. She didn't let go off my hand. When we came to the hotel, Hans and Sven were in the lobby. Greta wasn't. Sven and I shook hands and Sven asked Michelle.

"Are you Carl's wife?"

"We are engaged Sven and we will marry when we go back to New York."

"You are beautiful and young Michelle. Mom didn't have a chance to marry Carl." Hans and I laughed.

Hans asked me "Did you watch the news today?"

"I didn't Hans. We were out, but I don't like watching news or TV that much anyway."

"The news was that the Dreyfus family found the diamonds and Carl Hope was the person who help them to find them. They said that Carl Hope will marry Michelle Dreyfus who is the granddaughter of Louis Dreyfus and the niece of Simon Dreyfus. I am happy that finally the Dreyfus family found the diamonds, because now nobody will look for them anymore. Now they know that I didn't know where the diamonds were. Simon Dreyfus was the source of the news."

"Who is Simon Dreyfus, Carl?"

"You will meet him tonight, Hans. He is the brother of Louis Dreyfus."

We were in the restaurant at 7:00 p.m. I introduced Hans Weber to Simon Dreyfus. I told them that I am sorry for both of them, because Hans lost his father and Simon lost his brother Louis because of the diamonds. They were killed for them.

"You must be happy that the diamonds didn't kill you Carl", Simon told me. Simon asked Hans for his father.

"I have a letter in the safe box for Hans's father Simon. I will give him the letter when Hans come to New York. If you excuse me, I need to visit with other people that are here tonight for me" and I left them. I introduced everybody to each other. We sat on a table and I told them that Michelle and I are happy that everyone has joined us to celebrate our engagement. We ate, drank and spoke. Hans surprised us when he took the microphone and told us that he is happy to be on the table with the Dreyfus family and he will play a special song on the piano for two special people "Michelle Dreyfus and Carl Hope". Michelle kissed me and told me "Thanks Carl". She thought that I ask Hans to do that. Mom and Simon smiled. They thought that too. I didn't ask him. He did it, because he likes to play the piano. Hans wanted to make Michelle and me happy. We went to dance. I was surprise that Michelle likes to dance. She was dancing well.

"Carl, you don't know many thinks about me yet. I think that this is good because you will have a chance to discover everyday new things about me." We went back to our seats when the next song started. Patrik and Veronica were sitting next to us.

"You dance well Michelle", Patrik told her.

"Hey Patrik, yesterday you told me that I am beautiful. Today you told me that I dance well. Do you love me too?"

"You are rich Michelle. I am scared of going there."

"I am not scared to jump in bed with Carl", Veronica told us.

"You are engaged Veronica", Patrik told her.

"Carl is too Patrik." Michelle didn't realize that Veronica was jealous.

"I think that this is a good idea Veronica" and I winked at Michelle.

"May I kiss you Carl?" Veronica asked me.

"Of course Veronica" and she kissed my mouth. Patrik and Michelle laughed and Michelle said "If you love Veronica then I will take Patrik".

"Don't worry Michelle, I will stay with Veronica", Patrik told us. "Veronica is jealous Carl."

"She is Michelle. You need to think before you are joking."

Ethan came and asked Michelle to dance with her.

"Absolutely, she is your daughter."

When Michelle went to dance with her father, Kate came and sat next to me.

"You should stay far away from me Carl."

"You can count on that, Kate."

"I don't like to create a problem for you with Ethan."

"Do you think that I was wrong when I started this relationship with Ethan?"

"If you are happy then go for it. I will never tell you what is right or wrong. This is your life."

"He loves me Carl. I like Ethan, but it is so hard to say that I love him. I have been with him for a month and he asked me to marry him. I know that Michelle met you one and half month ago, but it is different… "

"Are you scared because you are twenty three years younger?"

"Ethan and I are different in so many ways Carl. He is so rich. Everybody will think that I am marrying him for his money."

"Don't worry about that Kate. Everybody thinks that I am marrying for Michelle money."

"You will marry Michelle, because you love her. I love Michelle, Kate, but if you ask Ethan, he will tell you that I want to marry her for the money."

"This is the problem between me and Ethan, Carl. I told Ethan the truth, but he told me that I am young and I don't understand."

"I suggest that you speak with Michelle, Kate."

"I will never return to Ethan's house. He hurt me so deep. Nobody had hurt me like that before."

"You need to know that Michelle and I support you."

Ethan and Michelle were coming back to the table from the dance floor.

"Carl, I need to go back to my seat."

Michelle sat next to me and she asked me "How is your future step mom Carl?"

"She is afraid to marry your father Michelle, but I told Kate that she can count on us for support."

"Kate is a good girl Carl."

"I know that Michelle." Simon came and asked Michelle to dance, so I went and I sat next to Hans.

"How do you feel Hans?"

"I am feeling good Carl. I have a Mom, a wife and two children in Germany. My mom and wife will come to Switzerland and we will live in Zug. We have been separated for one and half year. My children live with my mom. If you are staying in Switzerland or France, I would like you to meet her."

"I will ask your mom to tell me where the diamonds are." We laughed and he told me that she will reply that the diamonds are in the bank.

"I would like you, Sven, you and Greta to come to New York, Hans."

"I have to tell you that when Greta returned from Helsinki, she cried and she laughed. Sven and I didn't know what to do. I asked Greta, what happened with her."

"I cried, because I lost Carl. I laughed, because I was the last woman in bed with him before he is getting married."

"Greta is OK now." She told me that she doesn't know what she will do when she sees you with another woman.

"I love Carl, Hans. He will be with his girlfriend. I am not ready to meet him. You and Sven go to Geneva."

"I think that Greta will be ready when we decide to come to New York. She needs some time. "

"Maybe she will come with her future husband."

"If she forgets you, Carl", Sven told us and he laughed. I and Hans turned to see Sven. He was behind us. Mom came and asked Hans to dance.

When Mom and Hans left, Sven told me "Michelle is beautiful and a very nice girl Carl. I think that she loves you very much."

"She loves me Sven."

"My father loved Mom too, but I think that she will meet a another man who will love her. She lost three kilograms. She said that she will lose seven more. She will be sexy again." We laughed.

"How old are you Sven?"

"Thirteen Carl, but Hans is teaching me to think like seventeen or nineteen. Do you think that this is good?"

"It is Sven. I started to understand people when I was twelve. After seventeen, I started to build me own life. You need to listen to Hans. He loves you and he will help you to build your life. Would you excuse me Sven, I need to see Chris and Clara." I went to sit next to Clara.

"Carl, I couldn't believe it. I told Chris and he didn't believe it too. We think that Veronica loves you. Do you think that something happened between Veronica and Patrik?"

"Michelle and Patrik were joking and I think that they hurt Veronica. I told Michelle that Veronica is jealous and she needs to be careful with her."

"What should I tell her?" Chris asked me.

"Tell Veronica that I love Michelle. Veronica will understand, why I am saying that. Clara you need to dance with Patrik. I will dance with Veronica and tell her what Carl told me."

Sofia came and asked me to dance. While we were dancing she thanked me for helping her and Max yesterday, when we were in the restaurant.

"I wasn't ready to answer Julia's questions Carl. Today we spend the whole day talking about how to answer Julia's questions. I was prepared tonight. We spoke several times and she told me that she will be happy if I marry Max. You are so lucky, Michelle is a beautiful girl. When we move to New York, I hope to spend a lot of time with her."

"It will be good for you both to know each other, so you can be friends since you both will be part of the same family." The song finished and we went back to the table. I sat next to Simon.

"Boy, I am so happy to see all these people on the table enjoying. You make people happy Carl."

"There is one person that is not happy. It is Ethan."

"That is understandable. You slept with his girlfriend" and Simon laughed.

"I spoke with my lawyer this morning Carl. When you and Michelle return to New York, we will start to work on our new business. The documents for the new company will be ready."

"Ok."

"What do you think about Kate, Carl?"

"Michelle and I have decided to support her, but Ethan and Kate need to decide what they want to do. Ethan is a greedy and a cheap man."

"Michelle told me the same Carl. She is his daughter. She knows him well. My brother and I didn't talk about Ethan. He was his mom's boy."

"Hey Simon, I am my mom's boy too."

"You are, but Julia thinks before she gives an advice." Michelle came and asked Simon to dance and Mom took the opportunity to come and sit next to me.

"How are you feeling Carl?"

"I am happy Mom."

"I spoke with Sofia. She is a good girl."

"She is Mom. You must be happy, because Sofia will deliver

your first great grandchild. When Sofia delivers my first great grandchild, I will give my apartment to Max and her."

"That is great Mom. I know that you are a good Mom" and I kissed her. We stayed until the restaurant closed. Sven didn't drink at all because he is too young. Mom, Simon, Hans and Sven were OK. Hans drank a little because was with Sven. Mom and Simon drank a little too. The rest of us drunk a lot and we were all drunk. We were very loud. Before we parted, we decided that the next party will be in New York.

Michelle and I went straight to bed.

"I want to sleep Carl." I kissed her and took her in my arms, her head resting on my chest. Her breathing became even. She was asleep. Michelle looked so beautiful in her sleep.

I woke up in the morning to say good bye to Sven and Hans. They left at 9:00 a.m. Michelle came to the lobby around 10:00 a.m. She ordered breakfast and coffee. We talked about the night before. Mom, Simon, Ethan and Kate came to the lobby at 11:00 a.m. Mom kissed me and told me that I need to listen to Michelle.

"If he doesn't listen, you need to call me Michelle."

"I will Julia." Simon kissed Michelle and me.

"I am very happy that you will marry Michelle, see you in New York" Simon told me.

Kate said "good bye" and kissed Michelle. I shook her hand. Michelle laughed.

"Are you scared to kiss your step mom Carl?"

"I will be his step mom, if I marry Ethan, Michelle." Ethan kissed Michelle and told me that he counts on me to keep Michelle safe.

"You didn't tell him how to keep me safe Father. I think of the safest ways to keep me safe will be, in the bed with him father." Everybody laughed. Ethan too. Ethan was trying to keep a good relationship with Michelle, because Kate loves her. If Michelle tells Kate to marry Ethan, she will do it. Kate wants to, but she is scared. I think that Kate is waiting for Michelle to tell her that it is OK with it.

Mom, Simon Kate and Ethan left to New York. Michelle and I decided to stay two more nights and we asked the man at front desk, if we need to change to another room. He told us that we don't have to.

We left the hotel and spent the whole day in the city embracing the atmosphere and enjoying being together, getting to know each other better. We returned to the hotel after 10:00 p.m. We had sex for few hours. Michelle said that she was tired and after five minutes she was asleep. I kissed her cheek. Mom was right when she said "I am human being and I love Louis. Doesn't matter if he was death or alive". I think that Michelle and I are like my mom. Michelle fell in love with me when she saw me and she will love me forever. I knew that I loved her when I decided to ask her to marry. I think that will love Michelle forever. My life has changed a lot since I found out that I am a father. I heard people say that when you have children you see the world in a different way. Now I know that it is true. Before I didn't understand my feeling for Michelle. Since I mate her I often thought about her. Now I know that I love her and I am happy that I am engaged to her.

I can't believe how much has my life has changed in the last two months. The shark, Peter Volkov-Peter Volak tried to kill me, but I am alive. I thought to kill the shark. I didn't kill him, but he is death. Roger, Simon and Ben killed hm.

I found the diamonds, but I didn't see them. Simon, Michelle and Ethan did. I do not regret that, because I have the most expensive diamond next to me in the bed. Michelle is my diamond. I am so happy that I chose to marry her. Now I know that every night I will sleep with my diamond, Michelle. When I open my eyes, my Michelle will be next to me. I know that she will take control of my life. I don't need to think and write something for my future, because Michelle will think and write my future. I felt tired. I closed my eyes and went to sleep happy.

MORE BOOKS BY ANGEL JONSON

Who Kidnapped Holly Gold?